Praise for Barbara Dawson Smith and her novels

The Duchess Diaries

"With a strong mystery as the backdrop and sizzling sexual tension throughout, Smith's enthralling tale of murder and passion will keep you up all night."
—*RT BOOKclub Magazine*

"A wonderfully captivating tale . . . the mystery is well-crafted and will keep readers guessing to the very end."
—*Romance Reviews Today*

"Smith has penned a charming, easy-to-read novel . . . fans will find this a treasure."
—*Huntress Reviews*

The Wedding Night

"A great story! Barbara Dawson Smith is a wonderful story-teller and shows her talent especially well in this tale . . . fast-paced . . . a great book."
—*Affaire de Coeur*

"The story is loaded with lots of good dialogue and sexual tension."
—*Rendezvous*

"This book had me staying up late to finish it. This touching story of love and betrayal will go on the shelf to be read again."
—*Old Book Barn Gazette*

"A continuation of the Kenyon family series, but make no mistake, it's quite good all by itself. *The Wedding Night* is a cute and sexy read . . . lots and lots of intrigue and surprises are involved."

—romancereaderatheart.com

"Sexy, compelling, exciting, and with a deep vein of emotion, this is a story filled with the deeper meaning of family and respect, independence and feminism."

—*RT BOOKclub Magazine*

"Barbara Dawson Smith is such an accomplished author that we are assured of a quality read with interesting characters and vignettes of the previous families."

—newandusedbooks.com

With All My Heart

"A delightful romance . . . fabulous . . . one marvelous read."
—*Romantic Times* Top Pick

"Barbara Dawson Smith is a masterful storyteller of complex plotting and three-dimensional characters, making *With All My Heart* a delightful romance . . . fabulous . . . one marvelous read." —*Romantic Times* Top Pick

"A well-fleshed-out page-turner! . . . Ms. Smith is such a good writer." —*Old Book Barn Gazette*

Tempt Me Twice

"A fabulous hero who has finally met his match—the tension sizzles." —Christina Dodd

"Don't miss an extraordinary author, and one of the best romances of the year!"
—Doubleday Book Club

"A delectable, fast-paced tale with charming characters . . . great dialogue and heart-melting love scenes make this a book you don't want to miss." —*The Oakland Press*

"Another keeper from Barbara Dawson Smith . . . a wonderful mix of mystery, humor, and romance."
—*Heartland Critiques*

"Capturing both the era and the essence of suspense, Ms. Smith draws readers into her web and spins a tale that holds their attention and wins their praise."
—*RT BOOKclub Magazine*

"With Barbara Dawson Smith's deserved reputation for strong novels, Regency romantic suspense fans will not need a second temptation to read her latest tale . . . the story line is exciting, loaded with intrigue, and never slows down for a breather as the plot spins to a fabulous climax. Smith goes to the bestseller lists as usual." —*Reviewer's Book Watch*

St. Martin's Paperbacks Titles
by Barbara Dawson Smith

The Duchess Diaries

The Wedding Night

One Wild Night

With All My Heart

Tempt Me Twice

Romancing the Rogue

Seduced by a Scoundrel

Too Wicked to Love

Once Upon a Scandal

Never a Lady

A Glimpse of Heaven

Countess
Confidential

~

Barbara Dawson Smith

St. Martin's Paperbacks

Countess
Confidential

"Off with his head!"

—*King Richard III*, III:iv

Prologue

If Simon Croft, the Earl of Rockford, had discovered one truth in his years of covert detective work, it was that criminals always claimed to be innocent. This one was no exception.

As he methodically searched the tiny, two-roomed flat, Simon heeded the villain's protests with only half an ear. The gray light of a rainy morning showed a scene of cozy domesticity. A plate containing the remains of breakfast sat on a rickety table beside the unlit fireplace. The meager furnishings included a pair of brown upholstered chairs, a battered oak desk, and a narrow cot in the adjoining bedchamber. Heaps of books and papers covered every available surface.

Somewhere in the clutter lay the proof Simon needed to put Gilbert Hollybrooke behind bars. The diabolical thief was known as the Wraith for his uncanny ability to slip in and out of the houses of the nobility.

"This is preposterous," Hollybrooke said, pushing his wire-rimmed spectacles back up his thin nose. "I'm a scholar, not a jewel thief."

Guarded by a stocky Bow Street Runner, Hollybrooke sat on a stool in the middle of the room. He was a gangly man with pale blue eyes, his back slightly stooped, his receding fair hair dulled with gray. With his frayed cuffs and tatty brown coat, he looked as harmless as the dons who had taught Simon at Oxford.

But Simon knew better than to judge by appearances. He had learned that cruel lesson as a wild youth of fifteen when he had witnessed the murder of his father.

Grimly ignoring the man's protests, he crouched down to tap on the rough wooden floor, checking for a hollow hiding place. The Wraith had been responsible for a rash of robberies over the past two months. By peculiar happenstance, the latest incident had been a brazen theft from the bedchamber of Simon's mother.

The memory of her shock and distress gripped him with steely rage. She had endured enough suffering at the hands of brigands. If necessary, he would take the place apart, board by board. He would find the evidence to bring this criminal to justice.

"I'm an author of some renown," Hollybrooke argued. "If you'll allow me to show you—"

"I'm acquainted with your work." Simon stood up and went to a leather trunk by a window that overlooked the soot-blackened brick of a neighboring building. *"Everyman's Guide to Shakespeare."*

"Yes, indeed! So you see, I couldn't possibly be your culprit. You've made a terrible mistake."

Opening the trunk, Simon inhaled the faint scent of lavender. The interior contained a few articles of neatly folded female garments, nothing of interest. The man had a grown daughter who taught at a girls' boarding school in Lincolnshire. Because she lived so far away, Simon didn't view her as a viable accomplice. "It's no mistake," he said coldly. "A quotation from Shakespeare was left at the scene of each robbery."

"Do you mean . . . because I'm an expert on the Bard . . . you would think . . . ?"

"You also dropped a grocer's bill outside the last house you robbed. It contained your address."

Hollybrooke made a credible attempt at astonishment. "But that's absurd. Where was this house? In Mayfair? I never venture there. Perhaps the grocer was making a delivery and . . . and it fell out of his pocket."

"That isn't all. I know about your connection to the Marquess of Warrington. I know that you lured his daughter into marriage in the hopes of gaining her dowry. And I know that you've every reason to want vengeance on society."

Hollybrooke blanched. His ink-stained fingers gripped the edges of the stool. A succession of expressions played across his face: shock, alarm, and not surprisingly, bitterness. "So that's it. Warrington is behind this. He's trying to ruin my good name. I only wonder that it took him so many years to do so."

The argument left Simon unmoved. Gilbert Hollybrooke had been rejected and humiliated in his long-ago scheme to join the ranks of the upper class. In some people, malice never died.

Simon took a seat at a small desk littered with papers. Atop a stack of books sat a chipped earthenware mug that held the dregs of cold tea. One by one, he opened the drawers and searched through the ragtag contents. Extra quills and ink, a penknife, a ball of twine, reams of cheap paper. Then, in the back of the bottom drawer, he found it.

Triumphantly, Simon withdrew the piece of jewelry. Even in the dim light, there was no mistaking the cold glitter of his mother's diamond bracelet.

"Lord, what fools these mortals be!"
—*A Midsummer Night's Dream*, III:ii

Chapter One

Two weeks later

If they didn't change the subject soon, she was going to make a scene. A loud, unladylike scene that would ruin her disguise and foil her plans.

Her gloved hands clenched in her lap, the woman known as Mrs. Brownley sat in the grand ballroom near a group of gossiping matrons. All around her swirled the sounds and activities of the party. Hundreds of candles winked in chandeliers and wall sconces, the scene slightly blurred by her borrowed spectacles. Footmen bearing silver trays of champagne and punch circulated among the throngs of aristocratic guests. Rich perfumes scented the air, and at the far end of the vaulted chamber, an orchestra played music fit for the angels.

It was an extravagant feast of the senses for someone who had never set foot into society before tonight.

Until a moment ago, Claire had been enjoying herself, much to her surprise. At the sedate old age of five-and-twenty, she was supposed to have her feet firmly planted on the ground. She was conscious of her duty to keep a close eye on beautiful, young, flighty Lady Rosabel Lathrop, whose white gown and blond hair could be glimpsed on the dance floor among the two long rows of ladies and gentlemen.

Yet as Claire watched their graceful moves, a wistful yearning had struck from out of nowhere. Beneath her shapeless gray gown, her foot had tapped in time to the lively tune. She had found herself longing to join in the festivities instead of languishing here in the role of paid companion. She had even entertained the traitorous thought that if matters had been different, she too might have grown up in this world of wealth and privilege.

Then someone had mentioned the Wraith.

And her desperate purpose had come crashing back over Claire.

"It's a relief that criminal is behind bars at last," Lady Yarborough declared now, her vehemence jiggling the fleshy folds beneath her chin. The tight gray curls that ringed her rotund face looked too stiff to be real. "The effrontery of him to prey upon his betters, to steal our jewels from right beneath our very noses."

Clucks of agreement came from the other matrons. In this flock of old hens, the viscountess clearly ranked first in the pecking order.

"The Wraith made off with my ruby brooch," Mrs. Danby said in her gravelly voice. Her clawlike hands gripping the knob of her cane, she glanced around as if half-expecting a masked figure wielding a pistol to leap out from behind a potted fern. "I vow, my nerves shall never recover."

The woman looked too peevish to suffer from any such weakness, Claire judged. Mrs. Danby's features were gaunt with charcoal shadows beneath sunken brown eyes. She was like all the ancient beldams of society, haughty and pretentious, radiating self-importance.

"The Wraith filched my favorite diamond earbobs,"

wailed another lady, clad in a tight green gown more suited to a younger, slimmer figure. "Along with the pearl necklace Ralph gave me on our fortieth wedding anniversary last year. Yet that ruffian claims he didn't do it."

"There can be no doubt the fellow is guilty," Lady Yarborough pronounced. "The Runners searched his rooms and found a diamond bracelet belonging to Lady Rockford."

"And he *is* a Shakespearean scholar," said a pucker-mouthed matron. "Was not a quote from the Bard left at the scene of each crime?"

"Indeed, Gilbert Hollybrooke is a thief, a liar, and a beast." Mrs. Danby's nostrils flared in her cadaverous face, and she rapped her cane on the parquet floor. "A beast, I say!"

No, he's innocent! They've arrested the wrong man!

Her body rigid, Claire concentrated on taking slow, deep breaths. She didn't dare speak her mind here, not in this enemy encampment where no one knew her true identity.

"There is no need for histrionics," Lady Yarborough chided. "Do have a care for Lady Hester's sensibilities."

The gossip died down. A few ladies gasped. Everyone's eyes turned discreetly toward the plump woman sitting at Lady Yarborough's right. Several in the group looked genuinely concerned for Lady Hester Lathrop, and Claire supposed there must be a few good souls in society, for her own mother had come from these hallowed ranks.

Lady Yarborough addressed the lady at her side. "Do forgive us, dear Hester," she said, a trill of sympathy entering her voice. "The events of the past week must have come as a dreadful shock to you."

As one, the ladies leaned closer so as not to miss a single word of the exchange. Their jewels glowed in the soft candlelight, and their wrinkled faces showed varying degrees of distaste, pity, and curiosity.

In the background, the orchestra music swelled in a crescendo. The other guests danced and chatted, unaware of the drama unfolding in this corner of the ballroom, where wallflowers wistfully awaited a dance partner and sour old ladies condemned a blameless man.

Like an actress on cue, Lady Hester lifted a lace handkerchief and dabbed at imaginary tears on her florid cheeks. In her pink gown with the chocolate ribbons, she resembled a large bonbon. "You may speak as you will. It is no use pretending that ancient scandal never happened. Nor in denying my family's unfortunate connection to the Wraith."

A collective gasp met the statement, and Lady Hester paused—obviously for dramatic effect.

Her employer was every bit as formidable as the viscountess, Claire thought cynically. Lady Hester presented herself to the world as a frail, ineffectual female, but nothing could be further from the truth. She had found a brilliant way to turn the scandal to her advantage. Like the heroine in a tragedy, she would milk all the dubious glory of possessing inside information to feed the gossip mill.

In the face of such agonizing honesty, even Mrs. Danby subdued her strident tone. "Dear me, Hester. Do you mean . . . he is the one who . . . ?"

"Alas, yes." Lady Hester sniffled daintily. "Many years ago, Gilbert Hollybrooke was hired as a tutor for my dear departed John and his elder sister. John's parents trusted Hollybrooke, but he repaid their kindness by luring sweet, foolish Emily into an elopement." She pressed the handkerchief to her brow. "John said it was horrible . . . simply horrible! Poor Emily didn't realize until it was too late that Hollybrooke coveted only her fortune."

That's a lie! They were madly in love. Money didn't matter to them.

Claire clenched her teeth to keep from voicing those incriminating words. No one here knew that she was really Gilbert Hollybrooke's daughter, or that she had formulated a desperate scheme to free her father from prison.

Lady Hester musn't discover that Claire had taken a leave of absence from her position as a teacher of literature at the Canfield Academy in Lincolnshire. Or that she had forged her own references, attesting to be the respectable Mrs. Clara Brownley. But most importantly, Lady Hester mustn't know that the widow she had hired to chaperone her daughter was her own niece by marriage.

"Of course, John's father cut them off without a penny," Lady Hester went on sadly, as if she mourned the loss of the sister-in-law she had never met. "John never saw Emily again—nor ever even heard from her."

Another falsehood. Mama had written to her family many times.

Emily Hollybrooke had been a blithe, sunny person who had cast sunshine on everyone in her sphere. But one day when Claire was nine, she'd been shocked to find her mother weeping at Papa's desk while composing a letter. Mama had summoned a smile and contrived an excuse, but when Claire had told Papa, he'd said that Mama wrote once a year to her noble father, who had shunned her for marrying a commoner. Never once had she received a reply to her letters. Papa's fury at the Marquess of Warrington had stunned Claire, and he'd refused to answer any more questions.

But now was not the time to set the record straight. Especially to Lady Hester—*Aunt* Hester, though Claire scorned to claim any relation to the indolent, self-absorbed woman she had known for only three days.

Lady Hester's ample bosom lifted and fell in another

sigh. "It was by chance that we learned of Emily's death fourteen years ago. Oh, my poor, darling John suffered so at the news. Never will I understand how she could have abandoned her own family to run off with that . . . that villain."

"There now," Lady Yarborough said, reaching out a wrinkled, beringed hand to pat Lady Hester's arm. "Emily isn't the first lady to be taken in by a scoundrel. But at least now he'll get his just punishment."

"He'll be imprisoned for life," ventured a timid, gray-haired woman.

"Transported to the colonies," said a hunchbacked crone.

"He deserves far worse," Mrs. Danby declared, her gaunt features showing an unladylike relish. "I shan't rest easy until Gilbert Hollybrooke is sent to the gallows."

The gallows.

A small moan escaped Claire. She pressed her hand to her mouth, but luckily no one heard, no one saw, no one paid any heed to the hired chaperon. For once, she was grateful for the anonymity of her position. These ladies had no notion that her palms felt icy inside her kid gloves, that her stomach clenched and her heart pounded.

She had known the danger Papa faced, agonized over his desperate situation, wept to see him imprisoned in a cold, dank cell. She had conceived a reckless plan to clear his name. But to hear him condemned now so bluntly and with such spiteful intent struck straight into the center of her fears.

Her father could be executed. For a crime he didn't commit.

"Mrs. Brownley. *Mrs. Brownley.*"

It took a moment for Claire to surface from the depths of her dark thoughts, to realize that Lady Hester was addressing her.

She turned to gaze into the hazel eyes of her late uncle's wife. Lady Hester had a round face, seamed with wrinkles and flushed from the heat of the ballroom. The façade of defenseless debility was gone, and a thunderous frown furrowed her brow.

Claire froze. Had Lady Hester noticed Claire's distress? Had she seen a portrait of Claire's mother and realized Claire's identity?

Ridiculous. Emily Hollybrooke had had green eyes and blond hair, while Claire was a brunette under the voluminous widow's cap. She wore spectacles that dulled her blue eyes and a plain, high-necked gray gown that turned her complexion sallow. She had made herself mousy and meek and entirely unlike the vivacious Emily.

With studied humility, Claire said, "Yes, my lady?"

"The music has stopped," Lady Hester hissed under her breath. "Where is my daughter?"

Claire swung her gaze toward the dance floor. The lines of ladies and gentlemen had dissipated, the orchestra was tuning their instruments in the corner, and the guests chatted in clusters. But Lady Rosabel was nowhere to be seen.

"I'll go in search of her. If you'll excuse me."

Claire made to rise, but Lady Hester caught her sleeve. Her expression displayed the fierceness of a mother bear defending her cub. "You are to keep watch over Rosabel at all times. But I vow, I saw her dancing with that scoundrel Lewis Newcombe."

"Isn't he Lord Frederick's friend?" Claire asked cautiously, remembering a suave gentleman with fair hair and a charming smile.

"Not anymore," her aunt snapped. "My son no longer associates with rakes and gamblers. Especially not a villain like Newcombe. Good heavens, his mother was a common *actress*!"

Claire swallowed a retort about judging a person by his pedigree. "I'm sorry, I didn't know."

"Then you must make it your business to know, Mrs. Brownley." Leaning closer, Lady Hester added sternly, "I will not allow any blot upon my daughter's virtue. I've had to let go three other companions because they failed in their duties. Do I make myself clear?"

Nodding, Claire rose to her feet. It was abundantly clear. If she failed, she would forfeit her post in the Marquess of Warrington's house.

She would lose her one chance to prove that someone in her mother's estranged family had conspired to send her father to prison.

"The nursery noose."

The moment Simon uttered the phrase, he had cause to regret his rashness. In the dimness of the coach, the man opposite him straightened his languid posture. A puzzled frown flitted across his affable face; then a slow grin displayed a flash of white teeth beneath a large Roman nose and blue eyes.

"The nursery noose, eh? The time in a man's life when he must find a wife and beget an heir." Sir Harry Masterson slapped his gloved palm against his thigh. "By gad, that's a prime one. I must remember to tell it to the fellows at the club."

Simon grimaced. He had no interest in sharing witticisms. Nor in discussing the private issue that had sparked his pronouncement.

But Harry had known him too long to let the matter rest. As the well-sprung coach swayed around a corner, he gave Simon an amused stare. "Something tells me you've had another tiff with the dowager. No doubt she wants you to put the noose around *your* neck."

"My mother is not the dowager," Simon corrected.

"She remains Countess of Rockford until such time as I acquire a wife."

His smile broadening, Harry shook his head. "You shan't distract me with lectures on the fine points of etiquette, old chap. The *countess* won't rest until you're as happily shackled as your sisters."

Outside the coach, candles glinted in the windows of tall, stately town houses, and the occasional gas lamp appeared like a hazy moon against the misty darkness. *Happily* was a matter of degree, Simon reflected. Unlike his three younger siblings, he preferred his freedom too much to go willingly to the altar. But his mother was right; duty called. At the age of three-and-thirty, he needed to set up his nursery and ensure the continuation of his noble lineage.

He could accept his fate. He could take a rational approach to the obligations required of his title. But he wasn't looking for *happiness* in a marriage.

He would find that elsewhere. With a real woman, not the virginal milk-and-water miss he must select to be his countess.

One eyebrow lifted in casual hauteur, he corrected, "*I* have decided to take a bride. Perhaps you should do the same."

"Misery loves company, eh? But pray recall I have two younger brothers to inherit."

"Not all of us can be so fortunate."

"Indeed." Looking cheerfully carefree, Harry lounged against the burgundy velvet cushions. "Well, well. I never thought I'd see the day you'd consent to be joined in holy matrimony. So who's the lucky lady?"

"I'll find out tonight."

"Tonight? Good God, don't tell me you've allowed your mother to pick her out for you, too."

"Certainly not." Simon crossed his legs, matching his

friend's casual posture. "Stanfield will have invited most of the season's debutantes. It should be a simple matter to make my choice."

"Just like that?"

"Just like that."

His friend looked skeptical, and Simon knew Harry wouldn't understand. Harry threw himself exuberantly into love affairs, sampling women like fine wine, declaring each one his perfect mate, and in the next moment moving on to another pretty face. He wore his heart on his sleeve, flirted with everything in skirts, and in general, thrived on chaos.

Simon, however, thrived on order and logic. Passion, he believed, could be controlled through mental discipline. By keeping his perspective, a man could live in peace and avoid emotional turmoil. Consequently, he kept a mistress only for so long as she abided by his rules. The instant she became possessive or demanding, he extricated himself from the relationship.

He intended to handle a wife in the same manner, with firmness and detachment. If she grew tiresome, he would banish her to his country estate in Hampshire and visit her from time to time, enough to ensure the succession of his line. There, she could preside over local society, while he pursued criminals in London.

"But"—Harry waved his hands expansively—"there are so many to choose from, *I* wouldn't know where to start. Miss Gorham with her sparkling blue eyes. Lady Ellen Reed, so shy and sweet. Lady Rosabel Lathrop, who has the most exquisite bosom—"

"Lathrop?" Simon said sharply. "That's the Warrington family name." Pity and triumph warred within him. Pity for the marquess who had suffered the loss of his daughter to Gilbert Hollybrooke, only to have the old scandal rear its ugly head again. And triumph that the Wraith now awaited trial in Newgate Prison.

Harry gazed askance at Simon. "Lady Rosabel is Warrington's granddaughter. Have you a particular interest in her?"

Simon kept his expression bland. Not even Harry knew about his secret work as a fighter of crime. "Certainly not. Any girl of good birth will do."

Uttering a harumph, Harry folded his arms. "You must have some qualities in mind. Fair or dark? Short or tall? Quiet or loquacious? Let me guess. You'll prefer a tall, slim brunette, a woman with a tongue sharp enough to fence words with you."

"Short, blond, and naïve will be fine. So will average, auburn, and gauche. The point of the matter is not her appearance so much as her suitability for the role of countess."

"Do tell."

"She must have impeccable lineage, enjoy good health, and be malleable enough to train."

Harry whistled softly. "Excellent criteria, if you're seeking a pedigreed puppy."

"In a manner of speaking, I am." Annoyed by the way that sounded, Simon frowned. His sisters would have his neck if they'd heard him talk so cavalierly.

But of course, he thought highly of his younger siblings. Elizabeth, Jane, and Amelia were sensible and quick-witted, hardly qualities he expected to find in the current crop of giddy debutantes. Indeed, each of his sisters had been the stellar catch of their respective seasons, and he was damned proud of them, as proud as if they were his own daughters.

After his father's violent death when Simon was fifteen, he had seen to their schooling. In a society where most girls learned only womanly arts like playing the pianoforte and stitching needlework, *his* girls had read Plato in the original Greek and Cicero in Latin. They had studied mathematics and geography and astronomy—albeit grumbling at times—and now they could carry on an intelligent conversation.

When they weren't talking about babies and household matters, that is. It seemed not even an excellent education could dull a woman's interest in domestic topics.

Harry looked disgusted, so Simon clarified, "I would never imply that women are like dogs. But even you must agree that the typical girl has little rattling around inside her head beyond fashion and flirting."

"No, I don't agree. I wholeheartedly *dis*agree." Harry leaned forward, his elbows on his knees. "If you'd spend more time in society you'd see what I mean. Girls are mysterious and fascinating, each and every one of them. They're soft and sweet and—"

"Silly. Nevertheless, I intend to take one to wife and mold her into my countess."

Harry shook his head. "You're a coldhearted bastard."

"Quite the contrary," Simon said dryly. "My mother will attest to my legitimacy."

The coach slowed as they neared the magnificent façade of Stanfield House. Harry gave him that calculating look, the one Simon had known since their days together at Eton. "Since you regard every young lady as essentially the same, then you might as well choose the first one you meet."

Chuckling, Simon shook his head. "I won't be drawn into one of your challenges."

"Aha! Then you don't stand by your word. You'll admit you're wrong—or you'll accept my dare."

He was being manipulated, Simon knew. Only a fool would fall into such a scheme. But in all honesty, he had dug his own pit. He had proclaimed his beliefs in no uncertain terms. And although it was stupid and illogical, he felt compelled to prove he was right.

He fixed Harry with a cool stare. "As you wish, then. But certain standards must be met."

Harry flashed a wide grin. "Certainly! She must be pretty, I'll allow. I wouldn't expect the Earl of Rockford to wed a bucktoothed Amazon."

Simon ticked off each point. "Yes, reasonably attractive. From a good family. And no older than twenty."

"Thirty," Harry amended. "Look at Lady Susan Birdsall, on the shelf these past ten years, but not for want of suitors—"

"Five-and-twenty," Simon compromised. "And she must be a virgin. I will have no doubt about the paternity of my firstborn son."

"So you'll order her to have a boy first, eh? Very sensible of you, old chap." Glancing out the window of the coach, Harry rubbed his hands together with relish. "What do you say we hop out here and enter straight into the ballroom from the garden? Then all the young ladies will have a fair chance at winning your hand."

"I have no other but a woman's reason:
I think him so, because I think him so."
—*The Two Gentlemen of Verona*, I:ii

Chapter Two

Irksome girl! Where was she?

After a swift search of the house, Claire hastened out onto the loggia behind the Duke of Stanfield's house. Music lilted from the ballroom behind her. The chilly evening breeze tugged at her cap and sent a flurry of goose bumps over her bare arms. Shivering, she adjusted the spectacles lower on her nose and peered over the gold rims.

Although situated in the heart of London, the garden was quite decadently large. Strings of lanterns lent faint illumination to the pathways nearest the porch. Gloom shrouded the beds of flowers, and deep shadows lurked along the stone fence. The fine, cold mist further obscured the scene. The overgrown trees and the moonless night conspired to create many hidden places where a naïve young lady might be lured for a stolen kiss.

Or more.

Claire tamped down a flare of alarm. Only ten minutes had passed since Lady Hester had noticed her daughter's absence. Surely nothing untoward could have happened in so short a time.

But Rosabel had been dancing with Mr. Lewis Newcombe. He was a crony of Rosabel's brother, Lord

Frederick, and despite what Lady Hester had said to the contrary, Claire knew from downstairs gossip that the two knaves were as thick as thieves.

While interviewing Claire for employment, Lady Hester had spoken at length of her daughter's impetuous nature, but Claire hadn't realized the full extent of the problem. The truth was, Rosabel lacked the sense of a newborn kitten. She had a knack for getting into trouble, most often for wandering away on her own. On Bond Street, while Claire gave instructions to the coachman, Rosabel had vanished, only to emerge from a stationer's shop over half an hour later. On a walk, after sending Claire chasing after a windblown hair ribbon, Rosabel had veered off the path in pursuit of a stray dog. That time, it had taken Claire twenty minutes to track down the girl.

Now she had disappeared again. And in the doing, she'd put Claire's position in jeopardy. Heaven help them both if Lewis Newcombe enticed Rosabel into an indiscretion.

Hurrying down the marble steps, Claire kept her eyes peeled for a voluptuous blond in a white gown. Only a few couples wandered the pathways, but none included her quarry. Gravel crunched beneath her stiff new shoes. The scent of damp earth gave testament to the rain of the past few days, and she held up her heavy skirts to avoid the puddles.

Starting at the far end of the garden, she conducted a systematic search. She peered behind every hedge and bush, checked inside every alcove, even ventured into the grimy black depths of the gardener's shed.

While brushing off her hands, she glanced across the garden and something caught her eye. Was that a flash of pale skirt near the back wall? Yes, she could discern the outline of a man and woman embracing behind a miniature temple.

Claire headed straight for them. She splashed through

a puddle without a heed for the dampness that seeped into her cheap shoes. Within the faux shrine, the statue of a cherub poured water from an urn, and the burbling of the fountain masked her approach.

Nearing the couple, she slowed her steps. In the murky shadows, the two figures were locked in a shockingly passionate kiss. The man was rubbing the woman's backside, lifting her to him, and she was gasping, clutching at him.

Embarrassment stung Claire's cheeks. Under any other circumstances, she would have beaten a hasty retreat. But the lady had fair hair and a pale gown that glimmered in the misty darkness.

Rosabel!

She cleared her throat. "Excuse me."

Engrossed in their own private world, the two continued moaning and caressing. The man fumbled with the lady's skirt, drawing it up, reaching beneath it.

Claire had seen quite enough. Marching forward, she planted her hand on the woman's shoulder and gave it a stern shake. "Lady Rosa—"

In that instant, Claire realized her mistake. The woman's shoulder felt too bony, and she was a few inches taller than Rosabel. Her heavy perfume was unlike the flowery essence worn by the debutante.

Like a shot, the couple sprang apart. The woman spun around, fussing with her skirts. Her mature features were barely visible in the dimness. With a gasp, she ducked behind the man.

A portly man who was not Lewis Newcombe.

An angry man Claire recognized as their host, the Duke of Stanfield.

"What the devil—" he snarled. "Who are you?"

Feeling a ghastly thud in the pit of her stomach, she deemed it wise to withhold her identity. "Pardon my mistake, Your Grace. I'm terribly sorry."

Wheeling around, Claire plunged into the gloom of an unlit pathway. The last thing she needed was to bring herself to the attention of a duke.

But surely Stanfield wouldn't recollect her name—even if he'd had a good look at her in the darkness. There had been hundreds of people in the receiving line. So what if Lady Hester had introduced her as the poor, grieving Waterloo widow whom Lady Hester had taken in out of the goodness of her heart? No one had really noticed the mousy chaperon in her baggy gray dress . . . had they?

Oh, bother. She refused to be wary of a pompous peer who had gained his position not by hard work but by an accident of birth. A man who would carry on with one of his guests in the middle of his own party. Papa would have said the duke was like all of his kind, a lecher and a leech, bleeding profits from his estates while his tenant farmers starved.

Her throat squeezed, and rather than dwell upon her father, she held tightly to her resentment of the nobility. Glancing back over her shoulder, she spied the couple entwined again, much to her disgust. She muttered aloud, "A blight upon the soul of civilization—*oh*!"

Claire ran straight into something solid. The impact knocked the breath out of her. She would have stumbled if not for the hands that grasped her waist.

Male hands.

Disoriented, she clutched blindly at a pair of broad shoulders. Her cheek had landed against a starched shirt, knocking her spectacles askew. For one paralyzed moment, she stood jammed against him, unable to move, unable to think. Her heart tripped madly. The heat of his body and the firmness of muscle invaded her senses. His spicy scent filled her empty lungs, and a thrill of awareness prickled over her skin.

Automatically adjusting her spectacles, she tried to

step back, to put space between her and the stranger. But his grip remained fixed, as did the pressure of his masculine form against hers.

Panic flared. Having grown up near Covent Garden, she knew the dangers of footpads and other ruffians.

"Loathsome wretch. Let me go!"

She brought her heel down hard on his instep. He grunted in pain. His fingers flexed, locking her more securely in the shackles of his hands.

"Well, well," he said, his breath warm on her brow. "Who have we here? Not a servant girl, but a lady. A very spirited lady."

He had the deep, cultured voice of a gentleman, and it snapped Claire to her senses. Of course he was a gentleman. There were scores of them in the ballroom. This one had stepped outside, and she'd had the ill luck to run from one problem straight into another.

Leaning back, she wedged her arms against the wall of his chest. "Release me, sir. At once."

Although Claire used her most indignant tone, he ignored her command. His large hands continued to span her waist, bunching the fabric of her too-large gown as if measuring her slenderness. He appeared to be staring intently at her.

Not that he could see anything through the shroud of darkness. She herself could discern no more than the tall black shape of him.

Then the voice of another man startled her. "By the devil, that was fast work. Who is she?"

"I wouldn't know. We haven't been properly introduced."

Her captor's voice oozed charm . . . and menace. Claire's uneasiness increased. So there were two of them. And what did the other one mean by *fast work*?

She had no notion why these two scalawags had been

lurking in the dark. But caution kept her from identifying herself as a paid companion. Noblemen often preyed upon those who lacked the protection of status. Mustering the hauteur of a lady, she said, "If you're fishing for my name, I shan't tell you. And no true gentleman would ask."

"Oho," the second man said with a laugh, "she's put you in your place, Rockford."

"That remains to be seen," her captor said coolly.

Rockford. Where had she heard that name before?

Claire didn't know and she didn't care. "Unhand me," she ordered for the third time. "I wish to return to the ballroom."

"Allow me to escort you," Rockford said.

Without awaiting her permission, he shifted his hold to her upper arm and turned her down the darkened pathway toward the mansion. Though his manner was polite, he exuded arrogance, as if he were accustomed to getting his way. The fact that he had repeatedly ignored her wishes both angered and worried Claire.

She sensed something disquieting about him, something that made her fear he was up to no good.

But straight ahead lay the long porch and the ballroom where the orchestra played. The golden glow of candlelight beckoned, and the sounds of laughter and conversation floated from the row of opened doors. She could see people dancing in there. People who would hear her if she screamed.

Deciding it was more prudent to acquiesce than to quarrel, Claire fell into step beside him. She would watch for an opportunity to escape these men with a minimum of fuss.

From behind them, the second man spoke up in a jovial tone. "Do forgive us for startling you, my lady.

We'll have you back with the other girls in half a moment. Perhaps you'll even consent to dance with one of us."

"Unless you've a husband who might object," Rockford added.

He was staring at her again; against the darkness of the trees Claire could see his head tilted down toward her. The narrowness of the path caused their hips to brush, and the pressure of his hand on her upper arm made her feel flushed and strangely agitated.

Under normal circumstances, she set great store by honesty. But in her present situation, a small fib might be wise. "I do indeed have a husband," she asserted. "He's waiting for me inside."

"Dash it all, you're married?" the second man said with keen disappointment.

"It would seem so," Rockford said.

The trace of mockery in his voice gave Claire the uneasy suspicion that he saw through her pretense. Did he view her as a potential conquest?

The notion made her stomach clench. She was appalled and . . . angry. Extremely angry that this toplofty aristocrat would view her—or any other woman—as a resource to be exploited as he willed.

She couldn't count on his carnal intentions changing once he saw her dowdy disguise, either. Because then he would realize she was not of his class. To men like him, servants were fair game.

"Your assistance is unnecessary," she stated. "I'm perfectly capable of finding my own way."

"No doubt you are," Rockford replied. "However, considering our unfortunate collision, I must insist upon seeing you inside. It's my duty to make certain that you've suffered no ill effects."

"The only ill effect is the bruise you're causing on my arm."

He loosened his grip slightly. "Better now?"

"*Better* is having you remove your hand from my person."

He chuckled. "You'll run away. And I feel obliged to deliver you into your husband's keeping."

Claire tensed. They couldn't stroll through the ballroom in search of a nonexistent spouse. Lady Hester would see her. She would demand to know why Claire hadn't yet found Rosabel. At best, she would expose Claire as a liar; at worst, she might misconstrue the situation and accuse Claire of flirting with the gentlemen.

And if anyone discovered that Claire had been outside with these men, her reputation would be ruined. It wouldn't matter that it had been a chance meeting. She would be considered unfit to chaperone a young lady. She would lose her post and her one chance to free her father from Newgate Prison.

She gauged the distance to the ballroom. A few more yards and they would emerge from the darkness of the trees. Once they reached the safety of the porch, she would find some pretext to free herself.

"No clever retort?" Rockford asked. He leaned closer, crowding her, causing a lurch of warmth in the pit of her stomach. "You make me wonder if something is worrying you, my lady."

"I'm wondering how I'll explain you to my husband." In the hope of discouraging him, Claire embellished the lie. "He's a very jealous man. He's likely to come at you with fists flying."

"Ah, the possessive sort. Yet he allows his wife to wander alone outside in the dark." Rockford paused. "Or was he not aware that you'd left the ballroom?"

Claire stiffened. He was implying that she'd come out here to meet a lover. Abandoning caution, she said, "*You* were skulking out here, too. What was *your* purpose?"

"One might say I was seeking my fate."

The cryptic answer irritated her. "Your fate, sir, is to be an overbearing aristocrat who tramples upon the wishes of anyone in your path."

"It seems to me *I* was in *your* path. You nearly bowled me over back there."

The unexpected urge to laugh intruded on Claire's ill humor. Seldom did she meet a man who could take an insult in stride and turn it into a wry jest. Despite his domineering manner, Rockford intrigued her. She was curious to know if his quick wit would hold up in an intellectual debate, or if he would prove to be like all the others in society, vain and self-absorbed, interested only in frivolities.

Behind them, someone loudly cleared his throat. "I say, if you two would cease your squabbling, we could join the party."

Claire had forgotten about the other man. At the same moment, she realized they had paused in the gloom beside the long porch.

Inside the ballroom, the music had stopped, and she could see gentlemen escorting ladies back to their friends and family. The sounds of their laughter and conversation drifted into the chilly night air. Like a manacle, Rockford's hand lay warm and firm around her arm.

It was time to make her escape.

She started up the steps of the porch, and Rockford easily kept pace with her. The golden light from within the house gave Claire her first good look at him. She nearly stumbled on the top step—and wouldn't *that* feed his overweening conceit.

For conceited he must be. No man could be so gorgeous without suffering the taint of narcissism.

Tall and dark-haired, he had high cheekbones and intense brown eyes in a face etched with masculine character. A tailored dark blue coat fit his wide shoulders to perfection, and tight white breeches sheathed his long legs. He embodied wealth and elegance, but it was more than mere clothing that made this man. Rockford projected confidence and authority, the inbred right to rule. She could picture him playing in Shakespeare's *Henry V,* leading his troops into battle.

Claire realized he was studying her just as intently. His narrowed gaze roamed from the black cap that concealed her hair to the spectacles that perched on her nose, and then down the length of the high-necked, loose gray gown designed to make her appear matronly.

Judging by the grim look on his face, he had been expecting a fine lady, perhaps even a beauty. She felt an errant longing to be girded in gold muslin with her hair done up in stylish curls, so that he would view her with admiration.

Instantly, she was ashamed of her shallowness. Her wits must have been left back on the darkened path. She cared nothing for the approval of rude, domineering gentlemen who disregarded her wishes.

And how could she have forgotten—even for an instant—that her sole purpose in entering society was to unmask the Wraith and free her father?

"Thank you for the escort, Mr. Rockford," she said politely. "As I'm sure you'll agree, any further assistance is unnecessary."

With a deft twist, she dislodged his hold. But as she turned and started toward the ballroom, his friend stepped into her path.

He had light brown hair and a large nose that somehow

suited his affable features. Somewhat shorter and broader than Rockford, he wore a yellow waistcoat beneath a sky-blue coat and an intricate white cravat.

His blue eyes danced with merriment. "*Mr.* Rockford, indeed. It seems introductions are in order." He swept her a gallant bow. "I am Sir Harry Masterson. And my friend here is Simon Croft, the Earl of Rockford."

A knell of alarm resounded in Claire. An earl. She had been sparring with a peer of the realm.

At the same instant, she realized why his name had sounded familiar to her. She swung toward Lord Rockford. "It must have been your wife whose diamond bracelet was stolen by the Wraith. The Runners found it in . . . in Gilbert Hollybrooke's desk." She almost said *my father's*.

"The piece belongs to my mother," he clarified. His gaze sharpened. "Where do you come by your information?"

"Some ladies were discussing the case in the ballroom."

"But you said the bracelet was found in his desk," Lord Rockford persisted. "That fact wasn't reported in the newspapers."

Quaking inside, Claire held up her chin. Rockford was quick to have noticed that slip. But he couldn't possibly know she was Gilbert Hollybrooke's daughter.

"One of the ladies must have mentioned the desk," she said coolly. "Perhaps she heard about it from your mother."

Lord Rockford's face looked set in stone. "My mother has spoken to no one about the case. She's been ill this past week and hasn't received any visitors other than family."

Claire was determined not to show the slightest alarm. "Then someone else in your family let it slip. How am I to know? I can't imagine why it matters, anyway."

"I agree wholeheartedly," Sir Harry chimed in. He

rubbed his gloved hands together. "Come along, Rockford, my man. I'm anxious to go inside and see how our bargain plays out."

"Bargain?" Claire asked.

Both men glanced at each other, and an unspoken message seemed to pass between them. "Oh, it's nothing," Sir Harry said rather sheepishly. "Rockford agreed to—er—dance with the first lady he encountered here at the ball. But since your husband is the jealous sort, we'll just be on our way."

Lord Rockford put out a staying hand to his friend, though his dark gaze remained fixed on Claire. "On the contrary, I see no reason why her husband wouldn't allow a simple dance. Provided we can find the man in this crush."

Claire stared coldly back at him. His interest in her could only be unscrupulous. But he could hardly assault her in the midst of a party. The safest ploy might be to lead him around the perimeter of the ballroom, keeping far away from Lady Hester. Then at the first opportunity Claire could slip away into the throng—

"Brownie! Oh, Mrs. Brownley, there you are!"

The sound of that breathy voice jolted Claire. Spinning around, she spied Lady Rosabel waving gaily at her from one of the open doors. Everything about Rosabel was lush, from her elaborate blond curls to her hourglass form. The low-cut gown of white gauze enhanced her generous bosom. As she started forward, her hips swayed in a display of innocent sensuality that never failed to draw masculine attention.

The effect certainly worked on the two men with Claire. Sir Harry wore a huge, silly grin, while Lord Rockford scanned Rosabel's figure with keen interest.

Anxiety gripped Claire. She didn't believe for an instant that these two men had made an absurd bargain about dance partners. It was far more likely that Rockford had vowed to seduce the first available female.

And now his sights were set on Rosabel.

Leaving the men behind, Claire hurried toward Rosabel. "Where have you been?" she whispered.

The girl made a vague gesture at the house. "In there, of course. But who are those gentlemen? I do believe I may know one of them."

She hadn't really answered the question, Claire noted. "We met by chance when I was looking for you. Come, we must go to your mother straightaway. She's been frantic with worry."

She linked arms with Rosabel, but the girl dug in her heels and aimed a flirtatious smile over Claire's shoulder at Lord Rockford and Sir Harry. "Mama won't mind. She wants me to meet all the eligible bachelors. Who knows, one of those two gentlemen may be my future husband!"

"We'll let Lady Hester decide that," Claire said, using a firmness of manner that always worked on her pupils at the Canfield Academy. "I've been given strict orders not to let you talk to anyone without her approval."

But it was too late. The men had already strolled to their side.

"Good evening, my lady," Sir Harry said, bending in a courtly bow. "Sir Harry Masterson, at your service. Perhaps you won't recall, but we met a fortnight ago at the Drury Lane Theatre."

"I daresay I should pretend *not* to remember *you*, Sir Harry." Her lips forming a playful pout, Rosabel tapped him on the arm with her closed fan. "You were the one flirting with all the other ladies in the lobby."

He attempted an abashed expression, then gave up with a grin. "None among them can compare to you, my lady. Now, if I may be so bold, allow me to introduce you. Simon, this is Lady Rosabel Lathrop. Lady Rosabel, Simon

Croft, the Earl of Rockford. He's your most ardent admirer."

Lord Rockford looked somewhat startled. He must have heard of Rosabel's family connection to the Wraith, Claire thought. Maybe it would turn him away from the girl.

But he bent over Rosabel's hand and kissed it. "You are indeed lovely, my lady."

Her face glowed with pleasure. Turning the full force of her charm on him, she blinked her big blue eyes. "Oh! I am flattered. Though I must confess, I've not seen you at any of the parties this past month."

"I've been around. At these affairs, I often talk politics with the other gentlemen." Lord Rockford wore an indulgent smile, as a man might give an adorable puppy. "But with such beauty as an enticement, perhaps that will change in the days to come."

As Rosabel giggled and cooed, Claire tightened her lips. "I'm afraid we must take our leave," she said. "Lady Hester Lathrop has entrusted me to keep a very strict watch on her daughter. So has Lady Rosabel's grandfather, the Marquess of Warrington."

Lord Rockford arched one of his black eyebrows in cool amusement. His smirk relegated her to the lowly status of paid companion. "Is Warrington here, then? I should like to give him my regards."

"I, as well," Sir Harry added with alacrity. "He and my uncle served together at Trafalgar."

"Grandpapa's leg was bothering him, so he returned home early," Rosabel said blithely. "But Mama is sitting with the other ladies, and I know *she* would be happy to receive you."

"There," Lord Rockford told Claire, "we are all satisfactorily settled in the matter. You can have no further objections."

His air of superiority grated on Claire's nerves. She

would not be disregarded, not when he intended to misuse Rosabel in order to win a wicked wager. "I do object. I intend to watch over Lady Rosabel day and night."

"Your husband might have something to say about that."

A flush heated Claire from head to toe. "I—"

"Oh, dear me, didn't you know, my lord?" Rosabel broke in, her playfulness vanishing into a look of sorrow. "Clara lost her husband last year at Waterloo." Giving Claire a spontaneous hug, she added, "I *am* sorry, Brownie. It must be horrid to lose the man you love."

Lowering her eyes, Claire pretended to look distraught. Rosabel had no notion that Claire's widowhood was a fraud, designed to secure a position in the Marquess of Warrington's household. Claire had lied for the best of reasons, yet she couldn't deny a twinge of guilt. Perhaps because she hadn't expected to *like* her pampered cousin.

She had entered the household of her mother's estranged family prepared to detest each and every one of its occupants. Over the past few days, her patience had been tested to the limit by Rosabel's silly behavior. But how could she hate the girl when her blue eyes glimmered with unbridled sympathy?

"Pray forgive the misunderstanding, Mrs. Brownley," Lord Rockford said, his tone dismissive. "Please accept my sincere condolences."

Turning away, he offered his arm to Rosabel. The couple strolled into the ballroom, leaving Claire to follow with Sir Harry, who chattered nonsensical gossip about people she didn't know. She pretended to listen, though her attention remained fixed on the tall figure of the earl. She ought to feel relieved that he had lost interest in her.

But now he posed a greater danger. If he succeeded in

compromising Rosabel's virtue, Claire would lose her position.

He must never have the opportunity. She would make certain of that. No one, not even the powerful Earl of Rockford, must stand in the way of securing justice for her father.

"Fair is foul and foul is fair."

—*Macbeth*, I:i

Chapter Three

"You won't believe what Simon did at the Duke of Stanfield's ball last night," Amelia announced to their mother the following day.

Simon looked up from the *Times* to see his youngest sister breeze into the morning room, bedecked in a frilly green gown that set off her reddish-brown hair. Her face glowed with healthy color and the gentle mound beneath her gown gave evidence of her first pregnancy. With typical careless disregard, she stripped off her gold-trimmed pelisse and tossed it onto a gilt chair, where it fell to the blue patterned carpet.

Banishing her gloves to the same fate, she cast an impish glance at Simon before going to give Lady Rockford a kiss on the cheek. Their mother reclined on a chaise longue near the window and worked on her embroidery. She was recovering from another bout of the ague. Her health had been somewhat precarious ever since that long-ago night when she had been shot in the chest and Simon's father murdered . . .

Simon wrestled the dark memory back into its coffin. He couldn't change the past, but he could do all in his power to make her happy now. For that reason, he welcomed Amelia's arrival as a distraction for their mother.

He did not, however, relish this inevitable scene.

"*The Town Tattler* has a position open," he said, eyeing his sister over the top of the newspaper. "You might consider applying for the post."

She wrinkled her nose at him. "Don't be droll. It isn't gossip when it involves one's own family."

Lady Rockford regarded them with an exasperated smile. Dressed in a gown of maroon silk, her graying brown hair neatly pinned, she looked thin and pale from her illness. Yet she commanded attention by the simple act of setting aside her sewing and folding her hands in her lap.

"I can scarcely wait to hear this shocking news," she said with a trace of skepticism. "Simon has said nothing of it, and I can't imagine him doing anything to raise eyebrows."

"Yes, he *is* a dull old stick, isn't he?" Amelia said archly.

"I prefer to regard myself as a sharp young blade."

Ignoring him, his sister glided to the table to help herself to a cup of tea. "But now he's taken complete leave of his senses, Mama. It all started when he danced with the same girl twice—*twice*! I vow, everyone in the ballroom commented on it. He might as well have fallen to one knee and declared himself before the entire company!"

"Good gracious." Lady Rockford's brown eyes shone with keen pleasure. "Simon, this *is* a surprise. Why didn't you tell me?"

His mother had long encouraged him to marry, and the hopeful interest on her face made Simon glad that he had taken a step in that direction at last. His reluctance to announce his intentions to her over breakfast had to do with that stupid bargain. He had been loath to come up with a falsehood to explain why he had singled out Lady Rosabel from among all the other debutantes.

His sister chimed in before he could respond. "He didn't tell any of us," Amelia complained. "Not me, nor Elizabeth, nor Jane, either."

"Pardon the oversight," Simon said dryly. "I was unaware that I required the approval of my sisters."

"It would have been common courtesy." Amelia added cream to her teacup and stirred vigorously. "You put me in an unconscionable position, Simon. Everyone was pestering me for information. And I was forced to admit that I knew nothing whatsoever of the matter!"

"There is no need for dramatics, my dear," Lady Rockford chided. She shifted her vibrant gaze to her son. "Now, tell me about this girl without delay. Who is she?"

"She's good-natured, kind-hearted, and well-connected," he said. "Her name is—"

"Lady Rosabel Lathrop," Amelia broke in. Giggling, she sank onto an upholstered gold ottoman and balanced the cup of tea in her lap. "That's the crux of the matter, Mama. Of all the sensible, intelligent ladies he might have chosen to court, he has settled upon that buffle-brain, Rosabel Lathrop!"

Simon compressed his lips. Of course Lady Rosabel couldn't match his sisters in intellect; they had had the benefit of an excellent education. But Lady Rosabel had been raised to be the wife of a nobleman, and that was all he required. She was agreeable, pretty, and ingenuous—if utterly incapable of clever conversation.

Unlike her companion, Mrs. Clara Brownley.

His thoughts strayed to that impromptu meeting in the garden. The memory of how much he'd enjoyed their verbal sparring now irked him. But there was no denying that his interest had been snared from the moment she had come charging out of the darkness, straight into his arms. He had relished the feel of her shapely form, the scent of her lavender soap, the softness of her skin. Under the cover of night, he had foolishly envisioned a woman with the rare combination of beauty and brains.

And he'd been intrigued by the suspicion that she had been lying about her marital status. He had been determined to call her bluff. He had even blessed his luck in meeting the one woman outside his family who was capable of returning his every volley.

What had she called him? *An overbearing aristocrat who tramples upon the wishes of anyone in your path.*

At the time, he had laughed, but now he considered the cheek she'd had to talk to him so. Nothing could have jolted him more than seeing her in the light. His mysterious lady had turned out to be a dowdy, unattractive widow forced by circumstance to labor for her keep.

A woman totally unsuited to a man of his stature.

"Lathrop," his mother said with a frown. "That is the Marquess of Warrington's family name. I've met Lady Hester Lathrop, but I don't recall Lady Rosabel."

His mother didn't care much for huge society balls. Because of her uncertain health, she preferred quieter gatherings with a close circle of friends. Despite her tranquil nature, however, she was strong-willed and decisive in her opinions, and he knew the necessity of winning her over to his side.

"She's Warrington's granddaughter," he confirmed. "This is her first Season, which explains why you haven't met her yet. But I can assure you Lady Rosabel has all the qualities of an excellent wife and mother."

Amelia snorted. "Since intelligence was obviously not a factor in your decision, I can only presume her attraction is the considerable size of her—"

"Enough." Annoyed, Simon snapped his newspaper onto the table and glared at Amelia. "You will not disparage the lady. Henceforth, you will speak of her with the utmost respect."

Sipping her tea, his sister gave him a look of dewy-eyed innocence. "I was only meaning to say her considerable *dowry*. Isn't that what all men look for in a bride?"

"Her *dowry* is of little import," he said testily. "What does matter is that my future wife comes from a highly respectable family—"

"Wife?" In the doorway, two dismayed voices spoke in unison.

Simon watched in irritated resignation as Elizabeth and Jane entered the morning room. It was not yet ten o'clock, and the day was already going from bad to worse. But he might as well make his intentions clear to all three of his sisters at once.

"I came the instant Amelia sent the news," Elizabeth said, removing her plain blue bonnet. The elder of the two, she was willowy, dark-haired, and brisk. She had made a brilliant marriage to the Duke of Blayton's heir, a man strong enough to stand up to her bossy nature. "And it seems I have arrived not a moment too soon. Lady Rosabel Lathrop, indeed!"

"I knew I should have gone to Stanfield's ball," Jane fretted. The middle sister and the peacemaker, she wore a prim gown of amber silk, looking every inch the matronly wife of a viscount. "But Laura was suffering from a cold and I was afraid the baby might be catching it, too, and so Thomas and I decided to stay home, but oh, dear me, Amelia's note came as such a shock."

Simon poured himself another cup of coffee from the silver pot. "Good morning," he said. "It's always gratifying to be greeted with remonstrations."

Elizabeth and Jane had the good grace to look penitent. They went to kiss their mother and exchanged salutations with her and Simon before sitting down near Amelia. Then the three of them regarded him like judges on the bench.

Apparently Lady Rockford made the same comparison, for she warned, "Girls, do remember this is not a trial in which you decide the outcome. Simon is free to make his own choice."

"But he cannot marry Lady Rosabel," Elizabeth said decisively. "It would be remiss of me not to point out that she's completely frivolous, without a serious thought in her head."

"I fear he should be miserable within a week," Jane agreed with a worried frown. "But perhaps Mama is right. Perhaps we shouldn't interfere. Especially if he is in love with her." Her aghast hazel eyes pinned him. "Are you, Simon?"

The question made him defensive, and he didn't like the feeling at all. He had always been careful to show his sisters a good example. God help him if they found out he had attained Lady Rosabel on a bet. "That is neither here nor there. What matters is that I am firmly fixed upon courting her."

"There, you might as well say *no*," Amelia retorted. "You made certain each of us married for love, but apparently you needn't follow your own advice."

"The situation is sometimes different for gentlemen," he said. "As I'm older, I have the experience and judgment to choose a wife based upon specific qualities of family background and suitability."

"Pompous drivel," Elizabeth declared. "The situation is *not* different for men. Unless you're saying that Marcus has never loved me."

A clamor rose from his sisters as they each in turn berated him for doubting the affections of their husbands.

At times, Simon regretted having encouraged their debating skills. "You are all willfully misunderstanding me," he said sternly. "None of you loved your husbands at first sight. Affection takes time to grow and deepen."

He wisely withheld his doubt that he could ever feel any depth of sentiment for a girl who chattered endlessly about trivialities. But Rosabel met his qualifications for a countess, and once she bore him an heir, they could lead separate lives.

"I don't see how you could develop any fondness for her," Amelia said in a blunt echo of his own thoughts. "It's far more likely you'll grow to despise her."

"Why didn't you tell us you were looking for a wife?" Elizabeth added. "We could have helped you find someone more appropriate."

"It isn't too late," Jane ventured. "Truly, you haven't yet made her an offer, and there are any number of other ladies who are more suited to your temperament. The Honorable Miss Cullin, for one. She's an excellent conversationalist, and founder of the Society of Lady Painters."

"How about Lady Susan Birdsall?" Amelia suggested to her sisters. "Granted, she's a bit long in the tooth, but she *is* well-read."

"I like Miss Greyson," Elizabeth said. "She's the daughter of a minister and very sober-minded. She wrote a pamplet proposing that women be granted the right to vote."

A clamor of talking filled the chamber as the three of them bandied names and qualifications.

Simon gritted his teeth. If he hadn't committed himself to that bargain with Harry, he might have welcomed their opinions. But their bickering only served to underscore the fact that he had to make his intentions crystal clear.

Pushing back his chair, he rose to his feet. "Silence!"

Their faces showing varying degrees of surprise and alarm, his sisters gave him their full attention.

He walked toward them, his hands clasped behind his back. He glared at each one of them in the face, as he had often done while supervising their schooling. "Here are the facts. First, I intend to court Lady Rosabel, with or without your blessings. Second, I will not tolerate any further discussion of her suitability as my countess. And third, you will set aside your personal feelings when I invite her and her family here to dine in the near future. Provided, of course, that our mother is feeling well enough for company."

Lady Rockford, who had been quietly observing the quarrel, nodded approvingly. "I am quite recovered, thank you. And I must concur with your decision, Simon. I am more than happy to welcome Lady Rosabel into this house. I should hope my daughters would behave accordingly."

"We would never insult her to her face, Mama," Elizabeth said with an air of injury.

"Certainly not!" Jane added, looking aghast at the prospect. "How can you even imagine us so rude?"

"But we've always been candid among ourselves," Amelia pointed out. "And we do wish to ensure Simon's happiness—"

Lady Rockford clapped her hands. The room fell silent again.

"While I realize that you are speaking out of love for your brother," Lady Rockford said sharply, "he has made his choice, and *I* trust his judgment implicitly. All of you must afford him the same honor."

Her face softened as she smiled at Simon, gazing at him with such pride and faith that he felt humbled. He wondered uneasily what his mother would say if she knew the truth—that he had agreed to court the first eligible maiden he encountered at the ball.

That he had allowed fate to choose his bride.

While Rosabel slept late after the ball, Claire spent the morning nurturing friendships with the other servants. It was a vital part of her plan to prove that someone in her mother's family was responsible for sending Claire's father to prison. Through subtle flattery and the offer of a sympathetic ear, she hoped to secure valuable information from those who had served the Marquess of Warrington for years.

She especially sought proof to implicate her grandfather as the Wraith. She needed to find out if he still bore a grudge against Gilbert Hollybrooke for stealing his daughter all those years ago.

Consequently, Claire had assisted the humorless housekeeper, Mrs. Fleming, in tallying the contents of the upstairs linen cabinet. She had helped Lady Hester's gossipy French maid with the mending. And now she lent a hand to Oscar Eddison, Lord Warrington's skinny old valet, as he shined the master's shoes in the boot room.

But although Claire had encouraged them to ramble on about the family, she learned nothing more useful than the fact that they shared a strong loyalty to the marquess.

"The Lord Admiral, he runs a tight ship," Eddison informed her. Sitting on a stool, a buckled shoe resting on his knee, he rubbed blacking into the fine leather. "He likes order and schedules, just as he did back when he captained *The Neptune* in His Majesty's navy."

Perched on a straight-backed chair opposite the valet, Claire handed him a soft chamois buffing cloth. "He sounds fearsome. I do hope he doesn't mistreat any of the servants. That wouldn't say much for his character."

There, she had given Eddison an opening to confide his true opinion of the marquess.

The valet stiffened, and a scowl deepened the wrinkles on his leathery face. "He's a harsh man, aye, but he's fair. Make no mistake about that."

To hide her frustration, Claire made a pretense of adjusting her spectacles. Eddison had served in the navy under Warrington, a fact that explained his allegiance to the marquess. But Claire measured her grandfather by a different yardstick. She judged him by the heartbreak he had caused her mother. Warrington had to be cruel to cut his daughter out of his life as if she no longer existed.

Had a long-festering appetite for revenge prompted him to frame Gilbert Hollybrooke for theft?

Eddison looked suspicious, so Claire reluctantly postponed further probing. "Pray forgive my curiosity," she said. "It's only that I know nothing of his lordship. I've been employed here for nearly a week already, and I've yet to catch a glimpse of him."

"Spends his time in the library, he does." Buffing the shoe, Eddison appeared mollified by her explanation. "Of late, his scars have been the very plague of him."

"Scars?"

"Wounded bad at Trafalgar, ma'am. Would've lost his leg if he hadn't threatened that wretch of a sawbones with court-martial."

Claire refused to feel any sympathy for the marquess. If he had been injured in battle, it only proved there was some justice in the world.

Heading down the dimly lit passageway to the kitchen, she pondered her next move. It was time she spoke directly to her grandfather, and that task would require delicate planning. Along with the other servants, she had a rigid set of rules to obey. One of those rules forbade her to enter the formal rooms upstairs except in the company of Rosabel.

Although Rosabel joined her grandfather for tea most afternoons, she always went with Lady Hester. When Claire had offered to accompany them, Lady Hester had given her a long list of tasks to accomplish in their absence.

No, Claire had to find another excuse to visit the marquess. Every moment she delayed meant another moment

Papa spent in the cold damp confines of a prison cell. Every passing day brought him closer to his trial, which had been set for the following month. Every passing hour inched him nearer to the gallows.

Fear tore at her heart. Upon her father's arrest, she had dipped into her meager savings and consulted a barrister, an officious, impatient man who had said he could do nothing without solid evidence proving that someone had planted the diamond bracelet in her father's desk. Even then, she could not afford his hefty fee, so she had hired a young lawyer whose enthusiasm, at least, exceeded his lack of experience.

And she had devised this reckless plan to infiltrate her grandfather's household. It had been a stroke of incredible luck that Lady Rosabel's companion had been dismissed at that very time, leaving the post open for Claire.

But she had yet to find a single shred of proof to support her father's innocence. If she failed . . .

Her insides churned. She couldn't fail, she mustn't. The alternative was unthinkable.

As she reached the kitchen, a bell jangled impatiently, jolting Claire out of her dark thoughts. One of a row affixed to the wall, the bell bore a label identifying it as connected to Rosabel's chamber.

"Aye, yer ladyship, I 'ear ye," the undercook grumbled. A stout woman, she spooned clotted cream into a small porcelain dish. "Don't that girl know it takes more'n five minutes to fix breakfast?"

"Thank you for hurrying, Mrs. Bull. I'll take it to her." Claire collected the tray with its silver pot of hot chocolate, the rasher of toast, and an assortment of jams. Although it had been hours since her own breakfast, she was too upset to be tempted by the rich aromas. Using her shoulder, she pushed open the door to the servants' staircase and mounted the narrow, wooden risers. Her footsteps echoed in the chilly shaft like the relentless scourge of her thoughts.

She mustn't be blinded by her hatred of the marquess, Claire reminded herself. She must keep her eyes and ears open to other possibilities, too. Lady Hester, for one.

Yesterday evening at the ball, her aunt had tarred Claire's father as a villain who had seduced Emily in order to claim her rich dowry. Of course, nothing could be further from the truth. But if Lady Hester resented Papa for tarnishing the family honor, she might have plotted to implicate him as a thief. She could have hired someone to plant that bracelet in Papa's desk.

Then there was Lord Frederick, Rosabel's elder brother and Lord Warrington's heir. According to the downstairs gossip, at the age of one-and-twenty, he was already a seasoned gambler and often short of funds. He might very well turn to robbery in order to finance his wicked habits. Perhaps he'd thrust the blame onto a likely scapegoat—Gilbert Hollybrooke, a noted Shakespearean scholar and a man vilified by Frederick's family.

And although it seemed ludicrous, Claire couldn't discount Rosabel, either. Was it possible she hid a crafty mind behind a façade of childlike innocence?

But Rosabel had no need to steal jewels; she had plenty of her own. Her dressing room was stuffed with gowns in all the latest fashions. She could walk into any shop and purchase whatever she liked without even inquiring the price. Nevertheless, Claire intended to find out exactly where Rosabel had gone after dancing with Lewis Newcombe.

Reaching the second floor, she entered a long, luxurious corridor only to see Lady Hester rushing toward her from the grand staircase. Huffing and puffing, the older woman reached Rosabel's door at the same time as Claire. Her plump features were flushed with excitement, and her ample bust heaved within its shield of copper silk. The very haste of her approach was unusual, for she seldom exerted herself for any reason.

Holding the heavy tray, Claire managed a curtsy. "Good morning, my lady. Is aught amiss?"

"Amiss? Good heavens, no. I must see my daughter at once!"

Lady Hester hurried into the bedroom, and Claire followed close behind, placing the tray on a low table by the fire. The drawn curtains over the windows filtered the light of a sunny day, rendering the spacious pink-and-white chamber dim and shadowy.

Although it was nearly noon, Rosabel reclined against a nest of pillows in the huge four-poster bed. Her spun-gold curls tumbled over her shoulders and the frilly white nightdress hugged her generous bosom. She looked sleepy-eyed and out of sorts, as she often was upon wakening.

"What is it, Mama? Why are you in such a dither?"

Beaming, Lady Hester waved a piece of folded paper as she scurried to the bedside. "I bring the very best of news, darling. The Earl of Rockford has requested my permission to take you on a drive this afternoon."

Claire's hand jerked as she poured the hot chocolate into a dainty china cup. Luckily, neither woman noticed the few brown drops that spattered the saucer, and Claire surreptitiously wiped them away with her finger.

Lord Rockford. In her quest to find the Wraith, she had forgotten all about the earl and his vile plan to seduce Rosabel.

Her cousin yawned and stretched. "When is he to arrive? If 'tis before two of the clock, send him away."

"Send him away?" Lady Hester cried. "Why, the very idea! The man is a prize matrimonial catch. Even your grandfather approves of him."

Rosabel gave her mother a rather sly look. "Grand-papa's consent can only turn me from him. Anyway, *I* thought the earl rather old and stuffy."

"Three-and-thirty is the perfect age for a gentleman of means to marry," Lady Hester said in a wheedling tone. Leaning down, she stroked her daughter's golden curls. "Lord Rockford could have any lady he wishes. And he chose *you,* my beautiful, beautiful darling. You, from among all the other girls."

A simper curled Rosabel's mouth. "Yes, he did, didn't he? I daresay we make a handsome couple."

"A pretty picture, indeed," her mother gushed. "I vow everyone in the ballroom was watching the two of you dance."

As Rosabel preened, Claire considered blurting out exactly what had transpired out in the garden the previous night. Yet caution stopped her. Lady Hester might accuse her of flirting with Lord Rockford. If the slightest doubt was cast upon her character, she would be dismissed from her post.

Better she should keep a close eye on him herself.

Picking up the tray, she carried it to Rosabel and settled it on her lap. "Did his lordship say at what time we should be ready to depart?" she asked.

Lady Hester frowned. "You? Good heavens, you're to stay here."

"But I must chaperon them," Claire said in alarm. "Lord Rockford may be a rogue."

Rosabel's expression perked up, and she paused in the act of slathering strawberry jam on a slice of toast. "Do you really think so, Brownie? He seemed awfully dull to me—although he *is* wonderfully handsome. Did we not look splendid dancing together last night?"

They had made a perfect picture, she so fair and dainty, and he so tall and masculine. At the memory of those dark, penetrating eyes, a prickling ran over Claire's skin. The mere thought of him caused a heated tension in the depths of her stomach. "It is more important to examine a man's character than the comeliness of his face or the size of his bank account. While a gentleman may appear respectable in company, he may behave improperly when he is alone with you."

"I beg your pardon," Lady Hester said icily. "There is no man more honorable than the Earl of Rockford."

If only they knew. "Forgive me for erring on the side of caution, my lady." Seeing an opportunity to further her investigation, Claire added, "I can only recall what William Shakespeare wrote in *Macbeth*. 'Fair is foul and foul is fair.' "

She watched mother and daughter for any sign of recognition. The Wraith had left that quotation at the scene of one of the robberies, and Claire knew she was taking a huge risk by voicing it now. If either of them was responsible for her father's incarceration, they might become suspicious of Claire repeating that very same passage.

But both women wore identical blank expressions.

"I don't care much for Shakespeare," Rosabel declared, taking a sip of hot chocolate that left a brown rim on her upper lip. She daintily licked it off with her tongue. "I never quite understand what the actors are saying."

"That particular reference means to be careful not to judge by appearances," Claire explained. "Someone who is handsome on the outside might very well be wicked on the inside."

Lady Hester's hazel eyes were like cold daggers. "Mrs. Brownley, you overstep your bounds. It is perfectly acceptable for a courting couple to take a drive in Hyde Park. I will hear no more of these ridiculous objections."

That cutting tone made Claire fall silent. She was bitterly aware that she was a servant here, and servants were not supposed to have opinions—not even on so vital a topic as protecting a lady's virtue. She could take solace only in the fact that at least she had issued a warning to Rosabel.

But when Claire glanced at the girl, Rosabel winked. Her bright blue eyes were dancing with merriment. And Claire realized in dismay that she had done more damage than good.

If anything, she had piqued Rosabel's interest in Lord Rockford.

"By the pricking of my thumbs,
Something wicked this way comes."
—*Macbeth*, IV:i

Chapter Four

Lady Rosabel wasn't ready when Simon arrived at three, so he was forced to cool his heels in the drawing room with her brother, Lord Frederick, and her mother, Lady Hester.

Simon would have rather been out in the stews of the city, tracking down criminals. He preferred the vigor of a good chase to the dullness of polite conversation. However, taking a wife required a period of courtship. Although a rush to the altar might be a more efficient use of his time, it would also set tongues wagging.

Apparently suffering from a night of debauchery, young Lord Frederick slouched in a chair and examined his fingernails. Over the course of half an hour, he also played with the large gold buttons on his dandified yellow coat, plucked at his starched cuffs, and smoothed away imaginary wrinkles in his dark green breeches. With his tousled fair hair and jug ears, he resembled a chastened schoolboy forced to sit in detention.

It was clear his mother had coerced him into playing host—not that Frederick made any attempt to be sociable. He ignored her efforts to draw him into the conversation, which centered on Lady Hester enumerating her daughter's merits.

"Frederick, darling, do tell Lord Rockford how very lovely your sister looked at her debut ball last month."

"Lovely?" Yawning, he stretched out his legs and inspected the shine on his shoes. "If you say so, Mama."

Lady Hester frowned at him, but when she returned her gaze to Simon, an ingratiating smile creased her round face. "He was Rosabel's partner in her first dance, you know. Oh, what a vision she was in white silk, and with her dear departed grandmother's diamonds at her throat. And *all* the gentlemen were vying for her hand. Quite a number of them proclaimed her to be the belle of the Season." Lifting a lacy handkerchief to her cheek, Lady Hester made a credible attempt at abashment. "But perhaps, my lord, you think me boastful for saying so."

"I could never fault you for speaking the truth," Simon said politely. "Lady Rosabel is indeed a beauty."

A giggle came from the doorway. "Why, thank you, m'lord."

Simon stood up as Rosabel minced into the drawing room, looking fresh and charming in pale green muslin that outlined her splendid bosom. A straw bonnet with matching green ribbons framed her dainty features. Her pink lips formed a rosebud, and her clear blue eyes shone with delight. With that aura of innocent sensuality, she was every man's dream.

But instead of being struck by desire, Simon was jolted to see that she looked even younger than he remembered. In truth, she *was* younger than his sisters.

Then his gaze narrowed on the woman behind her.

Mrs. Clara Brownley looked like a drab shadow of her mistress. A gray cap concealed all but a glimpse of tightly pinned dark hair. A baggy gown in the same ugly hue cloaked her slender form. But there was nothing lackluster about the way she was glowering at him. Her blue eyes magnified by a pair of gold-rimmed spectacles, she skewered him with sharp disapproval.

Simon was unaccustomed to servants staring at him, disdainful or otherwise. That must be why he felt as if he'd been slapped awake.

He rationalized his strong reaction to her. Last night, he had held her close for much longer than was proper. He had been captivated by the feel of feminine curves, by the faint scent of lavender, by the softness of woman. He had enjoyed sparring words with her, too. The darkness had tricked him into believing her a lady—the lady he would court and marry.

He despised being tricked.

To be fair, though, he supposed she hadn't liked being trapped against her will, either. Their impromptu embrace had given her the wrong impression of him. No doubt she believed him a bounder who intended to ravish Lady Rosabel.

Nothing could be further from the truth. Yet a little devil persuaded Simon to embellish her mistaken assumption.

Going to the doorway, he bowed over Rosabel's gloved hand and pressed a lingering kiss to the back. "You shine like a spring day, my lady. Perhaps we shouldn't go to the park, lest you put all the flowers to shame."

Rosabel dimpled. "But I was so looking forward to our drive."

"Your wish is my mandate, then. Henceforth, I intend to devote myself to pleasing you." Lowering his voice to a husky murmur, he added, "Might I add, I can scarcely wait to be alone with you."

She playfully tapped him on the arm with her lacy reticule. "Oh, you *are* a rascal today, my lord."

Behind her, Mrs. Brownley compressed her lips. Censure deepened the rich blue of her eyes, and she took a step forward as if intending to chastise him.

Simon found himself relishing the prospect of her prim reprimand.

"Mrs. Brownley." Lady Hester's strident voice rang out as she lumbered toward them. "Have you finished all your mending?"

Mrs. Brownley's fine eyes widened; then she lowered her gaze to the marble floor. "No, my lady. I'll go upstairs at once."

Her abrupt switch from impudence to submissiveness intrigued Simon. At least she knew who paid her wages.

But as she turned to leave, she shot him another quelling glance. It warned Simon to keep his hands to himself.

Again, he was torn between irritation and humor. Mrs. Clara Brownley had not been born to the role of servant, that much was clear. In truth, she seemed to believe herself his equal. He wondered how she imagined she could stop a man of his stature from doing as he willed.

It might prove interesting to find out.

An hour later, Claire entered the first-floor corridor through a door hidden in the oak paneling. To her relief, the opulent passageway was empty in both directions. The cleaning was done early in the morning so the housemaids wouldn't disturb the family as they went about their daily lives.

But at present, Lady Hester was napping, Lord Frederick had gone out, and Rosabel hadn't yet returned from her drive with Lord Rockford. At least Claire hoped her cousin was at the park with him. If he had lured her away from the safety of the crowd . . .

Frowning, she started down the passageway. Her mistrust of the earl had not been unwarranted. He had behaved like a rake with Rosabel, turning her head with extravagant compliments and whispering suggestive comments in her ear. In his navy blue coat and snug-fitting tan breeches, he had looked as darkly handsome as the devil himself.

Even Claire, who knew better, had found herself breathless in his presence. In defiance of all common sense, she had felt a shameful warmth inside herself, a yearning to be pressed against his hard body again, to smell his spicy scent and to feel his hands gripping her waist.

And this time, to know the taste of his kiss.

Her carnal attraction to him mystified Claire. She scorned noblemen who had been born to privilege by a vagary of fate. They used the power of their position to subjugate people—and to prey upon them. Yet now she could understand how easily a woman could fall under the spell of such a man. In addition to wealth and a title, Lord Rockford possessed an abundance of charm and good looks. His cool, intelligent gaze had held a hint of amusement, as if he'd enjoyed the game of manipulating a naïve girl.

Resolutely, Claire pushed him from her mind. With all her duties, it was rare for her to have a moment of freedom. Better she should focus on accomplishing her purpose.

Her footsteps were silent on the thick carpet with its gold fleur-de-lis pattern. The only sounds were the rustle of her skirts and the muffled bong of a clock tolling the half hour. She passed a dining chamber, where a long table gleamed in the afternoon light, and then a ballroom, vast and shadowed, the draperies drawn. Mama had told a story of dancing secretly here in the darkness with Papa one night, and how he had fallen to one knee and declared his love for her.

A lump formed in Claire's throat. How strange to think that long ago, her mother had walked these corridors. She had been Lady Emily then, the privileged daughter of nobility. When Claire was a little girl, she had begged her mother to tell stories of the days when Lady Emily had owned an array of china dolls and had played with the children of the king. Obligingly, her mother had described this house, room by room. She had spoken fondly of her younger brother, John, Lady Hester's husband, now deceased.

Mama had seldom mentioned her parents, though. Her father had been gone at sea for much of her youth, serving in the king's navy before gaining the title of marquess. He was a cold, cruel man who had expelled his only daughter for the sin of marrying a commoner. He had cut her off without a penny. She had been dead to him.

He had never acknowledged Claire's existence, either. But now she would meet him at last.

At the end of the corridor, she turned a corner and stopped in front of a closed door. Her heart thumped heavily, and she dried her damp palms on the gray serge of her skirt. In all her planning, she hadn't expected to feel the slightest reluctance. Yet it was tempting to turn around, to escape back to the safety of her duties.

Briefly closing her eyes, Claire called forth the image of her father as she had seen him last, his thin hands gripping the iron bars of his cell, his normally smiling face haggard. She had vowed to do everything in her power to free him. This was no time for cowardice.

Lifting her hand, she rapped firmly on the polished oak panel. A muffled male voice, fraught with irritation, bade her enter.

Claire stepped into the lion's den.

The Warrington library was every bit as magnificent as her mother had once described it. A domed ceiling with panels of frosted glass brightened what might otherwise be a gloomy chamber. Tall bookshelves lined the walls from floor to ceiling, requiring a ladder to reach the uppermost volumes. Several tables held maps and dictionaries, and scattered chairs provided cozy places in which to curl up and read.

The room appeared empty. Where was the marquess?

Then she spied him seated in a wing chair facing the fire. She could see only his profile, a thatch of gray hair, a brown-clad arm, a leg propped up on a stool, the foot encased in a slipper. A book lay open on his lap.

Over his shoulder, he snapped, "You're a full quarter hour early. I don't want my tea yet. Go away and return when you ought."

"I doubt you're expecting *me,* your lordship."

A clock ticked into the silence. He didn't turn around, but made an imperious gesture with his gnarled hand.

Claire walked forward, her chin held high. Now that she was here, she felt sustained by icy resolve. Somehow, she would find proof that this man had schemed to destroy her father. Her only regret was that at present, Warrington would know her as a servant.

Not as the granddaughter he had shunned.

Reaching his chair, she took her first good look at him. Cornelius Lathrop, the Marquess of Warrington, was thinner and less robust than she had imagined him. His face was craggy and deeply wrinkled, as if the years spent in the wind and salt spray had sapped him of all softness. Except for the leather slippers, he was perfectly groomed in tailored coat and starched cravat. A pair of spectacles lay on the opened book in his lap, and he had just removed them, a fact betrayed by the red mark on the bridge of his hawk nose.

He remained seated, one leg propped on the stool. His cold gaze flicked over her ill-made gown, then returned to her face. He looked every inch the condescending curmudgeon. "Who the devil are you?"

Your long-lost granddaughter.

A noose of emotions choked Claire. Anger for the way he had treated her parents. Bitterness that he had kept himself a stranger to her. And shock that she could see her mother in the shape of his eyes and the tilt of his cheekbones.

Playing the servant, she dipped a curtsy. "I am Mrs. Brownley, Lady Rosabel's new companion."

"You're insubordinate," he snapped. "I've given orders for no one to disturb me."

His rudeness only fortified her low opinion of him. "Forgive me for intruding, my lord. Lady Rosabel asked me to fetch a book for her."

One bushy gray brow winged upward. In a tone heavy with skepticism, he said, "My granddaughter wishes to read, does she?"

"Actually, she wants *me* to read to *her*," Claire said, using the excuse she had formulated. "I thought perhaps something by Shakespeare would do. Would you happen to have a volume of his plays?"

She watched him closely for a reaction, for a flicker of awareness, some sign that Warrington knew exactly which quotations the Wraith had left at the scene of each crime. But he merely looked annoyed by her intrusion.

"Over there." He pointed to the row of shelves on the far side of the fireplace. "Take the sonnets instead. You'll do better with something short to hold her interest."

Claire went to the place he'd indicated. Neat rows of bound books gave off the heady aroma of leather and ink. Under any other circumstances, she would have been eager to explore the array of works contained on these shelves. Not even the Canfield Academy had such a vast library.

She scanned the titles while her attention remained focused on the marquess. "Pray understand, I wouldn't read

She co

the entire play all at once. Only one scene per day at the most."

"Rosabel hates plays. Can't sit through 'em, not even at the theater."

He looked thunderous that she would dare to contradict him, so Claire thought it prudent to compromise. "Then I shall take the sonnets as you suggest," she said, selecting the slim volume from the shelf. "But if you don't mind, I'll also take *Macbeth*."

"Too morbid. She'll despise it."

He was right. Rosabel was unlikely to appreciate Shakespeare's darkest work. But after her father's arrest, Claire had asked the magistrate for permission to see the quotations left at the scene of each crime. He had refused on the grounds that they were official evidence, until she'd begged and he'd relented enough to read them aloud. One had been from *Macbeth*.

"Gloom often appeals to young ladies," she said. "And certainly the dialogue is engaging. 'By the pricking of my thumbs / Something wicked this way comes.'"

Warrington clenched the opened book in his lap. "You'll give her nightmares reading about murderers and madness. I forbid it."

Claire knew she walked a thin line between the obedience expected of a servant and her own need to determine which plays he knew well. "Then perhaps *The Tempest*? It's an allegorical tale of good and evil."

"Allegorical, bah. It's full of faeries and frivolity."

"Yet there's a romance to hold Lady Rosabel's attention. And the language is beautifully lyrical. 'We are such stuff as dreams are made on.'"

"By gad, enough of your chatter. Take whatever you like and leave."

He shoved the spectacles back on his nose and glared at her over the gold rims. His scowl made it clear that she was keeping him from his reading. Then he turned his attention back to the book in his lap.

Claire's stomach sank. Now what? She had discovered little other than the fact that her grandfather was familiar with a few of Shakespeare's works, and that description would fit half the people in England. She couldn't leave yet, not until she had found some proof to implicate him.

Holding the book of sonnets in the crook of her arm, she looked over the scattered volumes. Each play was bound individually in fine calfskin, a needless expense when a collection of the Bard's works usually were published in one volume. As her fingers reverently traced the gold lettering on the spines, she grasped for an excuse to return here. "Your books are out of order, my lord. Perhaps sometime I could reorganize them for you."

He looked up, his bristly gray eyebrows perched like caterpillars atop his eyeglasses. "There is nothing out of order, madam. I know the exact location of every book in this library."

"Then where is *A Midsummer Night's Dream*?" She strove for a pleasant tone. "I do believe Lady Rosabel would enjoy the discourse in that one, don't you? 'Lord, what fools these mortals be!' "

This time, she managed to elicit a reaction from him, though not the one she had intended.

Warrington clapped his book shut and thrust it onto a side table. Stiffly swinging his leg off the stool, he reached for a polished wood cane that she hadn't noticed on the other side of his chair. He used the stick as leverage to rise. "By gad, woman, it's right there in front of your face—"

Halfway to standing, he lost his balance. He fell against the table and knocked it over. The cane went flying. Landing in a heap on the hearth rug, he cursed and gripped his leg.

Claire dropped the book of sonnets and rushed to his

side. Kneeling beside him, she scanned his crumpled form. "Are you all right—"

"Stop your fussing," Warrington snapped. "I'm perfectly fine."

His coldness banished her instinctive softening of compassion. She reared back on her heels as he braced his knobby hands on the carpet and struggled unsuccessfully to get up. His lips were thinned and white with pain, though he uttered no sound, probably from sheer stubbornness.

Despite her antipathy, she said, "Have a care, your lordship. You may have broken a bone."

"I'll be the judge of that. Now go away!"

A dark ruddy hue tinted his weathered cheeks. He was mortified, Claire realized. A proud man like him, accustomed to being in control of his world, would despise his own frailty. More than that, he would loathe the fact that someone had witnessed his weakness.

Blast him, she wouldn't let herself feel any sympathy.

She got to her feet, intending to help him up regardless of his irascible nature. Then the door opened, and Oscar Eddison entered with a tea tray.

The short valet set down the burden and hastened to his master's side. "Allow me, my lord."

A hand under Warrington's elbow, Eddison guided him back into his chair. From the manservant's efficiency, she gathered that Warrington's collapse was not an uncommon event.

Sitting upright again, his age-spotted hands wrapped around the knob of his cane, Warrington flashed her a furious glare. "There's the play down there," he said, stabbing the cane at a lower shelf where she hadn't looked. "Take the cursed thing and begone!"

Oscar Eddison frowned at her, too—as if he suspected her of deliberately pushing his lordship.

Recognizing the need for caution, Claire lowered her gaze. She couldn't afford to antagonize her grandfather any further. Not if she wanted to keep her post in this house.

She collected *A Midsummer Night's Dream,* along with the volume of sonnets that she had dropped. Spying her grandfather's book lying on the hearth rug, she bent down to pick up that one, as well.

She glanced at the brown leather cover and froze. An arrow of shock pierced her heart. Unable to believe her eyes, she ran her fingertip over the embossed gold lettering. *Everyman's Guide to Shakespeare.*

Lord Warrington had been reading a copy of her father's book.

"O villain, villain, smiling damned villain!"
—*Hamlet*, I:v

Chapter Five

Simon was annoyed after tramping halfway across Hyde Park to fetch a lemon ice. His ill humor increased tenfold when he strode back to his phaeton, which he'd left parked in the shade of a massive plane tree.

The carriage was empty. So was the stone bench in the garden where he had left Lady Rosabel to enjoy a bank of scarlet and yellow tulips. His groom, Hobson, stood by the horses and uneasily shuffled his large feet.

"Where is Lady Rosabel?" Simon demanded.

"Left t' see a friend, m'lord. Well on 'arf an 'our ago."

"A friend? Who?"

"Dunno. She went that way." The wiry, middle-aged servant pointed toward Rotten Row, then ducked his head. "She bade me wait right 'ere fer ye, m'lord. I din know what else t' do."

Simon couldn't blame him for obeying orders. He was fast discovering that his intended bride had a flair for charming men into doing her bidding. And for behaving exactly as she pleased.

He shaded his eyes with his hand. A short distance away, carriages and riders jammed the wide avenue. The balmy spring afternoon had lured virtually every member of society outside for a drive. The sun shone, the birds sang, and Lady Rosabel was nowhere in sight.

Where had the little fool gone?

Simon felt like the fool. At her request, he had walked back to a vendor they'd passed alongside the road. She had been weary of the carriage, she'd said, and had begged him very prettily to leave Hobson and the phaeton here to protect her from any ruffians. Grimly determined to please her, Simon had ignored his better judgment and had gone on foot all the way back to Grosvenor Gate.

Now he was sweating from the warm weather, and his hat felt glued to his head. Something cold plopped onto his wrist. With a grimace, he looked down to see the lemon ice melting over the rim of the glass.

He shoved the confection at the groom. "Wait here. Should Lady Rosabel return, instruct her to stay here by my command."

"Aye, m'lord."

Simon knew that if she had disobeyed him the first time, she would do so again, but he had no other option. He had to find her. From his work apprehending criminals, he knew too well the dangers that could befall a young lady on her own.

Leaping into the high seat, he took up the reins and directed the pair of matched grays toward the parade of fashionable aristocrats. The gentle breeze carried the modulated din of carriage wheels, horse hooves, and genteel conversations. Joining the procession, he watched for a voluptuous blond clad in pale green. But the gravel road extended more than a mile through the park, and he couldn't see Lady Rosabel anywhere.

Her truancy caused an irritating wrinkle in the neat fabric of his plans. He needed to woo the girl, not waste valuable time chasing after her. The sooner he got this business of courtship over with and done, the better.

Then he spied a familiar face. From out of the throng, Sir Harry Masterson guided his bay gelding alongside Simon's carriage. In a double-breasted crimson jacket with a matching band on his tall black hat, he looked like the dashing man-about-town. "Ho, old boy. Thought I'd see you here with Lady Rosabel." Grinning, he lowered his voice to a murmur. "Or have you conceded defeat already? I knew I ought to have put money on my challenge!"

Simon ignored the jibe. Rather, he welcomed another pair of eyes, for he was beginning to worry. "As a matter of fact, she *was* with me until a short time ago. She went to speak to a friend."

"Why did you not attend her?"

"I was fetching her an ice. When I returned, she was gone."

Harry gave a hoot of laughter. "What do you mean— she ran away?"

His voice caught the attention of a pair of old matrons in a passing landau. Their eyes sharpened on him with keen interest.

The plump one beckoned to Simon. "Lord Rockford, what a pleasure to see you out and about. We so seldom encounter you here."

Swallowing a groan, he lifted his hat and gave them a polite nod. It was just his luck to encounter the two biggest rumormongers in all of society. "Lady Yarborough. Mrs. Danby. A fine day, is it not?"

Lady Yarborough preened as if he'd voiced a clever witticism instead of a bland cliché. A lavender bonnet with far too many ribbons enhanced the roundness of her face. "Did I hear you say someone has run away?"

"Surely it wasn't Lady Rosabel," Mrs. Danby added, curiosity stark on her skeletal features. "Last evening, you two were as cozy as lovebirds."

Announcing Lady Rosabel's disappearance to these

old crones would be like taking out an advertisement in the *Times*. As anxious as Simon was to find her, he knew the value of protecting her from embarrassment.

He slowed his horses so that the landau moved ahead of his phaeton. "It's my sister I'm seeking," he lied smoothly. "We were to meet here, but I was unavoidably detained. Good day."

"Which sister?" Lady Yarborough called out, but they were almost out of earshot, and Simon pretended not to hear.

Still smiling for the benefit of any watchers, he muttered testily, "For God's sake, Harry, keep your voice down. And Lady Rosabel didn't run away. She's here somewhere. I could use your help in finding her."

"She must have had a reason for abandoning you," Harry said with a grin as he directed his mount around a muddy spot alongside the gravel road. "No doubt you offended her."

"I've never offended a woman in my life."

"You scolded Lady Burkington for leaving her jewels out for the Wraith to steal."

At the time, Simon had been frustrated in his investigation of the case. The thief had had the uncanny ability to slip in and out of the finest houses undetected—even Simon's, where his mother's diamond bracelet had gone missing during a dinner party. The only clues had been those taunting passages from Shakespeare left at the scene of each crime. Simon had wasted weeks pursuing leads and coming up empty. Now, he allowed himself a moment to dwell on the satisfaction of knowing that Gilbert Hollybrooke sat behind bars awaiting trial.

Only one fly lurked in the ointment. By a strange twist of fate, Hollybrooke was Lady Rosabel's uncle by marriage. Although the family had cut off ties long ago, Simon felt like a fraud for hiding the fact that he had been the one to arrest Hollybrooke. Yet informing Warrington meant Simon would have to reveal his secret work with the Bow Street Runners. That was something he was not prepared to do.

Harry's voice pulled him back to the present. "Tell me, what were you two conversing about when Lady Rosabel sent you away?"

"Devil if I remember—" Aware of the parade of people, Simon bit off the interjection. "We talked about the weather, the scenery, the park."

"A vague answer from one who prides himself on precision."

"All right, then, I was explaining to her how Rotten Row came by its name. The name dates back to the French phrase *'Route du Roi,'* meaning the king's road. Over the years the words were corrupted, in much the same way as Bethlehem Hospital became known as Bedlam."

"Aha!" Harry pointed his whip at Simon. "You were lecturing the poor girl. It's no wonder she contrived a means to get away. You bored her silly."

Simon gripped the reins, controlling his annoyance as deftly as he did the matched grays. "My future wife must learn to speak of something more substantial than fashion and other tittle-tattle."

"Ah, but the key to winning a lady's heart is to allow *her* to direct the conversation."

"I won't change myself to suit her."

"But you expect *her* to change for *you*," Harry said slyly. "Give it up, old boy. Admit that you cannot take any girl at random and train her as you would a puppy."

"I'll bring her to heel within the fortnight," Simon countered. "Now, you may assist me or not, but I intend to find the lady."

Determined, he scanned the throng again. Carriages jammed the road for as far ahead as he could see. Ladies in a rainbow array of bonnets and gowns rode in open coaches alongside gentlemen in top hats. Lady Rosabel had to be somewhere among them.

Because where the devil else would she have gone?

Claire sat sewing in her garret bedroom with a mound of mending in a basket beside her. Or at least she attempted to work. At the moment, her hands sat idly atop Lady Hester's enormous shift with its burst seam. Instead of minding her stitches, she stared out the small attic window at a sea of rooftops where pigeons sailed on waves of wind and chimneys chugged smoke into the oceanic blue of the sky.

For the past hour, she had been brooding about the encounter with her grandfather. It had shaken her deeply to see him reading *Everyman's Guide to Shakespeare*. His interest in a book written by Gilbert Hollybrooke could be attributed neither to sentiment nor to coincidence. Warrington had never made any attempt to contact Claire's family. He hadn't even attended her mother's funeral fourteen years ago.

His purpose in reading the book, then, must have been to gloat. He must have been reveling in the success of his villainy, enjoying the satisfaction of having sent Gilbert Hollybrooke to prison. He had hired someone to steal those jewels and leave the quotations—or perhaps instructed his weaselly valet, Oscar Eddison, to do the dirty work. It would have been simple enough for Warrington to drop that grocer's bill with her father's address outside the scene of the last robbery.

The thought made Claire's blood boil. She had burned to confront him with her accusations. But he had been in a foul temper, and the last thing she needed was to be thrown out onto the street before she had obtained iron-clad proof.

Fiercely, she attacked the shift with needle and thread, placing a battalion of neat stitches along the ripped seam. She was tying off the ends of the thread when a snooty footman poked his head inside and announced that she had a visitor waiting in the blue drawing room.

Startled, she straightened the spectacles that had slipped down her nose. "A caller for Lady Rosabel, you mean?"

"Nay, the gennelman asked for you. Told me to keep his presence a secret from all but you." As he left, the footman eyed her with a certain sly curiosity.

Claire frowned. She had met only a handful of gentlemen: Lord Rockford, who was out with Rosabel; Lord Frederick, who had no need for subterfuge since he lived here; and Sir Harry Masterson, who surely could have no reason to hide his identity.

That left one other possibility—Mr. Mundy, her father's barrister. He was the only person aside from Papa who knew she had taken a position in this household. But she had warned Mr. Mundy never to come here except in case of dire emergency.

Her heart lurched. Had something happened to Papa?

The mending forgotten, Claire dashed out of the room and headed down the servants' staircase. Her footsteps matched the quickened tempo of her heart. She mustn't think the worst. It could as easily be good news, a break in the case or a witness who could prove Papa was not the Wraith.

Reaching the ground floor, she made her way toward the front of the house along a vast corridor constructed entirely of marble. The house was silent except for the echo of her footsteps. Alabaster statues stared coldly from niches in the walls as if she were an intruder trespassing on hallowed ground.

How ironic to think she ought to have the right to walk here as freely as any other family member. Instead, Lady

Hester would be furious if she learned that Claire had re-ceived a caller in one of the formal chambers. Mr. Mundy should have come to the back entrance, and Claire had every intention of telling him so.

She opened one of the double doors and went inside. The drawing room exuded wealth from the elaborately carved mantelpiece to the blue-striped chairs with their gilt trim. Heavy brocade draperies with lace undercur-tains dimmed the sunlight and muffled the noise from the square. The air held a whiff of beeswax and something else, something spicy and masculine.

Something that aroused a warm, curling awareness in Claire even before she spied her visitor.

She came to an abrupt halt. He stood at one of the front windows, peering out at the street. His tall, distinguished form banished all thought of Mr. Mundy and her father.

"Lord Rockford!" Confusion eclipsed her surprise. "But where is Lady Rosabel?" If her cousin had gone up the grand staircase, they would have missed each other.

The earl approached with an arrogance of manner that made Claire dislike him on principle. It was as if he owned the world and expected everyone else to bow to his wishes. No doubt many worshiped him as a god, for he possessed a title, wealth, and a face too handsome for any mere mortal.

Fortunately, Claire had the sense to see past his splen-did façade. Only a demon could possess that sinful mouth, those dark burning eyes, the aura of sinister charm designed to beguile unsuspecting women.

Going past her, he shut the door and then turned, his expression grim. "I was hoping you knew."

She gazed uncomprehendingly at him. Then his mean-ing struck like a blow, and her suspicions about him came flooding back in full force. She rushed at him with her fists clenched. "Lecher! What have you done to her? If you've harmed even one hair on her head—"

"Don't be absurd." His stern voice stopped her cold. "If I'd compromised her, I'd hardly return here."

Mistrust kept her fingers curled into balls. "What happened, then?"

"At the park, I went to fetch an ice for Lady Rosabel. When I returned, she was gone. My groom said she went to speak to a friend. He didn't see who."

The earl's words carried the ring of truth. Surely he couldn't know that Rosabel had a habit of disappearing. "You swear to this?"

"On my life. I searched the entire length of Rotten Row, and she's not to be found. I thought she might have returned here."

His brown eyes bored into Claire, and he looked genuinely concerned, a concern she shared. It forged a peculiar connection between them, one she preferred not to acknowledge. But it was there in the thrumming of her heart and the warming of her breast. Despite the disastrous circumstances, her body instinctively responded to his masculine allure.

Disastrous, indeed.

She folded her arms in self-protection, and his gaze flicked down to her bosom. That confirmation of his vile nature prompted Claire to speak coldly.

"You must have missed her, then. She's probably in a panic right now, wondering where you've gone. You must return to the park at once!"

"Harry Masterson is there, looking for her. I lent him my carriage. If he finds her, he's to bring her back here straightaway."

The earl paced to the window, moved the curtain aside, and peered out at the street as if expecting the two of them to drive up at his command.

Anxiety induced Claire to follow him. She looked beyond his shoulder to see a workman's dray rattle past the house, then a trio of ladies riding in an open carriage. In the square, two nannies sat side by side on a wrought-iron bench, watching several children playing in the grass.

The serenity of the scene only underscored Claire's alarm. Was Rosabel in trouble at this very moment? "You should be there yourself," she repeated. "We gave her into your care. What sort of man are you, that her reputation and well-being mean so little to you?"

He regarded her coolly. "Your concern is duly noted. Now, have you any notion where she might have gone?"

It was on the tip of her tongue to admit that Rosabel vanished with annoying regularity. But Lady Hester would be livid. She would accuse Claire of ruining her daughter's chance to make a brilliant marriage. "No, but I'm sure Lady Rosabel did exactly as she said—she went to speak to a friend. And I won't have you blaming her. She's young and easily bored. You ought not to have left her alone."

Claire braced herself for the annihilation of his rebuke. No servant was allowed to voice such blunt opinions, let alone to a man of his stature.

But he merely said, "Who are her acquaintances?"

"I'm afraid I don't know. I've been employed here for only a few days."

Muttering what sounded like an oath, he released the curtain and prowled the chamber. "She must be friendly with other girls her age. What are their names?"

"Frankly, she's more interested in the gentlemen." When he raised an eyebrow, Claire amended, "I certainly don't mean to imply that she would go off with another man. She has more sense than that."

At least Claire hoped so. She truly didn't know what went on in her cousin's mind. And she had a worrisome hunch that Rosabel was not as frivolous as the world believed her to be.

"What about a relative?" he asked. "Does she have any aunts or cousins she might have gone to visit?"

Claire shook her head. "Her mother was an only child. And her late father had a sister, but she died long ago."

Lord Rockford said nothing. His eyes were narrowed on Claire, and she had the odd impression that he could see into her mind, that he knew all her secrets.

Ridiculous. He couldn't possibly guess at her connection to the family. She had been extremely careful in concealing her personal history. If he knew anything at all of Gilbert Hollybrooke and the Wraith, it had come from the newspapers or from idle gossip.

"I'll need to organize a search," he said. "But first I'll have a word with Warrington. Kindly inform him I'm here."

"No!"

"No?" he repeated, his voice coldly mocking.

She refused to cower. The Marquess of Warrington was a cruel, embittered man who would blame Claire for failing in her duty to chaperone Rosabel. It wouldn't matter to him that Claire had been expressly forbidden to accompany the courting couple.

Seeking an excuse, she said, "It would be foolish to raise a hue and cry when Lady Rosabel might already be on her way home."

"It would be more foolish to risk her safety."

"His lordship has given orders that no one is to disturb him."

"Not even if his granddaughter has gone missing?" Rockford regarded her with steely authority. "Go on now, there's not a moment to waste."

The childish urge to disobey seethed in Claire, but common sense kept her silent. Whether she agreed with his order or not, she was obliged to do his bidding. Giving him a stiff nod, she turned toward the door.

"Wait."

His voice was a blessed reprieve. But when she glanced back at him, he wasn't looking at her. His manner alert, he returned to the window and moved the curtain aside. An instant later, he came striding back with energized steps.

"They're here," he said with more grimness than pleasure. "Thank God, Harry's brought her back."

"Love looks not with the eyes, but with the mind."
—*A Midsummer Night's Dream*, I:i

Chapter Six

As Simon started toward the door, Mrs. Brownley took the lead. He doubted that she had rushed ahead to hold the door open for him. He found himself both irked and intrigued by the anomaly of a servant who clearly believed her status on par with his.

Without a doubt, there was more to her than met the eye. She was no mere commoner, for one. Her proud, prickly nature along with the fineness of her speech suggested that she had been raised as a gentlewoman.

Unfortunately, she hadn't been taught any flair for fashion. Her shapeless gray gown had all the style of a gunnysack. An ugly black cap hid all but a few fringes of dark hair. The wire-rimmed spectacles were more suited to a dowdy old matron. If not for their close encounter in Stanfield's garden, Simon would never have given her a second glance.

He wouldn't have known she had the curvaceous figure of a goddess. He wouldn't have realized that she smelled of lavender and that her blue eyes sparkled with intelligence. He wouldn't have noticed that she had the smooth, glowing skin of a woman in her twenties.

And at the moment he wouldn't be experiencing the heat of . . . lust?

Good God. He must be mad to feel even the slightest attraction to Clara Brownley, let alone to savor the fantasy of stripping off that hideous garb and exploring her naked body. His women were always cultured, beautiful, and well-versed in the art of pleasing a man. Only a fool would consider bedding a frumpy, temperamental shrew.

Especially when that shrew was employed by his intended bride.

Lady Rosabel. He fixed his thoughts on blond hair and a bountiful bosom. With her elegance and breeding, Lady Rosabel would make him a suitable wife. Her lack of maturity could be remedied by means of firm guidance. First and foremost, he intended to have a word with her on the dangers of a lady wandering away on her own.

Grimly, he followed Mrs. Brownley into the entrance hall. She marched straight to the front door and opened it, disregarding the young footman standing on duty. She strode out onto the porch, leaving Simon little choice but to trail behind her like a lackey.

Three marble steps separated the vast porch from the pavement. His phaeton was parked at the curbstone, alongside Harry's bay gelding, which Simon had left tethered to a post. Aided by Harry, the object of Simon's courtship was dismounting from the carriage. The afternoon sunlight lent a luminous quality to Lady Rosabel's skin. In the frothy green bonnet and form-fitting gown, she looked fresh and youthful, every man's image of virginal femininity.

So why the devil did his gaze stray again to Clara Brownley?

Her voluminous dress flapping, she flew down the steps and stopped in her mistress's path. "My lady, we've been very worried about you—"

"Pray step aside, Brownie," Lady Rosabel said, lifting a graceful gloved hand to her brow. "I am far too fatigued for a lecture."

Frowning, Mrs. Brownley obeyed, moving back to let Lady Rosabel glide toward the house. As Simon descended the steps, she greeted him with a woebegone smile.

Clasping her hands to her ample breasts, she said, "Oh, thank heavens you're here, Lord Rockford! What a relief it is to find you at last."

Bowing, he refrained from pointing out that *she* had been the one who was lost. "The relief is all mine. I trust you've suffered no ill effects from our separation?"

"I'm extremely weary from walking." She leaned on his proffered arm and gazed up at him. "You see, I went off to pay my respects to the Duke of Stanfield. I wanted to thank him for the lovely ball he gave last evening. And for giving us the opportunity to meet."

"I found her wandering along a pathway near Park Avenue," Harry said musingly, "quite some distance from Rotten Row."

A flicker of displeasure crossed her fine features. "As I already explained, I was looking for Lord Rockford." She returned her full, simpering attention to Simon. "After I spoke to the duke, I traipsed all over Hyde Park. But I couldn't find you anywhere."

"Didn't you return to the tulip garden?" Simon glanced inquiringly at Hobson, who held the horses. "I left my groom waiting for you there."

"Oh, but I couldn't *find* the tulip garden. Mama says I'm hopeless with directions." Lady Rosabel ducked her chin and regarded him through the fringe of her lashes. "My lord, I'm terribly sorry to have caused such trouble. Truly, I am. You will forgive me, won't you?"

He recognized that soulful look. His sisters used it

whenever they had done wrong and hoped to maneuver him. Just as with them, he felt an involuntary softening. But he covered it with a stern expression. Her lapse of judgment was no matter to be dismissed lightly.

Nor to be discussed on a busy street. A carriage clattered over the cobblestones, a horseman trotted smartly toward them from the direction of the park, and a curtain flicked in the window of a neighboring house. The two nannies sitting in the square were gazing straight at them.

"We are beginning to attract attention," he murmured. "Shall we adjourn to the house?" He drew Lady Rosabel toward the porch with its grand marble pediment.

She balked, and her lips formed a little-girl pout. "Oh, dear, you *are* angry, are you not? Will you not accept my apology?"

"In due course. I'd like a word with you first."

"Must we talk? I'm so exhausted by my long walk."

"It wouldn't matter if you're near swooning," Harry commented. "When Rockford sets his mind on something, there's no stopping him." When Simon glared at him, he added, "But never mind, I'll just toddle along now. Rockford, do try not to be too hard on the poor girl."

Harry untethered his bay gelding and vaulted into the saddle. With a jaunty wave, he headed off down the cobblestone street.

Simon returned his attention to Lady Rosabel. Contrary to her claim of tiredness, she looked in the pink of health, and he suspected she was exaggerating in order to escape a scolding. But he felt compelled to impress upon her the perils of a lone lady being set upon by ruffians. "I beg only a moment of your time," he said firmly. "If we might go inside—"

"She needs rest," Mrs. Brownley broke in. She stepped briskly to Lady Rosabel's side, taking hold of her other arm and tugging her away from Simon. "Come with me, my lady. Anything his lordship has to say can wait until the morrow."

Her sharp stare impaled him, sparking an irrational anger in Simon. This servant had placed him in an indefensible position. If he insisted, he would appear ungentlemanly. If he acquiesced, he would be giving her the upper hand.

Logic told him to postpone the lecture. He was allowing himself to be ruled by pride and emotion, which he had sworn never to do. Yet he found himself grasping Lady Rosabel's arm again. "I'll escort her inside. You may return to your other duties."

"With all due respect, my lord, *no*."

Mrs. Brownley held her ground. They stood on either side of Lady Rosabel, glaring at each other, both too obstinate to back down. He had the ridiculous image of them pulling at the girl like two children quarreling over a rocking horse. He could only imagine what an unfavorable impression he must be making on Lady Rosabel.

But she wasn't paying attention to him. She was looking over her shoulder, her blue eyes bright with interest. Turning his head, Simon realized that a stranger on horseback had reined to a halt in front of the house.

The young gentleman tipped his tall black hat with the curled brim. "Ho there, Lady Rosabel," he said laughingly. "Have you been naughty? Are they hauling you off to gaol?"

Simon assessed the newcomer at a glance. Wiry and fair, dressed with fashionable flamboyance in a dark green coat with gold buttons. His sharp, foxlike features looked vaguely familiar. With the panache of a storybook hero, he leaped down from the horse and tossed the reins to Hobson.

"Oh, Mr. Newcombe!" Lady Rosabel trilled. "What a pleasant surprise." She swiveled to face him, pulling Simon and Mrs. Brownley along with her.

Lewis Newcombe. Simon recognized the name with an unpleasant jolt. Newcombe was a scoundrel of the worst ilk. Although he was heir to Viscount Barlow, the clubs had banned him from the gaming tables for being too deeply in debt. The grapevine of gossip flourished on the fertile rumors of his duels. Even the matchmaking mamas shunned him for his thwarted attempt to run off with the underage daughter of a wealthy merchant.

How the devil did a gently bred lady like Rosabel know such a rogue? Simon's question was answered in the next breath.

"I intended to call on Freddie," Newcombe said, referring to her ne'er-do-well brother. "Instead, I must rescue a lady in distress." Lifting his arm, he pretended to brandish a sword. "Unhand her at once, varlet. I'll fight to the death to keep you from locking her away."

The nannies were craning their necks now and talking excitedly. An old woman next door pressed her nose to the window glass. Annoyed, Simon released Lady Rosabel, and Mrs. Brownley did likewise.

Lady Rosabel giggled. "Don't be silly, Mr. Newcombe. It is only that Lord Rockford wishes to rebuke me for getting lost in the park."

"Rather unsporting of him to browbeat a defenseless lady. And for such a flimsy cause. For shame, Rockford! If you dare to speak one cross word to this ideal of maidenly virtue, I shall call you out."

Simon refused to be goaded. "Whatever I say to Lady Rosabel is no concern of yours."

"Then perhaps we should meet at Hampstead Heath

tomorrow at dawn." With unholy glee, Newcombe rubbed his palms. "Name your weapons. Pistols? I've a new set of beauties I've been itching to try. Or do you prefer swords?"

"Neither," Simon said flatly. "If you'll step into the house, the footman will summon Lord Frederick for you."

"Oh, but Grandpapa has forbidden Mr. Newcombe entry," Lady Rosabel said, her mouth forming a moue of distress. "He called him a wicked, unscrupulous rogue."

"A wretched fiend, that's me," Newcombe added cheerfully. "I'm king of the rum coves."

He winked at Lady Rosabel, and she blushed like a girl receiving her first compliment. In truth, she looked entirely too taken by his unsavory reputation. Apparently she needed to modify her inappropriate behavior in more ways than one.

Frowning, Simon turned to Mrs. Brownley, who watched the proceedings with narrowed eyes. "Will you kindly fetch Lord Frederick?"

"He's gone out," she said. "More than an hour ago."

"You might have said so straightaway."

"It isn't a servant's place to interrupt her betters."

To a casual observer, she would look demure and humble. But Simon noted the mocking arch of one brow and the directness of her gaze. Despite his displeasure, her cheeky manner unexpectedly amused him.

Newcombe swept off his hat and made a theatrical bow. "Well, then, *au revoir,* my friends. Rockford, do keep a civil tongue with the lady, or you'll answer to me."

With a jaundiced eye, Simon watched him swing onto his mount. Nothing surprised him anymore, not even the colossal irony of being chastised by a blackguard. He had no intention of being forced into that duel. He was getting too old for such nonsense.

He turned to Lady Rosabel, only to see Clara Brownley murmur something in her ear. The girl flashed a wide-eyed glance at Simon, then scampered up the steps and vanished into the house.

Mrs. Brownley blocked Simon's path. "The lady requests that you return on the morrow. Good day, sir."

As she marched after her mistress, Simon distinctly heard her add under her breath, "And good riddance."

The moment they entered the pink-and-yellow bedchamber, Rosabel threw her arms around Claire. "Oh, Brownie, you're such a dear. You saved me from a horrid scolding."

The embrace caught Claire unawares. Enveloped by soft arms and floral scent, she stood frozen. The last thing she'd expected was a show of affection from her cousin. In all her planning to infiltrate this household, Claire had regarded her mother's family as the enemy. She had never even considered that Rosabel might exhibit any warmth toward her.

Perhaps, for the sake of the ruse, she ought to return her cousin's hug. But she felt too awkward and stiff to move.

Thankfully, Rosabel didn't appear to notice Claire's rigidity. She drew away, untying the ribbon beneath her chin and dropping the green bonnet onto a chair. "I do believe we shall get along quite well, you and I," she went on. "You aren't as stuffy as my other companions."

Uttering a noncommittal murmur, Claire collected her composure along with Rosabel's hat. It was foolish to imagine that such a frivolous girl could feel fondness for anyone but herself. Rosabel was relieved to have escaped so lightly from her latest escapade, that was all.

Little did she know the real reason Claire had thwarted Lord Rockford—she hadn't wanted him to question the girl too closely. What if Rosabel had been up to no good?

What if she was involved in a dangerous scheme . . . like jewel theft? What if she was the Wraith?

A ridiculous notion. And yet . . .

"It isn't the earl's place to rebuke you—" she began.

"Exactly!" Rosabel flounced to the dressing table and sat down to tidy her blond curls in the mirror. "One would think he was my father for the way he spoke to me."

"—however, I do wish to have a word with you myself. You should never have gone off on your own."

The looking glass reflected Rosabel's suddenly sulky expression. "Was I not to pay my regards to the Duke of Stanfield? Mama taught me it was proper to thank the host after a ball."

"It would have been proper for you to wait for Lord Rockford to escort you. He had every right to be alarmed when he returned to discover you missing."

"I already apologized. And even Mr. Newcombe thought it unsporting of him to chide me for getting lost."

Lewis Newcombe had a skewed notion of respectable behavior, Claire thought. Watching Rosabel closely, she smoothed the ribbons of the bonnet. "You were gone for well over an hour. With so many people in the park, could you not have stopped someone and asked directions?"

"There are many unattended pathways. And I was afraid to approach a stranger, anyway."

Claire wouldn't accept the flippant explanation. Not when her father's life was at stake.

Bonnet in hand, she walked to the dressing table. "On my first day of employment, you slipped away from me on Bond Street and I couldn't find you for over half an hour. Then, on our walk the following afternoon, I had to chase down the street after your hair ribbon, only to turn around and find you gone."

"I was following a stray dog. Such a darling little creature it was, all gray and fluffy."

By the time Claire had found Rosabel smelling the roses in a garden several blocks distant, the dog had been gone. "I distinctly remember you saying it was black with white spots."

Rosabel peered closer into the looking glass, turning her head this way and that. "Black or gray, what difference does it make?"

"It makes quite a lot of difference." Claire paused, choosing her words carefully. "Especially if you're engaged in secret matters unsuited to a genteel young lady."

The silver brush paused infinitesimally; then Rosabel touched up a curl. "And what if I am? Are you going to tell Mama? She'll never take your word over mine."

Claire's heart beat faster. Rosabel had as much as admitted that she had lied about her actions. But what exactly had she been up to all those times—and today? Could it be something other than thievery?

"Of course I wouldn't tell," she said coaxingly. "I'm only worried about you, my lady. Are you involved with another man? Someone inappropriate, perhaps?"

Rosabel smiled mysteriously into the mirror. "If I was, I certainly wouldn't admit so."

"It's my responsibility to ensure your safety. I cannot allow you to put yourself in danger."

"Ah, but danger makes life exciting, does it not? It's much more fun than trading gossip with the other girls."

The glib reply frustrated Claire. In all her years as a teacher, she had never encountered anyone as trying as Rosabel. "You've been disappearing quite a lot. Eventually, your behavior is bound to come to the attention of your grandfather."

Rosabel swiveled on the stool to face her. "Are you threatening me, Brownie?"

The petulance in those blue eyes startled Claire. Lowering her chin and hunching her shoulders, she assumed a nonthreatening pose. "Please be assured, I'm no tattler. You may trust me implicitly. Whatever you say here will remain confidential."

Unless, of course, Rosabel admitted to being the Wraith. If it meant clearing Papa's name, Claire would suffer no guilt over betraying her cousin.

"I suppose we all have our secrets," Rosabel said in a rather sly tone. "Even you, Brownie."

The statement struck like a lightning bolt from a clear blue sky. Claire stared over the rims of her spectacles. "I beg your pardon?"

"I saw you making eyes at Lord Rockford. Confess now. You admire him."

Claire didn't know whether to be relieved that her disguise was safe, or mortified to have shown an unseemly attraction to the earl. "You're mistaken, my lady," she said indignantly. "I can't imagine where you would come up with such a wrongful notion—"

"Oh, I'm not angry," Rosabel said with a wave of her hand. "He might be handsome, but he's a dull dog and you're welcome to him."

Nonplussed, Claire busied herself by straightening the bottles and jars on the dressing table. "This discussion is absurd. Not only is an earl far beyond my reach, but I'm in mourning. Not a year has passed since my husband's death."

"I *am* sorry," Rosabel said, not unkindly. She took a green vial from Claire's hand and returned it to the collection. "However, you cannot mean to grieve forever. How old are you? Five-and-twenty?"

"I hardly think it matters—"

"It does indeed matter." Getting up from the stool, she

walked around Claire, studying her critically. "You were raised a lady, were you not?"

"I come from a genteel family in York, though far less exalted than yours." Claire had purposely kept the story vague in case anyone checked into her background. "But you've turned the subject away from yourself—"

"I would speak of *you*, Brownie." Reaching out, Rosabel bunched the fabric at Claire's waist. "Why do you wear these hideous gowns? Your figure looks fine. Why do you hide it?"

Uneasy, Claire stepped back. "It would be improper for me to call attention to myself."

"Not even servants dress in sacks. Have you no money to pay for clothes? I will give you some of my castoffs. You're taller and slimmer, but they can be altered to fit."

Claire stiffened. She wanted no charity from her cousin. "I would be obliged to respectfully decline anything so fancy. I prefer my own garb, ugly as it is. Modesty is a virtue."

"Stuff and nonsense. How are you ever to attract a man if you make so little effort?"

Claire had had enough of the conversation. "My lady, I'm only interested in your mysterious disappearances," she said firmly. "You must realize you've only postponed Lord Rockford's lecture. If I'm any judge of character, he'll be back tomorrow."

A look of calculating interest lit Rosabel's delicate features. Watching Claire, she walked slowly around the bedchamber. "I believe I shall endure his scold for your sake, Brownie."

"For my sake?"

"Yes, henceforth you will chaperone us everywhere. I shall pretend to encourage his courtship. But only you and I will know that it is all a hoax."

The cunning half-smile on her cousin's face worried Claire. "I don't understand."

Rosabel laughed gleefully. "I've conceived a brilliant plan. If I pay heed to the earl, Mama will cease thrusting me at every old codger with a title. And then *I* will contrive to leave *you* alone with Lord Rockford."

"Some Cupid kills with arrows, some with traps."
—*Much Ado About Nothing*, III:i

Chapter Seven

"I can't possibly testify against Hollybrooke in a court of law," Simon objected. "That would mean revealing my work here at Bow Street."

Thomas Cramps spread his beefy hands wide. "I'm not pleased with the situation, either, m'lord. You've been essential in breaking these high-society cases. But I'm afraid we've no other choice. I very much doubt Islington will return in time to bear witness at the trial."

Simon frowned at the chief magistrate who sat across the battered oak desk. Islington had been Simon's partner in the case, the Bow Street Runner who had assisted him in arresting the Wraith. Now, Islington had gone to visit his father who lay dying in a village near the Scottish border.

Which left Simon the only eyewitness who could swear that the diamond bracelet had been found in Hollybrooke's desk.

"Perhaps the trial can be delayed," he said.

Cramps shook his head. "There's some in society clamoring for Hollybrooke's throat. Lord Yarborough, a Mr. Danby, even the Duke of Stanfield. Word's come down from on high to get the trial under way posthaste."

Simon cursed. "At least we have nearly a month. Islington may be back by then."

Looking ill at ease, the magistrate scratched the tightly curled white wig that was his badge of office. "Er, that isn't the whole of it. The trial date has moved up by request of the Regent himself. 'Tis set for less than a fortnight from now."

The chair legs scraped as Simon sprang to his feet. "The devil you say! That doesn't allow either side sufficient time to prepare their case."

"Aye, m'lord," Cramps said gloomily. "There's naught to be done but to have you testify. Hollybrooke's conviction depends upon you."

His mood grim, Simon departed the station by a rear door. A dark sky threatened rain. Bow Street was sufficiently distant from the exclusive district of Mayfair, where people might recognize him, but he took the precaution of scanning the alley, anyway. He saw only a housewife gathering in her laundry and a watchman marching off on his rounds.

Simon mounted his horse. Should he go to Carlton House and seek an audience with the Prince Regent? No, he sincerely doubted that Prinny would back down on his decision. Not if that wily bastard Stanfield had persuaded him otherwise.

Simon's blood ran cold at the thought of the notoriety in store for him. When the press got wind of the story, his name would be plastered over every news rag in town. A peer of the realm capturing a criminal would cause a sensation. His cover would be ruined.

And the reporters were bound to dig deeper. They might discover he had aided the Runners on numerous other occasions. They might even unearth the long-buried truth behind his crusade against crime. Once again, his family would be subjected to the horror of his father's death.

Breathing deeply of refuse-tainted air, Simon swung his mount toward home. He should have anticipated this event and taken steps to prevent it. But he had been too distracted by his courtship of Lady Rosabel.

Deliberately, he focused his thoughts on the girl. Yesterday's incident at the park had underscored her youthful impetuosity. In the coming weeks, he must devote a portion of his time to molding her into a proper countess. He might have already started on the task of correcting her behavior if not for Mrs. Brownley's high-handed interference. Any further meddling by that woman could complicate his courtship, especially if her waspish tongue poisoned Lady Rosabel against him.

He would not permit that to happen.

In the meantime, the looming trial brought another problem to the forefront of his mind. No longer could he ignore the unlucky fact that his potential bride was connected by marriage to Gilbert Hollybrooke.

He would soon need to tell Lord Warrington the truth about his son-in-law's arrest.

Lady Hester's maid was putting the finishing touches on Rosabel's hair when a footman brought word that Lord Rockford had come to call. He was waiting in the library with Lord Warrington.

With an impatient wave of her hand, Rosabel jumped up from the stool. "That's enough, Lucille. You may return to Mama."

"Oui, mam'selle." The diminutive, dark-haired maid bobbed a curtsy, then gave Claire another avid scrutiny before vanishing out the door.

Claire self-consciously smoothed her gown of dark blue gauze festooned with delicate gold scrollwork. Lucille would report to the other servants that the new companion was wearing one of Rosabel's castoffs, a privilege usually reserved for longtime members of the upper staff. They wouldn't know how grudgingly Claire had accepted this gown, or how cunningly Rosabel had maneuvered her.

"Your appearance is a disgrace, Brownie. Those gloomy colors add at least ten years onto your age."

"Pray recall that I'm in mourning. Besides, Lady Hester would forbid me to wear your garments."

"Then I shall tell Mama that I refuse to be seen with a companion who dresses like a frump. She will agree with me. She always does."

"She won't agree with me flirting with Lord Rockford. Nor will I agree to be used as a shield to guard whatever secrets you're hiding."

"Then we'll make a bargain. If you allow me to improve your wardrobe, then I won't ask you to distract his lordship."

With that, Rosabel had rummaged through her dressing room and produced several gowns that she declared too sober for herself. She had ordered Claire to spend the rest of the day letting down hems and adjusting bodices to accommodate her taller, slimmer figure. All the while, Claire had reassured herself that a single change in her appearance wouldn't jeopardize her disguise.

But now, as she glanced at her reflection in the mirror, uneasiness niggled at her. Despite the sober cap, she looked like a lady of means. A lady who belonged in this house.

What if someone spotted a family resemblance?

Impossible. The spectacles helped to camouflage her face, and she had inherited her father's features more so than her mother's. Besides, no one would be looking for Lady Emily's daughter here, especially not among the servants.

"That cap is far too matronly," Rosabel declared. She floated into view in the mirror, a voluptuous angel in a gown of pale gold gauze. "Next time, I'll have Lucille do your hair, too."

"No!" Taking a breath, Claire modulated her tone. "It's appropriate for a widow, my lady. I've no wish to call attention to myself."

"What a silly goose you are, Brownie. A woman should use her looks to get whatever she fancies."

"Being a servant, I fancy anonymity."

"Well, you can at least do without these." Taking Claire by surprise, Rosabel snatched off the spectacles. "There, that's better."

Anger and alarm choked Claire. "Give those back to me at once. How do you expect me to see?"

"I believe you need them only for reading or mending. I've noticed you peering over the rims when you wish to see in the distance."

Had she been so transparent? Fighting panic, Claire held out her hand. "I want them returned. This instant."

"No." Rosabel scuttled to the dainty writing desk, opened a drawer, and dropped the eyeglasses inside. Then she turned the key and dropped it into her bodice. "There, you've no choice in the matter. Now come quickly, we mustn't keep his lordship waiting."

"We? I'm not going anywhere without my spectacles."

"Oh, don't be cross," Rosabel said in a cajoling voice. "I'll return them to you later, I promise. But you look so much nicer without them."

Irritation made Claire immune to praise. For half a moment, she considered plucking the key from its soft, scented cradle. Then the practical side of her faced the futility of the situation.

"You may go alone," she said frostily. "I hardly think you need a chaperone in the presence of your grandfather."

Claire didn't know why the prospect of accompanying Rosabel made her stomach clench. She ought to seize the chance to observe Lord Warrington and possibly glean something of importance.

Or perhaps it was Lord Rockford she didn't care to encounter.

"You simply *must* go with me," Rosabel insisted, grabbing Claire's arm and pulling her out into the passageway. "I might need your help."

"Help?"

"With Lord Rockford. If he's told Grandpapa that I went wandering alone through the park yesterday, I shall be in dire trouble."

The comment caused Claire to forget about her stolen eyeglasses. Heading down the sumptuous corridor with her cousin, she said, "Surely he'll only scold you."

"Oh, yes. But believe me, Grandpapa's bark is far worse than his bite."

Claire doubted that. She would rather picture Lord Warrington as a cruel sea captain who would flog someone for the least offense. He likely hid his ruthless side from his family. "If he intends to give you a well-deserved rebuke, I don't see how *I* can stop him."

"You can convince him that I was merely lost. You see, Lord Rockford might inflate the whole event into a matter far more serious than it was."

It *was* serious. Rosabel was pursuing secret activities—possibly as the Wraith. But Claire opted to keep silent on that matter for now until she had the chance to catch her cousin in the act.

"Perhaps you're worrying too much. Since he seems determined to court your favor, I doubt he'll tattle to your grandfather."

"I'm sure you're right," Rosabel mused. "However, I do believe the earl is after something other than mere courtship."

Claire came to a halt at the top of the grand staircase.

Her fingers gripped the polished oak of the newel post. "Did he make improper advances yesterday? Is that why you sent him away?"

Rosabel released a tinkle of laughter. "Quite the opposite. He was as dreary and polite as a doddering old vicar." Then she pursed her lips in a grimace. "But what if he's asking Grandpapa's permission to marry me?"

Remembering his lecherous bargain with Sir Harry Masterson, Claire shook her head. "I cannot believe the earl's purpose is honorable. You must be on your guard against him."

"Then he'll contrive to get me alone. Heaven only knows what might happen." She gripped Claire's arm. "Please, Brownie. You must promise to protect me!"

Claire knew better than to trust that quivering lip, those soulful, pleading eyes. Nevertheless, she felt an unbidden softening. She could hardly protest, anyway, since she had been hired as chaperone.

"Certainly, I'll watch out for you. But remember your promise. There will be no slipping away and leaving me to entertain the earl."

"Whatever you say, Brownie. I'll be on my very best behavior." Rosabel paused, then added, "And you do look rather nice today. So don't be surprised if Lord Rockford notices!"

Reverting to her usual high spirits, she led the way down the broad flight of stairs and to the library. It was clear she wanted Claire to be attractive for a reason. The hint of self-satisfaction to her smile indicated that she hadn't given up on her wild scheme to encourage a romance between Claire and the earl.

An illicit romance. A love affair.

The notion sparked a deep-seated throb of warmth in Claire. It was shocking, appalling, *disgusting*. She ought to be repulsed—the only rational reaction—yet a thrill enveloped her body. She subdued the aberrant feeling by silently enumerating his many faults, as she had done the previous night.

He was arrogant. He was corrupt. He was condescending. His outer handsomeness masked the wicked depravity of a tyrant accustomed to having his every wish fulfilled.

He would *not* use Rosabel to fulfill a wager. Not if Claire had anything to say about the matter.

As they entered the library, she felt confident in her ability to face Lord Rockford with cool indifference. Since he considered her his social inferior, he would ignore her. She would keep to the background, study her grandfather, and formulate a plan to prove he had engineered Papa's imprisonment.

But Rosabel hooked her arm around Claire's and towed her straight toward the two men sitting by the hearth.

Lady Hester sat with them, an ingratiating smile fixed on her round face, the usual handkerchief clutched in her pudgy fingers, which she used to wave at her daughter. "Darling Rosabel," she trilled. "You're a vision of beauty today."

"Thank you, Mama," Rosabel said, then curtsied to Lord Rockford. She went to Lord Warrington and bent down to kiss his leathery cheek. "You're looking very well, Grandpapa. That blue coat perfectly matches your eyes."

His lips twisted in the parody of a smile. "I'm too old for compliments," he said gruffly. "Save them for your young man here."

"She makes such a pretty picture," Lady Hester said, reiterating her praise. "Do you not agree, Lord Rockford?"

The earl had risen to his feet and stood with his hands clasped behind his back. "Indeed, I do."

But his gaze skimmed past Rosabel and lingered on Claire in her fine new gown with its low bodice and flattering slimness.

Her heart tripped under the force of that scrutiny. Despite her resolve, she experienced another rush of involuntary heat. It made her skin prickle and her cheeks burn. It settled low in her belly with a persistent stubbornness that defied the stern rebuke of her mind.

The intensity of his gaze made her hot with embarrassment and cold with anger. How dare he look at her—or any other woman—when he was supposed to be courting Rosabel?

"Mrs. Brownley," Lady Hester said in a tone of sharp astonishment, "are you wearing one of my daughter's new gowns?"

Claire braced herself for a tirade. "It was a gift, my lady."

"Pray don't be vexed, Mama," Rosabel said. "You must agree, the color is too subdued for me. I should never have ordered it from the dressmaker."

"But the expense . . ." Lady Hester protested.

"One can only admire your daughter's generous spirit," Lord Rockford said. "And yours, Lady Hester, for inviting Mrs. Brownley to join us today."

Lady Hester looked momentarily confused. Then her bosom swelled with self-importance. "Thank you, my lord. Why, I took the poor widow into our family out of the goodness of my heart." When she shifted her attention back to Claire, her mouth pinched into a hostile smile. "Do your obeisance to our guest. It is a privilege for you to keep company with him."

Claire stiffened. Paying homage to a nobleman—especially this one—went against her staunch belief in equality, a belief that had been fostered by her parents.

Only the memory of Papa in prison could induce her to humble herself.

She dipped a curtsy, then rose to meet the earl's dark, sardonic eyes. She stared frigidly back at him. No doubt he relished having people bow and scrape before him as a means of impressing his importance on them. But if he lived to be one hundred, he could never be half the man her father was.

"Be seated, the lot of you," Lord Warrington ordered gruffly. "You're giving me a crick in my neck."

Rosabel drew Claire over to a chaise and contrived to make her take the spot right beside Lord Rockford's chair. Claire perched on the edge of the cushion and folded her hands in her lap. Despite her determination to ignore the earl, she could see him from the corner of her eye. A faint whiff of spice made her toes curl, and she scolded herself for noticing. It was shameful to be so aware of him when she ought to be concentrating on her grandfather.

Lord Warrington sat ramrod-straight in his dark green chair. Today, he had pushed the stool aside and planted both feet on the floor. A relaxed expression softened the craggy lines of his face. Despite his grumbling, he appeared to be in a favorable humor.

"Well, my girl," he said to Rosabel. "Rockford and I have had a most enlightening visit."

"How lovely," she said, sliding a suspicious glance at the earl. "Did he happen to mention our drive in the park yesterday?"

But Lord Warrington appeared unaware of Rosabel's misbehavior. "Yes, and I'm pleased to see you encourage a decent suitor at last. I was beginning to believe you had deplorable taste in men."

"My lord, I must object!" Gasping, Lady Hester clutched the handkerchief to her cheek. "Rosabel has done nothing to deserve such a remark. Her reputation is spotless."

"It won't be for long if you encourage her to associate with ne'er-do-wells." He slapped his hand onto the neatly folded newspaper beside his chair. "It says right here in the gossip column that she danced with that Newby fellow at Stanfield's ball."

"His name is Newcombe," Rosabel corrected sweetly. "The *Honorable* Lewis Newcombe, and it would have been rude of me to refuse him. But pray recall he's Freddie's friend, not mine."

Was that true? Claire wondered. The previous day, Rosabel's face had lit up on seeing Mr. Newcombe. Then later, she had professed an appetite for courting danger. Did that include secret trysts with unsavory rakes?

"That gamester is no longer Frederick's friend," Lady Hester corrected with an air of injury. "However, I *encourage* Rosabel to be friendly and considerate to everyone. Truly, she has done nothing more than enjoy her first Season, the same as any other girl—"

Warrington glared her to silence. "I've had enough of these young pups sniffing at her heels. They all want to get their greedy paws on her rich dowry so they can pay off their gaming debts. I won't have it."

"Oh, my," Rosabel said. "How lowering to think that men are interested only in my money."

She had to be mocking him. Yet she appeared so genuinely stricken that Claire couldn't be certain. It was another reminder of how little she understood the workings of her cousin's mind.

Warrington's thin lips crooked into another of those almost-smiles. "No insult intended, my girl," he said. "But you do need a steady, reliable fellow to keep you on the straight and narrow. Rockford has asked my permission to court you, and I've given him my blessing."

"Much to my pleasure," the earl said.

Lord Rockford turned his attention toward Rosabel. For the barest moment, his dark gaze brushed Claire, but it was enough to spark a combustive reaction. Her heart kicked into a wild rhythm. Her lungs felt starved for air. Her breasts tingled and her loins melted. His profound effect on her was exhilarating . . . and humiliating. It didn't seem to matter how much she despised him; her body had a life of its own.

Admittedly, she had never met any man as physically attractive as the earl. Growing up, she had known only the middle-aged scholars who were her father's friends, along with the men in her neighborhood, and those tended to be laborers and merchants with limited interest in books or learning. At the Canfield Academy, her acquaintance with the opposite gender had been severely restricted, as well. There was Master Josephson, the mathematics instructor, who had the pasty white skin of a cadaver and cold, damp hands that made her shudder with distaste. She also had been repelled by the local curate, a stout man who watched her with beady brown eyes and always stood too close during choir practice. Several times, she'd had to apply a sharp elbow before he'd learned to keep his distance.

Nevertheless, she had long nurtured a private yearning for love. Her parents had been a shining example of the happiness to be found in marriage. But Claire knew she would far rather live out her life alone than compromise her dream of finding the perfect mate. If ever she loved a man, he would be like Papa, steadfast and kind, easy to laugh, warm and loving.

He certainly would *not* believe himself the superior of other human beings. Nor would he plot to seduce a young lady on a wager.

"Mrs. Brownley! Do you intend to sit there all day?"

Jarred by her aunt's strident voice, Claire realized that

everyone was standing up except for her grandfather and herself. Hastily, she rose to her feet. "Forgive me, my lady."

"Come with me," Lady Hester commanded. "You'll have mending to do. We'll give the young couple a little time alone in the morning room. It's quite cozy there and no one will disturb them."

"That's most thoughtful of you, my lady," Lord Rockford said. "I would like very much to speak to Lady Rosabel in private."

He offered his arm to Rosabel. A hint of rebelliousness on her fine features, she accepted his polite assistance. But she shot Claire a pleading look that begged her to disregard Lady Hester's maneuvering.

Claire prepared to follow them. She racked her brain for an excuse to thwart Lady Hester. Claire had no intention of giving him an opportunity to work his wiles on Rosabel.

As they started toward the door, Lady Hester sailing in the lead, Lord Warrington beckoned to Rosabel. "Come back here a moment, girl. I wish to know if you are enjoying the play."

She and Lord Rockford stopped. Pausing just behind them, Claire took the opportunity to scan the table beside Lord Warrington. But the maroon leather volume lying beneath the newspaper was not the book written by her father, the one she'd seen here the previous afternoon.

"I haven't been to any plays lately," Rosabel said in confusion. Then her face brightened. "But I should like to see that new one at the Theatre Royal. It's about a gentleman who falls in love with a lady who has promised her heart to another—"

"I'm referring to *A Midsummer Night's Dream*. Mrs. Brownley has the grand intention of reading it to you." Lord Warrington fixed his self-satisfied gaze on Claire.

"Have you had second thoughts, then? I warned you not to attempt it."

Those ocean-blue eyes impaled Claire. She felt naked without her spectacles; conversely, she burned to have him recognize her as his long-lost granddaughter. She would relish nothing better than to blister him with recriminations.

"I haven't changed my mind," she said. "We have had no opportunity as yet to begin."

"Humph. You'll find out soon enough that you ought to have listened to me." He waved them all away. "Run along now. I can see that you wish to disagree, and I want my peace."

Claire hesitated, then followed the others. It would serve her ill to quarrel with him. He was probably right, anyway; Rosabel showed little interest in anything intellectual. And he couldn't possibly know that Claire had used the play only as an excuse . . .

To investigate him.

Struck by daring inspiration, she swung back around and returned to his side. When she reached his chair, he had already put on his spectacles.

He snatched them off in a show of irritation. "What is it now? I bade you leave."

"I wondered . . . if I might be permitted to borrow the book you were reading the other day."

"Speak up, girl. I read many books." He waved an age-spotted hand around the library. "Which one?"

"I believe the title was *Everyman's Guide to Shakespeare*."

A thunderous darkness descended over her grandfather's face. His bristly gray brows clashed over his sharp blue eyes. His lips thinned and his cheeks turned a deep ruddy hue. For an instant, she feared he might succumb to apoplexy.

And he was looking at her with fury. She wanted to trigger a diatribe against her father, to tempt Warrington into revealing his penchant for hatred and vengefulness, to wrest a clue that would fortify her belief in his guilt.

But not at the expense of losing her place in this household.

Her body tensed with the effort to appear innocuous. "Perhaps I should explain, my lord. I believe that particular work might give me guidance to interpret Shakespeare's play for your granddaughter."

"I'm not through with it," he snapped. "Go on now, get out." He shoved his eyeglasses onto his hawk nose and wrenched open his book.

Frustrated, Claire started toward the door. She was startled to see that the rest of the party had waited for her. Lady Hester and Rosabel were holding a spirited discussion about what to order for their tea.

Lord Rockford alone appeared to have overheard her conversation with the marquess. His dark head was tilted to the side in a listening pose. And he gave Claire a piercing stare that penetrated her to the bone.

"Heaven hath a hand in these events."
—*Richard II*, V:ii

Chapter Eight

The next morning, a flurry of cold raindrops spattered Claire as she hurried down the narrow lane near Lincoln's Inn Fields. Her hooded merino cape provided protection from the inclement weather, but she shivered nonetheless. Skinny clerks and stout lawyers hastened with their heads bent against the rain on their way to the various courtrooms and offices in the area.

The fine mist blurred her spectacles, and when she almost bumped into a passerby, she took off the eyeglasses and tucked them into her reticule. There was no need to disguise herself so far from Warrington House.

A sense of urgency dogged her heels. She walked at a swift pace through the maze of unfamiliar streets before finally locating the address in a row of buildings constructed of soot-blackened stone. Pushing open the door, she entered a small dreary foyer that felt almost chillier than outside. A staircase led to the upper floors, but Claire headed straight down a dimly lit passageway, her sturdy shoes clicking purposefully on the wooden floor.

The building housed a variety of small law offices. Some of the doors were closed; others stood open to reveal men laboring busily at their desks. The occasional murmur of voices drifted into the corridor.

She had been here only once before, the previous week, when she had secured the services of a barrister to defend her father in court. Mr. Mundy had been her last hope. The best lawyers had turned down the case, and not only because of her inability to pay their hefty fees. "It's a losing proposition," one of them had told her bluntly. "Too much incriminating evidence and too many powerful families out for blood." The pity in his eyes had told her he believed her father to be guilty.

The memory released a flood of anger and anxiety in Claire. What if others closed their minds to the possibility of her father's innocence? What if both judge and jury refused to view him as anything other than an unprincipled villain? The consequences could be deadly.

She rapped on the door to the last office and then clenched her gloved fingers in an effort to alleviate her tension. The few moments stretched out like an hour before a tall, gangly young man in an ill-fitting black coat and gray trousers ushered her into a minuscule waiting room. In the office beyond, another gentleman sat with his back to the door.

"Good morning, Miss Hollybrooke! I didn't expect you quite so soon, but of course you're very welcome, indeed. May I take your cloak?"

Too cold to give up the outer garment, she shook her head. "I came the moment I received your note, Mr. Mundy. But if you're busy—"

"Oh, no, no. We've concluded our business. As a matter of fact, come right in. I believe you are acquainted with my visitor."

As Claire followed the young barrister into his office, the other gentleman rose to his feet. Of middling height, he had sandy hair, pale blue eyes, and a thick mustache that overbalanced his receding jaw. He was dressed rather raffishly in a finely tailored blue coat with brass buttons, and she almost didn't recognize him.

"Mr. Grimes?" she said in surprise.

He bent at the waist in a courtly bow. "Miss Hollybrooke, do allow me to express my deepest sympathy concerning the plight of your dear father. I've only just returned from a research trip in Oxford, or I would certainly have contacted you sooner."

A lecturer at a boys' school, Vincent Grimes was an acquaintance of her father's. Claire judged him to be in his middle thirties. She puzzled only briefly over why he would have gone out of town in the middle of the school year; then her thoughts returned to more pressing matters.

"Thank you," she said, grateful to have another ally. "But how did you find Mr. Mundy? And why have you come here?"

"To offer you my help, of course. When I couldn't locate you, I made inquiries at the courts to determine the name of your father's barrister." Grimes picked up his tall black hat. "But pray don't let me intrude upon your meeting. I'll wait outside for you, if I may." Going out, he closed the door behind him.

Mr. Mundy held a straight-backed chair for her and hovered while she sat down. "Do forgive the state of the place," he said, exactly as he had the first time she had visited. "I know it isn't much, and I hope to be acquiring finer furnishings very soon."

As he spoke, he bustled around the small office, using the hem of his coat to dust the battered oak desk and then straightening the shiny gilt frame that enclosed a diploma attesting to his law degree. His white wig and black robe hung from a hook in the corner. They were the only new items in the dilapidated office, which clearly had been furnished with castoffs.

But what Mr. Mundy lacked in experience, he made up for with enthusiasm. With his big brown eyes and untidy hair, he reminded Claire of an overeager puppy. "Are you comfortable?" he went on. "May I fetch you anything?" He looked around as if expecting a fully loaded tea tray to magically appear on the empty side table. "A glass of water, perhaps?"

"Nothing, thank you." Claire gripped her hands in her lap. "Your message sounded terribly urgent. What's wrong? Is my father unwell?"

"Oh, no, *no*! He's in perfectly fine health." His smooth features aghast, Mr. Mundy sank onto the chair behind the desk. "I never meant to worry you, Miss Hollybrooke. I beg a thousand pardons for causing you the slightest distress."

Claire relaxed, and the aftermath of tension left her limp. "Never mind, it was a simple misunderstanding. Only do tell me the purpose of your note."

"Yes, well, I wanted you to know that I received a notification from the court yesterday." Mr. Mundy nervously shuffled through the papers on his desk, then plucked out one and held it up to the meager light from the single window. Clearing his throat, he read, " 'The Crown hereby orders the trial of one Gilbert Hollybrooke, on charges of nine counts of grand larceny, reassigned to May the twenty-seventh in the year of our Lord, eighteen hundred and sixteen. All parties are requested to be present in the docket at the Old Bailey precisely at the hour of nine o'clock—' "

"Reassigned!" Disbelieving, Claire sprang up from her chair. "Are you saying they've moved up Papa's court date? That he'll go before a judge in less than a fortnight?"

Mr. Mundy ducked his head as if the change in schedule were his fault. "Er, yes, Miss Hollybrooke, I'm afraid that is indeed the unfortunate state of matters."

"Why did this happen? *How* did this happen?"

"Trial dates are determined by the lord justice in charge of the case. Believe me, I am as appalled as you are!"

Weakened by shock, she wilted back down onto the chair. "They can't expect us to be ready by then. I haven't found any proof yet to clear Papa's name. Can you petition the court for more time?"

"I've already done so, but my request was denied." Planting his skinny arms on the desk, Mr. Mundy leaned forward earnestly. "You should know, I took the liberty of doing a little detective work of my own. I visited the office of the court and found out from a clerk that an order to speed up the trial had come from someone higher up."

Her blood chilled. "From Lord Warrington."

Mr. Mundy shook his head, dislodging a brown curl onto his forehead and making him appear younger than ever. "Now, we cannot know that for certain. One of the victims might very well have influenced the chief justice."

Claire remembered the vindictive ladies at the Duke of Stanfield's ball who had denounced the Wraith. But she thought it far more likely that her grandfather was behind this latest development. "How are your preparations for the defense proceeding?"

"I've done as you suggested and constructed a timetable of when and where each robbery was committed, along with a list of which quotation was left at each house. May I say, the Bow Street Office gave me a time procuring the information. The magistrate took some convincing to believe that I was representing so important a client. But never mind, I've copied it all out for you."

She took the sheet of paper and tucked it in her reticule for future study.

"What about the handwriting? Did the magistrate compare it to Papa's?"

"Yes, but I'm afraid the Wraith disguised his hand by using block letters."

She tried not to show her disappointment. "Thank you. You're very efficient."

Flushing, Mr. Mundy regarded her with the apologetic look of someone who bears bad tidings. "Perhaps not *so* very efficient. I have been interviewing your father's neighbors to see if anyone could verify his whereabouts at those times, but I've not yet found any witnesses who can attest to his innocence. Unfortunately, at the time of the robberies, your father says he was home alone, either asleep or reading."

Knowing her father's habits, Claire had feared as much. Hearing it confirmed made her heart lurch with dismay. Her voice husky, she asked, "Have you been allowed to see Papa, then? How is he doing? Are his spirits low?"

"Not at all! He's bearing up splendidly." Mr. Mundy spoke with a heartiness she suspected was at least partly due to wishful thinking. "He is most pleased to have a private cell and the extra food you've provided."

"I've written him a letter," she said, extracting a thickly folded paper from her reticule and placing it on the desk. "Will you give it to him on your next visit?"

"Certainly, and that reminds me." A drawer squawked as Mr. Mundy opened it. He produced a small packet, which he handed to Claire. "I provided Mr. Hollybrooke with pen and ink, and he's kept busy writing several letters to *you*."

Tears blurred her eyes as she looked down at the precious bundle inscribed with its familiar spidery penmanship. The barrister couldn't possibly know how much this gift meant. Her duties at Warrington House made it impossible for her to visit her father. It had taken some wrangling to get away this morning, and the housekeeper had warned Claire she would not be eligible for another free half-day until the following week. These letters would have to be her sole communication with Papa until then.

She rose from her chair and warmly shook Mr. Mundy's hand. "Bless you, sir. I'm so glad to have you on Papa's side."

The young man scrambled to his feet. He looked bowled over by her gratitude, and his Adam's apple bobbed up and down in his scrawny throat. "I shall continue to search for witnesses," he vowed. "You can count on me, Miss Hollybrooke. I will be your father's champion—and yours!"

Claire had the nagging suspicion that Mr. Mundy was half in love with her. The possibility discomfited her. She wanted him to concentrate his attention on the case, not on her. She didn't feel a smidgen of attraction to him, either, not like what she felt for—

She firmly shut her mind to all thought of Lord Rockford and his dark, smoldering eyes. She didn't have the leisure to indulge in foolish fantasies about inappropriate men. Especially not now, when time was running out.

Now, she must pray Mr. Mundy had the skill to win against the expert barristers employed by the Crown.

When she entered the waiting room, Vincent Grimes stood up. He clasped his hat to his broad chest. "My dear Miss Hollybrooke, may I speak to you for a few moments?"

"I'm rather in a rush, but you may certainly walk with me."

"Better yet, might I offer you a ride in my carriage?"

Claire accepted with alacrity. Free transportation would be a blessing from heaven. In order to be back at Warrington House by half past eleven to prepare Rosabel's morning tray, she had intended to spend one of her precious coins on a hackney driver.

She ignored a faint qualm. Although she knew Mr. Grimes only slightly, it wasn't as if she were setting out with a complete stranger. Papa regarded him as a trusted colleague, and she could do no less.

Outside, he led her to a smart black carriage parked at the curbstone. A small boy in gray livery held the horses, and he hopped onto the backboard. As Mr. Grimes helped her onto the seat and climbed up beside her, Claire found herself wondering how he could afford such splendid equipage.

He must have seen the question on her face, for as he took up the reins he said wryly, "It isn't quite what you'd expect of a poor teacher, is it? But I've recently come into a tidy legacy from my great-aunt. She died only a few months ago."

"Pray accept my condolences."

"Ah, it was bound to happen. She lived to the grand old age of ninety-eight, and I was her nearest relation." Mr. Grimes snapped the reins and the horses trotted briskly down the narrow street. In his tall black hat and fine coat, he might be mistaken for an aristocrat. "But enough about me. Shall I head toward Covent Garden? Or am I wrong to presume you're living at your father's flat?"

Claire bit her lip. No one except for Papa and Mr. Mundy knew of her true whereabouts. "I'm staying with a friend," she hedged. "But I'd be most grateful if you'd leave me off at Piccadilly and Regent Street."

"Mayfair, is it?" Mr. Grimes flashed her a keen look. "You must have acquaintances in high circles, then. If I may be so bold as to ask, is it possible you've turned to Lord Warrington for help?"

Claire stiffened. That was the last question she had expected from him—and the last one she wanted to answer. "No," she said flatly. "I presume my father told you about the connection."

"I've long known that your late mother was disowned for marrying beneath herself." Keeping his eyes on the road ahead, Mr. Grimes pursed his lips beneath the great sweep of his sandy mustache. "I fear your father has never forgiven Warrington for shutting her out of his life. You must realize, it doesn't bode well for the case."

"If you're suggesting that Papa is guilty . . ."

Mr. Grimes turned his head to regard her with an expression of chagrin. "Absolutely not. It's absurd to think that Gilbert could commit any such crime. However, if we're to solve this mystery we need to think like the fellows at the Bow Street Station."

We? Claire balked at bringing anyone else in on her plan. But it might help to get another opinion. "I do know how they think," she said. "I spoke to the magistrate over a week ago. He suggested that Papa wanted revenge on society for shunning him, that he felt deprived of my mother's dowry, and robbery was his way of getting his just due." Bitter frustration simmered to the surface of her emotions. "What blather! My father never wanted tuppence from Mama's family."

"You won't hear any argument from me on that count," Mr. Grimes said. "In fact, if you need a character witness, I would be more than happy to testify on his behalf in court."

For the second time that morning, she felt a surge of gratitude. "Thank you. I don't know if it will be necessary, but I'll mention it to Mr. Mundy."

A gust of cold rain sprinkled the carriage as Mr. Grimes guided the horses around a dray of beer kegs parked at the curbstone. "Miss Hollybrooke, may I speak frankly to you?"

"Please go ahead."

"I've been wondering what brought the law to Gilbert's doorstep in the first place. Certainly, he's a renowned

Shakespearean scholar, but that's hardly proof. *Was* it his connection to the nobility that tipped the scales?"

"It was a grocer's bill, of all things," she said. "At the scene of the last robbery, one of the Runners found it lying on the ground outside. My father's address was on it."

"Ah," Mr. Grimes said. "That wasn't reported in the newspapers."

"The magistrate is sure to present it as evidence at the trial. He won't even consider that it was planted there by someone else."

"Well, doesn't that beat all! It would be a simple matter for an experienced thief to have taken the bill from your father's flat, then come back later to leave the diamond bracelet."

Claire nodded grimly. "Papa is always gone during the day either lecturing or researching at the library. As for *why* he was chosen as the scapegoat, I can't say."

"Hmm." Frowning, Mr. Grimes deftly wove a path through the traffic. "Has your father ever mentioned having any enemies?"

"No, none." Except for Lord Warrington, she added silently.

"Then perhaps this Wraith fellow wished to throw the police off his scent by using a likely decoy. Your barrister should use that scenario to cast doubt on the Crown's case."

For the remainder of the ride, they discussed various other aspects of the case, including the Shakespearean snippets left at the scene of each crime. The purpose of the quotations was still a mystery to Claire, and she intended to apply careful study to the list Mr. Mundy had given to her. Until now, she'd known only a few of the passages from a brief glimpse the magistrate had given her. And in the meantime, it was a relief to talk openly with someone who knew her father well.

As Mr. Grimes drew the carriage to a halt half a block from the hustle and bustle of Piccadilly Circus, he handed her a small pasteboard calling card. "You must let me know if I can help you in any capacity, my dear."

"Mr. Mundy and I are working hard on finding witnesses who can vouch for Papa. I'm sure we'll be successful. We *must* be successful."

As if to mock her, a chilly wind whipped at her hood. Huddling deeper into her cloak, Claire sensed the hollowness of her words. Dread lurked in the shadows of her mind, but she wouldn't let herself even contemplate defeat.

Mr. Grimes helped her down from the carriage. Then, much to her surprise and chagrin, he brought her gloved hand to his lips for a lingering kiss. His thick mustache tickled the back of her wrist, and his fingers gripped hers for a moment longer than necessary. "I greatly admire your devotion to your father, Miss Hollybrooke. I look forward to seeing you again very soon."

He tipped his hat to her, then remounted the fine black carriage and drove away into the crush of vehicles in the busy intersection.

Claire stood in the misting rain and watched him go. Good heavens. Was he hinting that he felt more for her than concern for the daughter of a friend?

First Mr. Mundy, now Mr. Grimes had exhibited a decided romantic inclination toward her. She didn't quite understand what they saw in her, drab and soaked from the rain, her hair stuffed inside the gray mobcap that formed part of her disguise. Perhaps the notion of helping a lady in distress had awakened a sense of gentlemanly chivalry in them.

But that explanation couldn't possibly apply to Lord Rockford. He knew nothing of her situation, yet he had eyed her far too often yesterday while he had been speaking to Rosabel. His intense gaze had had the dual effect of angering Claire and weakening her knees.

As she stepped back to avoid being splashed by a passing cart, she almost stumbled. The mere memory of him made her legs shaky. What nonsense to think of the earl when her father's predicament should be uppermost in her mind. No man must distract her from her purpose, especially not a lecherous, aggravating, too-handsome lord—

"Mrs. Brownley. What a surprise to see you here."

That deep, mocking voice resonated from the depths of her most secret fantasies. Her heart pounding, she spun around and saw Lord Rockford sitting tall and proud on a fine bay horse.

She blinked, willing him to be a figment of her imagination. But the cold, steady drizzle assured her she was wide awake. And the earl looked larger and more intimidating in real life than any dream lover.

Like a swashbuckling pirate, he wore a black caped greatcoat over tan buckskins and black kneeboots. His insulting gaze skimmed over her form as if he were imagining her without the encumbrance of clothing. Against all logic, she experienced a deep, shameful throb of desire. It made her want to turn and run.

A horrible thought held her riveted in place.

Had he seen her with Mr. Grimes?

He swung down from the saddle and came straight toward her, leading his horse. The sense of purpose about him alarmed Claire. Perhaps he merely wanted to ask her about seeking to borrow *Everyman's Guide to Shakespeare* from her grandfather. The prospect didn't worry her; she could explain that she hadn't been aware it was written by the Wraith.

But in the next breath, Lord Rockford confirmed her worst fear.

"It isn't like you to have nothing to say," he went on. "So tell me, who was that gentleman you were speaking to a moment ago?"

"I do suffer love indeed, for I love thee against my will."
—*Much Ado About Nothing*, V:ii

Chapter Nine

Instinct told him she was hiding something.

By the widening of her blue eyes and the paling of her rain-damp skin, Simon knew he had alarmed Clara Brownley. Clearly, she hadn't expected to be observed by anyone familiar to her. For that matter, Simon hadn't expected to be the observer.

He had gone to Bow Street Station as he did most mornings, but aside from a petty forger hauled in by one of the Runners, the docket had held only a few pickpockets and drunks arrested the previous night. High society crime had dwindled now that the Wraith was safely behind bars. The current batch of misdemeanors was being handled by the other officers. Craving the stimulation of another difficult case, Simon had left the office and headed down the Strand toward his club in St. James's Street.

It was then, utterly by chance, that he had spotted Mrs. Brownley. He had been startled to see her riding in a fine carriage with a stranger. Startled, then puzzled, then suspicious.

From their first meeting in Stanfield's garden, he'd noticed inconsistencies that separated her from other servants: her bold speech, her disdain for the upper class, the baggy gowns she wore—at least until yesterday. This latest situation only deepened the mystery.

He had followed them for some distance, trying to determine the nature of her relationship with the man. A relative? A friend? She might very well have family ties here in town.

Then the man had kissed her hand. In a way that was anything but brotherly. And Simon had wanted to plant his fist in the middle of that mustachioed face. The irrational lust for blood still resonated in him.

"Well?" he prompted. "Cat got your tongue?"

Mrs. Brownley returned his stare with cool aplomb. "That's a ridiculous cliché," she said. "It's unbefitting a man of your cleverness. Now, do pardon me, I must return to Warrington House."

She pivoted on her heel, but he caught her arm. Though not conventionally pretty, she had compelling features framed by the hood of her cloak, with dark delicate brows that complemented her keen blue eyes and a mouth too luscious for sarcasm. "Answer me."

She scornfully raised her chin. "You're not my employer. I needn't account to you for my actions."

"Is he your lover?" The thought of her occupying another man's bed enraged Simon, though he countered the gut reaction with logic. She was a widow, an experienced woman, and what she did on her half-day off was none of his business.

Color flooded her cheeks. "How ironic that you would voice such a vile charge—you, who think nothing of making wagers to seduce young ladies."

"A promiscuous woman isn't a suitable companion for Lady Rosabel."

"Nor is a promiscuous man. You should be ashamed of yourself for pretending to court her. Now I *must* go or I'll be late."

She wrenched out of his hold and hurried down the street, leaving Simon standing on the curbstone, holding the reins of his horse and swearing under his breath. How had she managed to twist matters and make him the one at fault? Not even his sisters dared to chastise him so soundly.

Or maybe they did—sometimes

And maybe he *had* misled Mrs. Brownley into thinking him a rake. But dammit, what gave her the right to throw it in his face? She had to be covering up for her own sins. Hoping to distract him by lashing out with an attack of her own.

She wouldn't succeed.

Leading the gelding, Simon strode heedlessly through the puddles along the edge of the street. A few people glanced curiously at him, though most of the passersby were intent on getting to their destinations and out of the bone-chilling drizzle. For once, he didn't give a damn about attracting attention.

He caught up to Clara Brownley at the busy corner, where she waited for an opening in the traffic. Carriages and carts vied for position in the steady stream of vehicles flowing in both directions. The cacophony of noise held the rattle of wheels, the clop of hooves, the shouts of drivers and street vendors.

She must have heard him coming, for she swung to face him. "He's a friend of my father's," she said in a low, fierce tone, "*not* my paramour. There now, you have no reason to question me any further."

Was she telling the truth? Or lying to protect herself from being dismissed? He suspected the latter. After all, why would a family friend not drive her straight to Warrington House, thus saving her a twenty-minute walk in the rain?

Simon knew from hard experience to follow his

hunches. But it occurred to him that grilling her like a suspect in a crime would only serve to bolster the wall she kept around herself. If ever he hoped to unravel the puzzle of Clara Brownley, he would have to change his tactics.

A clearing appeared in the roadway. He took hold of her arm again and bustled her across the wet street. "I was going your way myself," he lied. "I'll accompany you."

She scowled, but said nothing, apparently recognizing the futility of arguing. Releasing her arm, he easily matched her brisk steps, his mount following close behind. The prim line of her lips conveyed displeasure. Clearly, she was intent on reaching her destination as swiftly as possible.

He was equally determined to figure out the enigma of her. "Yesterday," he said, "you attempted to borrow a book from Warrington."

Her steps faltered. Her sharp eyes pierced him, then darted away to stare fiercely at the roadway. "Do you object to my reading from his lordship's library? Have I overstepped the bounds of a servant?"

Hiding his irritation, Simon shook his head. "I'm wondering if you're aware of the reason why he was angered by your request."

"No doubt he considered me cheeky. *You* certainly do."

"That isn't what I mean. *Everyman's Guide to Shakespeare* was written by his estranged son-in-law, Gilbert Hollybrooke."

The wings of her eyebrows flew together in a shocked frown. "Do you mean . . . the Wraith? Are you quite certain?"

"Yes, and I must advise you not to ask for that particular book in the future."

"Your counsel is unnecessary. I certainly have the sense not to repeat my mistakes."

The tartness of her tone underscored her animosity toward him. Somehow, he had to convince her to drop her defenses. "I suggest we call a truce," he said in his most charming tone. "My sisters accuse me of being far too autocratic at times, so I can't blame you for taking offense."

She shot him a wary glance. He braced himself for another diatribe on his tyrannical behavior, but she surprised him by saying, "I'm trying to picture you with sisters. Are they older or younger? Younger, I'd guess."

"And why would you think that?"

"Older sisters would have taught you to be more respectful toward ladies. Younger ones would have honed your skill at giving orders."

A grin tugged at his mouth. "They *are* younger, all three of them. And yes, I did give them a fair number of orders. After our father died, someone had to guide them."

The dark memory of the murder lurked at the edge of his consciousness, but Simon refused to acknowledge it. Instead, he kept his mind firmly focused on the aftermath. Overnight, he had left his wild ways behind and shouldered the responsibilities of an earl. He had provided the best physicians for his mother and seen to the education of his sisters. And he had done his utmost to put criminals behind bars.

A hint of interest softened Mrs. Brownley's expression. "How old were you when he died?"

"Fifteen. It was by far the most horrifying experience of my life."

Instantly, he clamped his teeth shut. Now why had he admitted that? It was a private matter, one he had never discussed with anyone. Not even his mother realized the full burden of the guilt he carried.

Mrs. Brownley parted her lips as if to question him further, so he said quickly, "Where are your spectacles?"

"My—oh!" She blinked in momentary confusion, then searched in her reticule, drew out the eyeglasses, and perched them on her nose. "The rain was spotting them."

He wondered if she realized how the glass magnified the glorious blue of her eyes. "You weren't wearing them yesterday, either. Do you not need them to see?"

She adjusted the hood of her cloak, partially hiding her face. "My sight is only somewhat imperfect. But yesterday Lady Rosabel took it into her mind to improve my appearance."

"Ah, so that would explain your new gown."

"What else?" she said, sounding prickly again. "I haven't the funds for frivolities."

Simon led his horse around a bend in the street. They had entered the rich bastion of Mayfair, passing a number of shops that catered to the wealthy. Ahead, a row of magnificent town houses looked gray and dreary, the eaves dripping from the rain. The traffic here had diminished to an occasional carriage or bundled-up pedestrian.

Clara Brownley's closed expression discouraged further conversation. He wondered if she wore the gold-rimmed spectacles as a form of disguise, along with the shapeless garb. For some reason, she wanted to camouflage that heavenly body of hers. Was it simply a way for her to appear older and more suited to the task of chaperone? That was a reasonable supposition, yet he sensed she was too complex a woman for simple explanations.

She kept her gaze pointed downward as if fascinated by the stone pathway. The sodden hem of her skirt showed an occasional glimpse of mud-spattered petticoat. Her rapid footsteps betrayed her eagerness to reach home.

Simon, however, had no intention of wasting the next ten minutes. "Do you not have a pension from your late husband?"

Her head snapped up. Her fine eyes narrowed, but not

before he saw a spark of something like alarm. She countered, "Do you always ask impertinent questions?"

"I beg your pardon," he said smoothly. "But you mentioned your lack of funds, and I have connections in the government. If for some reason you're not receiving the money you deserve, I'd be happy to check into the matter. In what branch of the military did your husband serve?"

She stared at him frostily, and he thought for a moment she wouldn't answer. "I've received my compensation," she said in a clipped tone. "My husband was a foot soldier, not an officer, so the pension is small. I sought the post of companion to supplement my income."

Did she also sell her favors for the same reason? Was that why the bastard had dropped her off so far from her place of employment, because she didn't want anyone to discover her immoral activities? One fact continued to bother him. She hid her beauty instead of enhancing her assets, thereby denying herself the opportunity to earn much more as a wealthy man's mistress. If she would sweeten her tongue and use it for the right purpose, he himself might consider . . .

From behind them, the bay gelding snorted a protest. Realizing his fingers were clenched around the reins, Simon halted the dangerous direction of his thoughts. It would be despicable for him to pursue a liaison with the companion of his intended bride. He would never allow lust to rule him. Indulging one's base urges only clouded a man's rationality.

He took a deep breath of chilly air to clear his head. "You must have family who could help you," he said. "You mentioned your father—or at least his friend."

"Papa is all I have left." Those expressive eyes revealed raw agony; then she dipped her head, the hood concealing her face. "But I'm afraid he can't work at present. He's . . . ill."

The picture was becoming disturbingly clear. "Do you need money for his care? I would be happy to—"

"No!" She cast him a horrified glance. "I could never accept tuppence from *you*, my lord. Pray, don't even suggest such a thing."

Simon understood pride, and Clara Brownley had pride up to the brim of her ugly gray cap. "As you wish, then. Where does your father live?"

"In York, where I grew up."

Her diction was too crisp for the north of England. She spoke like a lady of the upper class. Of course, she might have been taught by tutors. "Tell me about the city. Did you like it there?"

"Yes, I had a very happy childhood. The people are warm and friendly. But of course when I married, I moved away."

Her vague answer only made him more curious. "Whereabouts in York did you live?"

"Just outside the city walls. Near enough to see the tall steeple of the Minster."

"I visited there not long ago. Perhaps I went past your house. What was the name of your street?"

Her mouth tightened. "Does it matter? One would think you were interviewing me for the position of your wife."

Her coupling of the two of them, even in mockery, both startled and intrigued Simon. And it hinted that she was more than mere gentry. Clara Brownley considered herself his social equal.

Who the devil was she? And why was he imagining her naked beneath him in the marriage bed?

As they passed beneath the spreading limbs of a plane tree, a flurry of cold raindrops pelted his overheated skin. Mrs. Brownley lowered her chin and peered over the rims of her water-spotted spectacles at the walkway. She looked bedraggled and tight-lipped and . . . tantalizing. The sight of her brought to mind hidden curves and veiled secrets. It would be the ultimate challenge to transform the thorny vixen into a passionate lover.

Irked with himself, he felt compelled to make a clear distinction between them. "I wouldn't ask such questions of a potential bride," he said tersely. "I would know her family background before I courted her."

"Quite so. That is how grand alliances are made."

"By your scornful tone, I would presume you married for love."

"By *your* scornful tone," she countered, "I would presume you're too toplofty to feel such a plebeian emotion."

He surprised himself by chuckling. "You make me out to be a monster, Mrs. Brownley. The fact of the matter is, love can be a dangerous way to choose a bride. Burning passion dies quickly, and one is left with only ashes. I've seen it happen to my friends."

"So you've embraced a life of debauchery? You would misuse a young lady of good name? I wonder what your sisters would have to say about that."

"Actually, they think me rather a dull dog." When she parted her lips in an instant rebuttal, he held up his gloved hand. Perhaps it was time to apprise Clara Brownley of her mistake lest she turn Lady Rosabel against him. "You've made a wrongful assumption about me, I fear. That wager you heard Harry Masterson mention had nothing to do with seducing the first girl I met."

She stopped walking and faced him with fists clenched. "I don't believe you."

Simon came to a halt, too. They stood on a quiet street with rows of stately, red-brick residences on either side. Droplets of rain dripped ceaselessly from the somber sky. Around the next corner lay Warrington House and the end of their conversation. He found himself strangely intent on lingering with her.

"The agreement," he said, "had to do with me *courting* the first eligible girl I encountered at Stanfield's ball. That's all there was to it."

He kept quiet about his intention to marry Lady Rosabel. God, wouldn't Clara Brownley lash him if he admitted that he'd decided his future on a quirk of fate?

She released a huff of incredulity. "You're attempting to put me off my guard."

"If you don't believe me, ask anyone in society. My reputation is unblemished. Even you must admit that it's highly unlikely I'd wait until the grand old age of three-and-thirty to begin corrupting virginal young ladies."

Her brilliant eyes appraised him over the rims of her spectacles. "If this is true—"

"It is, I assure you. My intentions toward Lady Rosabel are completely honorable."

Unlike his intentions toward Clara Brownley.

In the gray light, her high cheekbones bore a sheen of dampness from the rain. She was wavering, he could tell by the way her teeth nibbled her bottom lip. The sight riveted him. He could close the distance between them in one stride. He could take her into his arms and kiss her right here on the street. No, he could sweep her up onto his horse and ride hell-bent for the town house he kept in Belgravia for the purpose of such discreet liaisons. There, he could make love to her until she uttered only the sighs and moans of ecstasy—

"So this is your method of choosing a *wife*?" Her critical voice burst the bubble of his fantasy. "On a whim, a wager?"

To his chagrin, a flush heated his neck. He should have known Clara Brownley would guess the whole of it. "It's merely a starting point," he said brusquely. "I have every intention of ensuring that she and I are compatible."

"Then allow me to save you the trouble. You're not compatible. For one, you're far too old for her. You'll make her unhappy."

As if the matter were settled, Clara commenced walking again, heading toward the corner where the green umbrellas of trees brooded over the deserted square.

Once again, Simon found himself stalking after her like a lackey trailing after a queen. He didn't want to acknowledge that the age gap troubled him, too, so he focused on his anger. What right had she to pass judgment on him? More to the point, why did he feel so compelled to explain himself to her?

Leading his mount, he caught up to her as she turned into the mews behind the row of houses, where stone fences guarded small gardens and protected the residents from prying eyes. The odor of horse droppings hung in the moist air. Simon walked alongside her down the graveled pathway that led to the stables.

"Lady Rosabel will benefit from my firm guidance," he stated. "She has impeccable breeding, she's good-natured, and she knows the duties of a nobleman's wife."

"What is that, a code to judge a woman's suitability?"

"Yes. A man of my position must have high standards."

All of a sudden, Clara Brownley slowed her steps, threw back her head, and laughed merrily. "No wonder . . . I didn't understand before, but now I do." Like a child caught speaking out of turn, she clapped her gloved hands over her mouth.

Mirth transformed her. The spectacles had slid down her nose and she watched him with sparkling eyes. Being the target of her humor irritated Simon beyond measure. So did the jolt of heat that assailed his loins. Through clenched teeth, he said, "What great insight have I inspired, pray tell?"

She shook her head, dropped her hands to her sides. "I'll offend you."

"There's a new state of affairs," he bit out. "Go on, speak up."

She nibbled her lip again in that unconsciously come-hither style, then said, "I just now realized why you asked me so many questions in the duke's garden. And why you looked so disappointed when you saw me in the light. *I* was the first woman you met, not Lady Rosabel. You were assessing *me* by your Countess Code."

She giggled again in a completely ingenuous manner.

That blasted flush returned with a vengeance. He felt hot all over, embarrassed that she knew the truth and livid with lust in spite of it.

For once in his adult life, Simon didn't stop to think. He dropped the reins and backed Clara Brownley against the stone wall.

Sliding his hands inside her cloak to grip her slim waist, he bent his head to her startled face. "Tell me," he murmured, "were *you* disappointed when you saw *me*?"

All trace of amusement deserted her expression. Her gaze flitted to his lips, then skittered away. "Let me go, or I'll scream."

The breathy feebleness of her voice betrayed his effect on her. So did the way she stole a second glance at his mouth. He wooed the sensual nature that struggled within her. "I wanted you the moment you ran into my arms, Mrs. Brownley. I wanted you then and I want you now."

Her eyes rounded. "But . . . you're courting Lady Rosabel."

That ought to matter to him, but holding Clara inflamed him to the point of eradicating all common sense.

He burned to discover if her sour tongue could be coaxed into yielding sweetness. "I'm still a free man." He traced her lips with his gloved finger. "Free to take pleasure where I will. And free to give it in return."

Denying her any more objections, Simon brought his mouth down on hers. Her cool skin tasted of raindrops, then warmed with satisfying swiftness. Not surprisingly, she stood stiff and rigid within his embrace. Her fingers dug into the fabric of his greatcoat, but at least she made no attempt to push him away. Taking that as an invitation, he nudged her lips open, then delved inside and tasted her for the first time, exploring her secrets, concentrating on arousing her.

A tremor rippled through her body, and with a faint, thrilling sigh, she slid her arms around his neck, pressing herself more closely to him. To his delight, she returned his kiss with an untutored ardor that made him wonder if she had ever known a skilled lover, if her husband had been a fumbling boy without a care for her pleasure. By God, *he* would see to her pleasure.

The single-minded thought dominated Simon, even as the eagerness of her response fed the flames within him. His greedy hands found the womanly curves of breasts and hips. With lightning-bolt velocity, his desire surged into the need for skin-to-skin contact. He craved the sweat and vigor of lovemaking. Clara would be a vixen in the bedchamber, and he hungered to tame her.

But he had the presence of mind to recall their surroundings. A filthy alleyway in the rain was no place to initiate their love affair. They needed privacy in the warm confines of his town house, a sanctuary in the luxurious comfort of his bed. And they needed it *now*.

Breaking the kiss, he murmured, "Come, Clara. I've a better place for us."

Her lashes lifted to reveal the bemused passion of a

woman in lust. He recognized the necessity of preserving that expression for the fifteen minutes it would take to reach their love nest. Supporting her lithe form with his arm, he planted little kisses over her face as he urged her toward the gelding that cropped a patch of grass a short distance away.

His mind worked feverishly. Clara didn't need to labor for a pittance. He would take care of her, set her up in his house, buy her a carriage and a roomful of gowns, give her money to provide for her ill father. And Simon alone would enjoy the right to plumb the heaven between her thighs. No other man could touch her. Not even in his randy youth had he felt so energized over the prospect of taking a mistress.

"I can't go anywhere." She halted, still leaning against him as if unable to hold herself upright. "I'm late as it is."

"Your time here is over, darling." Tenderly, he brushed his lips over hers. "Come with me, and I'll make sure you never want for anything."

Turning, he vaulted into the saddle, then reached down for her. She ignored his gloved hand and stared up at him with the beginnings of alarm. "My lord, what . . . what are you saying?"

"Simon. Call me Simon." Too late, he saw the danger in letting her go. He was desperate to feel her warm body nestled against him, desperate to keep her spellbound. In a commanding voice, he said, "Take my hand now, and I'll help you up. Trust me, Clara."

Wordlessly, she shook her head and backed away, her gaze locked to his. As he maneuvered closer, she whispered forcefully, "No!"

Then she turned on her heel and ran for a wooden gate in the stone fence. She fumbled with the latch and vanished inside, leaving Simon cursing and frustrated in the alley.

• • •

Someone flew through the doorway to the servants' stair-case, almost knocking Freddie flat. He grabbed the wooden railing to catch his balance. In a glimpse, he iden-tified her plain, rain-drenched features as belonging to his sister's latest companion, Mrs. Somebody-or-Another.

"Hey," he snarled. "Watch out, there."

Still hurrying, she turned her head around long enough to gasp out, "I do beg your pardon, my lord." Then she raced upward, her footsteps echoing in the hollow shaft of the stairwell. A moment later, he heard the click of a door opening and closing.

Freddie scowled down at his highly polished Hessians in the dim light, examining the boots for signs of a scuff mark. Luckily for her, he couldn't find a single blemish. Then another thought wiped out all concern for the pris-tine state of his garb.

What if the chit tattled on him?

The thought sent him scuttling for the door. He crept out into a corridor, looking both ways to make certain it was deserted. The last thing he needed was for someone to sound the alarm. Sneaking out of the house was the only way to escape another confrontation with his mother. He hadn't had an easy moment since the old bat had found out about what he'd stolen.

Freddie quelled a pang of guilt. He had taken no more than his due. A fellow who couldn't pay his gaming vowels couldn't hold his head up in the clubs. So what if his debts were a bottomless pit, threatening to suck him under? Mama ought to trust him. A few lucky rolls of the dice, and he'd win it all back.

Instead, Lady Hester had been threatening to haul him down in front of the admiral. Freddie hated even thinking about *that*.

He'd always considered his grandfather not as the

marquess, but as a pinchpenny tyrant who barked orders to his crew. Why couldn't his grandsire be a bacon-fed old fart like the fathers of his friends? Why did Freddie have to put up with a bully who made him feel like a tyke in leading strings rather than a grown man of one-and-twenty?

Passing the library, he made a face at the closed door. The admiral had been born with an iron rod up his arse. He didn't understand Freddie's need to gamble because he didn't know how to have fun.

The click of an opening door almost made Freddie jump out of his skin. He dove into the nearest chamber and hid behind a pillar in the darkened ballroom. His heart chattered in time with the rapidly approaching footsteps. Risking a peek, he spied Eddison walking past, the valet's sour face a mirror of the admiral's.

His palms perspiring, Freddie waited a few minutes. Then he hurried for the back door before his spate of bad luck brought him face-to-face with his mother. Or his grandfather.

The admiral would never tolerate a thief. If he found out the truth, he would cut off the last of Freddie's funds—and his ballocks in the process.

"The course of true love never did run smooth."
—*A Midsummer Night's Dream*, I:i

Chapter Ten

"Do you not think, Brownie," Lady Rosabel said as the Warrington coach lumbered toward home late that night, "that it would be great fun to join a troupe of traveling players?"

"Mmm-hmm," Claire murmured. Along with Lady Hester, they had attended the theater, but Claire couldn't remember much about the play. All evening, her attention had been focused inwardly on the events of the morning.

Simon—Lord Rockford—had *kissed* her. He had wanted her to be his mistress. And for one horrifyingly madcap moment, she had been tempted to accept his vile offer. She had nearly fallen like a ripe plum into the cunning hands of a nobleman.

"Don't be silly, darling," Lady Hester chided her daughter. Adopting a more forceful tone, she added, "Mrs. Brownley, why on earth would you encourage my daughter to ruin herself?"

Startled, Claire said, "Forgive me, my lady. I never meant to imply such a thing."

She made an effort to concentrate on Rosabel, who sat beside her mother on the opposite seat. A lighted lamp inside the coach cast a golden glow on the girl's pretty features, which were framed by a stylish green bonnet. To the casual observer, her expression might look innocent, but Claire noted the sparkle of mischief in those blue eyes.

Leaning forward, Rosabel admired her reflection in the darkened glass of the coach window. "Drama fascinates me," she declared. "I wouldn't care a jot for my reputation so long as I had the attention of adoring spectators."

"Have you gone mad?" Lady Hester squawked. In her gown of gray silk with a matching feathered hat, she resembled a well-fed goose. "You can't associate with theater people. I forbid it."

"I daresay Lady Rosabel has given little thought to the consequences," Claire said. "She wouldn't enjoy huddling under a wagon during rainstorms or washing her own clothes in a cold stream."

"Oh!" Wrinkling her nose, Rosabel lolled against the cushions. "Of course, I cannot live without servants. But it does sound lovely, does it not? To glide about the stage and have the audience hanging on to my every word."

"You would have to memorize long passages," Claire pointed out. "And spend weeks practicing your lines for hours and hours until you were heartily sick of them."

"Bah, it cannot be so dreadful as all that," her cousin said airily. "Mr. Newcombe's mother used to be an actress, and *she* liked it. She even married a viscount and lived happily ever after."

Lady Hester huffed with disapproval. "Lady Barlow is vulgar. That is precisely why her son is such a scoundrel. Bad blood will tell."

"I wouldn't be so quick to accuse others of bad blood, Mama. We Lathrops have had our share of scandals, too. Just look at my aunt Emily."

Claire froze. Beneath the cloak, her fingers dug into the gauzy folds of her skirt. Her first impulse was to leap to her mother's defense, to assert that her parents' love should have been celebrated, not reviled. Mercifully, shock stayed her tongue.

Lady Hester fanned her flushed face with a handkerchief. "Good gracious, darling, must you speak of that woman? You'll give me an apoplexy."

"But she *was* my blood relation, Mama, and *your* sister by marriage. Not everyone can claim such a notorious connection." Turning to Claire, Rosabel went on enthusiastically, "You see, a long time ago, Aunt Emily ran away from home to marry the Wraith. Of course, back then Uncle Gilbert was only a poor tutor, not a thief—unless you consider that he stole my aunt right from the bosom of her family."

"I've heard the story," Claire said woodenly. "Some ladies spoke of it at the Duke of Stanfield's ball."

"Did you know that Grandpapa disowned Aunt Emily? No one in our family ever heard from her again."

That isn't true! Mama wrote to her father many times, but he refused to answer. Claire held back a blistering condemnation of Lord Warrington and forced a note of sympathy into her voice. "It's always a tragedy when parents are estranged from their children."

"Perhaps, but *I* think it's terribly romantic that Aunt Emily gave up everything to be with the man she loved." Rosabel clasped her hands to the green-and-gold pelisse that hugged her generous bosom. "She was very pretty, you know. She had dozens of suitors, and I daresay she could have married a duke or even a prince if she'd pleased. If you like, I can show you her portrait sometime."

Claire sat immobilized by breathless amazement. A likeness of her mother existed? Papa had always planned to commission a miniature, but then Mama had died in childbirth along with Claire's infant brother when Claire had been only twelve years old . . . "Yes, my lady," she murmured, trying not to sound overly eager. "If you wish it."

"Here, now, you are not to encourage my daughter," Lady Hester said, shaking her handkerchief at Claire. "Portrait, indeed! That painting should have been put in storage, even though my dear John is depicted in it, too. I vow, it *will* be put in storage after that dreadful Holly-brooke fellow is convicted at his trial."

The fervor left Rosabel's face, and she looked suddenly forlorn. "Poor Uncle Gilbert. I've never met him, but I cannot like to think of him going to the gallows."

"He will reap what he has sown," Lady Hester averred. "He has brought shame upon our family, and for that I can never forgive him."

Fighting a powerful fear, Claire shifted her gaze to the night-darkened window of the coach. She'd had time to read only one of the letters Papa had sent to her. Rather than dwell upon the horrors of prison, he had described the essay he was writing about his search for a lost Shake-spearean play. His cheerful manner had been enough to break her heart.

Now, her aunt's harsh judgment served as a grim reminder that someone other than her grandfather might be responsible for Papa's imprisonment. What if Lady Hester had stolen the jewels? What if she had incurred large gaming debts like some of the ladies? No, it was far more likely that her son Frederick had the debts. Had Lady Hester turned to robbery in order to help him? As soon as Claire had a chance to study the list Mr. Mundy had given her, she would try to find out if her aunt had been present at the parties where the thefts had occurred.

And what about Rosabel? If *she* was the Wraith, it might explain why she looked distressed. She might be feeling remorse for having conspired to put an innocent man behind bars.

As the coach swayed around a corner, Rosabel perked up again. "Perhaps Uncle Gilbert will dig a tunnel and escape from Newgate. Or bribe a guard to open the door of his cell. That is what *I* would do in so dire a circumstance."

"Enough," Lady Hester said sternly. "I will hear no more about that man."

"But Mama—"

"Not one more word. You must especially watch your tongue when Lord Rockford is present. I won't allow the scandal to drive him away."

Pouting, Rosabel lapsed into sulky silence.

Claire's mind stole inexorably to that kiss. The mere mention of Simon's name brought a flush to her skin, a tightness to her breasts, an ache to her loins. *Simon.* Try as she might, she could no longer think of him as Lord Rockford. He had become Simon with the first glorious touch of his lips to hers.

And she had become someone she didn't recognize, a woman of passion and fire. For a few moments, she had forgotten the outside world, forgotten she was standing in the mews in the rain. It was as if another entity had inhabited her body. A wild, sensual creature who reveled in the pleasures of the flesh.

What a fool she had been!

Outside, a street lamp loomed like a golden moon against the night, shining over the wet cobblestones and the dark, dripping trees. The familiar surroundings of the square came into view; then the glimmering of candlelit windows revealed their approach to Warrington House.

As the coach slowed to a stop, Lady Hester said, "It's a pity the earl couldn't attend tonight. I can't imagine how a family dinner could be more important than escorting *you,* my darling."

Rosabel yawned daintily. "I don't mind. He needn't change his plans on *my* account."

"You *should* mind. Lord Rockford is the foremost catch of the season. Should you take him for granted, any number of girls will gladly step into your place."

A footman opened the door of the coach. Waiting for Rosabel and her mother to exit, Claire thought how shocked they would be to discover the method by which Simon had settled on his bride. Despite his immoral nature, she believed he had told her the truth about his wager with Sir Harry Masterson. Simon couldn't have feigned that look of mortification. He really *had* agreed to woo and marry the first eligible lady he met at the Duke of Stanfield's ball. What a preposterous way to choose a wife!

And what a strange twist of fate that Claire had encountered him in the garden first. He would never know that like Lady Rosabel, she too had noble blood, she too was the granddaughter of the Marquess of Warrington.

A dark bitterness crept through Claire. It took a moment for her to recognize it as jealousy. As galling as it was to admit, she coveted her cousin's position in society. *She* longed to be the favored young lady of the house. So that Simon would court *her*.

How could she be so shallow? Had that kiss taught her nothing about his true character?

She stepped out of the coach. The rain had stopped, but the cold damp air chilled her to the bone. For a short while, Simon had had her believing that she had misjudged him, that he was not a villain but an honorable man who had made a foolish wager. But apparently he reserved his principled behavior for the ladies of his own exalted class.

Any lesser female was fair game for seduction.

Anger sizzled through Claire. She fervently regretted not slapping his face and scalding him with fiery invectives. How was it that she could be outspoken on other matters, but reject his heinous offer with a simple *no*? And then she had run from him like a frightened schoolgirl!

He had caught her off guard, she reminded herself. His sensual assault had taken her completely by surprise. She had never imagined that he might view a dowdy servant as a prospective mistress.

Or that she herself could be so susceptible.

For that reason, she wouldn't make the mistake of believing that he had given up on her. The Earl of Rockford had proven himself to be a man who aggressively pursued what he wanted. Next time, she wouldn't underestimate him.

Next time, she would make him regret his callous treatment of her.

"So tell me," Harry Masterson said, helping himself to the decanter of brandy. "Have you decided on the next step in your campaign to win the lady's heart?"

The question pulled Simon from his contemplation of the brandy glass in his hand. He sat in his study with his stocking feet propped up on the fender of the fireplace, the coal blaze toasting his soles. He had shed his coat and cravat hours ago. All evening, he'd been preoccupied by the image of Clara Brownley as he'd last seen her, drenched from the rain, her lips reddened from his kiss, her expression changing from impassioned to appalled.

"Apologize," he muttered. "Dammit, I should never have—" He stopped abruptly, realizing in his bleary state that Harry was giving him an odd look. *Lady Rosabel.* Harry had just arrived, and he had no idea what had happened with Clara. Nor would he. "Never mind," Simon amended curtly. "It's none of your concern."

Grinning, Harry settled into a chair and crossed his legs. The gaudy ginger coat and yellow breeches suited his flamboyant nature and big-boned frame. "Ah, I begin to understand why you're hiding here. The two lovebirds have quarreled."

Simon subjected him to a cold stare. "I came here to be alone. Mrs. Bagley should never have let you in."

"No woman can resist my charm. And I certainly wouldn't have intruded if she'd said you were entertaining."

Simon didn't doubt either statement. He had purchased this house as a place to bring his mistresses, and gentlemen respected each other's privacy. The only servants were Mr. and Mrs. Bagley, a devoted middle-aged couple who asked no questions and kept the place ready for the master's arrival on a moment's notice.

Unfortunately, Harry had long ago ascertained that Simon also used the study as a retreat, that sometimes he came here alone. But no one—not even Harry—knew Simon's true purpose on those occasions. Here, in the confines of this book-lined office, away from the distractions of daily life, he worked on confidential cases for Bow Street. Sitting at the polished mahogany desk across the room, he had scrutinized the list of Shakespearean quotations left by the Wraith, trying futilely to find meaning in the random selections.

Tonight, however, Simon had no such official objective. He had been heading home for a family dinner after spending the afternoon at his club, and somehow he'd ended up here. It was an illogical destination. This house only served to remind him that he wasn't upstairs in bed with Clara Brownley.

He took a long swig of brandy. Dammit, he didn't want to think about Clara—or Lady Rosabel. "What are you doing in Belgravia, anyway?" he asked.

"Visiting my grandmother, of course," Harry said. "It *is* Thursday night, you know."

Harry had a long-standing appointment for dinner

each week, Simon remembered fuzzily. "Is she still threatening to cut you out of her will if you don't marry?"

"Same as ever. And same as ever, I extolled the virtues of being a free man." Harry raised his glass in a mock salute. "I don't suppose *you'd* want to join me in a toast to bachelorhood?"

"Certainly. Women are more trouble than they're worth." The words slipped out, and Harry jumped right on them.

"So you *did* have a row with Lady Rosabel. Did you scold her for running away from you in the park the other day? Perhaps she's too young and frisky for an old stallion like you."

"It was nothing." Hiding his annoyance, Simon let his friend believe whatever he wanted. "A minor disagreement, that's all."

"Hmm. You ought to be over there groveling, then."

"She and her mother attended the theater tonight."

"Then you should have accompanied them." Looking amused, Harry arched a sandy-brown eyebrow. "Unless, of course, she's too flighty to hold your interest. Are you ready to admit that you can't mold just any girl into your countess?"

"Our wager is still intact. I'll be calling on her tomorrow."

Turning away, Simon reached for the decanter and poured himself another generous splash of brandy. Dammit, he *would* court Lady Rosabel. She possessed everything he required in a wife: blue-blooded lineage, an agreeable disposition, and an upbringing that had prepared her to fulfill the role of his countess. What was the term Clara had used to describe his criteria? *The Countess Code.*

He grimaced. She had found his method of choosing a

bride highly amusing. Especially the part about him assessing *her* as a potential wife in Stanfield's garden.

How ironic that Clara had been the first woman he'd encountered after making that blasted wager. From the moment she'd run straight into his arms, he had felt a powerful attraction to her. Her quick wit and cheeky manner had intrigued him, not to mention the lushly female curves he had held so briefly. If circumstances had been different . . .

Dangerous thought. Even in his half-drunken state, Simon knew better than to play wishing games. He'd be damned lucky if Clara hadn't told Lady Rosabel about that kiss. His thoughtless action could jeopardize Clara's position in the house. For that reason, what had happened between them must never happen again.

Yet he remembered the way she had melted in his arms. He was looking forward to hearing her veiled rebukes. She would be furious that he had taken liberties, furious that he had assumed her willingness to be his mistress. How he would enjoy teasing her out of her ill humor. Perhaps if Lady Rosabel left the room—

Disgusted with himself, he rose to his feet and walked unsteadily to the window. The parted curtains revealed a night as black as his thoughts. Only a scoundrel courted one lady while making love to her hired companion.

"You're scowling," Harry observed. He had put down his glass and steepled his fingers beneath his chin. "If it isn't the quarrel with Lady Rosabel, then I'd swear you had something else weighing on your mind."

"Meddlesome friends who intrude on a man's peace and quiet."

Harry laughed. "Well, whatever it is, I haven't seen you so foxed since the time we nicked a bottle of gin from the groundskeeper's shed."

Simon leaned against the window frame as the old

memory from their days at Eton swam into his mind. He latched on to the distraction like a drowning man to a wooden raft. "We were still drunk in the morning. You dozed off during our history examination."

"You tried to wake me up, remember? And Bertie Thatcher told the dom that you were cheating off my paper." Harry shook his head. "What a bloody fool. He should have known you were far cleverer than me. And he also should have known you'd haul him outside after hours that night."

Back then, Simon had had a white-hot temper, and fist-fights had been his favorite sport. He had spent the past eighteen years making up for the mistakes of his youth. Now, he fought only in the practice arena at Gentleman Jim's boxing establishment—and occasionally in the line of duty.

"It was a fair fight," he said.

"Except for that wicked right of yours. I vow, Thatcher never saw it coming." Looking self-satisfied, Harry lounged in his chair with his hands folded over his broad chest. "I made half a crown in wagers that night. Back then, you were my prime source of income, you know."

At least until Simon had been sent down from school for one too many brawls. To add to the humiliation, both of his parents had come to fetch him home. His father had been coldly furious. The earl had been in the midst of a tirade when their coach had slowed down—

Simon slammed the door on that memory. He was sweating, his heart pounding, the gorge rising in his throat. Turning, he stared blindly out the darkened window. He wouldn't be a mawkish drunk who dwelled on the low points of his past.

Clara. He would think about Clara with her sparkling blue eyes and passionate kisses. After an initial stiffness, she had found pleasure in his arms. She had been sensual, responsive, eager. And then horrified by his offer of *carte blanche*.

Dammit, he had learned long ago the dangers of acting on impulse, of letting emotion rule him. For that reason, he usually took a more logical approach to choosing his mistresses. Certain discreet brothels catered to discriminating men of his class. There were plenty of available women in the demimonde, women who earned their living by gratifying a man's desires. They were not employed in respectable houses as companions of ladies.

And if he had taken the time to think the matter through, he would have anticipated Clara's reaction. She was too proud a woman to exchange her body for goods.

Or was she?

His thoughts veered to the man who had given Clara a ride in his carriage. Her father's friend, she'd told Simon. She had looked Simon straight in the eye, yet he'd had the nagging suspicion that she wasn't telling him everything. So what was the true nature of her relationship with that man? *Was* she his mistress?

The possibility made Simon livid. His only consolation was that the fellow fell far short as a lover. He hadn't taught her how to kiss, nor had her late husband. And Simon hadn't fared much better. He had behaved with all the finesse of a green youth with his first girl. Rather than taking the time to woo Clara, he had abandoned all self-discipline. She could have no notion of the pleasure that lay in store for her if only— . . _____

God! What was he thinking? He was courting Lady Rosabel. He must put all other women out of his mind.

"Flowers," Harry said sagely.

Simon spun around. "What?"

Lounging in the chair by the fire, Harry grinned wryly over the rim of his brandy glass. "I really shouldn't help you win this wager, should I? But you're looking rather glum, old fellow, so I'll advise you to purchase red roses for lovely Rosabel. A nice bouquet never fails to put a female into a better frame of mind."

"An excellent idea." Harry didn't know it, but Simon was thinking that Clara wouldn't care for hothouse blooms. She'd prefer wildflowers gathered from a meadow, a riotous array of colors. He'd like to sprinkle the petals over his bed and make love to her . . .

He set his glass down sharply on the windowsill. Damn, he was a fool for drinking so much brandy.

He'd be an even bigger fool if he acted upon his desires.

"O, what men dare do! What men may do! What men daily do, not knowing what they do!"

—*Much Ado About Nothing*, IV:i

Chapter Eleven

Seated at a small writing desk in a corner of the morning room, Claire attempted to do three things at once. She addressed invitations to an upcoming ball according to the guest list given to her by Lady Hester that morning. She puzzled over the set of Shakespearean quotes from Mr. Mundy that she kept hidden beneath her pile of papers. And she strove to ignore Simon, who sat talking to Rosabel a short distance away.

Or rather, Rosabel was doing most of the talking.

"Mama wanted to give an ordinary ball, but I insisted upon a masquerade. Doesn't that sound like great fun? I daresay, it shall be the grand event of the season." She giggled in a silly, self-effacing manner. "Oh, you will think me immodest for saying so, will you not? But you must admit, it is quite an occasion for a girl to celebrate her eighteenth birthday."

"Indeed, I'd find it odd if you took no pleasure in it."

Simon's deep voice caused a flurry of gooseflesh over Claire. Keeping her gaze glued to the folded square of paper on the desk, she dipped her quill in the silver inkpot and wrote "Lord and Lady Yarborough, Number Twelve Curzon Street." The monotonous tapping of rain on the window should have lulled her senses. But her traitorous body betrayed a keen awareness of Simon. Her skin felt sensitized and her heart thrummed at a rapid pace.

The reaction only enhanced her sense of outrage. Yesterday, his vile proposal had confirmed her low opinion of his character. Yet today he had greeted Claire without a second glance before sitting down for a casual chat with Lady Rosabel. Exhibiting no sign of guilt, he acted as if his despicable behavior had been erased from his memory.

That could mean only one thing. Seducing female servants must be second nature to him. It was as unremarkable as shaving the dark stubble from his face every morning.

From out of nowhere, her mind produced the image of Simon half-naked, standing before a mirror and wielding a razor. A shudder of heat bathed her. Dear sweet heaven, she had to stop thinking about him!

"If I may confide in you, my lord," Rosabel prattled on, "Grandpapa wanted me to wait another whole year to make my come-out. He thought me a bit young to join society, but Mama and I prevailed. Can you imagine how dreadful it would have been to turn *nineteen* during my first Season?"

"It isn't so uncommon as you might think. My middle sister Jane managed to survive the circumstance."

"Oh! You will not understand me, then. But I suppose age doesn't matter so much for men. *You* needn't worry about being left on the shelf. Why, you've passed your thirtieth year, and no one calls *you* a spinster."

"No one would dare."

The dry mockery in Simon's tone grated on Claire's nerves. She wanted to spin around and say that *she* would dare to call him all manner of humiliating names. Instead, she moved the invitations slightly to the side. Holding the quill in a pretense of writing, she examined the paper Mr. Mundy had given to her the previous day. With so many duties to perform, she had had precious little time to study it.

The barrister's precise script revealed a detailed list of all nine robberies committed by the Wraith, including dates, places, items stolen, and the quotation left at the scene of each crime. The first entry read, "By the pricking of my thumbs / something wicked this way comes."

The passage from *Macbeth* had been left in place of an emerald necklace in the bedchamber of a Lady Pemberly. Apparently, the theft had occurred while a large party was going on in the ballroom. If Claire's grandfather had orchestrated the burglary, had he merely chosen a phrase at random, his only purpose to lead the law to a noted Shakespearean scholar? Or had the quote meant something in particular to him?

Claire suspected the latter. "Something wicked this way comes." One of the witches had spoken that phrase in the fourth act of the play, directly before Macbeth's entrance on stage. Perhaps Lord Warrington was implying that like the murderous king of Scotland, Claire's father had committed wicked deeds—

"What do *you* think, Brownie?"

Rosabel's voice startled Claire out of her dark thoughts. Unwilling to be drawn into their conversation, she said over her shoulder, "I beg your pardon, my lady. I was busy writing."

"Do turn around," her cousin begged prettily. "I dislike talking to your back."

"But I'm addressing the invitations to your masquerade ball."

"Surely you can spare a moment to settle a dispute between Lord Rockford and me."

Claire could see no way to avoid it. Reluctantly laying

down the pen, she moved the invitations back over Mr. Mundy's list. Only then did she turn around on her chair to view the couple who sat at either end of a gold-striped chaise. On the cushion between them lay the extravagant bouquet of spring wildflowers that Simon had given to Rosabel.

The sight galled Claire. Only yesterday, he had kissed her lustfully and made the despicable offer of a liaison. Today he courted her cousin with respect and admiration. What a deceitful blackguard!

Sustained by righteous anger, she turned her eyes to him. He gazed back with a gravity she attributed to arrogance rather than any remorse for his actions. A crisp white cravat set off his dark handsomeness. In a form-fitting coat of deep blue superfine, tan breeches, and polished black boots, he was the epitome of understated elegance. Yet he was more than just an extraordinarily attractive man. His face bore the hard stamp of experience, and his dark eyes hinted at intriguing depths . . .

Nonsense. He had all the mystery of a garden slug. Yesterday, she had learned her lesson about being susceptible to charming rogues.

In contrast to his sinister presence, Rosabel looked like a breath of spring in a yellow gown with a pale green ribbon threaded beneath the bodice. A smile lit her youthful face, displaying the innocent exuberance of a girl who knew nothing of the faults of her suitor. At least Rosabel had no intention of marrying Simon, which saved Claire the obligation of revealing that passionate scene.

"You wished my opinion?" Claire asked.

The brightness in her cousin's clear blue eyes had to be mischief. "Lord Rockford claims that an unmarried lady isn't considered to be firmly on the shelf until age five-and-twenty. *I* say it is one-and-twenty. So what do you think? Am I right or is Lord Rockford?"

"I believe shelves are for books and dishes, not ladies."

Rosabel giggled. "Do not be so contrary, Brownie. Surely *you* must have married at a young age. You cannot be a day over five-and-twenty yourself."

The guess was disturbingly accurate. Even more disturbing was Simon's scrutiny of her, as if he were very interested in her counterfeit past. "Age is but a number," Claire stated. "And it is impolite to go on about such matters."

Rosabel turned her smiling attention on Simon. "Brownie is not always such a scold, my lord. But she seems determined to agree with neither of us."

"Then I must commend her diplomacy."

How perfectly proper he was today, Claire thought, when yesterday he had seen no need to behave himself. "It isn't diplomacy," she said coldly. "Rather, it is my way of saying that any such rule is arbitrary to the point of being silly. Which means you are *both* wrong."

"There, you see?" Rosabel said. "There is no reasoning with her at all. She's in a very willful frame of mind today."

"One can hardly blame her. We've distracted her from her duties."

"Yes, you have." Claire didn't care if she was rude to him. "Now, I really must finish the invitations. Lady Hester wishes for them to be sent out by tomorrow morning."

"Pooh, you have plenty of time. There will be no drives in the park today, what with all the rain." Rosabel cast a crafty glance at Simon, then at Claire, before rising to her feet. "Perhaps, Brownie, I might beg a favor of you. I hope you won't mind entertaining Lord Rockford for a few minutes."

"Where are you going?" Claire asked in alarm.

"To fetch a vase for the flowers the earl brought. They'll wilt without water."

Claire sprang up. "I'll go, my lady. I should have thought to do so when he arrived."

Rosabel gave an imperious wave that was reminiscent of her mother. "No, sit back down. I've a fancy to handle the matter myself." With that, she sauntered out of the morning room—and closed the door.

Claire stood frozen. Clearly, her cousin had not relinquished her scheme to throw Claire into Simon's path. Rosabel would be shocked to know how well her plan had already succeeded.

Simon had stood up politely, and now he made no move to resume his seat on the chaise. With a look of unnerving intensity, he gazed straight at Claire.

Her muscles felt stiff, her tongue paralyzed. She had the panicked suspicion that he was thinking about kissing her again, that he would pull her into his arms and she would be too weak-willed to resist him. But she wouldn't run away this time as if *she* were the one in the wrong. This time, she must seize the advantage and state her position in no uncertain terms.

"Pray keep your distance, my lord," she said frigidly. "I refuse to associate with a man of your dissolute nature. Nor will I suffer any attempt at persuasion. If you dare to lay one finger on me, I shall scream."

Turning her back, Claire sat down at the desk, picked up her pen, and dipped the sharpened tip into the inkwell. Her hand trembled as she wrote another name and address on a blank invitation, but she persevered in the task. Concentrating on her work would show Simon that she had absolutely no interest in him.

Yet her senses were keenly attuned to his presence. She strained to detect any sign of movement behind her, but could hear only the hissing of the fire and the rattling of raindrops on the windows. Was he still standing there, staring at her? Was he formulating a new plan of attack?

Would he disregard her wishes and force his attentions on her?

Surely not. Surely he had the sense to leash his desires while under another man's roof. Besides, gentlemen set great store on their wagers, and he wouldn't want to ruin his chance to win Lady Rosabel.

But if he *was* so brash, Claire would fight him tooth and nail. She had no intention of succumbing to the passion he had awakened in her. To do otherwise meant compromising her honor, ruining her reputation, and most of all, losing her place in this house, squandering her only chance to find the proof of her father's innocence—

Simon stood beside her. From the corner of her eye, she saw him and gasped. Her hand jerked, and the quill left an inkblot on the invitation. He had moved with the silent stealth of a predator. Where had a nobleman learned that skill?

She glared up at him. From her point of view, he looked far too tall and far too intimidating. To hide her turmoil, she snapped, "I told you to stay away from me."

"I've no intention of touching you. I merely wanted to give you this." Gravely, he held out a sprig of violets.

She stared at the blooms, then back at him, appalled at his audacity. "That's from the bouquet you brought to Rosabel."

He shook his head. "The wildflowers reminded me of *you,* Clara. They're yours—though circumstances kept me from giving them to you directly. I hope you'll view my gift as a peace offering."

"You handed the flowers to Rosabel, but now you say they're for *me*?"

"Yes," he said, his dark eyes concentrated on her. "Because I wanted to apologize for my actions yesterday."

"Apologize." A swarm of emotions assailed her: incredulity, anger, and a trace of softness that she crushed without mercy. "And this is your way of doing so, by spouting lies about flowers?"

"It's the truth. I could hardly give them to you in front of Lady Rosabel—"

"Precisely. You came here today to court *her*. But the instant she leaves the room, you betray her by trying to beguile another woman."

"It isn't a betrayal, it's an attempt to make amends." His voice lowered to a husky murmur. "I don't know what came over me yesterday. It isn't like me to act without thinking. But I was wrong to press my attentions on you, Clara. I hope you can forgive me."

Leaning down, he placed the violets on the pile of invitations. The tiny purple petals taunted her, as did the spicy scent that belonged uniquely to Simon. Against her will, desire curled its dark, seductive fingers around her heart. Perhaps he truly meant what he said . . .

But though Simon's expression was remorseful, he didn't act humbled in the least. His aura of superiority intact, he gazed down at her expectantly, as if he waited for her to show gratitude for his act of contrition.

Fury choked Claire, fury at him and at her own gullibility. She swept the flowers off the desk, scattering the invitations along with it. Thrusting back her chair, she surged to her feet. "You would *dare* to make romantic gestures to me? In the midst of expressing regret for taking advantage of me? You must think me a dupe, that I'll fall into your arms and beg for another chance to be your mistress."

His expression hardened. "I've offered a simple apology, no more, no less. I expect nothing in return."

"So you would have me believe a nobleman would give flowers to a servant merely to ask her pardon." Lest she succumb to the urge to slap him, Claire kept her fists clenched at her sides. "I'm sure you aren't accustomed to denial. You feel entitled to take whatever you like, and you'll do or say whatever is necessary to get it."

"Don't call yourself a servant, Clara. You were raised a lady."

"You certainly didn't treat me like one yesterday. I was no better to you than a whore."

The memory stung more than it ought. She did not care what this haughty, too-handsome nobleman thought of her. *She did not.*

Uttering a sound of frustration, Simon ran his fingers through his hair, mussing the black strands. "For pity's sake, you're a widow. I know of many ladies in society who enjoy discreet affairs. I meant you no disrespect."

Would he have behaved differently if he'd known she was a virgin? Claire saw no reason to excuse him. "I'm *not* a member of society," she said. "I am paid a monthly wage to work as a chaperone to Lady Rosabel. I mend clothes, pick up her clutter, and perform any other tasks I'm ordered to do. That would certainly classify me as a servant, no matter what my background."

His eyes softened unexpectedly, and a slight lift at one corner of his mouth made him look devilishly attractive. "Prickly Clara. No true servant would dare to speak to me the way you do."

Claire felt more threatened by that smile than she would if he had pointed a pistol at her. It turned her insides to warm treacle. She despised the involuntary effect he had on her, causing desire to corrode her principles. "Then you may think of me as an advocate for all the maidservants who have been preyed upon by gentlemen like you. No doubt you've worked your charms on many women of my stature. Women who are too helpless and fearful to refuse you."

"I've never seduced a servant. Nor have I ever forced any woman against her will."

"You did so yesterday."

That hateful half-smile deepened. "Now who's the liar, Clara? You can't deny the passion we shared. You wanted to take that kiss to its completion as much as I did."

She blushed, heat rising up her throat and into her cheeks. Not wanting him to guess the reason for her embarrassment at his frankness, she said forcefully, "Anything I felt was wrested from me against my wishes. Let me tell you very plainly, I will never be your mistress. There is nothing in the world that would disgust me more."

All softness vanished from his face, leaving his eyes a fathomless brown. Once again, he looked aloof and implacable, the almighty Earl of Rockford. "You have my word that I won't lay a hand on you again."

"Your word," she scoffed. "I could never trust a man who has proven himself to be completely without honor."

His eyes widened slightly as if she had startled him. Then his mouth tightened. "That is quite enough, madam. Since my presence offends you, I won't disturb you any longer."

Yet he stood there, frowning, and Claire had the uneasy feeling that she had hurt him. Had she been too harsh? If so, it was no more than his due. Because of her lower rank, he had judged her to be an easy mark for his seduction. It didn't matter that he believed her to be an experienced widow.

She told herself to move, to sit down at the desk and resume the tedious task of addressing invitations. Certainly she had more vital things on her mind than an arrogant aristocrat who viewed servants as fair game. Simon was nothing but an irksome distraction; her thoughts should be focused on freeing her father from prison. Right now, she ought to be studying Mr. Mundy's list . . .

Claire glanced down at the desk, and her heart jolted. The polished rosewood surface contained only the discarded quill and the silver inkpot. The invitations to the masquerade ball lay scattered on the carpet, where she had swept them in a blind rage.

On top of the untidy heap rested the sprig of crushed violets—and the document that revealed her interest in the Wraith.

"Was ever woman in this humour woo'd?
Was ever woman in this humour won?"
—*King Richard III*, I:ii

Chapter Twelve

Simon crouched down to help Clara collect the spilled papers. She looked pale and stiff as she snatched up the uppermost one—a guest list, no doubt—and folded it into a square before reaching for the invitations. Although kneeling right in front of him, she didn't look at him or speak, and he felt a surprisingly sharp sense of loss.

He had bungled a simple apology. Rather than atone for his misjudgment of her morals, he had made matters worse.

Moodily, he watched as she reached up to toss the posy of violets onto the desk. The bodice of her matching violet gown stretched over the perfection of her breasts. Although she wasn't voluptuous, she had more than enough to fill a man's hands. But he wouldn't want her to catch him looking, not in her present state of mind. What sort of damn foolish impulse had caused him to tell Clara those wildflowers belonged to her? He should have known she wouldn't believe him.

After checking in at Bow Street Station that morning, Simon had stopped at Covent Garden and searched every stall for the perfect assortment of fresh-picked blooms.

He had felt compelled to purchase a bouquet that would be pleasing to Clara. At the time, his plan had seemed perfectly logical. What difference did it make if he handed them to her or not? Flowers didn't belong to anyone in particular. They just sat on a table where everyone could look at them.

But he had shrugged off the notion that giving the bouquet to Lady Rosabel first would make Clara feel like secondhand goods. He had only reinforced her conviction that he viewed her as unworthy of his respect.

Reaching under the desk for a lost invitation, he faced an uncomfortable truth. He *did* consider Clara beneath him. Not because of any conscious judgment on his part, but because class divisions were a fact of life. He'd had the good fortune to be born at the top of the tier, and he had been taught to take pride in his rank.

I could never trust a man who has proven himself to be completely without honor.

Nothing Clara had said had cut him so deeply. She didn't know it, but those words echoed the censure his father had voiced after Simon had been tossed out of school for fighting. *You have failed in your reponsibility to adhere to a higher standard of behavior. People will never look up to a man who has shown himself to be without honor.*

The memory left him raw and angry. Dammit, he resented Clara's denunciation of his character. Although she scarcely knew him, she had painted him a villain. But he had spent the past eighteen years on a straight and narrow path. After his father's violent death on that long-ago night, Simon had had to grow up fast. He had shouldered the duties that came with his title, he had committed himself to chasing down criminals, and he had seen to the education of his three younger sisters. He had worked devilishly hard, and it rankled for Clara to belittle his efforts.

She didn't know it, but since the age of fifteen he had always had perfect control of his actions—except with her.

He reached for an invitation under the desk chair at the same time she did. Their hands brushed. It felt as if a hot spark ignited his veins, sending liquid fire straight to his groin.

Both of them paused with their fingers on the square of stiff paper. Clara stared at him, her eyes so dark a blue they were almost lavender. For a woman who professed to despise him, she sent him strong signals to the contrary. Her lips were parted slightly as if in anticipation of his kiss. Her breathing was fast, her gaze full of fascinating secrets.

The moment spun out into an eternity. He wanted to pull off that severe black cap she wore and allow her luxurious brown hair to tumble past her shoulders. The urge to press her down to the floor almost overwhelmed him. She would be furious at first, but even the wildest mare could be tamed with determination and a skilled touch. Then, when she was ready, he could draw up her skirts, sink into her tight warmth, and ride her to the pinnacle of pleasure.

The fantasy wreaked havoc with his restraint. *Madness*. It was sheer madness even to consider making love to Clara in Warrington's house where anyone might walk in on them. Madness to crave her when it would only confirm her belief that he had no honor.

Yet with complete disregard for logic, he found himself leaning closer to her. Today he was stone-cold sober, and still he couldn't scour her from his thoughts. In the throes of intense frustration, he muttered, "Clara, I wish—"

A rapping on the door cut him off. The handle rattled and Lady Rosabel poked her head into the room.

Simon pulled back instantly. Clara sat bolt upright on her heels and clutched the invitations like a shield to her bosom.

Thankfully, Lady Rosabel didn't appear at all offended to see them kneeling together. She strolled inside, a silver vase cradled in her hands. "Hullo again. I'm glad to see you two are becoming better acquainted. It would be awkward indeed if you disliked each other."

Rising, Simon offered Clara his hand. "We've had a very enlightening chat," he said, giving her an ironic glance.

She rose nimbly to her feet—without his help. "It was clumsy of me to drop the invitations, my lady. The earl was helping me pick them up."

"How gentlemanly of him." Lady Rosabel went to the chaise to fetch the bouquet and stuck it unceremoniously into the vase. Without bothering to arrange the flowers, she dusted off her hands and turned to face Simon and Clara. "Well! I have something very important to show the two of you."

Clara frowned at the flowers before returning her gaze to her mistress. "If it's all the same, I'll stay here and put the invitations back in order."

"But you simply *must* come. Remember what I promised you last evening? In the coach as we were driving home."

Clara looked puzzled for a moment, then her eyes widened with unexpected interest. "Are you certain that's wise? Lady Hester will disapprove."

"Mama is napping," Lady Rosabel said breezily. "My lord, will you be so kind as to escort us?"

"Only if you tell me where we're going."

"It's a secret. You'll see in a minute."

Simon had intended to depart, as he had promised Clara. But he offered an arm to both women. "Faced with such a mystery, I can hardly refuse."

Surprisingly, Clara didn't hesitate to curl her fingers around the crook of his elbow. She seemed impatient to go. What was it that had caught her interest so completely?

As Lady Rosabel led them out into the corridor, he was conscious of Clara's hand nestled against his side. The faint flowery scent of her made him want to bury his face in the valley between her breasts. With effort, he forced his attention to Lady Rosabel.

She had pretty features with smooth white skin, pouty pink lips, and light blue eyes that constantly looked for new amusements. The gauzy yellow gown hugged generous breasts more suited to an opera singer than a well-born lady. Undoubtedly, she attracted male attention wherever she went. If he was her father, he'd keep her under lock and key.

Simon frowned. He wanted to be her husband, not her parent. Nevertheless, there was something faintly incestuous about the notion of bedding the girl. Seventeen, by God! He hadn't known she was *that* young.

But he would see the matter through, and for more reason than that ill-advised wager. By seeking Warrington's permission to woo Lady Rosabel, Simon had made a commitment of sorts, and he never shirked his obligations. He planned to wait a few weeks before he declared himself. Her birthday would have come and gone by then. And he could always press for a long betrothal, perhaps six months, to allow her more time to mature and him the chance to accustom her to the duties of being his countess. Yes, the Christmas holidays would be soon enough to wed.

The plan satisfied him—until he made the mistake of glancing at Clara Brownley.

As they walked down the wide corridor, she kept her gaze trained straight ahead. She appeared to be deep in thought. When her teeth nibbled at her lower lip, he had the violent urge to kiss her again. If he were marrying Clara, he wouldn't wait six days, let along six months. He'd ride hell-bent to the archbishop and pay the price for a special license. Better yet, he'd take her with him and—

Simon banished the delusion. Nothing could be more unthinkable. His rank required him to wed a blue-blooded virgin. Not a widow of questionable background.

He aimed his full attention at Lady Rosabel. "Will you come to dinner tomorrow evening? I'd like you to meet my family."

"Is Brownie invited, too? I shan't go anywhere without her."

"My lady!" Clara chided. "It's ungracious to place stipulations on an invitation. I'm perfectly content to stay here."

The flush of her cheeks displayed her embarrassment. Clearly, she preferred to keep as far away from him as possible, but Simon could only think how much his sisters would enjoy sparring with her. "The invitation certainly includes you, Mrs. Brownley, along with Lady Hester and Lord Warrington."

"Then it's settled," Lady Rosabel said, as they entered a picture gallery at the rear of the house. "And just in time, for here we are."

The crimson-and-gold carpet muffled their footfalls. Although the heavy gold draperies had been drawn back from the tall windows, the overcast day made the long room dim and gloomy. Groupings of chairs had been placed at strategic intervals to allow comfortable viewing of the many portraits that lined the wood-paneled walls.

The Warrington ancestors, Simon observed. This gallery was a testament to Lady Rosabel's noble pedigree. It was similar to the one at Holyoke Park in Hampshire, the family seat of the Earls of Rockford, where he often spent the summer months, providing there were no criminal cases requiring his attention in London.

Clara released his arm and dropped back to follow them as Lady Rosabel led him straight to one of the two fireplaces. Even though it was the proper behavior for a companion, the deferential gesture disturbed Simon. Imprudent though it might be, he wanted Clara beside him. Then Lady Rosabel tugged on his arm, demanding his attention.

"Look," she said, her eyes sparkling as she pointed at a portrait that hung above the marble mantel. "There's what I wanted to show you."

Baffled, Simon gazed up at a family garbed in the style of the previous century. A distinguished man in blue naval uniform stood beside a chair that held a smiling woman in a powdered wig and a blue satin gown festooned with lace. At her feet, a girl of perhaps ten and a younger boy played with a floppy-eared spaniel.

The sight riveted Simon. The man's gruff features belonged to a younger Lord Warrington, which meant the little blond girl must be his daughter, Emily. Simon had thoroughly researched her story in his investigation of the Wraith. Some seven years after this portrait had been done, that innocent girl had fallen into the clutches of the man hired to tutor her and her brother, John.

Gilbert Hollybrooke.

Simon's gut tightened. The memory of Hollybrooke's capture several weeks ago remained fresh in his mind. How innocuous the Wraith had looked in his small flat near Covent Garden, how vehemently he had asserted his innocence. He had continued to protest even after Simon had discovered the diamond bracelet hidden in the bottom drawer of Hollybrooke's desk.

Simon knew from experience that the cleverest of criminals were chameleons adept at disguising their true nature. But even clever criminals sometimes made mistakes. At the last house he'd robbed, Hollybrooke had been careless enough to drop a bill from the grocer.

That one simple error had been his downfall.

"Do you know who they are, my lord?" Lady Rosabel glanced over her shoulder at the open doorway, then answered her own question, "Those are my grandparents. The little boy is my father. And the girl is my aunt Emily. She's the one who ran away from home and married the Wraith."

Simon inclined his head in a nod. "I'd surmised as much."

"Mama thinks you ought not be reminded of our family's connection to a notorious jewel thief. But *I* find it deliciously exciting."

Lady Rosabel couldn't possibly know that Simon had been instrumental in capturing Hollybrooke. Therefore, the sly quality to her gaze meant she was trying to provoke a reaction from him. It was a trick his sisters had sometimes used as children, and not one he cared to nurture in his future countess.

He kept his expression bland. "Such a man might appear to be a romantic figure. But make no mistake about it, he's a dangerous criminal."

Behind them, Clara drew in a breath as if to speak. When she remained silent, he wondered what acid comment she had subdued. Perhaps she had intended to agree with him, then decided not to give him the pleasure of it.

Lady Rosabel sashayed to a nearby bench and sat

down. She patted the seat beside her, and Simon walked closer to her, but stayed on his feet since Clara remained standing. The position gave him a better view of her. Seemingly oblivious to them, she stood with her hands clasped in front of her and gazed at the portrait.

It surprised him that she would show such interest in the girl Hollybrooke had duped. Clara didn't strike him as someone who thrived on gossip—but then again, he didn't know much about her. She kept her personal life inviolate. Perhaps they were alike in that respect.

Lady Rosabel sighed. "When I was growing up, I never even knew I *had* an Aunt Emily and Uncle Gilbert. And when I found out last summer, Mama and Grandpapa refused to talk about them. I was reduced to wheedling the story out of Mrs. Fleming."

"Mrs. Fleming?" he asked.

"Our housekeeper. She's been with the family forever."

Clara turned around. "Are you saying she was employed here at the time Lady Emily ran off to marry her tutor?"

Lady Rosabel nodded. "Yes, and it's such a tragic tale. She said they were madly in love, but Grandpapa called Uncle Gilbert a fortune-hunter. He cut off Aunt Emily without a penny."

"As well he should," Simon said flatly. "Hollybrooke wanted her dowry, along with any future inheritance she might receive."

Clara frowned. "How cynical of you to assume he married her only for her money."

"I'm merely reiterating the statement given to the newspapers by the magistrate." Simon was careful to say only what had been reported. "Hollybrooke wanted to claim what he considered to be his rightful legacy."

"Then why did he not steal jewels from *this* house?"

she asked scornfully. "Why would he take a diamond bracelet from *your* mother? Did *she* know Mr. Holly-brooke? Maybe he tutored her, too."

"Don't be ridiculous. Lady Emily ran off with him some twenty-six years ago. My mother had already been married for eight years."

"There, you see? It makes no sense at all."

"It makes perfect sense. All this time, he nursed a grudge against society for shunning him. He wanted revenge against the aristocracy."

"Well, that seems a shaky reason to me. I cannot help but wonder if the Runners have been thorough in their investigation."

Offended by her disdain for his work, Simon clenched his jaw to keep from snapping at her. But it was better not to encourage Clara. She relished being contrary, especially today when she was already angry at him, ready to disagree even if he said the sun rose in the east.

"I do believe Brownie is right. We *should* give Uncle Gilbert the benefit of the doubt." From beneath her lashes, Lady Rosabel showed Simon a winsome look. "Do you know, I've never met him? Perhaps I should pay him a visit in prison."

Clara's eyes widened. She took a step forward, her hands clenched at her sides. "No! My lady, you can't possibly do such a thing."

"Whyever not? He must be very lonesome. I could bring him tea and cakes. It is the charitable thing to do."

Lady Rosabel was too innocent to realize the realities of life behind bars, Simon judged. "Newgate is no place for a lady. It's cold, damp, and filthy, and the cells are full of brigands and murderers."

She batted her lashes at him. "But I'd be perfectly safe if I had a strong man like *you* to escort me."

He could only imagine her reaction when Hollybrooke identified *him* as the arresting officer from Bow Street. "Absolutely not. You're to put the matter out of your mind. I won't hear another word about it."

Her smile turned pouty. "Oh, bother, I'm sure you're right. I must not allow my curiosity to get the better of me."

Lady Rosabel held out a dainty hand, and Simon assisted her in rising from the bench. As they strolled the gallery, she turned the subject to society gossip. He felt satisfied that she had abandoned her rash plan to visit her uncle. She had the impetuousness of youth, but he felt confident in his ability to correct any such deficiencies in her character by using patience and firm guidance.

Only one problem nagged at him. Although he appreciated her beauty, he felt the detached admiration he might afford a lovely woman on the streets. He experienced no quickening of his blood, no flash of heat that made him burn to get her into his bed.

Unlike with Clara Brownley.

Across the gallery, Clara walked slowly from painting to painting, stopping before each one to read the engraved brass plate at the bottom of the gilt frame and then study the portrait. The slim-fitting violet gown swayed with her movements, hinting at hidden curves. Annoyed by the tightening of his groin, he almost wished she wore that gunnysack again. Was she pretending an interest in the family history as a means of avoiding him? Or was she simply being polite in allowing him time alone with Lady Rosabel?

I could never trust a man who has proven himself to be completely without honor.

Her thoughts and opinions held no significance to him, Simon grimly reminded himself. What he felt for her was lust, pure and simple. For some unknown reason, he was drawn to her unique combination of boldness and beauty.

She was as unconventional a woman as he had ever met—and more prickly than a hedgehog. Maybe it was the challenge he relished. He wanted to soothe her barbs and make her purr like a kitten.

Luckily, he had the self-discipline to restrain himself. If it killed him, he had no intention of touching Clara Brownley ever again.

"All that glisters is not gold."
—*The Merchant of Venice*, II:vii

Chapter Thirteen

"I make my own polish from linseed oil," Mrs. Fleming told Claire as they headed down the upstairs corridor the following morning. "None of that cheap stuff from the shops for me. The recipe was handed down from my mother, who was housekeeper at Windsor Castle. I believe in caring for the marquess's furniture as if it belongs to the king himself."

"That's very admirable," Claire murmured.

As the housekeeper intoned the excellence of her other cleaning products, Claire listened with only half an ear. She could scarcely believe her good luck. Since it was barely eight o'clock and Lady Rosabel likely would sleep until noon, Claire had offered her services to Mrs. Fleming.

Twice a week, the stern, middle-aged woman did a thorough cleaning of Lord Warrington's private apartments. She always worked alone, deeming that particular task too important for the upstairs maids. Claire had used a skillful blend of flattery and charm in order to persuade Mrs. Fleming to accept her assistance.

Anticipation made her fingers tighten around the basket

of cleaning supplies. At last, she would have the chance to explore her grandfather's chambers and search for the evidence of his guilt.

"Here we are," Mrs. Fleming said, stopping before a closed door trimmed in gilt. She had narrow features, heavily creased with age, and sharp gray eyes that could spot a speck of dust from thirty paces. With a hint of misgivings, she peered at Claire. "Are you certain you wish to dirty your hands, Mrs. Brownley? Seeing that you have the manners and speech of a lady, I wouldn't think ill of you for changing your mind."

"I'm accustomed to hard work. Since I've finished the invitations to the masquerade ball, I would rather keep busy than sit idly."

Mrs. Fleming nodded in approval. "Come with me, then."

Claire followed the housekeeper through a dim antechamber and into a large, gloomy bedchamber. A massive four-poster bed with dark velvet hangings dominated the room. A strange but pleasant aroma tinged the air . . . sandalwood? Mrs. Fleming stepped briskly to the window and drew open the draperies to let in the watery sunlight.

Claire halted in the middle of the Turkish carpet. If she had expected anything at all, it had been a room as austere as its occupant. Not . . . *this*.

Her eyes wide, she turned slowly around, trying to absorb it all. On every available surface rested exquisite, exotic objects. A jade figurine of a plump man. An ornately decorated brass vase. The golden mask of an Indian god. There were statues and bowls, urns and shields, and even a huge fan of vivid peacock feathers.

Mrs. Fleming returned to Claire's side, her manner prideful. "'Tis a spectacular display, is it not? Now you know why I never allow the housemaids in here. If anything were to break, the blame would be mine."

"I had no idea the marquess was such an avid collector. Where did all these things come from?"

"Lord Warrington served for many years in His Majesty's navy. These are souvenirs from his travels around the world."

Claire tried to imagine her grandfather searching out treasures in foreign bazaars. The image clashed with her view of him as a cold-blooded curmudgeon without any redeeming characteristics. Yet the man who had purchased these items had an eye for grace and beauty.

That didn't mean Lord Warrington possessed the warmth of a human being, she told herself. Clearly, he cherished these inanimate objects more than he had loved his own daughter.

Nevertheless, Claire found the eclectic exhibit enthralling. She wanted to wander throughout the chamber and examine each piece, but Mrs. Fleming handed her a pair of soft, folded cloths and motioned her over to the old-fashioned mahogany bed.

A pale green coverlet embroidered with dragons had been neatly drawn up and the pillows plumped, probably by Oscar Eddison, the dour valet. The image of her grandfather lying in this bed disturbed Claire. She didn't want to picture him in so vulnerable a state as sleep.

"You may start over here," Mrs. Fleming said. "Put the polish on the flannel, not directly onto the wood." The housekeeper demonstrated by tipping a brown bottle and pouring a dribble onto the cloth. "Rub the area hard until the oil is absorbed, then buff with the clean linen. And mind you, don't leave any excess that might soil the master's clothing."

Claire set to work on the scrolled post at the foot of the

bed. The oil gave off a pleasant, nutty aroma and made the old wood shine. This morning, she had purposefully donned an apron over one of her old gowns, so it didn't matter if she got dirty.

Out of the corner of her eye, she watched Mrs. Fleming bustle around the bedchamber, dusting the valuables. The housekeeper chattered as she worked, continuing her monologue on the best methods for getting ink spots out of cloth and singing the praises of her recipe for silver polish made with rainwater and hartshorn powder.

She was a wiry, energetic woman with an air of command and a reputation among the servants as a disciplinarian. But she also liked to talk, and Claire suspected it was lonely at the top of the staff hierarchy. Mrs. Fleming wouldn't lower herself to gossip with underlings, but Claire's position put them on more or less equal footing.

It was a fact that Claire intended to exploit.

The previous afternoon, she had been taken aback to discover that Mrs. Fleming had been employed here when Claire's mother was young. Rosabel had said so while they were viewing that painting in the gallery.

Claire's throat tightened. Seeing Mama as a girl had been an extraordinary moment. Since Papa had been unable to afford to commission a portrait, she had viewed no other likeness of her mother, who had died when Claire was twelve. She had wanted to stand there forever, absorbing her mother's smile, imprinting that familiar face on her memory.

Then Simon had spoken harshly of her father. *Make no mistake about it, he's a dangerous criminal.*

Anger had caused Claire to come perilously close to revealing herself. She wouldn't make that error again. She would question Mrs. Fleming, coax her into telling the story of Claire's parents falling in love. Mrs. Fleming would have witnessed the uproar when the marquess had found out. And she might know something to incriminate him now as the Wraith.

"You must have dusted these treasures countless times," Claire commented. "How long have you been working for the family?"

"I was ten when my mother secured a position for me as a scullery maid." Mrs. Fleming picked up a carved ivory box and ran her cloth over a side table. "That was nigh on forty years ago."

If the woman was now around fifty, she would have been twenty-three at the time of Mama's marriage. "I imagine you were promoted from washing pots very quickly."

"I was, indeed," Mrs. Fleming said proudly. "Made my way up the ranks through hard work, I did. I was an up-stairs maid by the time I was fifteen and housekeeper by age thirty."

Claire crouched down to polish the bottom half of the bedpost. "Then you must have been here during the scandal long ago."

Setting down the box, Mrs. Fleming pursed her lips. "I do hope you're not a gossipmonger, expecting me to betray family secrets."

"Certainly not! I only brought up the subject because Lady Rosabel took Lord Rockford to the picture gallery yesterday. She showed us both a painting of Lady Emily."

"Good gracious." The housekeeper's suspicious expression altered to a frown of concern. "Lady Hester will be beside herself. She has her heart set on a marriage between those two. She wouldn't want him frightened away by any reminders of that upcoming trial."

Feeling guilty for tattling on Rosabel, Claire said, "I

don't believe there's any harm done. The earl didn't seem bothered by the scandal."

"Then bless him for it. I've heard nothing but good about his lordship, and this does seem to confirm it. Heaven knows, young Lady Rosabel could use a steadying influence in her life."

Nothing but good about Simon? A steadying influence? Mrs. Fleming wouldn't say those things if Claire told her about that passionate kiss outside in the rain. Or that yesterday he had tried to charm her while Lady Rosabel was out of the room. While they were kneeling on the floor, picking up the invitations, there had been a moment when he'd wanted to kiss her again. She had seen it burning in his eyes and had felt her own yearning threaten to defeat her better judgment. Rosabel's return had been providential, saving Claire from disgracing herself.

Clara, I wish . . .

What had Simon been about to say? That he wished he'd treated her with more respect? Or that he wished she was of his class so that he could court her properly?

Blast him. He'd probably been wishing she'd agree to be his mistress, though Claire couldn't understand why. For the most part, she had been rude and unfriendly toward him. A handsome, wealthy nobleman surely could find a multitude of willing women. Did he view her as a challenge? Was it the very fact that she scorned him that nurtured his interest in her?

Perhaps if she tried being more civil, he would withdraw his attentions. But the notion of letting down her guard disturbed her. She had no desire to associate with a man who viewed her as his social inferior.

Now who's the liar, Clara? You can't deny the passion we shared. You wanted to take that kiss to its completion as much as I did.

Claire expended her anger on the bedpost, rubbing hard to work the oil into the carved wood of the footboard. Yes, he *did* kindle her bodily desires. But it was nothing more than the instinctive reaction of a woman to an attractive man.

Searching for a way to make the housekeeper reveal the past, Claire said, "I'm concerned that Lady Rosabel seems so fascinated by her late aunt. She finds it very romantic that Lady Emily fell in love with her tutor and gave up everything to be with him."

Mrs. Fleming had been wiping down a collection of figurines in a curio cabinet, but she turned around and shook her head in disapproval. "Lady Rosabel has no notion of the realities of life. She sees the world with stars in her eyes, just as Lady Emily did."

Claire privately objected to the suggestion of any resemblance. Her mother had been wise, sensible, and unselfish—and not at all inclined to stealing off on her own to make mischief. But Mrs. Fleming had to be encouraged to talk. "Are they really so much alike, then?"

"Well, perhaps not entirely," the housekeeper conceded. "Lady Emily was not quite so fickle, at least not until she fancied herself in love. She devoted herself to books and would spend the day in the library rather than go out to the shops—especially after Gilbert Hollybrooke was hired to tutor her and her brother." Dusting a small gold dragon with emerald eyes, she added in a huff, "That man! I certainly misjudged him."

"What do you mean?"

"When he first came to this house, he seemed like a decent fellow, always polite and respectful. He wasn't high-and-mighty like some tutors who fancy themselves a step above the other servants. I never imagined he was the sort to lure Lady Emily away from the bosom of her family."

Claire clenched her teeth. "But if they were truly in love—"

"In love!" Mrs. Fleming stuck her hands on her hips, the dust rag dangling from her fingers. "Does love pay the rent? Does love feed the hungry mouths of children? Lady Emily had no notion of the hardships of living as a commoner. Why, she never even put away her own clothes, let alone did the washing and the cooking and the cleaning. To think of her living in shabby, rat-infested rooms just breaks my heart."

Their little flat had been cozy and warm and spotless, thanks to Mama, who cheerfully had worked hard to make a good home for her husband and daughter. The only time Claire had ever seen her mother unhappy was when she'd been writing to her father, as she did faithfully once or twice a year.

Claire moved to the other post at the foot of the bed. "I suppose," she said, "there are no insurmountable obstacles when a girl is young and romantic and willing to make sacrifices to be with the man of her dreams."

But Mrs. Fleming didn't seem to hear. She picked up a blue porcelain vase and stared down at it. "If only I'd been able to stop her. I knew she fancied Mr. Hollybrooke, but she swore me to secrecy, and I thought for certain she'd warn me before she did anything rash . . ."

"You were friends with Lady Emily?" Claire asked in surprise.

Mrs. Fleming stiffened, as if realizing she had revealed too much. "I was the upstairs maid assigned to clean her chambers. I didn't ask for confidences, but she gave them to me anyway."

Claire's heart wrenched. How difficult it must have been for Mama to hide her feelings for Papa, how isolated she must have felt. The ladies of her own class would have been horrified had she disclosed her affection for a man they considered inappropriate. Yet like any young woman in love, she must have been bubbling over with excitement and sorely in need of a friend. "She must have trusted you very much."

"Not nearly enough," Mrs. Fleming said with a trace of bitterness. "You can imagine my shock when I came to light the fire one morning and discovered her bed was empty, the covers as neat as I'd left them the previous night. I immediately suspected that she'd run away with Mr. Hollybrooke."

"What did you do?"

"Luckily, Lord Warrington was on leave from his ship. I hastened to notify Mr. Eddison, and he woke the marquess at once. His lordship organized a search party, but Lady Emily wasn't found for three days. By then, it was too late. She'd been ruined."

Finishing at the foot of the bed, Claire moved her supplies to the table beside the headboard. She struggled to keep her voice neutral. "Isn't *ruined* a bit harsh? Mr. Hollybrooke married her, did he not?"

Mrs. Fleming gave Claire a glare reminiscent of the marquess. "She belonged with a man of her own rank. Perhaps they are more lax about such matters in the north of England where you are from."

"Perhaps." Claire made a show of diligently polishing the dark mahogany of the headboard. "Lady Rosabel said the marquess cut off Lady Emily without a penny, and that he refused to see her ever again. He must have been furious to erase her so completely from his life."

"'Tis my observation that men use anger to hide their pain," Mrs. Fleming said as she dusted a free-standing brass tiger with a tray on its back. "His lordship was distraught, make no mistake about that. For days, he hardly slept or ate. He'd lost his wife only the previous year, you see, and he'd doted on Lady Emily."

Claire swallowed a harsh exclamation. Papa had told her an entirely different tale, that Lord Warrington had tried to push Mama to wed a doddering old duke. If anyone had been hurt, it had been Mama, who had only sought to marry the man she'd loved.

Injecting a note of sympathy into her voice, Claire said, "It's such a tragedy for a family to be separated. Perhaps if his lordship could have brought himself to forgive her—"

"Forgive? It was *she* who should have begged for *his* forgiveness." The housekeeper wiped the tiger's feet with a vengeance. "After Lady Emily left, the master shut himself in his library for weeks on end. Then he went back out to sea and seldom returned until after Trafalgar, where he injured his leg most grievously. He never heard from her again."

That wasn't true! "Surely she would have written to her father. Did he never receive any letters?"

"If he did, I never heard anything of it." Mrs. Fleming shook her head in sorrowful disgust. "Lady Emily was always the sweetest, most considerate of girls. I can only think Mr. Hollybrooke changed her. He wasn't the honorable man I thought he was. Still, you could have knocked me over with a feather when the news came out that he was the Wraith. Somehow, I can't picture him creeping into fine houses and stealing jewels." She tut-tutted. "These days, you just can't tell about folks anymore."

Claire wanted nothing more than to set the housekeeper straight. Instead, she forced herself to consider the problem of the missing letters. What could have happened to them? Had the marquess received Mama's correspondence, but concealed that fact from the rest of the household?

Although Claire had never been in the front entrance hall when the post came, she had seen the footman carrying a silver tray of mail upstairs. "Speaking of letters," she said casually, "I'm expecting one from a friend in York. Who distributes the post in this house?"

Mrs. Fleming dusted the carved ivory tusk of an elephant. "One of the footmen brings it to Mr. Eddison. He takes care of the matter."

Claire didn't know everything about the division of labor in a typical wealthy household, but such a task seemed more suited to the butler, rather than her grandfather's personal valet. "Isn't that a bit . . . unusual?"

"'Tis the way things have always been in this house. Now, do pay heed to your polishing, or we'll be late leaving here."

A hint of distrust tightened Mrs. Fleming's lips, and Claire thought it wise to abandon the subject of her parents. As she applied herself to shining the headboard, she broached the topic of the upcoming masquerade ball for Lady Rosabel's eighteenth birthday.

But all the while, a different dialogue occupied Claire's mind. Was it possible that Mr. Eddison had destroyed her mother's letters? If so, he would have been acting under orders from Lord Warrington. The marquess had cut his own daughter out of his life as if she were dead.

But apparently that hadn't been enough to satisfy his craving for revenge. Now, he would punish Claire's father—unless she could find the evidence to thwart his wicked plan.

Surreptitiously, she eyed the drawers of the bedside table. Her grandfather might have hidden the stolen jewelry somewhere in this bedchamber. She had memorized the descriptions of the pieces from Mr. Mundy's list. If only Mrs. Fleming would leave the room . . .

Unfortunately, the housekeeper took her responsibilities seriously. She systematically rid the bedchamber of every speck of dust while Claire continued polishing until her arms were sore. Then Mrs. Fleming went around the room and scrutinized every surface, running her fingertip over the glossy wood of the bedstead to check for any missed spots.

Claire formulated a desperate plan. While the older woman's back was turned, she folded the oily cloth and dropped it inside a blue-and-white Chinese vase.

The housekeeper completed her inspection, gave a nod of approval, then closed the tall draperies again, chasing away the brightness of the day. As Claire collected the basket of supplies, Mrs. Fleming said, "You've done well, Mrs. Brownley. I must admit, I had my doubts about accepting your help. But it was quite pleasant to have your company."

Going down the servants' staircase, they chatted about various members of the staff. When they had almost reached the kitchen, Claire stopped as if in surprise. She made a show of searching through the basket of cleaning materials. "Oh, dear."

"What is it?"

"We were talking and . . . I'm afraid I left my polishing rag upstairs on the floor by the bed. I'll run back and fetch it."

Mrs. Fleming frowned. "I'll go. None of the staff is permitted in the master's chamber unless Mr. Eddison or I are present."

"Please, I can be in and out in a moment's time. I'd feel dreadful to inconvenience you when you've scores of important duties to oversee."

Mrs. Fleming puffed up with importance. "Well . . . if

you promise to hurry, then. I wouldn't want the marquess to come upon you there."

Nor would Claire.

Hurrying back up the stairs, she knew she had only a few minutes to retrieve the rag and search through her grandfather's things in hopes of finding incriminating evidence. And if she discovered the cache of jewels stolen by the Wraith? What then?

It might not ensure her father's release from prison, Claire knew. The court would demand eyewitnesses to confirm she hadn't planted the gems herself. Could she persuade some of the other servants to venture into the bedroom? Could she smuggle Mr. Mundy into the house? Or perhaps an officer of the law? And how was she to convince the magistrate at Bow Street Station to arrest the Marquess of Warrington?

If all else failed, she would take her accusations to the newspapers. She would create a scandal that would cast doubt on her father's guilt. She would make sure the world knew the true story if she had to print a handbill herself and stand on a street corner, giving it out to passersby.

Hastening through the antechamber, she entered the enormous bedroom. The faint scent of linseed oil lingered in the air. With the curtains drawn, the dim room had a malevolent quality, the exotic figurines staring at her from the shadows. The ruby eyes of the large bronze tiger seemed to track her every move.

Shaking off her uneasiness, she went straight to a small writing desk and looked through the drawers. A pile of cream stationery imprinted with the Warrington crest. A handful of quill pens. A ball of string. Nothing of interest, not even a packet of old letters written by the marquess's disowned daughter.

Claire moved to a black lacquered cabinet and opened

it to find stacks of loose artwork. Exquisitely rendered in thick black ink, the drawings showed Chinese ladies in flowing robes and men in Mandarin garb with long, curled mustaches. Under any other circumstances, she would have felt tempted to linger over the pictures, but not now. She tucked them back onto the shelves, careful to leave them undisturbed.

From there, she hurried to the bedside table with its two drawers. The topmost one held an eclectic collection of books: a holy Bible, an anthology of old poetry, and a volume written in a foreign script that looked like Hindi. The bottom drawer held a man's folded handkerchief, the stubs of several beeswax candles, and a brown bottle, which she uncorked and sniffed.

The sweetish odor of laudanum stung her nose. Did her grandfather have trouble sleeping? Did the old wound in his leg ache in the middle of the night and keep him awake?

Claire shoved the medicine bottle back into the drawer. All that mattered was finding the proof of his guilt.

Conscious of the clock ticking on the mantelpiece, she searched through every drawer, every trunk, every possible hiding place, but the stash of jewels was nowhere to be found. Of course, it was likely her grandfather kept his valuables secured in a wall safe.

Starting at one corner of the bedchamber, she moved each picture aside to peer behind it. Tension screamed inside of her. A good ten minutes had passed, and Mrs. Fleming might come looking for her at any time.

Why had she thought to find the evidence so swiftly? The booty might be anywhere in this house—or elsewhere. For all Claire knew, the marquess might have deposited the purloined jewels in a bank vault. Or hired someone to sell them, possibly overseas. She would have to ask Mr. Mundy to investigate all the possibilities.

Near the bed, she lifted a bronze shield away from the wall and saw the square outline of a small safe. Her heart jumped with excitement . . . then fear.

Voices sounded from outside in the corridor. The doorknob rattled. And the door to the antechamber opened.

> "No legacy is so rich as honesty."
> —*All's Well That Ends Well*, III:v

Chapter Fourteen

The pawnshop was located on the edge of Seven Dials, a seedy district known for its trade in secondhand goods, including contraband brought in by thieves looking to gain a quick profit from their nightly work.

As Simon entered the dim cavern of the shop, a bell tinkled over the door. The place hadn't changed from his last visit nearly a month ago. The shelves held the same clutter of miscellany: porcelain vases, a set of silver-backed brushes, an assortment of cheap jewelry.

Like a rat emerging from its hole, the proprietor scuttled out of a back room. Henry Taggert was a small, stout man dressed in a shiny brown coat and yellow breeches marred by black smudges. His sharp nose twitched as if he were sniffing the musty air for danger.

His toothy smile died when he recognized Simon. "What're ye doin' back 'ere? I tole ye, I don't know nothin'."

"I've come to have another look around."

"I've naught t' 'ide. Run a clean business, I do. Ye've no call t' be pesterin' me."

"Nevertheless, you'll answer my questions—"

The bell over the door announced the arrival of a

customer. While Taggert haggled with a stooped old man wanting to purchase a chipped decanter, Simon curbed his impatience. He had a lot of ground to cover today, and he didn't appreciate the delay.

I cannot help but wonder if the Runners have been thorough in their investigation.

Clara's acid comment seared him. He had sat up late the previous night, and the more he'd pondered the matter, the more he'd acknowledged an uneasy feeling in his gut. He couldn't deny the fact that other than the diamond bracelet belonging to his mother, none of the jewelry stolen by the Wraith had been recovered.

But it had not been for want of effort.

Weeks ago, Simon had scoured the well-known receivers of the city from Covent Garden to Cheapside, places where thieves sold their stolen booty. Pawnbrokers like Taggert processed the valuables under the guise of legitimate business. In under five minutes, they could break down a jeweled necklace into individual stones. The pieces would then be marketed to unscrupulous jewelers throughout the city, men who asked no questions in exchange for a bargain. Unless a gem had a particular identifying characteristic, like an unusual color, it was nearly impossible to trace.

But a nagging sense of unfinished business had caused Simon to return to this squalid pawnshop, the first of many he had decided to revisit. He would attempt again to track down the money, too, for he had been unable to discover what Hollybrooke had done with his ill-gotten gains. None of the banks had any record of a large deposit by a man of his description. Nor had there been any hiding place in his flat. Simon had spent the better part of a day searching the place himself.

His hands in the pockets of his greatcoat, he scowled at a poorly rendered landscape painting that sat on a dusty shelf. He shouldn't let himself be goaded by Clara. She had no notion of his involvement in Hollybrooke's arrest, no notion of the long hours he had already put into the case. She had probably disagreed with his assessment of the matter for the sole reason that she was furious at him.

Let me tell you very plainly, I will never be your mistress. There is nothing in the world that would disgust me more.

She *did* desire him, he could see it in the quickness of her breath, in the flitting of her gaze to his mouth, in the charming blush of her cheeks. But the possibility of an affair genuinely horrified her. Had he thought his offer through beforehand, he would have proceeded more cautiously. Not quite a year had passed since her husband's death at Waterloo, and she might very well view her lust for another man as a betrayal.

The prospect of convincing her otherwise tempted Simon. If he took his time in arousing her, perhaps—

No. He had set his life on a course that included marriage to Lady Rosabel Lathrop. Seducing her companion would lay waste to his plans. It would mark him as a scoundrel when he had sworn long ago to become a man who would make his father proud.

The bell tinkled again as the customer left, bearing the cracked decanter. Simon returned to the counter, where the pawnbroker was counting the pennies he had been paid. His nostrils twitched like the snout of a rat. Looking up, he shoved the coins into his pocket as if he feared Simon might snatch them out of his grubby palm.

"Still 'angin' about, are ye?" he sneered. "If ye ain't buyin', I got no time fer the likes o' ye. I'm a 'onest man, I am. I got business t' do."

"Your prison record is no tribute to your integrity. Five years in Newgate for petty larceny."

Taggert thrust out his chin belligerently. "I paid me

dues. Been on the straight and narrow ever since. A law-abidin' citizen, that's me."

"Then you won't mind if I take a look in the back."

Simon walked behind the counter, but the thickset man moved swiftly. Arms akimbo, he blocked the doorway. "This 'ere is private property. Ye got no right t' poke around."

"I've a warrant from the magistrate at Bow Street Station." Simon withdrew the paper from an inside pocket of his coat and flashed it at the man. "Move aside now, or you'll be jailed for obstruction of justice."

Taggert hesitated, then obeyed, muttering curses under his breath.

Simon stepped past him. If Taggert was guilty, any evidence would be long gone. But there were ways to wrest a confession from a closemouthed perpetrator, and Simon intended to use any method necessary to accomplish his purpose.

The cramped, cluttered back room was hotter than the shop, due to the small furnace located in the rear corner. The heavy odor of metal tainted the air. Wending his way past piles of junk, he stopped in front of the large iron crucible that had been set over a coal fire. Beside it sat a wooden form filled with newly minted silver ingots.

Simon picked up a silver tray from a grimy table and inspected it. "I see you're up to your old tricks. Dealing with thieves and then melting the evidence."

Like a cornered rodent, Taggert bared his teeth. "Ain't no law against buyin' old silver. Ye can't prove nothin'."

"Quite the contrary." Seeing the tiny hallmark on the bottom, Simon replaced the tray. "You and I both know there's a good chance I could trace the unmelted pieces here. Someone will have reported their theft."

"'Ow am I supposed t' know where people gets things? It ain't my place t' ask 'em."

"I've been interrogating the Wraith," Simon lied. "He claims to have fenced some of the stolen jewels in this very shop."

The falsehood was a calculated risk. If Taggert was hiding his compliance, he would show it through the twitch of a muscle, the blanching of his skin, a flicker of his eyelids.

Taggert merely sneered. "Bugger's lyin'. 'E's playin' ye fer a fool. An' ye're too fine an' fancy a chap t' know it."

Simon sprang forward, caught Taggert by the throat, and shoved him against the wall. Metal clinked and glass rattled. "But not too fine and fancy to send you to the gallows."

Alarm flashed in that beady brown gaze. His face turned a mottled red. "Lemme go," he choked out. "I ain't never seen no Wraith."

"Then maybe you know who did. Word gets around."

"Don't . . . know . . . nuthin'."

Simon dug his fingers into that thick neck. "If you're lying, I'll see to it that you swing on Tyburn Hill."

"I ain't! I swear it . . . on me mam's grave."

Taggert was too much a coward to withhold the truth, Simon judged. He released his grip, and the pawnbroker staggered backward, clutching his throat and coughing.

Frustrated, Simon strode out of the shop and mounted his bay gelding. The stink of sewage tainted the dark, dreary neighborhood with its ramshackle buildings. He felt the mad urge to ride hell-bent for Warrington House to see Clara, to touch her smooth skin and smell her lavender scent, to seek oblivion in the wild pleasure of her kiss.

He crushed the impulse. It was Lady Rosabel who deserved his full attention. Tonight, in the next step of his campaign to win her as his bride, she and her family would dine at his house. He would see to it that his mother and sisters enjoyed her company.

Clara would be present, too. Clara, who would never know how her sharp criticism had changed his plans for the coming week.

I cannot help but wonder if the Runners have been thorough in their investigation.

He reminded himself that he already had irrefutable proof. A grocer's bill had been found in the bushes outside the site of the final robbery. The address had led Simon straight to Hollybrooke and the stolen diamond bracelet in his drawer, a man who carried a grudge against the nobility.

But wasn't it all a bit too convenient? Wasn't Gilbert Hollybrooke the antithesis of the hardened criminal?

Uneasiness clenched Simon's gut again, and he turned his mount toward an adjacent lane. At least a hundred pawnbrokers and jewelers awaited him. If for no other reason, he owed it to Warrington and his family to be absolutely certain of Hollybrooke's guilt.

For two ticks of the clock, Claire stood frozen as the measured footsteps came closer. Panic gripped her limbs. Should she hide in the dressing room? Under the bed? Behind the window draperies?

There was no time; she would have to brazen it out. Rushing to the Chinese vase, she extracted the oily rag and swung around just as her grandfather shuffled into the bedchamber, followed by his sour valet, Oscar Eddison.

The marquess leaned heavily on his polished cane, his clawlike fingers gripping the carved ivory top. His jaw was clenched as if his leg pained him. He took another slow step, his cane thumping against the carpet. In the doorway, he spied Claire and stopped.

It was the first time she'd seen him standing upright. He was somewhat shorter than she'd thought, only an inch or two taller than herself.

His sharp blue gaze stabbed her. "What the devil are *you* doing in here?"

Claire sank into a deep curtsy. "Forgive me, my lord. I assisted Mrs. Fleming with the cleaning this morning. By mistake, I forgot one of my rags."

Rising, she strove for a humble expression. Heaven help her if he doubted her story. She walked toward the two men, but they remained in the doorway, barring her escape.

Behind her grandfather, Mr. Eddison lifted his chin and glared at her down his nose. "She may be a thief, m'lord. May I suggest—"

"I'll handle the matter," Warrington snapped over his shoulder. To Claire, he said, "*Are* you a robber, Mrs. Brownley? A confidence woman pretending to be a Waterloo widow? Have you fooled all of us?"

Not in the way you think.

Donning a cloak of affronted dignity, she said emphatically, "Certainly not! You may review my references if you like."

Unbeknownst to him, she had written the letters herself, pretending to be the parents of several pupils at the Canfield Academy. She had carefully chosen those who lived farthest from London so that if anyone here should decide to check her credentials, it would take days, even weeks, to receive a response. By then, she would have found the proof that someone in this house had planted the evidence to incriminate her father.

The coldness on Warrington's weathered face made her suppress a shudder. Balancing on the cane, he turned to his servant. "Eddison, take a look around and see if anything is missing."

"Yes, m'lord. I'll fetch the list." The officious little valet bustled over to the desk, pulled out a sheaf of papers, and stalked to the far corner to begin checking the exotic valuables.

At that moment, clenching the rag, Claire hardly knew which of the two men she detested more. How dared they accuse *her* of burglary when the marquess himself was likely the Wraith? Or rather, Mr. Eddison must have committed the crimes on his master's behalf since her grandfather's limp would have prevented him from sneaking around in strange bedchambers during society parties.

"You, there," her grandfather said. "Follow me."

"Follow—"

"Are you daft, girl? Or just hard of hearing?" Warrington hobbled toward a pair of overstuffed chairs near the window.

Claire glared at his back as he propelled himself forward with the cane, his crippled right leg all but useless. He maneuvered carefully, teetering a moment before awkwardly lowering himself into one of the chairs.

She felt an unwilling stab of sympathy. At one time, he had been captain of his own ship. How galling it must be for a proud man like him to endure such an infirmity.

He glowered at her. "Stop gawking. Open the curtains and sit down."

The brief spark of compassion vanished. Claire did as she was told, drawing back the draperies so that daylight flooded the chamber. She wondered if he would still bark orders if he knew she was his granddaughter.

He would do worse then; he would throw her out of his house.

But whether he approved or not, she *did* belong to this family. That poignant fact had struck her yesterday, when she had viewed the old portraits in the gallery and realized they were her ancestors, too. A fierce sense of pride in her heritage had startled her. No matter how much this bitter old man denied it, he could never take away her blood relations.

Claire sat down, her posture erect, the rag balled in her

fingers. She would not fidget, would not show any sign of guilt, no matter how much tension squeezed her insides. At least Mr. Eddison wouldn't find anything out of order. She had been very careful to leave things undisturbed. But what if the marquess decided to accuse her of conspiring to steal, anyway?

"Mrs. Fleming will confirm my reason for being here," she said. "Pray send for her if you don't believe me."

Warrington gave her a forbidding stare, his eyes a chilly ocean blue beneath bushy gray brows. "I'll be the judge of what to do."

"I assure you, there is nothing missing from this chamber."

"You look offended, Mrs. Brownley. A pity, for I'd believed you a woman with a brain, someone who would understand the necessity of safeguarding these priceless objects of art."

Stung by his belittling assessment of her, she said frostily, "I've every right to be offended at being treated like a criminal. And it is uncivil of you to question my intelligence."

Across the room, Mr. Eddison turned to stare in shock.

Claire clamped her lips shut. Dear God, had she really called the marquess rude? She was a servant here, not a family member, free to express her unguarded opinions. Swallowing her pride, she said, "Forgive me, my lord. I spoke out of turn."

That rigid mouth twisted slightly. "So you would correct me, would you? Perhaps you think I shouldn't find it at all suspicious when a lady's companion is polishing my furniture instead of attending to my granddaughter."

"Lady Rosabel sleeps until noon. I prefer to stay busy at whatever task I can find, so I offered my services to Mrs. Fleming."

"You must have other responsibilities."

"None that can be accomplished without entering Lady Rosabel's chamber—and she has asked me not to disturb her."

He harrumphed. "How's that play going?" he asked, changing the subject. "Is she enjoying it?"

Fortunately, Claire had started reading aloud the first act of *A Midsummer Night's Dream* the previous evening. Unfortunately, Rosabel had fallen fast asleep within five minutes. "We've only begun. It's too soon to judge."

"Hah! So she didn't like it. I was right."

"That remains to be seen, my lord."

He made a rusty sound in his throat halfway between a grunt and a chuckle. "You certainly aren't a toady, Mrs. Brownley. There's nothing worse than a groveling female."

Was he saying that he *liked* Claire? With a bittersweet jolt, she remembered the disappointment she'd felt on her tenth birthday, when she had posted a letter inviting her grandfather to visit. He had never responded, and Mama had taken Claire in her arms to soothe her. *He and I quarreled years ago, long before you were born. But if he knew you, darling, I'm sure he would love you every bit as much as Papa and I do.*

That one statement had had a powerful effect on Claire's young mind. It had kept a kernel of hope alive in her heart. Maturity had laid waste to the fantasy, but now she was appalled to realize that somehow, somewhere deep inside of her, that dream had survived. In spite of all that had happened, she longed for her grandfather's approval.

Claire buried the vulnerability. She wanted only to make the marquess pay for what he had done to Papa— and to Mama long ago. But first she had to find a way out of her present predicament.

"If you believe me to be plainspoken," she said, "then I couldn't possibly have stolen anything."

"Impertinent chit. I've no intention of letting you off so easily."

"These artifacts would be extremely difficult to hide. It would be more logical for a thief to take small items—like jewelry."

"You could have pried a gemstone out of something, perhaps that tiger over there." He pointed a gnarled finger at the brass table that Mrs. Fleming had dusted earlier.

"Rest assured, it still has both its ruby eyes." For a moment, curiosity overtook her. "Where did you find something so unusual?"

"It was a reward from the maharajah of Jaipur. I captured a robber who was creeping through the palace one night."

Claire lifted an eyebrow. Was he trying to provoke her? She wouldn't show any sign of irritation. "Why do you keep your treasures hidden away here? Why haven't you decorated the house so that everyone can enjoy them?"

"It's my own private museum, that's why. I won't have them lying about where any servant might steal them."

In spite of her antipathy, Claire found it sad that he mistrusted everyone. "That seems a rather cynical view of mankind. Not everyone is interested in taking your wealth."

"The poor always want what the rich possess. 'Tis human nature."

"The poor can have principles, too. The Bard himself said, 'No legacy is so rich as honesty.' "

" 'The lady doth protest too much, methinks,' " Warrington quoted in reply. He studied her closely, his fingers gripping the carved ivory knob of the cane. Almost as if he were thinking aloud, he added in an undertone, "I must say, it would be most curious to discover another thief who is so interested in Shakespeare."

Claire's heartbeat faltered, then took off racing. Her

throat felt dry, her limbs rigid. Had she given herself away? Had that astute gaze spotted the slight resemblance to her father—his son-in-law?

No, Warrington must be bluffing, trying to determine if she had discovered *his* secret. He reminded her of a spider wrapping its silk around its victim. But Claire could play that game, too.

Pretending astonishment, she said, "Good heavens . . . are you comparing *me* to the Wraith?"

He stiffened. "Never mind. It doesn't signify."

"I *do* mind, my lord. I'm deeply aggrieved to know that you think so little of me. I've heard Mr. Hollybrooke is the most wicked of men—"

He banged his fist down on the arm of the chair. "By gad, woman! You'd dare to say his name in my presence?"

"I beg your pardon," she said, injecting sympathy into her voice. "I've heard about his connection to your family, and I'm sure you wouldn't wish to dwell upon the man who lured away your daughter. However—"

"Enough!" His face stark, Warrington pointed at the door. "Go on, get out of here. Find yourself an occupation other than pestering me."

Claire sat unmoving. She had hoped to trigger an outburst of wrath directed at her father—and to get her grandfather to drop his guard long enough for her to gain a clue. But once again, she had been thwarted by his refusal to speak about her father.

From across the room, Eddison objected, "M'lord! I've not yet completed the inventory."

Warrington ignored him, staring fixedly at Claire until she rose to her feet. A part of her was anxious to leave; another part mistrusted both him and his servant. But she could hardly insist upon staying to make certain Eddison didn't pocket a rare item and then claim she had stolen it.

She bobbed the obligatory curtsy. "I'm truly sorry for

disturbing you, my lord. Good day." Turning, she started toward the door.

"Mrs. Brownley."

The lash of her grandfather's voice brought Claire swinging around again. She was unprepared for the lightning bolt he hurled at her.

"Henceforth, you will spend your mornings organizing the books in my library," he snapped. "I'll expect you there tomorrow precisely at eight."

"Is love a tender thing? It is too rough, too rude, too boist'rous, and it pricks like thorn."

—*Romeo and Juliet*, I:iv

Chapter Fifteen

"Good evening, Mrs. Brownley. Welcome to Rockford House."

As Simon bowed over her gloved hand, Claire experienced a flush of desire at odds with her resolve to remain cool toward him. The heat of attraction she felt in his presence had no basis in logic, nor did she seem able to control it through willpower. But she refused to belabor the irksome reaction. She would be gone from society—and his company—the instant she found a way to clear her father's name.

"It's a pleasure to be here," she said politely.

She attempted to tug her hand out of his grasp, but Simon held firmly a moment longer. His dark eyes twinkled at her, and one corner of his mouth curled, causing an extremely attractive dimple. "Still angry at me, are you?" he murmured under his breath. "You needn't be. I promise not to make the mistake of giving you any flowers tonight."

His self-mockery tickled Claire with the urge to laugh out loud. But that would attract undue attention from the other guests, so she merely lifted an eyebrow.

A lavish array of candles lit the entrance hall with its tall marble pillars. A short distance away, Lady Hester and Rosabel were handing their wraps to a footman in blue livery. Lord Warrington removed his top hat while leaning on his cane. Despite his crippled leg, he had the bearing of a military officer, shoulders squared and chin held high.

"Has my son arrived, Lord Rockford?" Lady Hester asked with a girlish trill unsuited to a woman of her broad girth and advanced years.

"Not yet," Simon replied.

"Ah, well, Frederick intended to stop at his club, and I'm sure he'll be here very soon. In the meantime, I'm looking forward to renewing my acquaintance with your dear mother and sisters. I would love for our families to become *very* close."

As Lady Hester bore down on Claire and Simon, Rosabel seized her mother's arm and drew her toward Lord Warrington. "Come, Mama. We must assist Grandpapa up the stairs, you on one side and I on the other."

"But my dear"—Lady Hester flashed a significant glance at Simon—"you may wish to accompany *someone else*."

"I can manage," Warrington objected at the same time. "I certainly do so at home."

Gorgeous in a pale pink gown that complemented her blond curls, Rosabel gave him a pouty look designed to charm. "Oh, don't be a crosspatch. I hoped you'd enjoy being escorted by your two favorite ladies. Or will you refuse our company and disappoint me terribly?"

"Fiddle-faddle," he grumbled. "You shouldn't waste your time on an old man." But the half-smile on his craggy face showed him to be in a better humor than that morning, when he had ordered Claire to begin working in the library. It was clear he wanted to keep an eye on her because she had stirred his suspicions. Little did he realize, however, she welcomed the opportunity to investigate *him*.

Yet a pang struck Claire's breast as she watched him fuss over Rosabel. He seemed to have a soft spot for the girl. If circumstances had been different, would he have regarded Claire with such affection?

She didn't care to know. His cruel actions toward her parents had proven him to be a villain without a drop of kindness in his withered heart.

"You heard your grandfather," Lady Hester said coaxingly to her daughter. "He doesn't need help, and *I'm* certainly of little use to him." As if about to swoon, she fanned her plump face with her handkerchief.

"Stop playing the invalid, Hester." Warrington made an imperious gesture. "Take my other arm now, unless you intend to stand there gawking all night."

Looking miffed, Claire's aunt complied.

Rosabel cast an impish glance over her shoulder—and winked. Simon didn't see it since he had turned to say something to the footman, but Claire saw. The minx had maneuvered the situation so that Claire was forced to accompany Simon. The girl seemed determined to play her little games, though to what purpose, Claire had yet to discover.

"Mrs. Brownley?"

Simon stood waiting, and it would have been churlish not to slip her fingers into the crook of his arm. His muscles were hard beneath the dark gray coat, and another uninvited thrill swept through her. Ignoring him, she gazed straight ahead as they led the others toward a grand staircase that curved gracefully upward to the reception rooms.

In contrast to the gilded opulence of her grandfather's mansion, this house had a classic simplicity of design. The décor showed exquisite taste, from the pale green walls to the wrought-iron balustrade with its ivy leaf pattern. Wax-lights flickered in recessed sconces, enhancing the glow from the crystal chandelier suspended from the domed ceiling.

"Nothing to say, Mrs. Brownley?"

Simon bent his dark head closer, making her aware of his spicy scent. As they mounted the broad steps, she grasped her skirt to keep from tripping. "Forgive me," she said coolly. "I'm not well-versed in social prattle."

"It would be polite to comment on the weather—or on my home."

"The weather is cold and chilly, as well you know. As for your house, I've never before seen one so well-lit. Your monthly bill for candles must be outrageous."

He grinned. "I can afford it."

"If you practiced thrift, you could donate the savings to charity."

"And put the candlemakers out of work? It would weigh on my conscience to know they couldn't pay for food to feed their children."

A clever point, but she wouldn't let him win. "I begin to understand how the rich justify their extravagant way of life. However, the fact remains that you're an idle man, born to privilege. You can't possibly know what it's like to labor for a living."

A secretive look narrowed his eyes, though his smile lingered. "Your knowledge of my character is astounding, considering our short acquaintance."

Their conversation was masked by Rosabel's chattering several steps behind them. Nevertheless, sound carried in the huge entrance hall, so Claire spoke quietly.

"You're mocking me because you don't want to admit the truth. You consider yourself entitled to take whatever you like from those beneath your rank."

"So you told me yesterday. I can only hope that time will exonerate me in your eyes."

"You needn't trouble yourself on *my* behalf. I have no interest in you whatsoever."

His smile deepened to a smirk.

His gaze dipped to her lips.

His voice dropped to a whisper. "Don't be cross, darling. It was only a kiss."

Claire blushed. As much as she tried to stop it, the burning sensation spread over every inch of her body. The memory of his mouth on hers fanned the flames of anger—and desire. She was furious that he would bring up their encounter—and thrilled that he had called her *darling*. He had given her his word that he would not touch her again—yet his flirtatious manner told a contrary story.

Finding her voice, she said in a wintry tone, "If you value your life, do not ever mention that incident to me again."

This time, he chuckled outright. "You're as full of empty threats as my sisters. You'll get on especially well with Amelia. She's the youngest and every bit as irreverent as you are."

"Am I supposed to be reverent in your presence, then? I'm afraid you've chosen the wrong partner."

"And *I'm* afraid I enjoy your company far too much." As they reached the top of the stairs, he settled his hand over hers, trapping her fingers against his sleeve. That one touch made her pulse race and her breasts tighten. Then he made matters worse by adding, "Have I told you how lovely you look tonight, Clara?"

Her heart glowed with spontaneous pleasure. Rosabel had confiscated all of Claire's ugly caps—and her spectacles—and had directed a maid to do Claire's hair in a sophisticated arrangement of brown curls. A gauze gown in a rich, dark shade of bronze skimmed her curves, and she had stared at herself in the mirror, unable to believe that stylish lady was herself.

Now, she drew back her hand and crossed her arms. How was it that she had become so foolishly susceptible to this charming rogue?

She glanced over her shoulder, but due to her grandfather's infirmity, the others were only halfway up the long, curving staircase. "You compliment with the ease of practice," she murmured.

He kept his voice as low-pitched as hers. "Or perhaps I speak with the ease of truth."

"The truth is seldom easy, my lord. It's time you accepted the fact that there will be no liaison."

"I *have* resigned myself," he said, his face sobering. "I gave you my word, and I've no intention of breaking it."

She didn't trust his word. Especially not when he placed his hand at the small of her back and guided her down a wide corridor. The feel of his palm pressing against her waist caused a heavy ache in her privates. It felt scandalously as if he were caressing her naked flesh, touching her in places no man had ever known . . .

The forbidden fantasy shocked Claire to her maidenly core. Simon was an earl, a man with no purpose in life but the pursuit of his own pleasures. At her father's knee, she had been taught to despise the aristocracy and their exclusive rules of society. She respected only those who labored to put bread on the table, those who improved their minds through study, those who worked hard toward achieving a worthwhile objective. Handsome as he was, Simon could hold no allure for her.

Now who's the liar, Clara? You can't deny the passion we shared. You wanted to take that kiss to its completion as much as I did.

Yes, it was true, much to her chagrin. In that one exhilarating moment, Simon had made her realize what she was missing in her life. He had awakened the desire in her to experience the fullness of womanhood.

Yet he was too rich, too privileged, and too self-indulgent to realize the difference between *wanting* and *doing*. He could enjoy an illicit encounter and walk away a free man. She, however, would lose her reputation, her pride, her very livelihood. Who would want a fallen woman to teach their daughters? Who would employ her if she became pregnant and had a baby to feed?

And who would defend her father if she let herself be distracted by a love affair?

The chill of reality tempered the fires of lust. Yet the longing lingered, simmering deep inside of her, a warning to the dangers of lowering her guard.

Thankfully, she could hear voices coming from a room just ahead, the deep tones of a man and the throaty sound of female laughter in reply. Simon appeared to be intent on strolling straight inside, so Claire stopped just outside the arched doorway. "We should wait for the others. It *is* Lady Rosabel you wish to present to your family, is it not?"

Simon scowled as if he had forgotten his intended bride. He gave Claire another penetrating look before turning toward her grandfather, who slowly advanced down the corridor, flanked by his two escorts.

At that moment, a dazzling young woman with copper hair and inquisitive brown eyes emerged from the drawing room. A forest-green gown accentuated her milky skin, and she rested her hands on the gentle swell of her pregnancy.

"I thought I heard talking out here, Simon." She gave Claire a startled glance, looked at the approaching trio, then back at Claire. Keen interest lifted one dainty brow, and she held out her hand in welcome. "Hullo, I'm Simon's sister Amelia. Forgive me if I'm interrupting."

That blush returned to plague Claire. Clearly, Lady Amelia was trying to puzzle out the relationship between Claire and her brother. Blast Rosabel for maneuvering them!

Stepping away from Simon's side, she briefly touched Lady Amelia's extended hand. "It's a pleasure to meet you, my lady. Lord Rockford has spoken highly of you."

"Indeed?" A droll expression curled Lady Amelia's mouth. "I couldn't begin to imagine what fables he's invented. Perhaps later, I'll tell you his true opinion of me. And mine of him."

Claire found herself smiling. She decided then and there that she liked Simon's irreverent sister.

Laughing, he kissed his sister's cheek. "Amelia, may I present Mrs. Clara Brownley?"

"She's my daughter's hired companion," Lady Hester added, as the other three joined the group and made their greetings. Breathing hard from climbing the stairs, she directed her fawning attention at his sister. "You were so very kind . . . to include her in your invitation."

"The earl asked her," Rosabel declared, causing Lady Amelia's eyebrow to arch higher. "Brownie lost her husband last year at Waterloo. She's a dear, sweet lady. Don't you agree, Lord Rockford?"

His indulgent smile enhanced his dark attractiveness. "Since your knowledge of her is superior to mine, I must concede the point. Come now, I'd like you to meet the rest of my family."

He offered Rosabel his arm. No hand at the small of *her* back, Claire noted acidly. With Rosabel, he behaved as the consummate gentleman. On the outside, they made the perfect couple, she the petite, fair princess and he the tall, commanding prince. On the inside, however, they were poles apart. Rosabel didn't know that Simon was courting her on a wager, and Simon certainly didn't know that Rosabel had no intention of marrying him.

Beaming at the couple, Lady Hester waved the handkerchief at her rosy cheeks. "Go on in now, I'll be there directly. First, I'd like to have a word with dear Mrs. Brownley."

Claire tensed. Had her aunt overheard her conversation with Simon? Or had she simply noticed the intimate manner in which he had behaved toward Claire?

Lady Amelia glanced curiously from Lady Hester to Claire, then turned to Lord Warrington. "That leaves the two of us, my lord."

Leaning on his cane, he fixed her with a forbidding stare. "I knew your grandmother a long time ago. You're the very image of her. She had a temper as fiery as her hair."

"So do I—or so Simon tells me. But never fear, I shall be on my very best behavior tonight."

Her breezy manner wrested a gravelly chuckle from the marquess as they strolled through the doorway.

Lady Hester's smile vanished at once. Motioning Claire a short way down the corridor, she hissed, "I would like to know what you were whispering about to Lord Rockford."

"We were speaking of his house, the placement of candles in particular."

"Candles, bah. It didn't look that way to me. You were working your wiles on him, were you not?"

If only Lady Hester knew the truth. It required little

acting skill for Claire to look offended. "Certainly not! I would never conduct myself in so improper a manner."

Lady Hester harumphed. "Then why are you now garbing yourself as a lady? It can only be in the hopes of attracting a wealthy husband . . . or perhaps a paramour."

"No, you're mistaken. It was Lady Rosabel who insisted—"

"Lord Rockford is courting *my* daughter, and you will do nothing to distract him. Is that clear?"

"Of course, but—"

"I don't pay you to contradict me, Mrs. Brownley. However, since I'm a kind woman, I'll give you a piece of advice. Men of his rank don't marry females of your reduced station. If you entice him, he may very well use you as he pleases. And you'll have only yourself to blame for it!"

Clenching her teeth, Claire meekly lowered her head. "Yes, my lady."

"Henceforth, I intend to watch you very closely. Mind your step if you wish to keep your position."

Like a great warship, Lady Hester sailed into the drawing room, leaving Claire mired in frustration. She resented being called a flirt when Simon was the one at fault. And how had she managed to get herself into trouble again? In just one day, first her grandfather and now her aunt had reprimanded her.

She couldn't afford to make any more wrong moves. In particular, she had to be careful not to speak to Simon, which could prove awkward if he sought out her company again.

Maddening man. Why wouldn't he leave her alone?

The moment she entered the drawing room, Simon noticed that Clara was upset. The signs were too slight for the casual observer, but he had trained himself to identify subtleties of expression. From his stance by the fireplace, he saw the stiffness of her bearing and the firmness of her lips. Lady Hester had spoken to her in the corridor, and he had a strong suspicion their conversation had to do with him.

Damn the old biddy for chastising Clara. And damn himself for teasing her. He had been tense and irritable after spending all day traipsing through the stews of the city on a fruitless search for evidence against the Wraith. He had resolved to put Clara out of his mind. But the moment he'd seen her, the darkness in him had lifted. He had craved the stimulation of her quick wit, hungered for the touch and scent and sight of her with a fervor that had obliterated all logic.

What the devil had possessed him to call her *darling*? He had been so intent on Clara that he'd almost taken her into the drawing room ahead of Lady Rosabel, a breach of protocol that would have had serious consequences for his marriage plans.

Moodily, he watched as Amelia linked arms with Clara, drawing her away from a chair against the wall, where she would have been safely out of his sight. They walked slowly toward the group, Amelia murmuring questions and Clara making brief responses. His busybody sister must be trying to discover the nature of his association with Lady Rosabel's companion.

He sincerely doubted that even Amelia had the skill to pry the truth out of Clara.

Dragging his attention away from them, Simon told himself to feel satisfaction. The small party was proceeding according to plan. His three brothers-in-law gathered with Warrington by the sideboard, sharing hearty laughter and a round of brandy. Lady Hester and his mother conversed on the blue-striped chaise by the fireplace.

Nearby, Elizabeth and Jane sat in a circle of chairs with Lady Rosabel.

"Have I told you about my difficulty in finding exactly the right pair of slippers to match my gown?" Lady Rosabel was saying. When his sisters looked blankly at her, she went on blithely, "I spent days searching through every shop in the city. And only imagine where I finally found them!"

"Do tell," Elizabeth said. The eldest of his sisters, she was dark-haired and brisk, with little patience for guessing games.

"In my own dressing room," Lady Rosabel said, giggling as she wiggled the toes of her dainty pink shoes. "I'd completely forgotten that I'd already purchased these to match another gown. Aren't I silly?"

"Certainly not," Jane assured her. His middle sister was the peacemaker, always quick with a kind word. "Although I *am* sorry to hear you had to waste so much time. It must have been quite a trial."

"Oh, not in the least! I simply adore shopping, don't you? I can't think of a nicer way to spend the day!"

"Indeed," Elizabeth murmured.

Simon suppressed a grin. Elizabeth found shopping an ordeal on par with having a tooth extracted. It was a family joke that she had chosen her wedding gown with legendary speed, in and out of the dressmaker's shop in under ten minutes.

True to their word, his sisters were on their best behavior. Nevertheless, Elizabeth wore a slight frown as if she were trying very hard to keep her mind on the conversation. Jane smiled, though her fingers twirled the blue ribbons beneath her bodice, a betrayal of her wandering thoughts.

Simon wanted nothing more than to join the men, to

talk politics and horses and business. But he resigned himself to taking the empty chair beside Lady Rosabel. Determined to help her fit into his family, he said, "Perhaps you share an interest with one of my sisters. Aside from shopping, what are your favorite pursuits?"

"Oh, my, you *would* ask that." She pursed her lips, and in the soft pink gown, she looked like a pouty little girl. "I never had the patience to learn the pianoforte properly, and Grandpapa says my singing is simply not to be borne."

"Then perhaps you enjoy drawing. Jane is a gifted artist."

"Simon, you'll make me sound more accomplished than I am," Jane protested. "I'm strictly an amateur."

"Don't be so modest," Elizabeth chided. "Your work was displayed in a museum last year."

"It was only a small watercolor at a private exhibit." But Jane's hazel eyes shone brightly with pleasure. "If you like, Lady Rosabel, we could attend the new showing at the Royal Academy."

Lady Rosabel fluttered her eyelashes. "Oh, my, I cannot say that I've ever set foot in an art gallery. Is it a fashionable place? Whatever shall I wear?"

"A gown will do nicely," Amelia quipped, as she and Clara joined the group. "I suggest we all go together next week, Simon and Mrs. Brownley included."

He frowned at his youngest sister. Had she linked their names on purpose? She wasn't looking at him, though, so he couldn't be certain.

Of its own accord, his gaze flashed to Clara. She sat down in a chair directly opposite him, looking cool and uniquely beautiful. Without that ugly widow's cap, her hair shone a rich dark brown in the candlelight, the perfect foil for her intense blue eyes. The bronze silk of her bodice tenderly cupped her breasts and revealed a hint of cleavage. Lust flared, and for one mad moment, he considered enticing her away from the others, finding a private place where he could coax her and caress her . . .

Grimly, he banished the fantasy. It was time he put Clara Brownley out of his mind once and for all. He was no reprobate who ogled other women while in the company of his bride-to-be.

He turned to Lady Rosabel. "Do you enjoy reading or writing?" he asked. "Amelia is the family correspondent. On occasion, she writes plays and poetry, too."

"Most of my attempts end up in the rubbish bin," Amelia said with a laugh. "Benjamin claims I'll squander his fortune at the stationer's shop."

"I've never before met an author," Lady Rosabel said in goggle-eyed amazement. "Why, I can scarcely bear to write a thank-you note, and reading puts me straight to sleep."

"Then perhaps astronomy interests you," Jane said. "Elizabeth is a founding member of the Society for Lady Astronomers."

"Astron—"

"Star-gazing, my lady," Clara explained. "It's the study of the night sky. Lady Elizabeth, have you a telescope of your own?"

A glow of zeal lit Elizabeth's handsome features. "I most certainly do. Marcus is forever complaining that I prefer the rooftop to . . . well, to anywhere else in our house."

His sisters laughed, Clara blushed, and Lady Rosabel looked prettily confused. "Do you mean that—instead of going to parties—you spend your evenings on the rooftop?"

Elizabeth gave a crisp nod. "As often as weather

permits. Watching the heavens is extremely rewarding work. My hope is to someday discover a new star—or perhaps even a comet."

Lady Rosabel cocked her head to the side. "But . . . whatever would one *do* with another star? There are so many in the sky already."

His sisters had to be amused, but they hid it well. Elizabeth sat with a pleasant smile on her face. Jane's eyes implored him for guidance. Amelia bit her lip and lowered her gaze to her lap.

Hiding his own irritation with his intended, he said, "Perhaps one evening we'll join Elizabeth, so that you may view the spectacle for yourself."

Lowering her chin, she gazed at him with big, china-blue eyes. "Alas, I've a terrible fear of heights, my lord. Brownie will go with you, though. Then she can tell me all about it."

He had believed Lady Rosabel to be more adventuresome, judging by the way she'd gone off on her own in Hyde Park. But he supposed irrational fears could plague anyone. And he had no intention of going up on a roof with Clara to gaze at the night sky. He could only imagine the result of *that*. "Perhaps Elizabeth can show you the charts she's made of the constellations."

"Better yet, the telescope can be brought down to the garden," Clara suggested. "My lady, I daresay you'll enjoy imagining the pictures that the ancient Greeks and Romans saw in the stars."

Over the course of the next half an hour, Clara kept the conversation flowing smoothly by questioning Elizabeth further about astronomy, asking Jane to describe her favorite paintings, and inquiring if Amelia preferred sonnets to epic poems. She took care to clear up Lady Rosabel's occasional confusion, and Simon had to admit that

Clara's supply of patience and diplomacy far exceeded his.

Lady Rosabel was very young, he grimly reminded himself. She would celebrate her eighteenth birthday very soon. Like most ladies, she had been taught from the cradle to be nothing more than a pretty ornament. Her intellect had not been encouraged in the way he had done with his sisters. But surely maturity would come with marriage and children.

And if it did not? If he faced a lifetime of inane chatter about shopping and fashion?

He felt stifled, thrust into a cage of his own making. What had possessed him to make that ridiculous wager with Harry? He had agreed to court the first virginal young lady he encountered—and fate had given him Lady Rosabel Lathrop.

But fate had first played a cruel trick by tantalizing him with Clara Brownley. She had run straight into his arms, tied him into knots, and roasted him over the coals of her opinion. Yet he had never felt more alive than he did in Clara's presence. He wanted her—craved her. If she gave him one signal that she too desired an affair, he'd be tempted to call quit to the bargain and the marriage and set her up as his mistress . . .

Murdock entered the arched doorway of the drawing room. The elderly, white-gloved butler announced the evening meal.

Lady Hester hoisted herself up from the chaise. "I cannot imagine what could have happened to Frederick," she said fretfully. "I ought to have insisted he ride with us."

"I'm sure he was merely delayed," Lady Rockford said comfortingly. "Shall we hold dinner until he arrives?"

"Absolutely not," Warrington said. Gripping the knob of his cane, he hobbled toward the women, looking every inch the admiral despite his disability. "My grandson is unpardonably late. I won't have our food going cold on that pup's account."

Simon helped his mother to her feet. After her latest bout of the ague, she felt alarmingly thin, and a too-familiar combination of worry and guilt weighed on him. She had not enjoyed good health since that long-ago night when a bullet had pierced her lung. Yet she never complained, never remonstrated him for his role in her injury.

Now, she gave him a warm smile, her brown eyes alight with pleasure. "The evening appears to be going quite well," she murmured, casting a telling glance at Lady Rosabel.

His mother's innocent words were the key that locked the door of the cage. It was her dearest wish to see him settled with a wife and children. He owed her that much and more.

For her sake, he must escalate his courtship of Lady Rosabel. But first he needed to finish the task of tracing the stolen jewels. Tomorrow, he would go to Newgate Prison and drag the truth out of Gilbert Hollybrooke.

Returning his mother's smile, Simon patted her frail hand. "Things are going very well, indeed."

Freddie rubbed the pair of dice between his damp palms and blew on them for good luck. With desperate hope and a flick of his wrist, he flung the small cubes onto the table. They tumbled across the green baize and stopped.

His heart plummeted. A pair of threes.

He sat back, ran his fingers through his hair. Bile stung his throat. "Bloody nothing again."

Lewis Newcombe clapped him on the shoulder. "Cheer up, old chap. Your luck is bound to turn soon."

Lewis was the only jolly one at the table. He had alert, foxlike features beneath a thatch of fair hair. Despite hours of play, he had a rakish air of insouciance that Freddie had always admired.

The other two men looked glum, puffing on their cheroots and guzzling their brandy. Freddie knew them only as regulars here at the club. The elegant room with its dark green furnishings held a scattering of other gamblers who played other games, mostly cards.

Freddie gazed enviously at them. He should've gone for faro as he usually did. He'd had a gut feeling about that game, but Lewis had been intent on dice.

His friend scooped up the little cubes. Like Freddie, he had shed his coat hours ago and rolled his shirtsleeves up to his elbows. Unlike Freddie, he had been enjoying a winning streak.

Radiating confidence, Lewis threw a five and a two.

Freddie checked a groan. *Seven. Bloody seven.*

Had the majordomo not provided the dice, he'd've suspected Lewis of using dispatchers. Back in school, Lewis had been caught with the weighted dice, though his father had managed to hush up the matter. Freddie had no intention of confronting his friend now. One didn't accuse another gentleman of cheating without serious consequences. They would be obliged to fight a duel—and Lewis was a crack shot in addition to being the luckiest bastard in the room tonight.

"That's it, I'm done up," announced a thickset fellow named Cogsworth. He drained his glass, then lurched to his feet, swaying. "You staying, Vickers?"

Barely eighteen and rail-thin, Lord Vickers shook his head, dislodging a lock of gingery hair. "I won't be eating again until my stipend next month. 'Course, you've won my marker on that, too, Newcombe. Dash it all, you've the devil's own luck tonight."

As the two men ambled away, Freddie slumped in his chair and watched as Lewis gathered up his winnings.

The clink of coins sounded like the tolling of funeral bells. Gawd, the evening had started out so well. For once, he'd had money jingling in his pocket. His hopes had been higher than his mountain of debts.

But now he didn't own tuppence to his name. He had lost the handful of gold guineas his mother had slipped to him on the promise that—

He sat up straight, looking wildly around the smoky room for a clock. "Holy hell. What time is it?"

"Near ten, I'd guess," Lewis said as he folded several markers and stuck them in his pocket.

Freddie swore under his breath. "That stinking dinner party at Rockford's. I forgot all about it." He shoved back his chair. "Maybe I can make it in time for drinks afterward."

"Hold on, it won't do for you to arrive in the middle of a meal. How about we get our own dessert by visiting that new bawdy house near the opera? I hear the doves are delectable."

The thought appealed to Frederick, yet his gut was twisted so tightly that he felt sick to his stomach. "I'm a bit low in the pocket."

"I'll charge the night to my account," Lewis offered.

Envying him the grand gesture, Freddie comforted himself with the reminder that his friend owed even more than he did. "Maybe you ought to save your winnings for the dun collectors."

"You're sounding like my father now," Lewis jeered. "So what's it to be, old boy? A dull dinner or naked women?"

The temptation was too great. Figuring his mother would be furious, anyway, Freddie scrambled to his feet. She'd tell him he'd made a horrid impression on Rockford's family, and that it was all his fault if the cursed earl didn't offer for Rosabel. Mama had been Queen of the

Scolds ever since she'd discovered the thefts he'd committed. After tonight's loss, she would have all the more whip to lash him.

And if the admiral found out . . .

He quailed at the thought of his grandfather, then rebuked himself for being so hen-hearted. He was already up to his neck in hot water. What did a little more trouble matter?

"There's daggers in men's smiles."
—*Macbeth*, II:iii

Chapter Sixteen

As Claire stepped out of the dim coach and into the sunlight, she froze in disbelief. Instead of a broad street lined with fashionable shops, a great granite fortress loomed against the blue sky. A few small, barred windows broke the grim façade. Visitors traipsed in and out of the tall central tower with its iron gate, and the familiar sight sent a chill down her spine.

Newgate Prison.

Rosabel collected a covered basket from the coachman. "Wait on the next street," the girl instructed him, and the burly manservant tipped his hat and drove off into the throng of drays and carts.

Too late, horrified anger flooded Claire. Too late, she found the strength to move. "So *this* is why you summoned me from the library. It wasn't because you wanted my help in purchasing a new fan."

All morning, she had been cataloging books for Lord Warrington. She had been there on the dot of eight o'clock, determined to dig the truth out of her grandfather. But once he'd barked out instructions to her, he had left the library on the warning that he'd return at noon to check on her progress. It had been ten minutes shy of that time when Rosabel had sent for her.

"I truly *do* need a fan," Rosabel said ingenuously. "We'll go to the shops on our way home."

At the moment, Claire had no patience for wide-eyed naïveté. "You drew the shades in the coach. You said the brightness of the sun hurt your eyes. You purposefully deceived me."

"I'm truly sorry," Rosabel said, dipping her chin in a shamefaced manner. "But what else was I to do? I wish to meet my uncle, and I knew you wouldn't approve."

Claire fought off a wave of panic. They couldn't visit Papa. He might reveal her disguise before she had the chance to warn him. He had only to call out her real name . . .

"You should never have come here. We'll fetch the coach at once. We'll go to Bond Street, as we ought—"

In the midst of Claire's scolding, Rosabel dashed across the cobblestones toward the prison gate. Claire hastened in her cousin's wake, catching up to her as she entered the gatesman's lodge and joined the short queue of people inside the dimly lit, stone-walled room. They were an unsavory lot, mostly coarse women visiting their husbands, and a few shifty-eyed men who looked as if they belonged behind bars themselves.

By contrast, her cousin was a red rose among the weeds. A straw bonnet with cherry ribbons framed her china-doll features and blond curls, while a deep gold pelisse clung to a fine gown of crimson silk. Dainty kid gloves enclosed the hands that clutched the covered basket.

The presence of ladies attracted a number of greedy looks and lascivious stares.

Claire leaned close to Rosabel. Incongruously, the smell of fresh bread wafted from the basket. "This is madness. What if you're seen here? Your mother will be furious if you spoil your chance to marry Lord Rockford."

"Then *you* may have him all to yourself." The girl gave her a knowing smile, looking far older than her seventeen years. "He seemed to pay special attention to you at dinner last night. I vow, the man couldn't keep his eyes off you."

Claire battled a blush. Despite the dire circumstances, the memory of his dark, direct gaze caused a melting warmth inside of her. She couldn't deny Simon's interest in her—or her own wayward reaction to him. The visit to his house had only made matters worse.

Watching him banter with his sisters had opened up a whole new dimension to his character. He had not behaved as a callous, haughty aristocrat; rather, he had been relaxed and affectionate with his family. Seeing him with his mother had touched Claire's heart, too. Lady Rockford apparently suffered from ill health, and Simon had taken care to escort her into the dining chamber, to encourage her to sample every dish, and to walk her back to the drawing room afterward, even though the other men stayed at the table to drink their brandy. By the end of the evening, Claire had found herself half-believing he might actually possess a heart.

A heart he reserved for those of his own kind. Simon was a cad who saw nothing wrong with flirting with the lowly companion of his intended bride. In spite of his avowal to the contrary, he had made it clear he still wanted Claire in his bed.

And much to her shame, she felt a lurch of deep-seated longing to be there with him.

The people in line shuffled forward, and she returned her attention to Rosabel. "You are not to change the subject," she chided in an undertone. "If we don't leave right now, your reputation will be ruined."

"Oh, pooh, no one from society is here. We're perfectly safe."

"We're anything *but* safe. You're in danger from murderers and thieves and all manner of villains." She took firm hold of Rosabel's arm. "We're going, and I won't hear any more about it."

"I'm staying," Rosabel whispered, equally firm. "If you try to stop me, I shall kick and scream and make a scene. It will be reported in the newssheets and then everyone really *will* know I was here."

As a teacher, Claire had dealt with headstrong pupils, but never one so spoiled—or one so determined to disregard authority. The fire of zeal in those china-blue eyes made her hesitate to put the threat to the test. Silently begging her father's forgiveness, she said, "Mr. Hollybrooke is an accused felon. He isn't proper company for a lady."

"But he's my uncle—and the most notorious thief known to London society. I simply must meet him, or I'll die of curiosity."

"It's more likely you'll die at the hands of one of these ruffians. And if you don't care about yourself, think of me. I'll lose my post if your mother or your grandfather finds out you were here."

The corners of Rosabel's mouth drew downward in genuine sympathy, and she patted Claire's arm. "Dear Brownie, don't fret. We won't be caught. And even if we are, I'll defend you. I'll tell Mama it was all my fault and you tried your very best to stop me."

Claire doubted that Lady Hester would heed Rosabel in the matter. But that was the least of Claire's worries. If Rosabel found out they were cousins, she would never be able to keep the secret. She would blurt it out to her family. Claire would be dismissed . . .

They neared the front of the queue. Thankfully, the guards present had not been on duty the one other time she had come to visit her father. A balding official with a beaky nose patted down each man, searching for weapons, while a stout matron drew the female visitors into an adjoining room. Claire had faced that indignity before, and she murmured in her cousin's ear, "There's a nasty woman who will lift your skirts to make sure you don't have a knife or a pistol hidden somewhere. You'll be offended and disgusted—unless we leave straightaway."

"Never mind," Rosabel whispered back. "I have a plan."

She smiled prettily at the turnkey, slipped him a handful of coins, and achieved their entry into the prison with a minimum of fuss. The fellow didn't even glance into the basket, Claire noted in disgust. As if they were royalty, he bobbed several bows and sent them on their way, escorted by a burly gatesman.

With each step down the long, shadowed passage that led into the bowels of the prison, Claire felt her anxiety increase tenfold. The odors of filth and foulness permeated the air, and the damp chill penetrated her bones. From her previous visit, she knew the barred doors on either side led to various wards and common yards where master felons were housed separately from debtors, female prisoners apart from the male.

Her father, however, was being held in a private cell in a section reserved for those who could afford to pay the hefty fee. To secure the funds, Claire had depleted her life's savings and sold a string of pearls that had belonged to her mother. After paying a retainer to Mr. Mundy, she had nothing left with which to provide Papa luxuries, but at least he hadn't been thrown into the company of murderers and other riffraff.

Their guide lumbered up to a thick oak door, and with a rattling of keys, pushed it open. Without a word, he jerked his thumb inside, and then retraced his steps down the passageway.

Strolling into a small windowless room, Rosabel swung the basket at her side as if she were going on a picnic. A hulking guard sat playing cards at a rough wooden table. He gawked at the ladies, then scrambled to his feet.

Claire's heart kicked into a high rhythm. He was the same guard who had been here over a week ago. Staying behind her cousin, she prayed he wouldn't recognize her. At least last time, she had been a commoner in a cheap gray gown beneath a hooded cloak, rather than a lady in the fine blue pelisse and silk frock she now wore.

Rosabel gave him a jaunty smile. "Hullo, we're here to visit Mr. Gilbert Hollybrooke."

He clomped forward in hobnailed boots. His shoulders were massive beneath a shirt so dirty it looked gray, and tattered brown breeches hung from his thick waist. "Wot's in yer basket?"

"Bread and jam for the prisoner."

"Lemme see. Mayhap ye've brung a bit o' brandy fer the Wraith."

Foolishly, Rosabel didn't remove the cloth. "Oh, but I haven't. I assure you, sir, I've passed inspection at the front gate."

"I'll jest 'ave a look fer meself, then."

His meaty fist lashed out to grab the basket. Squealing, she backed up, clutching the prize to her bosom. "Brute! Stay away!"

Without thinking, Claire sprang into action. Her elbow

jabbed hard into the man's stomach. At the same moment, she lifted her hem, hooked her foot behind his ankle, and tripped him.

Doubled over and unbalanced, he staggered backward. His huge form thumped into the stone wall. He slumped there in a daze, trying to catch his breath.

She fixed him with her most haughty stare. "If you dare to bother her again, you'll answer to her grandfather, the Marquess of Warrington."

Cheers and whistles came from the cells along the adjacent corridors. Prisoners strained to look past the iron bars. Claire couldn't see her father; he must not have heard the clamor.

The guard looked furious, though he kept a wary distance. His shaggy eyebrows were lowered over beady brown eyes. Peering closely at Claire, he accused, "Ye been 'ere once afore."

"You're mistaken," she said, her voice dripping scorn. "If it isn't too much trouble, direct us to Mr. Hollybrooke's cell at once."

His sneer revealed a mouthful of blackened teeth. He pointed a stubby finger down a corridor. "Last one on yer right. An' mind, no fancy tricks, else I'll toss ye both out on yer fancy arses."

As they proceeded down the murky passageway with its iron-barred doors on either side, Rosabel clutched Claire's arm. "You were so very brave," she whispered. "Where did you learn such tricks?"

"I grew up in a poor neighborhood. It was necessary for a woman to know how to defend herself from footpads."

"I thought you came from a nice family in York."

Blast. "I'm afraid we didn't have much money."

"Oh, how dreadful—but how fortunate for us today. I knew I was right to bring you along!"

"You were wrong to come here, that's what." Seeing a

chance to impress her point, Claire added severely, "Perhaps now you'll see what I meant. You cannot trust anyone here, not even the guards. They're every bit as brutal and unprincipled as the prisoners."

Rosabel peeked back over her shoulder. "What a dreadful man. I vow, I am beside myself with fear."

The girl looked more excited than afraid. Her blue eyes sparkled in the dim light, and her voice had a lilt of enjoyment. She even smiled at the rough-looking prisoners who begged her to come closer for a kiss.

Did she lack the sense to realize the dangers here? Or did she only pretend to be so childish?

Not for the first time, Claire wondered if she'd made a mistake in subtracting the girl from the list of suspects. She had decided that Rosabel lacked the brains to execute a series of daring thefts. The girl seemed too tenderhearted to pin the blame on an innocent man who had a connection to her family. Unless . . .

Unless Lord Warrington, who was too crippled to sneak around during society parties, was the mastermind. Dear God, what if he'd recruited Rosabel to steal the jewels? What if Rosabel had come here today to revel in her success?

The thought turned Claire's stomach. Over the past week, she had developed a certain fondness for Rosabel and her exuberant silliness. Claire didn't want to believe her cousin could be so devious. Yet she dared not overlook the possibility, either.

As they approached the last cell, she lagged slightly behind. Her emotions veered between anxiety and fervor. Even though they wouldn't be able to speak freely, she was keen to see her father again. If only he wouldn't inadvertently betray her identity.

They reached the narrow, tomblike chamber with its slit of a window high in the stone wall. Papa sat hunched on a bare iron bedstead, a tattered brown blanket wrapped around his shoulders. He looked so dear and familiar that tears stung her eyes. His attention was focused on the sheaf of papers in his lap, which explained why he hadn't noticed the commotion. When he was involved in his writings, a riot could erupt outside his window and he wouldn't blink an eye.

He dipped his pen into the inkpot beside him and scribbled madly on the parchment. A lock of graying brown hair had fallen onto his forehead, and she remembered her mother brushing it back in a loving gesture. How Mama would grieve to see him locked in prison!

Rosabel dropped the basket to the pitch-coated floor. Clutching the bars with her neat white gloves, she asked in a breathy tone, "Mr. Gilbert Hollybrooke? Is it really you?"

He looked up at her. A puzzled frown wrinkled his high brow, and his round spectacles magnified the weariness of his pale blue eyes. Then his gaze moved to Claire.

Bittersweet joy lit her heart, as bright as the smile that bloomed on his haggard face. A scruffy beard lined his jaw, his clothing was disheveled, and his hair mussed, yet he looked wonderful to her. She fought the need to rush up to the bars and reach out to him.

When he opened his mouth to speak, she frowned a warning and shook her head. He flicked a glance at Rosabel, then returned his gaze to Claire. To her vast relief, he gave an almost imperceptible nod of understanding.

Setting the writing materials aside, he rose to his feet. The iron chain and the manacle around his ankle clanked against the floor. The contraption was fastened to a heavy ring embedded in the stone wall, permitting him to walk about the cell, but preventing his escape.

Despite the shackle, he swept a courtly bow. "Forgive me, my ladies. You seem to have the better of me."

"We've never met," Rosabel said in a rush, "although if circumstances had been different, we would have been very close, indeed. You see, I am your niece by marriage, Lady Rosabel Lathrop. And this is my companion, Mrs. Clara Brownley. We've come to give you comfort in your time of need."

He stared long and hard at the cousins as if searching for a resemblance. Claire bit her lip. He was a kind, gentle, friendly man—except when it came to aristocrats, in particular, Mama's family. She wouldn't be surprised if he refused to speak to Rosabel.

Claire had gone against his wishes in seeking a post in her grandfather's house. Papa had vehemently opposed the scheme, judging it far too dangerous. In the letters that Mr. Mundy had given to her, Papa had urged her to quit Warrington House at once. For him to see her with Rosabel must be an extremely difficult dilemma.

"You shouldn't be here," he said gravely. "Prison is no place for young ladies."

"That's what Brownie said, too. But I did so wish to meet you, Uncle Gilbert—I may call you that, mayn't I?" Rosabel smiled rather uncertainly. "Why, I never even knew you existed until recently. I was led to believe that my aunt Emily died when she was just my age."

"She *was* dead to Warrington."

The bitterness in her father's voice prompted Claire to step up to the bars and offer a distraction. "Lady Rosabel has been worried about your well-being, sir. How are you faring?"

She let her eyes convey a private message of love and concern. He had lost weight; she could tell by the way his clothing hung on his lanky frame. Lines of fatigue were etched into his too-gaunt features, and she feared that the meager prison diet of bread and water, with a small ration of meat once a week, had taken its toll on him.

His gaze softened. "Set your mind at ease," he said with a smile. "The accommodations are excellent"—he indicated the hard iron cot—"the view is superb"—he waved at the high window—"and at the moment, the company is unparalleled."

Wrinkling her nose, Rosabel peered into the cell. "But where is your mattress and pillow? And why do you not have a brazier of coals to keep you warm? Oh, dear, this is dreadful, indeed."

"My needs are few," he reassured her. "Private quarters, and pen and paper. There's nothing more I could want."

Except your freedom, Claire thought in despair. *If only I could give that to you.*

"I daresay you've too much pride to accept anything from me," Rosabel declared. "It's because of my grandfather, is it not? You must despise him tremendously for disowning Aunt Emily."

"Perhaps Mr. Hollybrooke doesn't wish to speak of the past, my lady," Claire admonished.

Rosabel lowered her chin in a little-girl pose. "Pray forgive me for being rude, Uncle. It's just that I know so very little about you."

His face grave, he stepped closer, the chains rattling. "I suppose your curiosity is understandable. But I can't imagine you're here with Lord Warrington's permission."

"The marquess is a very strict, unforgiving man," Claire added. "And that is precisely why we should leave here at once."

Rosabel shook her head, setting her curls to bouncing along with the cherries on her bonnet. "I won't go, not yet." Her voice dropped to a stage whisper and she cast a furtive look over her shoulder. "Not until I give you something very important, Uncle Gilbert."

On that cryptic statement, she crouched down and whisked the bleached linen cloth off the basket. Inside lay a loaf of crusty bread, and beside it, a pot of raspberry jam and another of golden butter.

He raised a questioning eyebrow. Claire did as well. Why would Rosabel make a fuss over a small gift?

"It smells delicious," he told the girl. "That's very kind of you to bring me bread."

"It's more than delicious, it's enormously *useful.*" Passing the loaf through the bars of the cell, she gave him an exaggerated wink. "You might wish to admire all sides of it."

Claire and her father exchanged a slightly puzzled glance. Then he turned the loaf in his ink-stained fingers and frowned. The bottom showed a long, narrow slit. Reaching inside, he withdrew a thick metal file with corrogated edges.

Claire stifled a gasp. She glanced down the corridor, and thankfully the guard was engrossed in his solitary card game. "You can't smuggle that into a prison."

"I just did," Rosabel said, looking pleased with herself. "I found it in the gardener's shed. It was very cunning of me, wasn't it?"

"It was extremely rash, that's what. If you're caught, you could be thrown into jail yourself."

Foolish, foolish girl! And Claire herself was even more foolish for not realizing her cousin had planned such a trick. Yet the deed did seem to exonerate Rosabel as her grandfather's pawn. Because why else would she make such a misguided attempt to help her uncle?

Unless she'd felt guilty . . .

"You shouldn't have endangered yourself," Papa said, stuffing the file back into the loaf of bread. "As much as I appreciate your effort, I cannot possibly keep this."

A crestfallen expression chased away Rosabel's smile. "But you must use it to dig a tunnel. Or to saw through these bars. It's your only hope!"

"No, the truth is my only hope. An escape attempt would be the act of a guilty man."

Rosabel gazed blankly at him. "But you *are* guilty. You're the Wraith. You're a dashing thief who crept into the finest houses in society. Everyone knows you took Mrs. Danby's ruby brooch and Lady Burkington's pearl necklace and lots of other jewels, too."

Claire sent her father a cautionary look. "This is not a matter that involves you, my lady," she said. "I'm sure Mr. Hollybrooke has people working on his behalf."

"I do, indeed," he said. "Rest assured, I have excellent associates who are gathering evidence to support my case."

He gave Claire a faint, encouraging smile that tied her heart into a knot. Papa was speaking to her more than Rosabel. He trusted Claire, yet he didn't want her to worry, either. It made her all the more determined not to fail him.

Her hands trembled as she took the loaf of bread from him and replaced it beneath the cloth in the basket. There were so many things she wanted to say to him, so many things she needed to do . . .

Rosabel gawked at him. "I don't understand. You were found with Lady Rockford's diamond bracelet. Everyone has been talking about it."

"Things are not always as they seem, my lady. But I've said enough. The rest must wait for the judge."

"And now we really *must* go," Claire insisted. "Good day, Mr. Hollybrooke. We will keep you in our prayers."

Seizing Rosabel's arm in one hand and the basket in the other, she steered the girl back down the corridor. She looked back over her shoulder one last time to see her father standing there, gripping the bars and watching them go.

The band around her rib cage twisted tighter. The next time she saw Papa, it would very likely be in court. His trial was scheduled to begin in slightly more than one week's time, and she felt a nip of panic.

The guard glowered at them as they left the ward, but mercifully he made no attempt to check the basket again. Once the door clanged shut behind them and they retraced their steps down the dim corridor, Rosabel burst out, "Did you hear that, Brownie? My uncle has been falsely accused. Can you believe it?"

With all my heart and soul. "He did seem very convincing," Claire couldn't resist saying. "And he certainly looks more like a scholar than a common criminal."

"Then that means"—Rosabel paused, her eyes lighting with a disquieting fervor—"that means the real Wraith is still out there somewhere. If I find him, I can free my uncle!"

Alarmed, Claire swung to face her cousin. "You'll do nothing of the sort," she said in a fierce undertone. "This is a matter best left to the proper authorities."

"But I can help. Tonight, at Lady Havenden's ball, I can question the guests and find out who witnessed the robberies—"

"No!" The notion horrified Claire. As much as she craved her father's freedom, she couldn't allow Rosabel to interfere. "If you say anything to anyone, even the slightest word, the marquess will find out you've come here."

"I'm not afraid of Grandpapa. Perhaps I shall convince him to lend a hand to Uncle Gilbert."

"It's far more likely that his lordship will banish *you* to the country for the next twenty years." Needing to impress the seriousness of the situation on the girl, Claire took hold of Rosabel's arm. "You must put your uncle out of your mind completely. And you'll mention this visit to no one at all. *No one*. Promise me now."

Rosabel wore a sulky expression, her lower lip sticking out. "Oh, all right. But you do know how to spoil all the fun."

Fun. That was how Rosabel viewed the world, as one huge carnival for her own entertainment. Claire would have to keep a close watch on the girl to make certain she kept her word.

As they turned the corner, heading toward the entrance of the prison, Claire spied a man speaking to the beak-nosed official in the shadows at the end of the corridor. The visitor's back was turned, but she could see he was a tall gentleman with broad shoulders and dark hair. He had an arrogance of manner that seemed somehow familiar . . .

Recognition bolted her in place. A clutch of disbelief halted her heartbeat. Her mind wrestled with the impossible.

Simon?

"If music be the food of love, play on."
—*Twelfth Night*, I:I

Chapter Seventeen

"Ouch!" Rosabel complained. "I promised to be good. There's no need to hurt me."

Heedless, Claire dragged her cousin backward by the arm. If they could retreat around the corner, they might have a chance to avoid discovery. "Lord Rockford is here," she whispered. "He must have seen the Warrington coach outside."

Rosabel craned her neck to look at the main entrance. In a perky voice, she said, "And now he's seen *us*."

Sure enough, Simon had started to walk in their direction when he broke stride in obvious astonishment. For one dizzying moment, they stared at each other down the dim corridor, and he made an odd move as if to withdraw from their sight. The fleeting impression vanished as he headed straight toward them.

He looked like a warrior marching into battle.

Cowardice urged her to turn tail and run. Logic argued it was too late to hide—or to lie.

After his conversation with Rosabel in the picture gallery the other day, he had to know who they had come to visit. Her stomach lurched. He would blame Claire for allowing Rosabel to talk to an accused felon. Worst of all, he might inform Lord Warrington.

"Lady Rosabel, Mrs. Brownley. What an unexpected sight."

Despite his biting sarcasm, he bowed courteously. His head was bare, his black hair mussed by the wind. He was dressed rather plainly in tan breeches with a coat in a deep coffee hue that enhanced the dark brown of his eyes. His black knee boots had no embellishments, nor did his white cravat sport its usual intricate design. At a casual glance, he might have passed for a common man of the streets.

Claire wondered what stroke of ill luck had brought Simon in the vicinity of Newgate Prison on this of all days. And why did he look so . . . nondescript?

Then he raised his head and she realized her mistake. There was nothing nondescript about Simon Croft, the Earl of Rockford. His chiseled features had been sculpted by a master. His face bore the hard hallmark of experience, and his eyes held a depth and mystery that must draw women to him in droves.

He certainly took *her* breath away. The force of his attraction made her knees quiver and her heart stutter. A deep inner heat threatened to melt her common sense.

Claire stiffened her spine lest she turn into a simpering idiot. Rather than wait for his attack, she threw the first punch. "Good day, my lord. What on earth brings you here?"

His gaze flicked to Lady Rosabel, who watched in dewy-eyed innocence, before returning to Claire's face. In an ominous tone, he said, "Better I should ask that of *you*."

"Charity work," she said glibly. "And you?" She wouldn't let him off without answering.

His eyes narrowed slightly at her impertinence. "I was on the way to my solicitor's office when I spied your vehicle."

"Oh, bother," Rosabel piped up. "I told Jarvis to wait out of sight."

"Because you knew it was wrong to come here." Simon's voice lost its mocking edge, reverting to the stern tone of a father. "And by your reckless behavior, you've put yourself in danger."

She gave him that pouty, little-girl look. "I wanted to give comfort to my poor uncle. He's cold and lonely and without any friends or family to visit him."

"Gilbert Hollybrooke is a devious criminal who will play upon your sympathies. I thought I'd made that very clear to you. To both of you."

He glowered at Claire. She wanted to shout that her father was a good man who had been unjustly accused. Instead, she gave Simon a cool stare. If he was blind enough to think this visit had been *her* idea, then he knew nothing of his intended bride.

"You mustn't blame Brownie. It was all *my* fault. I tricked her, and I'm ever so sorry." Dipping her chin, Rosabel performed a credible act of contrition. "You won't tell Grandpapa, will you?"

Distant voices echoed through the passageway. Simon's gaze remained closed, but after a moment, he shook his head. "Not if you've learned your lesson."

"I have! This is a dirty, smelly, vile place and I can't wait to leave." Wrinkling her nose, Rosabel gave a delicate shudder that apparently convinced Simon of her sincerity.

"Henceforth," he said crisply, "you must listen to those who have more experience in the world. Come along now, I'll escort you home."

He offered Rosabel his arm, and she accepted it. But as they started down the corridor, she glanced back and rolled her eyes at Claire.

The irreverent action coaxed a smile from Claire. Then she felt abruptly dispirited, her fortitude vanishing. She had a suspicion it had to do with seeing tall, dark, gorgeous Simon paired with an equally dazzling Rosabel.

She ought to be relieved at her easy escape, Claire thought as she followed them down the passageway, past the gawking guards, and out into the sunshine. She ought to be thinking ahead, planning how to finagle her way back into her grandfather's bedchamber to check out that safe or to search the library for a hiding place. She ought *not* to be remembering the passionate way Simon had kissed her that day in the rain. And she most certainly ought not to be eyeing him from behind and admiring the way his breeches outlined the lean muscles of his thighs or the way his dark hair brushed the back of his white cravat.

It was then that she sensed an unusual alertness in him. While he chatted with Rosabel, he scanned the busy street with its drays and cabs. He glanced right, then left—as if he were looking for something. As he led them to his bay gelding, untying the reins from an iron post, his keen eyes continued to survey the area around the prison.

A startling thought popped into Claire's head. *Simon didn't know their coach was waiting on the next street.*

But that was absurd. He must have seen it earlier, as he'd claimed. Because why else would he have come into the prison—except to find them?

"We've decided she's all wrong for you," Amelia announced.

Simon frowned at his youngest sister. They stood near a screen of potted ferns on a balcony overlooking the crowded ballroom at Havenden House. It was a small antechamber once used for minstrels. The sounds of the party swirled up to them: music and conversation and laughter. No one could overhear them in this oasis.

Nevertheless, he was annoyed that Amelia would confront him in the midst of a ball, so he took his time draining his champagne glass. He didn't have to ask her to explain herself. *We* referred to his three sisters. *She* referred to Lady Rosabel.

"Indeed?" he said. "I can't imagine how I would survive without you to direct my private life."

Predictably, his sarcastic tone failed to discourage Amelia. She had a determined look in her green eyes, which boded ill for his moment of respite from the obligations of dancing. "Lady Rosabel is the wrong wife for you," Amelia repeated firmly. "Elizabeth and Jane and I have all agreed you'll be bored halfway through the honeymoon. Once you've satisfied your lust for her body, you'll—"

"That's quite enough." His champagne glass made a sharp click as he set it down on the marble edge of the balcony. "I won't discuss the matter." The truth was, he felt uncomfortable hearing his sister speak so frankly— even if she *was* resting her hands on the gentle mound of her pregnancy. In his mind, Amelia would always be a precocious little girl, looking up at him as a father, clambering onto his knee and begging him to tell her a story.

She went on as if he hadn't spoken. "—be stuck looking at her over the breakfast table for the next fifty years—"

"You show great faith in my charm."

"—and attempting to hold an intelligent conversation, which will be virtually impossible—"

"I'll read the newspaper, then."

"—and you'll be desperately unhappy, and truly, Simon, I couldn't bear that." She finished with an earnest frown of distress.

His irritation evaporated. Leaning over, he kissed her cheek, just as he'd done every night at bedtime during her childhood. "I appreciate your concern. But I'm perfectly capable of choosing my own bride."

His sisters didn't know—would never know—that he had not strictly *chosen* Lady Rosabel. Fate had thrust her in his path as a result of that bloody wager. He had been stupidly determined to prove to Harry Masterson that any young, giddy debutante could be molded into the perfect countess.

However, Lady Rosabel didn't seem to be responding very well to molding. Her childish conduct already was beginning to grate on him. She behaved more like a spoiled little girl than a woman ready to step into the role of wife and mother. He was still livid about that encounter at Newgate Prison that afternoon.

Seeing her and Clara lurking in the corridor had been a jolt akin to running into an invisible wall. He had been obliged to abandon his plan to grill Hollybrooke again about the missing jewels—and forced to invent the lame excuse of having seen the Warrington coach. Then outside, like a fool, he had walked in the wrong direction, and Clara had had to correct him. The look she had given him had been very sharp, indeed.

For the barest moment, he'd had the impression she knew his true purpose. But she couldn't possibly guess why he'd gone to the prison. No one knew of his secret life.

At least not until he was forced to testify in Hollybrooke's trial next week, he thought grimly. Islington still hadn't returned from his ailing father's bedside in some godforsaken village near the Scottish border.

Nevertheless, Simon couldn't shake the notion that Clara knew *something*. The suspicion gnawed at his gut. He had been careful never to reveal his true identity in the line of duty. But had Hollybrooke described his arresting officer in such vivid detail that she'd recognized Simon?

Nonsense. Not even Clara Brownley could be so perceptive.

His gaze flashed across the crowded ballroom to the

corner where the old biddies sat and gossiped. Beneath the light of a crystal chandelier, Clara's rich brown hair shone against that sea of white and gray coifs. A dark blue gown showed off her cleavage and slender neck. She looked like a princess sitting among all those duchesses and countesses, and the sight of her fired his blood. It was an intensely frustrating condition, considering she wanted nothing to do with him.

Damn, he had it bad. He had seldom in his adult life encountered a woman who refused him, and the temptation of the forbidden must have honed an edge to his lust. He'd move heaven and earth to make her his mistress—

"She's quite the original, isn't she?"

Amelia's voice startled him; she sipped on a glass of lemonade and watched him. "Sorry?"

"Clara Brownley. You were staring at her."

"I was looking for Lady Rosabel," he said tersely. Peering downward, past the wall of palm fronds, he scanned the long line of dancers. His intended bride must be somewhere in that throng—because she certainly wasn't with her chaperone.

Lady Hester was speaking to Clara now, shaking her forefinger in a way that made Simon want to leap off the balcony and give the old biddy a piece of *his* mind. Clara, however, seemed to accept the scolding with aplomb. Giving a regal nod, she rose from her chair and made her way toward one of the huge arched doorways.

Simon hungrily tracked the sway of her hips. Instantly, he could have kicked himself.

"There, you see?" Amelia was gloating. "You know exactly where she is at every moment. And do you realize why you fancy her?"

"Save your imagination for your writing."

He wondered where Clara was heading. Thank God his sister was standing here, or he might be tempted to . . .

"Because she's clever and incomparable, that's why," Amelia answered for him. "She isn't the sort to be browbeaten or intimidated. She'll speak her mind and keep you on your toes."

"Every man's nightmare."

Amelia arched a reddish-brown eyebrow. "So Benjamin is to be pitied for marrying *me*? And Marcus for marrying Elizabeth? And Thomas for marrying Jane?"

Her meaning struck Simon like a knock to the head. He swung fully toward her. "Good God. You can't possibly be suggesting I should *marry* Clara Brownley."

"Why not? And don't give me any more of that nonsense about bloodlines and virgins."

"You're the one spouting nonsense." He chuckled, turning her absurd scheme into a jest. "She's a widow of dubious background employed as a paid companion. There isn't a more *un*suitable female in this ballroom."

The eyebrow lifted higher. "Why, Simon, are you prejudiced? After all the time you spent preaching to your sisters about keeping an open mind?"

"I was referring to politics and gossip."

"Oh, really? You made me invite Penelope Thornberry to my tenth birthday party because you said it wasn't her fault she was painfully shy and didn't have any friends."

"That was entirely different."

"Quite," Amelia said scathingly. "Penelope is the daughter of a duke, while Clara is a nobody, and therefore unworthy of your godlike notice."

"Don't be obtuse. I'm obliged to marry a well-bred maiden. A widow of Mrs. Brownley's reduced position is more suited to be my—"

Simon clamped his mouth shut. He had never so much as hinted to his sisters about his mistresses, although he had kept one on and off since the age of two-and-twenty, when he had lost his appetite for ploughing nameless women in brothels. He always chose his partner carefully, ensconcing her in the house in Belgravia for a few weeks or months, until inevitably she became too demanding or possessive. Then she was given an expensive piece of jewelry and shown out the door.

Clara wasn't like those women. Clara would be difficult from the moment she walked *in* the door. She would needle him with her pointed remarks rather than pander to his every need. Nevertheless, he craved the notion of taming her in bed. Every breathy sigh would be hard-won, every moan an achievement, every cry of ecstasy a triumph.

"Your mistress," Amelia accused. "That's what you were going to say. You want Clara to be your *mistress*."

Her disgust shamed him. It wasn't a pleasant sensation, so he spoke with a finality he had once used to stop quarrels in the schoolroom. "Stay out of it, Amelia. I've heard quite enough."

"So you'll marry Lady Rosabel and ruin her companion at the same time, is that it? I thought only rakes behaved so vilely. Certainly not my own brother." A look of loathing on her face, she spun away from the balcony and vanished into the corridor.

Simon stood clenching and unclenching his fists. He despised knowing he had upset Amelia. But she didn't truly believe he would carry on an affair while he was married, did she? Or that he could ever wed a woman like Clara? The notion was ludicrous.

Ludicrous!

Clearly, his sister had no appreciation for the duties that weighed on him. She had been only three when their father had been murdered, too young to understand the grief of loss, too young to realize that Simon's reckless behavior had created the circumstances for that tragedy. At fifteen, he had become head of the family. He had

vowed to mend his undisciplined ways and become a man
who could make his father proud. And he had succeeded—
until Clara Brownley had come rushing out of the darkness
to disrupt his well-ordered life.

*I could never trust a man who has proven himself to be
completely without honor.*

Clara's criticism still rankled. Yes, he was wrong to
lust after her while he was courting Lady Rosabel, but for
once he couldn't seem to control himself. Maybe he
didn't *want* to control himself. Maybe he ought to find
Clara and give vent to the ferocity of his feelings once
and for all.

Spurred by a sharp sense of purpose, he stalked out of
the antechamber. By God, if he was being condemned as
a rake, he might as well enjoy himself in the process.

Claire curled her fingers around the mahogany newel
post. A few guests strolled the sumptuous corridor, too
busy chatting with each other to notice her. Before she
went up to check the bedchambers, she tried to think of
somewhere else she'd forgotten to look.

She had searched every one of the reception rooms.
She had peeked into the dining chamber, where liveried
footmen were laying out a vast array of dishes for the
midnight supper. She had ventured into the library to see
a group of old codgers—her grandfather among them—
drinking brandy and arguing politics. She had visited the
drawing room with its tables full of guests laughing and
playing cards, including Lord Frederick, whose pale,
worried countenance suggested another run of bad luck.

But she had found no Rosabel. And no Lewis Newcombe.

When last seen, they had been dancing together, Rosabel looking gorgeous in pale blue with gold spangles,

and Mr. Newcombe elegant in a burgundy coat with a gold waistcoat, his fair hair in artful disarray. He wasn't supposed to be Rosabel's partner; she had been led onto the dance floor by graying, stoop-shouldered Lord Farley. But toward the end of the set, Mr. Newcombe had appeared in the line and somehow commandeered her hand. From her seat with the older matrons, Claire had been jolted by the sight of them, blond heads together, smiling and murmuring in a way that looked . . . *intimate*. Then they had been swallowed up by the swarm of departing dancers.

To make matters worse, Lady Hester had spied them, too. In between dabbing a handkerchief at her flushed face, she had shaken her pudgy finger at Claire.

"I warned you to keep an eye on her. I won't have my daughter in the company of such a man. Why, his mother was a common actress."

Her aunt had seemed more appalled by his impure bloodline than his ne'er-do-well reputation, Claire reflected as she started up the staircase. If Rosabel had gone off with Simon, Lady Hester probably would have told Claire to shove the two of them into a bedchamber so that he would be forced to offer for Rosabel.

Simon had certainly paid court to Rosabel this evening, dancing twice with her in his determination to win that disgusting wager. Claire had tried to keep her gaze averted so she wouldn't have to watch the two of them together. A discomfiting twinge gripped her insides, a sensation she didn't care to examine lest it be jealousy. She had more important concerns than mooning over a haughty, too-handsome nobleman . . .

"I say, is that you, Mrs. Brownley?"

Claire held on to the polished oak banister and looked down at the man who stood at the foot of the stairs. She recognized him at once as Simon's friend, the one who had been in the garden on the night they'd met. He had a friendly face with a large nose, hazel eyes, and light brown hair that curled wildly around his head. His hands rested on his hips, thrusting back his claret-red coat to reveal a yellow waistcoat and brown breeches. Everything about him was big, flamboyant, and unforgettable.

And it occurred to her that he could help her.

She descended the steps. "Sir Harry Masterson," she said warmly. "It's a pleasure to see you again."

His white teeth flashed in a smile. "It *is* you, by George. I vow, I nearly didn't recognize you without your widow's weeds."

"I'm afraid this transformation is Lady Rosabel's work," Claire said ruefully. "She can be very strong-willed at times. By the way, you wouldn't happen to have seen her in the last half an hour, would you?"

Keen interest lit his eyes. "Don't tell me Rockford has lost her again—like that day in the park."

"No, it's her mother who wants her."

"I see." Glancing around at the guests strolling through the corridor, he drew her to a doorway where they could speak in relative privacy. "Tell me, how's the old fellow doing with Lady Rosabel? Has he managed to bring her to heel yet?"

"For heaven's sake, she isn't a dog."

"I couldn't agree with you more! In fact, I said that very same thing to—er—"

"To Lord Rockford," Claire guessed. The nerve of Simon! "I suppose he thinks he can train Lady Rosabel according to his ridiculous Countess Code."

Sir Harry threw back his head and laughed, drawing the attention of a pair of young ladies, who snootily eyed Claire as if she were the cause of the racket. "Now, that's a rich one," he said, wiping his eyes. "The Countess Code, indeed. You've pegged exactly the way he thinks. It's quite perceptive, considering you barely know the man."

From out of nowhere came the memory of Simon's mouth on hers, his hands caressing her bosom, his body pressed to hers . . .

Feeling the rise of a hot blush, she said lightly, "I've learned a little while chaperoning his visits with Lady Rosabel this past week. Now, pray excuse me. I really *must* go and find her."

Bidding Sir Harry good-bye, she noticed him eyeing her with a speculative curiosity. But as she hastened up the staircase, she had no time to wonder at his thoughts. She could think only of Lewis Newcombe luring her cousin into one of the bedchambers. Despite her silliness, Rosabel deserved better than to be forced into marriage with a scoundrel.

Reaching the top of the stairs, Claire paused to determine which way to go. Unfortunately, Lady Havenden lived in a mansion rather than a small town house. Three passageways stretched out, one straight ahead and the others to either side of her.

Choosing the corridor to her left, she headed for the row of closed doors. It was deserted, though the lilt of music and the hum of conversation drifted from the ballroom below. A series of flickering lamps on pedestals against the wall cast an eerie light that left pockets of deep shadow.

Claire decided against going into each bedchamber without knocking. It would be awkward indeed if she disturbed someone other than her quarry.

Just as she raised her hand at the first door, a movement at the end of the corridor caught her attention. A man emerged from one of the chambers, then turned to pull the door shut. As he did so, the light from one of the lamps illuminated his profile. Of average height, he had sandy hair and a thick mustache that overbalanced his receding jawline.

Recognition slammed Claire. Her heart stumbled to a stop. He was a colleague of her father's.

Mr. Vincent Grimes.

"That man that hath a tongue, I say is no man,
If with his tongue he cannot win a woman."
—*The Two Gentlemen of Verona*, III:i

Chapter Eighteen

Claire ducked into a dim, deserted bedchamber. She shut the door as quietly as possible. Leaning against the oak panel, she inhaled deeply to clear the panic from her brain.

What was Mr. Grimes doing at Havenden House? Like her father, he was a scholar and a teacher. Encountering him in this rarefied setting was as incongruous as seeing an elephant sipping tea with a group of ladies.

Of course, when they'd last met at the office of her barrister, Mr. Grimes had mentioned inheriting a tidy sum from his late aunt. He had been fashionably dressed and driving a fine carriage. But he'd never uttered a word about being well connected enough to enter the high circles of the aristocracy.

She pressed her ear to the door. Only the faint sound of music emanated from the corridor. Had he left yet? Was he heading down to the ballroom to find a dance partner or to the drawing room to play cards with the other men?

Belatedly, Claire realized she ought to have gone straight to him and explained her situation. She could have entrusted him with her secret. He wouldn't betray her or her father. Instead, she now faced the danger of running into him in the midst of the party, where he might unconsciously address her as *Miss Hollybrooke* and ruin her disguise.

Another thought chilled her. What if Simon encountered Mr. Grimes? Would he recognize him as the man who had given her a ride in his carriage a few days ago? What if Simon quizzed Mr. Grimes and discovered her true identity?

Simon might feel compelled to inform Lord Warrington. And yet he had held his tongue about that meeting at Newgate Prison today. Something about *that* whole incident made Claire uneasy.

She shelved the problem until later. It was more vital at the moment that she find her cousin.

Opening the door, she stepped out into the corridor. The plush green carpet cushioned her footfalls as she hurried to the neighboring room. She rapped lightly, and when no one answered, she peeked inside without venturing past the doorway.

On the bedside table, a lone candle flickered inside a glass chimney. Scattered belongings gave evidence of habitation. A lady's scarf draped the back of a chair. A gentleman's walking stick lay propped against the fireplace. The coverlet of the stately four-poster had been turned down neatly, the pillows plumped in readiness for slumber.

There was no sign of Rosabel or Lewis Newcombe.

Stepping back, Claire drew the door shut. Numerous bedchambers stretched out along this corridor and the other two. She had to hurry—

Turning, she bumped into a man. Her shoulder struck his hard chest. She yelped in surprise.

Her first thought was that the occupants of the room had returned. In the next instant, her shocked eyes took in his dark hair and chiseled male features.

"Simon!"

"Well, well, Mrs. Brownley. It seems we're fated to meet in unexpected places."

Although her back was flat against the closed door, he stood close, far too close. A tailored gray coat framed the broadness of his shoulders, and a crisp white cravat enhanced the swarthiness of his skin. A tremor of attraction unsettled her. How had she not heard his approach? More to the point, what was he doing here? Was he looking for Rosabel, too?

Lifting her chin, Claire decided to use the opportunity to question him. "It was more surprising to meet you at Newgate today. Especially since you quite obviously didn't see the Warrington coach."

His mouth twisted wryly. "So you noticed."

"You also looked startled upon spying us inside the prison."

"You're entirely too perceptive."

"And you're being evasive, my lord." When his brow furrowed slightly, she modulated her schoolmarm tone. "I'm curious about the real reason for your being there."

"It's nothing mysterious. I wanted a word with Hollybrooke, too. After all, he stole my mother's diamond bracelet."

The hard flatness of his brown eyes made her suppress a shiver. She hadn't thought him a vindictive man, out for his pound of flesh. But his unmistakable aura of menace suggested otherwise. Simon was a powerful man who would stop at nothing to punish those who had wronged him. It frustrated her to be denied the chance to speak out in her father's defense.

"Why did you not tell Lady Rosabel the truth?" she asked.

"He's her uncle. I didn't wish to remind her of the crime he committed against my family." With that, his gaze dipped to Claire's bosom. His grim expression vanished, and a faint smile played at the corners of his mouth. "But enough about him. You'd do better to ask me why I came upstairs just now."

Her stomach performed a cartwheel. His sudden shift of mood made her aware of a different sort of peril. She was conscious of his nearness, the allure of his spicy scent wafting through the air. Dear God, had he already wrested the truth from Mr. Grimes? Would he use the information as a lever to force her into his bed?

She folded her arms defensively. "So tell me."

"I wanted to find you, Clara. To beg the pleasure of your company."

His silken tone gave her gooseflesh. He exuded a seductiveness that both frightened and fascinated her. Despite his avowal to the contrary, he hadn't given up on his scheme to make her his mistress.

"I'm sorry to say you've wasted your time," she said. "Now, I've duties to perform for Lady Hester and Lady Rosabel. If you'll excuse me."

Simon easily blocked her escape by planting one hand on the door and the other on the gilt molding. She found herself caught against the wood panel with the knob pressing into her backside. Although he didn't touch her, the radiant heat of his body felt disturbingly like an embrace.

Cocking a black eyebrow, he said, "It's your turn for explanations. Tell me why you came out of a bedchamber during a party."

"I was looking for Lady Rosabel."

"In the bedrooms?"

Lady Hester would be furious if Claire revealed that Rosabel had vanished with Lewis Newcombe. "I couldn't find her anywhere else in the house. I thought perhaps she'd taken ill."

"You probably overlooked her in the ballroom." His tone dismissed her absence as unimportant.

If Claire moved an inch, her breasts would touch his chest. Already, her nipples felt tight and aching. "I'm sure you're right," she said to placate him. "Nevertheless, Lady Hester has set me to the task of finding her. So do step aside."

A dangerously attractive smile curved his lips. He leaned closer, crowding her into the corner. "Darling Clara. I can't possibly let you go."

The romantic declaration melted her legs. When he reached around her, encircling her waist, Claire felt a wild leap of excitement. He intended to kiss her again, she knew it. And worse, she *wanted* it. With complete disregard for common sense, her body made demands and her mind invented excuses. What did one kiss matter? Why couldn't she simply enjoy it and see if it matched the combustive memory of that first one? She needn't go any further—

Abruptly, she lost her balance as the door gave way behind her. In a smooth move, Simon had twisted the knob. He caught her to him and hustled her into the dimly lit bedchamber.

Kicking the door shut, he pressed her to the wall and settled himself over her so they were joined from shoulders to thighs. She was tall, but he was taller. The blissful feel of his large body depleted the air from her lungs. The semidarkness of the chamber enhanced their closeness, making them the only two people in the world. His mouth trailed warmly over her brow, while his fingers caressed her bare arms.

"Clara," he said, his voice low and raspy. "I vowed not to touch you again."

"And I vowed not to let you," she said, clinging to the illusion that she meant it.

Her palms were splayed against his coat, and the feel of his hard muscles made her nerves thrum with impatience. At any moment, he would join his mouth to hers. He'd transport her to a realm of bodily pleasure. He'd put an end to the burning fantasies that had plagued her since their first kiss. She shouldn't want him to do so—but she did.

"I've tried to stay away from you," he murmured. "Believe me, it hasn't been easy. When it comes to you, I have the very devil of a time restraining myself."

"Yes, you do." Claire had troubles of her own. Until Simon, she had never known the true power of temptation. The weight of his chest against her breasts stirred the longing to move, to snuggle closer to him. She resisted, while at the same time wishing he'd lower his mouth to hers.

But he continued to talk in that persuasive, seductive manner. "You must understand, I had no intention of pursuing you tonight. But when I saw you leave the ballroom, I had to go after you."

"So you followed me." It thrilled her to know Simon had been watching her from afar. Just as she watched him now and suffered through the torture of his explanation.

Never before had she met a man so gifted by the bounties of nature. The sound of his voice hypnotized her. The scent of him was intoxicating. And his form . . . he could have been the archetype for the statue of a Greek god. Maturity had etched hard lines and angles into his face, imbuing the cold marble with the warm breath of life.

His fingers feathered over her bare neck and played with the tendrils there. His eyes were incredibly dark and intense. "It's wrong of me to break my word. I know that. But I want you, Clara, even if it damns me to hell."

Did he make such passionate declarations to all his

women? She no longer cared. "Please, Simon. Just kiss me."

Unable to bear the suspense a moment longer, Claire succumbed to boldness. She looped her arms around his neck, arched up on tiptoes, and touched her mouth to his. He went still, but only for an instant. Then he returned the kiss with a tender ferocity that surpassed her romantic dreams. His fingers slid into her hair to cup her head while his lips and tongue cast a devil's spell. If anything, the kiss was more marvelous than the first time. This time, she hadn't been taken by surprise as she had that time in the rain.

This time, she was a willing participant.

Desire subdued rational thought and transformed her into a creature of sensuality. It freed her from the restrictions of caution and prudence, encouraging her to touch him, to learn the muscled contours of his body, to express her delight with small moans and sighs.

It seemed only natural for him to shift his hand to her bosom. He cradled one breast, caressing her through the silk of her gown, rubbing his finger over the peak. Her skin contracted with a shock of pleasure that descended to her loins. Though her limbs were weak, she felt energized by his touch and hungry for more.

His lips left hers to lay a trail of kisses down her throat and over the flesh exposed by her low décolletage. All the while, he continued to touch her in a variety of ways designed to wreak exquisite torment. His mouth followed a path along the upper slopes of her breasts. His tongue slipped into the valley to taste her skin. His teeth nipped lightly at the covered peak; then he soothed her with a stroke of his thumb.

Her heart drummed at a dizzying pace. She leaned her head back against the wall, the air cool on her fevered skin. Awareness lurked at the edge of her passion. "Simon," she murmured. "We mustn't . . ."

"We must," he corrected, his finger tracing her lips. "You and I belong together."

Did they? The concentration of his eyes made her a believer. He subjected her to another deep, soul-stirring kiss. His hands moved down to her hips to draw her tightly against him. Through the layers of their clothing, she grew aware of the hard length inside his breeches. It should have embarrassed her, but instead it made her wild with longing. If he hadn't been holding her, she would have slid to the floor in a molten pool.

Catching her around the waist, he guided her across the chamber and stopped at the foot of the bed, where he turned her in his arms. With his chest against her spine, he curled her fingers around the bedpost. "Hold on, darling. Just for a moment."

As he unfastened the row of tiny buttons down her back, Claire clung to the post in a near swoon. The glow from the candle inside the glass chimney spilled onto the bed, leaving the rest of the room in shadow. The blue coverlet had been turned down to reveal crisp white sheets and a pair of plump feather pillows.

Realization arrowed through the sensual fog. Simon was undressing her. He intended to have relations with her. Right here and now.

In a panic, she whirled to face him. "Stop! We can't do this. *I* can't."

His gaze burned into her. Placing his hands on her shoulders, he looked deeply into her eyes. "It's been a long time for you, hasn't it, Clara? It's only natural to be frightened."

He believed her a widow. He thought her experienced. How foolish she'd been to imagine they would share only a kiss. She fumbled for an excuse to deter him. "There are guests staying in this room."

"Not at the moment."

"They'll return soon."

"It's scarcely midnight. Supper hasn't even been served. We've hours to ourselves."

He tried to kiss her again, but Claire turned her head away. She put her hands behind her neck to close the few buttons he'd undone. "I'm afraid we don't," she said, forcing steel into her voice. "If I've misled you, pray forgive me. I'll be going now."

He stepped behind her to help with the buttons. Then his fingers lightly caressed her arms and she felt the warmth of his breath against the nape of her neck. "I'll go with you," he murmured. "You're right, we don't want to be interrupted. We'll find somewhere else to be alone."

His touch felt far too good. She stepped away from him, away from the bed. "I told you before, I won't have an affair. Not now, not ever."

His jaw tightened, yet he seemed intent on convincing her. "I won't pry into your past. I don't know what happened in your marriage. But I can promise you bliss, Clara. Far beyond anything you've ever known."

A blush bathed her skin. What did he mean? It might be folly, but she was sorely tempted to learn the secrets of lovemaking. She wanted to lie with Simon, to allow him the liberties of a husband.

But he wasn't her husband, and he never would be. He used women like her for his pleasure. If she didn't go now, she might never find the strength.

"Good-bye, Simon," she said firmly. "I'll thank you to wait here for a moment. If I'm seen leaving a bedchamber with you, I'll sacrifice my post."

She started toward the door, but he stepped in front of her. "Clara," he said, tenderly stroking her face. "You shouldn't be a servant. Allow me to take care of you. I've a house in Belgravia where you can live in comfort. You'll have a carriage at your disposal, servants, all the jewels and gowns you could ever desire."

His words were a slap of cold water. A violent current of anger swept away the last of her warm feelings for him.

She struck his hand from her. "I *desire* my good name. I *desire* my self-respect. Those are the things you would rob from me."

He uttered a growl of frustration. Running his fingers through his hair, he asked, "Are you afraid I'll mistreat you? I'll devote myself to your happiness. Do you want books? I'll purchase an entire library for you. Music? You'll have the finest pianoforte. Better yet, I'll hire an orchestra to play for you every day—"

"Nothing! I want nothing from you. Nothing at all." Much to her chagrin, tears prickled her eyes. They were tears of rage, of course. She didn't want a future with this nobleman—not under any circumstances. "You should be ashamed of yourself for pursuing me. How can you seek a mistress when you're marrying Lady Rosabel?"

He stared fixedly at Claire. "I'm not."

"Not—?"

"I've changed my mind. I'm ending my courtship of her. I should never have agreed to that ridiculous bargain in the first place."

The news flummoxed Claire. "You can't mean that."

"I do," he said in a harsh, uncompromising tone. "Despite what you think of me, I'm not a man who can be with two women at the same time. And I choose you, Clara."

The charming rogue had vanished. He spoke with fierce conviction. For that reason alone, she found herself believing him. He meant what he said. He would abandon his wedding plans and lose a wager . . . for her.

I choose you.

None of his polished phrases had affected her as powerfully as that simple statement. But it didn't change matters.

She'd be a fool to allow the softness of yearning into her heart. She'd be an even bigger fool to wish she was a lady of his class so that he would make her an honorable offer.

He stood in the shadows, and something about his solitary figure hinted at a depth of loneliness that he kept hidden from the world. Did he feel only lust for her? Or did he also feel the aching need for companionship and love—as she felt?

Then fate intervened to save her from replying.

Far in the distance, a woman screamed.

"Double, double toil and trouble;
Fire burn, and cauldron bubble."
—*Macbeth*, IV:i

Chapter Nineteen

The cry of terror pierced Simon.

Without conscious decision, he sprang past Clara and wrenched open the door. Where lust had burned only a moment ago, raw urgency pumped through his veins. Memory conjured the image of his mother and father lying in a pool of blood.

Never again.

He ran down the passageway and turned the corner. A screeching maidservant almost collided with him. A smudge of coal marred her pale cheek and her plump hands clutched at him. "Oh! Oh, m'lord!"

He caught her by the shoulders. "Has someone been injured?"

"N-nay . . ." She broke off into noisy sobs.

Relief swamped Simon. Having no patience for hysteria, he gave her a hard shake. "Calm yourself. Tell me what's happened."

"Sumthin' turrible. M'lady . . . her jewels . . . they been nicked!"

"Whose jewels?"

"Lady Havenden, m'lord." Glancing back over her

shoulder, the girl quivered with palpable fear. " 'Twas the Wraith, m'lord. The Wraith!"

Clara hurried up to them. Her beautiful face displayed shock at the girl's unfounded claim.

Behind her, a rumble of voices sounded from the floor below. Guests would be hastening up the grand staircase to see about the commotion. He had to prevent the wildfire of rumor. "You will not repeat that to anyone," he commanded the girl. "The Wraith is in prison. Someone else did this deed. Do you understand me?"

She nodded jerkily, though her enormous brown eyes showed disbelief. But there was no helping that now. He needed to gather information before a swarm of gawkers impeded him.

He dashed down the corridor to an open door at the end. A pair of female voices, one distraught, the other submissive, emanated from within. Without bothering to knock, he entered an enormous, stately bedchamber decorated in white and pale blue.

A fire flickered on the hearth. Groupings of dainty chairs huddled in the shadows. Near the brocade-draped bed, a silver branch of candles illuminated the women.

A mobcapped lady's maid stood by the bedside table and searched frantically through a large, leather-bound strongbox. A thin, elderly woman in a green silk gown perched anxiously on a stool, clutching a small white terrier in her lap.

Spying Simon, the dog set up a shrill yapping.

"Hush, Daisy," Lady Havenden scolded. "It's Lord Rockford. You remember him." She turned her distressed face to Simon and held out a hand. "My jewels have been stolen. What shall I do?"

He gently massaged her cold, bony fingers. She was a widow, an acquaintance of his mother's, and he'd take great pleasure in strangling the villain who had wronged her. "Tell me what's missing."

"My emerald necklace. The clasp on my diamonds broke. So I . . . I came upstairs to exchange it for the emeralds . . . but they were *gone*."

Clara appeared beside Lady Havenden. "Perhaps you've merely misplaced the piece, my lady."

"No," the old woman said brokenly. "I never put my jewels anywhere but in that strongbox. It's always safely hidden in the drawer by my bed . . ."

Safely. Simon refrained from pointing out that a skilled thief could have found the coffer and sprung the lock in under five minutes. "When was the last time you saw the emeralds?"

"Earlier this evening, while I was dressing for the party."

"You're absolutely certain of that?"

"Yes. They were very special to me." Her blue eyes filled with misery, and tears rolled down her wrinkled cheeks. "Hugh gave them to me to celebrate our first Christmas together."

Sinking to her knees beside the stool, Clara handed Lady Havenden a folded handkerchief. "I am sorry, my lady. This must be terribly difficult for you."

"I considered wearing the emeralds tonight, and I wish I had. I wish I had!" Her voice trembling, Lady Havenden dabbed at her face. The terrier put its paws on her bosom and whined.

Clara made sympathetic sounds, too, and Simon was relieved to step away. Despite growing up in a house full of females, he felt unnerved by weeping women. He would sooner face a gang of ruffians in a dark alleyway with no weapon but his fists.

He examined the windows, but could see no sign of

forced entry. God! Hollybrooke had been apprehended less than a month ago. Now there was another burglar invading an upper-class house in the midst of a party. If he didn't know better, he'd be tempted to ask—

"My lady," Clara said, "did you by chance find a quotation from Shakespeare left in place of the jewels?"

"What nonsense," Simon snapped. Nevertheless, he found himself tensely awaiting the answer.

Lady Havenden clutched the handkerchief to her ashen cheek. "Do you mean . . . this could be the work of the Wraith? But I thought he was in prison."

"Indeed he is," Simon assured her. He glared a warning at Clara. "Mrs. Brownley must have forgotten that fact."

She gazed coolly at him. Although kneeling on the floor, she exuded an air of challenge, and he felt an inopportune stab of lust. By God, she was a fine woman, proud and passionate, willful and invincible. Was he wrong to expect her to compromise her moral code for him? *She* certainly thought so. Her defenses hadn't crumbled even when he'd made the snap decision to end his courtship of Lady Rosabel.

But he had a sinking suspicion that the strength he admired in Clara signaled doom for his campaign to make her his mistress. Which meant the only path into her bed was by way of a church.

He refused to consider *that*.

"I remember you now, Mrs. Brownley," Lady Havenden said. "You're companion to Rosabel Lathrop. Forgive me for taking you from your duties."

"It's quite all right. Now, *did* you find a written note in the strongbox?"

"Why, no. What about you, Prufrock?"

The maid shook her head. She was a sturdy, middle-aged

woman with worried gray eyes. "Nay, m'lady. I didn't see no papers at all."

"Then there is no connection to the Wraith," Simon said in satisfaction. The case went to trial next week, and he had enough complications already without further doubts being cast into the mix.

Clara, however, frowned at the strongbox as if she'd hoped for a different answer. The fleeting impression vanished as she stood up. "Prufrock, her ladyship has suffered a shock. Please be so kind as to fetch her a pot of strong tea and some brandy, as well."

"Aye, ma'am." Prufrock scurried out of the bedchamber.

"My lady, if you'll come with me, we'll sit by the fire. You'll be much more comfortable there."

"Thank you, my dear." Clutching the terrier, Lady Havenden accepted Clara's hand in rising slowly from the stool. "I would enjoy having a chat with you."

As they headed toward the chaise, Simon was struck by two observations at once. One was the way Lady Havenden readily accepted Clara as an equal—and Lady Havenden was one of the premier hostesses in society.

The other was the buzz of voices out in the corridor.

Harry Masterson poked his head through the doorway. As he stepped inside and closed the door, Simon went straight to him. Harry's usually jovial features looked grave.

He glanced at Clara, who was settling Lady Havenden onto a chaise by the hearth. Keeping his voice low, he said, "I heard the screams. The maid said there's been a robbery."

"Yes. An emerald necklace is missing."

"You'd better tell me everything. I need some ammunition to hold off the crowd out there."

"Lady Havenden is shaken, but otherwise well. The culprit is still at large."

"Good God. It's the Wraith all over again."

Simon clenched his teeth. That name kept cropping up tonight. "Others are bound to think so, too. Tell them that no passage from Shakespeare was left here. This robbery is unrelated."

"Righto. And I'll be sure to say that Lady Havenden wants them all to go back downstairs and enjoy the ball."

As Harry turned to leave, Simon grabbed his arm. "If you'll do me another favor."

"Name it."

"Send to Bow Street at once. Tell the magistrate we'll need a team of Runners here at once to get statements from any witnesses."

"I'm one step ahead of you, old boy. I've already dispatched a footman."

Harry departed, and Simon returned to the bedside table. It struck him that this wasn't the first time Harry had offered his assistance after a burglary. Most of the thefts by the Wraith hadn't been discovered until the following day. But on two occasions, the victim had raised the alarm during the party. Harry had kept the other guests calm, allowing Simon time for his investigation. And tonight, Harry didn't seem at all surprised to find Simon at the scene of the crime.

Had he guessed that Simon worked for Bow Street? And if Harry had surmised the truth, what about other people?

Simon always took great care to work behind the scenes. The most visible investigating was done by other Runners. But if an immediate situation arose—as it had tonight—then he drummed up a reason to explain his presence. He was in the vicinity, he was a friend of the victim, he was adept at taking charge. Not that an excuse was even necessary. It would be inconceivable to any member of the upper class that one of their own would dirty his hands by hunting common criminals.

But Harry was another matter. Harry knew about Simon's past.

Ignoring the knot in his gut, Simon filed away the issue until later. At the other end of the large chamber, Clara sat beside Lady Havenden on the chaise. While they conversed in muffled tones, he concentrated on assessing the scene.

The strongbox stood open. Against the crimson velvet interior lay an assortment of rings, necklaces, and brooches. He examined the lock, but could see no faint scratches to indicate the use of a pick. He'd have to find out where the key was kept.

Picking up the branch of candles, he surveyed the surrounding area for anything out of the ordinary. There was always a chance that the perpetrator had carelessly left a clue—just as Hollybrooke had dropped that grocery receipt outside the site of his last robbery.

Simon peered behind the bedside table, inside the opened drawer, and behind the window curtains. Then he crouched down to inspect the floor more closely. The blue-and-gold rug appeared to have been recently swept. Not even a speck of dust marred the pristine wool.

But something glinted in the shadows under the bed. Reaching out, he grasped a small, round object.

It was a brass button decorated with fine scrollwork. A man's button, he judged, and a fine one at that. A few dark threads dangled from the bottom.

Since the underside of the bed looked spotless, the button could not have lain there for long. That ruled out Lord Havenden, who had died more than a decade ago. The footmen in this house sported silver buttons on their livery. So unless Lady Havenden had recently been entertaining lovers—a circumstance he sincerely doubted—the button might have fallen from the burglar's coat.

He restrained a surge of excitement. Glancing at the fireplace, he made certain neither woman was watching him before slipping the button into an inner pocket of his coat.

If his conjecture was correct, then by the excellent quality of the button, he could also surmise that the culprit dressed well. Could the thief have been bold enough to sneak into the ball and pretend to be one of the guests?

Another thought arrested Simon. Or was the perpetrator a member of society? If Simon went downstairs, would he find a gentleman who was missing a brass button? The prospect left a bad taste in his mouth. He didn't want to think that someone from his own circle had preyed upon Lady Havenden.

There was only one way to find out.

It was only as he stood up that Simon noticed the sliver of white beneath the strongbox. He set down the branch of candles, lifted the coffer, and spied a folded piece of paper. He picked it up. The size and texture were identical to—

His heart thumped erratically. It couldn't be.

He stared at it for a long moment. Then slowly, he unfolded the paper. An inscription in block letters read, *Words without thoughts never to heaven go.*

The snippet was from Shakespeare's *Hamlet*.

While Simon had talked with Sir Harry, Claire had done her best to comfort Lady Havenden. They sat side by side on the chaise, and the old woman seemed eager to speak of anything but the robbery. She had deftly drawn out Claire's fictitious past about the husband who had died at

Waterloo, requiring her to take the post at Warrington House.

After Sir Harry departed, Simon spent some time examining the area around the jewel box. Lady Havenden's back was to him, but Claire had a clear view of his actions. She found it difficult to concentrate when her mind and body still reeled from the intensity of that kiss. But she noticed that his methodical manner seemed odd for a nobleman.

Of course, Simon was no ordinary aristocrat. She had glimpsed facets of decency in him: the affection he held for his mother and sisters, the concern he'd shown for Lady Havenden . . . and his declaration that he couldn't be with two women at the same time.

I choose you.

Her heart soared with shameful exuberance, but Claire dragged herself back to earth. She had no intention of embarking upon an illicit affair—even if she *was* flattered. What woman wouldn't be thrilled by the attentions of a handsome, charming man?

A woman who knew he regarded her as too inferior to merit an honorable courtship.

"I'm delighted to have this chance to talk to you, Mrs. Brownley." Lady Havenden spoke in a quiet, conspiratorial tone as she stroked the dog in her lap. Although age had woven a web of fine seams over her face, her blue eyes were sharp and inquisitive. "You must know Lady Rosabel quite well."

"Only a little," Claire murmured. "I've been at Warrington House for less than a fortnight." She agonized about Rosabel. Had she returned to the ballroom? Or was she off somewhere with Lewis Newcombe? Were they doing what Claire had been doing with Simon? Heaven forbid!

"Tell me, how is Lord Rockford's courtship of her progressing?"

Claire's heart lurched. "Perhaps that's a question for his lordship."

"Bah, men prattle about politics and horses. They haven't the slightest interest in important matters like marriage—except when it comes to the siring of children."

Claire reddened. She had immediately pictured herself entwined with Simon in bed. The covers were up to their necks and the details were sketchy, but she felt flushed with curiosity. And embarrassment.

Her gaze crept back to Simon. He had knelt down to examine the carpet. Stretching his arm under the bed, he withdrew a small object, which he studied for a moment.

"The marriage would be a grand alliance of families," Lady Havenden whispered in the sociable manner of someone fishing for information. "I wonder if Lady Rosabel realizes how very fortunate she is. The earl has eluded the matchmakers for quite some time, you know."

Simon glanced at Claire, and she pretended to be engrossed in conversation. "So I've heard."

To her surprise, he slipped the object inside his coat. What was it?

"At least he'll be a steadying influence on the girl. She does seem a bit fickle to me."

More than a bit. Claire kept her voice neutral. "She's very young."

"Perhaps, though I've always believed eighteen is the ideal age for a lady to marry." Lady Havenden looked at Claire expectantly. "I wonder if they'll make the announcement at her birthday ball."

"She's said nothing of it to me, my lady."

But Claire's insides twisted. What would happen once Simon realized she wouldn't succumb to his seduction?

Would he return to his pursuit of Rosabel? Would he propose to her on bended knee, pledging his heart and offering the honor of his name?

Rosabel professed not to care for Simon, but Lord Warrington would pressure her to accept. He had tried to coerce Claire's mother into marrying a duke—but Simon was no repulsive old codger. He was a man in his prime, handsome and charming, and if he set his mind to convincing Rosabel, he might very well succeed.

Across the chamber, he rose to his feet. The faint sound of music drifted from the ballroom. Lifting the jewel box, he retrieved a small square of paper. He held it folded in his hand, frowning down at it.

His manner intrigued Claire. Why did he appear so . . . intense?

Petting the terrier, Lady Havenden eyed Claire as if suspecting her of harboring a secret. "Perhaps they're keeping it as a surprise."

"A surprise?"

"Their betrothal, of course. It's bound to happen. Lord Warrington favors the match, doesn't he?"

"Yes." Claire could sense Lady Havenden's eagerness to hear confirmation of the engagement. She was a terrier on the hunt for gossip. Wouldn't she be shocked to know that Simon had renounced Rosabel in order to pursue Claire?

Out of the corner of her eye, she saw Simon unfolding the paper. Again, he stared at it as if transfixed.

"His mother favors the match, too," Lady Havenden whispered knowingly, "and she wields considerable influence over her son. He's been very protective of her ever since that terrible tragedy."

"Tragedy?"

Sadness replaced the avidity on Lady Havenden's withered face. "Many years ago, his parents were shot by a highwayman. His father was killed instantly. As for Lady Rockford, well, I fear she's never fully recovered."

The revelation jarred Claire. Dear God. Simon had told her he was fifteen at the time of his father's death. She wondered if he'd been away at school when he'd heard the news, if he'd rushed home in an agony of grief and fear that his mother would be taken from him, too. No wonder he was so attentive toward her. He must love his mother very much.

"It must have been dreadful for him and for his sisters."

"Indeed, it makes me ashamed to have carried on so about my emeralds," Lady Havenden said, her shoulders drooping. "After the way my dear friend suffered . . ."

Daisy whined, licking Lady Havenden's hand, and she bent down to croon to the dog.

Claire murmured a sympathetic noise. Her heart considerably softened toward Simon, she turned her eyes to him—just in time to see him slip the piece of paper into an inner pocket of his coat. The furtiveness of his actions confused her. Why would he take a note that clearly belonged to Lady Havenden?

Then a chilling thought drove all else out of her mind. Perhaps the paper had been left by the burglar. Perhaps by . . . the Wraith.

Had Simon found a quotation from Shakespeare?

Her heart beat at a dizzying pace. Wild to confront him, she was rising to her feet when Lady Havenden spoke again.

"Ah, there's Prufrock now. Will you be so kind as to pour, Mrs. Brownley? I'm afraid my hands are still a bit shaky."

Claire stood paralyzed. The stout maid scurried forward with a silver tray, which she set down on a low table in front of them. Oblivious to them, Simon remained standing by the jewel box. Perhaps he didn't want to upset Lady

Havenden with the news. But Claire had to read that note before he gave it to the authorities.

Concentrating to keep from spilling, she poured the steaming tea, added a spoonful of brandy, and handed the cup to Lady Havenden. "This should restore you, my lady."

"Will you join me, my dear?" the old woman asked plaintively. "And Lord Rockford, too."

In addition to a rose-patterned teapot, the tray held several plates full of food from the party—plum tartlets dusted with sugar, cubes of ham glistening with glaze, fresh bread with dewy pats of butter.

None of it tempted Claire. Her stomach felt tied in a knot. But she seized the excuse. "I'll . . . I'll go ask him."

She started toward Simon. He prowled the chamber now, his steps restless, his hands on his hips. He appeared deep in thought. If indeed he had found evidence that the Wraith was still at large, it would prove her father was innocent. The courts would have to let Papa go!

Giddy hope sustained her—but only for a moment. Did this mean the Wraith was *not* her grandfather? If Lord Warrington had achieved his revenge on Papa, then why would he steal again, thereby casting doubt on her father's guilt?

Perhaps she was assuming too much. Perhaps the paper was nothing more than a blank scrap that Simon intended to discard.

And yet . . .

She stepped into his path. He stopped, scowling at her as if resenting the interruption. His face was a frosty, unfriendly mask. She might have been gazing at a stranger, rather than the man who had kissed her senseless only a short time ago.

"Yes?" he said tersely.

His coldness cut deeply. But she wouldn't be daunted, not when her father's freedom was at stake. "Simon, I need to speak to you—"

A knocking interrupted her.

Without a word of apology, Simon left her standing in the shadows. He strode to the door and a footman spoke quietly to him. At a nod from Simon, a robust man in a dark coat and red vest stepped into view.

Claire's mouth went dry. A Bow Street Runner! If Simon gave him that paper, she would never have the chance to see it.

She hastened up to them in time to hear the Runner explaining his swift arrival. " 'Twas fortunate her ladyship's man spied me round Piccadilly. I was just off duty and on me way home."

When the man paused for breath, she said urgently, "Lord Rockford, I do need a word with you."

Simon's cool glance skated over her. "In a moment."

He proceeded to relate the situation to the officer, the screams of the maid and Lady Havenden's account of what had happened. Claire clenched her teeth to keep from exploding. At any moment he would hand the note to the Runner. And by the heavens, she would snatch it out of his hand and read it. She would make certain everyone knew the wrong man had been arrested. Her father's life depended upon it.

With a pencil stub, the balding officer scribbled in his notebook. "So you were first on the scene, m'lord. Did you find anything out of the ordinary? Anything that might be a clue?"

Claire steeled herself for action. But to her surprise, Simon didn't reach inside his coat. He didn't hand over the note—or the other object he'd found.

Instead, he aimed a condescending stare at the officer.

"May I remind you, searching for evidence is *your* job. And you had best move quickly. I want this thief apprehended at once."

"Aye, m'lord," the Runner said, bobbing his head. "I'll take a statement from her ladyship first."

While the men proceeded inside the bedchamber, Claire remained frozen in the doorway. Simon introduced the Runner to Lady Havenden and stood guard while she answered the questions. At any moment he would surely surrender the evidence.

But he didn't. Was Claire mistaken about the paper?

No. He had looked too stunned for the note to be blank. It *must* have contained a message from the burglar—the Wraith. So why had he withheld the vital information? *Why?*

The answer came to her in a blinding flash. What if he had taken the evidence to protect someone? What if Simon knew the true identity of the Wraith?

The ugly thought sank its claws into her disbelieving mind. Try as she might, Claire couldn't shake it loose. He wouldn't want anyone to know that the wrong man had been arrested.

But who would he shield? Was it her grandfather—or someone else? Lord Frederick? Lady Rosabel? Lady Hester? Or was it someone outside Claire's family?

And more puzzling, who would go to the trouble to implicate her father, then unravel the elaborate ruse by stealing again?

None of it made sense. But Simon's visit to the prison now took on a more sinister cast. He'd wanted to berate the criminal who had stolen his mother's bracelet—or so he'd claimed. But what if he'd had a darker reason? What if he'd felt guilty that an innocent man languished behind bars?

Claire's mind whirled with possibilities. Only one fact

was certain. Without a doubt, *something* was going on, something that connected Simon to the Wraith.

Perhaps the arrival of the law had been a blessing in disguise. If she had asked Simon about the note, he would have denied finding it. Then, at the first opportunity, he would have destroyed it.

Rigid resolve stiffened her spine. He held the key to free her father from prison. She would do anything to secure the proof that lay hidden in an inner pocket of his coat.

Even if it meant seducing Simon.

> "Tempt not a desperate man."
> —*Romeo and Juliet*, V:iii

Chapter Twenty

As Simon fitted his key into the lock of his house in Belgravia, he was keenly aware of Clara standing beside him on the step. A mixture of moonlight and shadow gave her face an aura of mystery. He kept one hand splayed over the small of her back. Although she'd chatted easily with him on the short ride here, a trace of tension had emanated from her, too.

He feared she might change her mind and vanish into the night.

Only half an hour ago, he had been leaving Lady Havenden's bedchamber, intent on finding the owner of that lost button, when Clara had stopped him in the passageway. His mind had been reeling from the reappearance of the Wraith, but her sultry blue eyes had distracted him. Sliding her hands inside his coat, she'd murmured, "I've made my decision, Simon. I want to be your mistress."

The fire of lust flamed to life. In an instant, he was consumed by sexual excitement. But circumstances forced him to put a damper on the blaze. He had a duty to investigate the robbery. He had to solve the riddle of who had left that quotation.

What a cursed inopportune moment!

He caught her wrists and brought her hands to his mouth to kiss them. The softness of her skin tortured him. "Clara, darling, you won't regret it. I'll make all the arrangements for tomorrow night—"

"No! Tonight. It must be tonight. If we wait, I'll—I'll change my mind. I know I will!"

She meant it. The quivering of her body showed how perilously close he was to losing her. It must have taken all of her courage to step over the line into sin. Although Clara was a widow, she was too principled to engage in light affairs. In fact, he would venture to guess he was her first—and that meant her desire for him must be powerful, indeed.

The thought was an irresistible aphrodisiac. He made his decision at once. "I'll have a quick word with Lady Havenden."

"Must you?"

"She asked me to return," he lied. "I'll need to tell her I'm leaving."

While Clara had waited out in the corridor, Simon had covertly given the stray button to the Runner with instructions to search for its owner. Then Clara had insisted on writing an excuse to Lady Hester and giving it to a footman to deliver. As they'd finally slipped out a side door, she had seemed eager, happy. Yet her warmth had been tempered by a hint of caution.

As if she doubted her decision.

Even now, through the darkness, Simon sensed her nervousness. It made him all the more impatient to start her seduction. Once he had her naked beneath him, she'd forget all her misgivings.

He'd make certain of it.

He turned the key and opened the door, ushering her

into the dimly lit foyer. An oil lamp burned on a small table beside the staircase. Clara took a few tentative steps, then stopped to survey the still-life paintings on the pale ocher walls, the tan marble floor and tall white columns.

"It's rather like a Roman villa," she said.

Amused by her surprise, Simon enfolded her in his arms. "Did you expect crimson velvet and portraits of naked women?"

Her prim blue eyes regarded him. "Something tawdry and crude, yes. To reflect the activities that go on here."

He gave her a brash grin. "Crude? I'll take that as a challenge to change your mind."

Lowering his mouth to hers, he subjected her to a per- suasive kiss. Her body felt tight with resistance. But her lips were soft, parting to allow him access, and that one concession drove him wild. He held himself in check, giving her the time she needed to trust him. With light strokes, he touched her face, her neck, her hair. Only as she melted against him did he allow himself to explore further, moving down her slim back and to her hips, rev- eling in her womanly shape.

She slid her hands inside his coat, and the surge in his heartbeat caused a hitch in his breathing. The tentative movements of her palms against his shirt felt more erotic than the practiced strokes of a courtesan. Their clothing was suddenly too restrictive. Unfastening her pelisse, he ran the pads of his fingers over her bare throat. She would be even warmer and more silken between her legs.

He ached to be there, filling her, their bodies joined as one.

As if she shared the thought, Clara moaned into his mouth. The erotic sound amplified his passion. He burned to possess her, and the nearest bed seemed miles away.

Without breaking the kiss, he walked her backward, heading toward the gloom of the adjacent drawing room.

Through a sensual haze, he heard distant footsteps tap on the marble floor, then abruptly retreat.

Clara stiffened, turning to peer down the darkened corridor beyond the stairway. "Who's there—"

Simon cuddled her close, nuzzling her face. "It's only Mrs. Bagley, the housekeeper. She must have heard us come in."

"I didn't think anyone else would be here."

"She and her husband are the only servants. They're extremely discreet."

"But she must have seen us." Clara looked unnerved by the intrusion. Frowning, she sank her teeth into her lower lip.

His groin responded with spontaneous combustion. Damn, he had to master himself. What was he thinking, anyway, to take her on a chaise in the drawing room? He wanted their first time together to be perfect. If he went up in smoke in the first two minutes, he'd never achieve her seduction in the manner he'd planned.

But first he had to get rid of that blasted note. He couldn't take a chance on it falling out of his pocket. Clara was too sharp not to realize its significance, and he intended to show it only to the magistrate.

"Come," he said. "I've something for you."

Taking the lamp in one hand and encircling her waist with the other, Simon drew her toward his study. He opened the door and guided her inside. Ordinarily, he forbade his mistresses to cross into his sanctum, but tonight was an exception.

Clara was an exception.

Her eyes alight, she gazed around with interest at the mahogany desk, the comfortable chairs by the hearth, the floor-to-ceiling walls of books. Pulling him to one of the shelves, she tilted her head to read the spines. "Chaucer, Cicero, Congreve. Alphabetized—though it would make more sense to arrange them by subject matter."

"Bagley catalogued them for me."

"Hmm."

Clara had a keen look on her face that told him she itched to start reorganizing. He saw himself sitting by the fire—not now, but sometime in the future—chatting with her while she sorted through his books. He'd help her get a volume down from a high shelf, but instead, he'd stroke her breasts and kiss her until they ended up on the hearth rug making love . . .

Her voice interrupted the fantasy. "But why do you have a library here of all places?"

"This house isn't only for entertaining. I'm often here alone. This room is my retreat."

It wasn't information he shared with many. In fact, only Harry had ferreted out his secret. But no one, not even Harry, knew that Simon had sat at that desk untold times and worked on cases for Bow Street. It was here that he'd struggled—and failed—to find meaning in the quotations left by the Wraith.

But the latest one had not been left by Gilbert Hollybrooke.

Simon wondered if he was responsible for imprisoning the wrong man. The thought was sobering enough to dampen his ardor.

Leaving the lamp with Clara, who was engrossed in his library, he walked to the desk. In his mind, he reiterated all the reasons why Hollybrooke had to be the guilty party. Hollybrooke had cause to resent the nobility. His grocery receipt had been dropped at the scene of his last crime. The diamond bracelet belonging to Simon's mother had been hidden in Hollybrooke's drawer.

To imagine that another culprit had planted those items was simply too incredible to accept.

Which meant that someone must be copying Hollybrooke. An enterprising thief had decided that a grand party was the perfect opportunity to stage a jewel heist. The penmanship looked eerily similar, yet there were differences, too. He would compare the note to the others in the morning.

Simon shrugged off his coat and dropped it onto the chair, along with his cravat. His contact, Thomas Cramps, wasn't on duty until tomorrow, which freed Simon for the entire night.

He intended to enjoy himself to the fullest.

Going to the sideboard, he took a glass and poured from a decanter. He returned to Clara, and her fingers were lightly touching the leather volumes in a way that made him instantly hard.

She swung to face him. Her large blue eyes scanned his white shirt with its opened collar, and her startled expression seemed oddly virginal. Had her husband been so prudish a man that he'd undressed in the dark? If so, her experience with lovemaking was about to take a change for the better.

Nevertheless, jealousy twisted in Simon. He didn't want to think about any other man touching Clara, not even in her past. His possessiveness was stupid and irrational—because if she were an untried maiden, he would never have brought her here.

She recovered with aplomb and smiled at him. "You said you had something for me. Was it a book?"

"No, this. You could use a bit of liquid courage."

Simon offered the glass, but she shook her head. "I don't drink spirits."

"Go on, take a few sips. It'll help you relax." The drink was merely a ploy to leave his coat—and the note—in his study. He had no doubts about his ability to pleasure her without the aid of external props.

He guided the glass to her lips, tilting it so that a few drops of the amber liquid trickled into her mouth. She swallowed and coughed, waving the glass away. "What is that?"

"The finest French brandy."

"It's swill and it burns."

"In certain situations, burning can be quite enjoyable." Turning the glass, he drank from the same place as she had, his gaze holding hers. He scarcely noticed as the liquor glided over his tongue and down his throat. He was too intent on Clara's reaction.

Her lips were parted slightly. Her eyes became the deep, dreamy blue of the ocean. She must be remembering their kiss. And anticipating the coupling to come.

By God, *he* certainly was.

Without looking, he set the glass on the nearest bookshelf. Then he wrapped his arms around her slender form. His mouth brushed hers, the contact flavored with the tang of brandy and the urgency of desire. "Let's go upstairs," he murmured.

Picking up the lamp, he steered her toward the door. But when they reached the threshold, Clara balked. She gazed back over her shoulder. "Aren't you taking your coat?"

"I doubt I'll be needing it tonight."

She didn't laugh at his wry jest. Evading another kiss, she ducked under his arm, scooped up his coat and cravat, and clutched them to her bosom. "I won't have Mrs. Bagley finding our garments strewn everywhere."

It had been a long time since Simon had met a woman who embarrassed so readily. That must be why his chest squeezed with tenderness. He felt a powerful compulsion to please Clara, to grant her every wish.

But not this time.

Gently wresting the coat from her, he tossed it back onto the chair. "Don't worry, darling. No one comes in here without my permission."

"But—"

"No one," he repeated firmly, maneuvering her out of the study and closing the door behind them.

Simon didn't want her to feel even one more twinge of hesitation. So he set down the lamp on a table. He swept her up into his arms and headed straight for the staircase.

Gasping, she looped her arms around his neck and clung with satisfying closeness. "What are you doing?"

"What I should have done on the night we met." God, she felt good in his arms, solid yet soft, her breasts cushioned against his chest. Her blue skirts draped his arms, and he could smell her tantalizing lavender scent. Mounting the stairs, he added aggressively, "I should have carried you here to this house and never let you go."

Her frown gradually changed into a tiny smile. Her eyes sparkled up at him. "You wouldn't have done so. I was a horrid frump."

"Yes," he agreed, sensing that honesty would get him further with her than declarations of instant attraction. "But you forget, I held you close when you bumped into me. Did you think I didn't notice the curves beneath that baggy gown?" He more than noticed now. He was on fire with the knowledge of what lay hidden beneath a few layers of fabric. And tempted by the insane urge to lay her down right there on the stairs. "Why *did* you disguise your beauty?"

Her lashes lowered slightly. "I wanted to look older, more matronly. I wouldn't have been hired otherwise."

Clinging to his neck, she stole a wary glance at him. "Do you really find me pretty?"

With any other female, the question would have been a bid for praise. But Clara spoke with the wistfulness of someone who doubted reality. Her unusual strength of character made her vulnerability all the more winsome. Once again, that sweet constriction gripped his chest—and it seemed to have risen to his throat, too, for his voice turned husky. "*Pretty* is far too tame a word for you, Clara. Flowers are pretty. The moon is pretty. But you . . . you're the most gorgeous woman I've ever known."

For a moment, she appeared gratified by his compliment. Then she ducked her head and stared at his shirt. "Thank you."

"You don't believe me."

"Superlatives are seldom believable," she said, sounding like a governess. "But pray don't think me unappreciative . . . oh, never mind. It doesn't matter."

"Yes, it does matter." Simon felt compelled to convince her of his sincerity. Reaching the top of the stairs, he bore her down the corridor and into the darkened bedchamber. There, he set her down gently and shaped his hands around her face. "You fascinate me, Clara. You're a magnificent woman—*my* woman. Make no mistake about that."

She gave him an intent look. "Then you're mine, too."

His heart soared—although if any other of his mistresses had said that, he'd have ushered her straight to the front door. "Hold that thought, darling. I'm off to fetch the lamp."

Simon had to force himself to leave her. It was downright painful to withdraw his hands from the softness of her skin. But he refused to make love to her under a shroud of darkness. He wanted to see every inch of her flesh, to watch her face come alive with passion, to revel in the glow of her ecstasy.

Spurred by erotic fantasy, he raced out of the chamber and back down the stairs. He seized the lamp and mounted the steps, taking them two at a time. That familiar, illogical fear dogged his heels.

Clara would be gone. She would disappear, leaving him with the cold comfort of his dreams.

When he reached the bedchamber, sharp relief bolted him to the threshold. She stood facing the bed. In the moonlit shadows, her figure was tall and slender, her posture erect.

She had removed her pelisse. Her arms gracefully raised, she worked at the buttons at the back of her slim-fitting blue gown. The sight held him transfixed.

She cast a shy look over her shoulder. "I'm having a bit of trouble. Would you help me, please?"

Simon almost dropped the lamp in his haste. He kicked the door shut, sprang forward, and deposited the lamp on the bedside table. "It would be my pleasure. In truth, I was looking forward to undressing you myself."

Clara instantly lowered her arms. "Oh! I'm sorry. I didn't think . . ."

Why did she sound so surprised? Had she never known the enjoyment of shared disrobing? Her husband must have been truly inept in the bedchamber, Simon thought, rejoicing at his own good luck. If she was innocent in some ways, she'd be all the more susceptible to his seduction.

But at the moment, he felt inept himself. He was all thumbs, fumbling with a simple task. Somehow, he managed to wrest open the back of her gown. As he delved inside to circle her waist, he felt as short of breath as a randy youth fondling his first girl.

He pulled Clara flat against him, his mouth buried in the fragrance of her hair. No doubt, the scent of lavender would arouse him for the rest of his life. Despite the impediment of her shift and corset, his fingers climbed a path up her abdomen to tease the undersides of her breasts.

Tilting her head back, she buried her face in the crook of his neck, her breath warm and ragged. Her hand reached up to stroke his jaw. "Touch me, Simon. Please touch me."

The raw need in her voice sent him to the verge of explosion. The powerful reaction chagrined him. If he didn't maintain his control, he'd embarrass himself—and they were both still fully clothed.

Slow down. Slow . . . down.

By force of willpower, he subdued his own needs. He worshiped at the altar of her breasts, devoting himself with the zeal of a celebrant. The globes fit his adoring palms to perfection, and the tips jutted against the stiffness of whalebone and linen. He traced reverent circles there while Clara sighed and moved sinuously.

As she brushed against him, his erection strained and throbbed, demanding release. But Simon kept the tyrant safely buttoned up. At the moment, he was determined to make the act memorable for Clara.

He drew the pins from her hair, one by one. The rich dark mass tumbled down to her waist. It was a sight he had imagined, but reality was so much finer. Leaving her gown on, he untied the lacings of her corset and slid his hands inside her undergarments. Her skin felt warm and soft as he touched her hidden places for the first time.

"How can you not know how beautiful you are?" he whispered against her ear. "You're flawless, and I've dreamed about touching you. Here"—he cradled her naked breasts—"and here"—he followed the indentation of her waist—"and here." He gave a feather-light brush to the juncture of her thighs so that she shuddered with yearning. "I've desired you since the moment we met. Scoff all you like, but it's the truth, Clara. I've never wanted a woman as much as I want you."

It *was* the truth, Simon realized in hazy surprise. He couldn't remember ever feeling as if his insides were tied into a knot. His groin, yes, but not his heart. He could imagine himself living with Clara, making love to her for the rest of his life.

He shut the door on that dangerous thought. The future could be decided later. Tonight was all that mattered.

"Oh, Simon. I've felt the same way about you. Would it be too forward of me to . . . ?"

Clara tugged at her gown like a woman possessed. Realizing he was obstructing her, Simon withdrew his hands from inside her garments. Her frantic state transmitted to him, and he abandoned his plan to undress her slowly, kissing every inch of her flesh along the way. Instead, he helped her strip, at the same time discarding his own clothing and letting everything fall to the floor.

When they stood naked by the bed, she made an anxious move to slip beneath the covers, but he held her back. "Wait. I want to look at you."

His hands on her shoulders, he gazed at the full breasts with their tight coral tips, the curve of her hips, the dark nest that guarded her entrance. She had long slender legs, trim ankles, and . . . hell, even her toes were adorable, curling into the thick blue rug. And her face . . . he couldn't imagine ever tiring of her lively features, the pert nose, the rare smiles, the deep blue eyes that could penetrate his very soul.

She was looking at him, too. Her gaze traveled over his shoulders and chest, moving downward to stop on the proud jut of his member. He wanted desperately for her to

touch him. But she didn't. She stared, briefly closed her
eyes, then stared again. In the golden glow of the lamp,
her cheeks were pink with discomfiture.

She drew a shaky breath. "Simon . . . I don't know if I
can . . ."

"You can. It's been a long time for you, that's all. Trust
me, darling."

As he spoke, Simon peeled back the coverlet and
pressed her down onto the cool white sheets. His body
settled over hers with such keen pleasure that a groan rose
from deep within his chest. Her eyes were a dark, sensual
blue, the lids half-closed. She sighed, a sound of needy
contentment.

He understood the dichotomy of her feelings—he too
felt both enervated and energized by the contact of flesh to
flesh. He kissed her again, long and deep, while he moved
slowly against her, reveling in the softness of her womanly
form. Ironically, now that he had her where he wanted, he
found the strength to hold his own desire at bay.

Especially when Clara touched him almost shyly. Her
fingertips ran lightly over his shoulders and biceps, exploring him with a curiosity that was highly stimulating.
She was eager and aroused, yet still somewhat reserved,
and he wanted her as primed and ready for the consum-
mation as he was.

A man could get drunk on the taste of her skin, he
thought, kissing a path downward over her throat. Breathing deeply of the fragrance between her breasts, he
rubbed his cheek against her, letting the beginnings of his
beard stimulate her. Then he applied himself to laving
one peak and blowing gently on her dampened flesh.

Moaning, Clara threaded her fingers into his hair.
When he laid his cheek against her bosom, he could feel
the swift beating of her heart. He shifted his attention to
the other nipple, already drawn into a tight bead. Taking

care not to frighten her, he moved his hand downward over the flatness of her belly and between her legs to ply her dampness with a feather-light touch.

With blessed swiftness, her breathing grew uneven and her hips undulated in the rhythm of love. Her thighs opened wide to encourage him. The sight of her arching on the bed, her eyes closed, her body taut and quivering, filled Simon with hard, driving need. She looked flushed and on the verge of climax—and so was he.

Bracing himself on his forearms, he plunged into her, met a barrier and breached it. Clara uttered a small fierce sound of pain, and when he would have paused in contrite confusion, she held him close, hooking her legs around his. Moaning his name, she rotated her hips, seating him more fully into the tight, silken heat of her inner depths.

The floodwaters of passion eroded his control. He lost himself in the exquisite friction of their joined bodies. Clara's desire mounted to a feverish height—he made certain of that—and he took fierce pleasure in watching the joy on her face as she tumbled into ecstasy, crying out his name. In one mighty thrust, he emptied his seed into her. The explosion was so powerful his entire body trembled. Drained of strength, he collapsed on top of her.

On top of Clara.

A bone-deep contentment radiated outward to his fingers and toes. The feeling was far richer than anything he'd ever experienced. It was happiness, Simon realized vaguely. He wanted to lie here with Clara forever, his face nestled in her hair, their damp bodies still joined.

Then he remembered.

He disengaged himself and sat up.

Clara rolled onto her side. She smiled up at him with a sweet adoration that should have made him flush with pride. The beauty of her supple form should have lured him back on the road to arousal.

But his attention was occupied elsewhere. Her movement had revealed a rusty splotch on the white sheets.

The shock of disbelief sucked the warmth from him. "A virgin. Dammit, Clara, you were a virgin!"

"Can one desire too much of a good thing?"
—*As You Like It*, IV:i

Chapter Twenty-one

Simon's thundering tone struck away the haze of bliss surrounding Claire. In her vulnerable state, she could only stare up at him. Conscious of her nakedness, she scooted up against the pillows and yanked the covers over the telltale spot and up to her chin.

Why had she so foolishly thought Simon wouldn't realize the truth?

Because she hadn't thought at all. Once he'd kissed her, she had changed into a mindless creature of sensuality. She had completely forgotten that he was a nobleman—and the enemy.

She could easily forget now, too. Her body hummed with the aftermath of pleasure. Never had she dreamed that intimacy with a man could be so amazingly wonderful.

He glowered at her. Clearly, he was waiting for her confession. Gathering the tatters of her dignity, Claire lifted her chin. "Yes, it's true. But I had a reason—"

"And it had damned well better be a good one."

"I *won't* explain if you curse at me," she snapped.

A muscle worked in Simon's jaw. He raked his fingers through his hair, further mussing the dark strands and making him heartbreakingly handsome. When he spoke, his voice was taut, controlled. "Forgive me."

Claire swallowed dryly. With the lamplight gleaming on his broad chest and rumpled black hair, he looked so strong and capable that she wanted to throw herself on his mercy, confess the truth about Papa, and beg for his help. How she despised all the lies!

But Simon had taken that note. He had hidden it from the law. He had left it downstairs, out of her reach. He must be protecting someone—the real Wraith.

Looking him in the eye, she walked a tightrope between truth and falsehood. "I'm destitute, and I needed the post at Warrington House. I already told you, it was necessary for me to appear matronly, or I wouldn't have been hired as a chaperone."

"So you aren't a grieving widow. Your husband didn't die at Waterloo. You've never even been married."

Simon's blunt assessment made her want to curl up into a self-protective ball. Was he hurt by her dishonesty? Or simply infuriated that she had duped him?

Whatever the case, she yearned to reach out and hold him in her arms. But he looked far too forbidding. "I'm sorry," she murmured. "You can't imagine how much. But please try to understand my situation. I didn't dare tell anyone the truth for fear of losing my position."

"You might have told *me*."

"I was afraid you might turn me away—because I lack the skill of your other women. I couldn't have borne that. You see, I—I wanted to experience life to the fullest. With *you*, Simon. I've never been tempted by any other man."

The words poured from Claire in a rush of sincerity. He needn't know that in her work as a teacher at a school for girls, she met very few men. Or that she had agreed to be his mistress for the sole purpose of stealing that note.

No, not the sole purpose. She would have come up to his bedchamber regardless. Because somehow her feelings for Simon had grown too rich and deep to resist.

His face remained blank. "Is Clara Brownley your real name?"

Startled, she spoke quickly. "Yes. Why would you doubt me?"

"One falsehood can breed others. Maybe you hoped to trap me into marriage."

"No!" The horrified denial burst from her. "I would never do that."

"The world is full of women who would trick a rich nobleman into wedlock." He settled his hand over the covers, at the juncture of her thighs. "Though they usually don't take the ruse quite so far as you did."

The pressure of his hand caused an untimely shock of desire. But at the same time, she felt sick with hurt—and anger. Could he really believe her so greedy? That she would give him the gift of her maidenhood in exchange for material gain and social status?

His hard expression confirmed it. The joy of their union died a bitter death. How quickly she had forgotten that her warm, loving Simon was also the arrogant Earl of Rockford.

She rolled out of bed, yanked the covers along with her, and returned his haughty glare. "You may fall to your knees and beg, my lord, but I'd never be your wife. It was a mistake for me to come here. I won't trouble you any longer."

Turning her back, Claire reached for her undergarments. The spurt of temper vanished, and her throat tightened. It was her own fault for lying to him, but he had secrets, too—that note, for one. After the closeness they had shared, how could he think her so mercenary?

And how could she still want him so desperately?

Dropping the counterpane, she pulled the shift over her head. The tingling between her legs served as a reminder of that marvelous coupling. She felt on the verge of noisy sobbing, and wouldn't *that* make him think she was angling for sympathy?

Gritting her teeth, she turned her mind to securing that paper, perhaps by sneaking into his office on her way out. Simon was a gentleman, and no matter how livid he was, he'd want to see her home safely. But she'd refuse his company and—

His arms enfolded her from behind. His unique aroma of spice and leather surrounded her. He had moved without making a sound.

She stiffened against the powerful lure of his hard body. Her mind went blank to all but the way his palms were flattened low on her abdomen. Only a thin layer of linen prevented him from touching her flesh. All the foolish, reckless passion came flooding back, weakening her knees and wreaking havoc with her pride.

His warm breath fanned her neck. "Tonight wasn't a mistake, Clara," he said gruffly. "Don't go. Stay with me."

She couldn't—she shouldn't. If they continued the affair, he would discover the whole truth. Very soon, he—along with the rest of the world—would find out that her father was Gilbert Hollybrooke. It was best to make a clean break. *Now*.

Instead, her vision blurred. She closed her eyes tightly, but the moisture defied her best efforts and slid in hot silence down her cheeks.

Simon rotated her to face him. With one hand, he tilted up her jaw. With the other, he wiped away her tears.

"Don't weep, darling, please don't." The words sounded wrenched from him. "I'm sorry—I shouldn't have been so mistrustful."

But you should be mistrustful. You should be.

"I don't want your wealth." She spoke fiercely to his bare chest with its matting of dark hairs over sculpted muscles. "I don't care about your rank, either. I would far rather you were a shopkeeper or a servant . . . or . . . or even a rubbishman."

"Not a rubbishman. Only think of the smell. You might never allow me near you again."

His unexpected levity drew her eyes to his face, where a lopsided grin melted away her defenses. She was left with the weakness of yearning . . . and a sweet ache that could only be love. Her heart swelled with the newness of it. The feeling was so pure and intense that it outshone even her doubts and fears.

A tremulous smile fought its way onto her lips. Slipping her arms around his lean waist, she stood on tiptoes to rub her cheek against his, relishing the rasp of his skin on hers. "I don't really want you to change, Simon. You're wonderful just the way you are."

He made a sound deep in his chest, then held her close for a long, lingering kiss. They returned to the bed and for a very long time communicated only in sighs and whispers and, eventually, the cries of glorious passion. Afterward, she lay replete in his arms, treasuring the gentle stroke of his fingers on her hair.

A clock ticked softly on the mantelpiece, a relentless reminder of reality. She would wait until Simon fell asleep before making her escape. But her eyelids were so very heavy. Claire let them drop, promising herself she'd rest for only a few minutes.

But when she opened her eyes again, bright morning

sunlight streamed through a crack in the draperies. And Simon was gone.

He sat alone in the breakfast room, drinking coffee and finishing a hearty plate of bacon and eggs. A vast satisfaction filled him in body and spirit. When Mrs. Bagley had delivered his food, Simon had rewarded her with an uncustomarily cheerful grin.

He couldn't remember ever feeling so happy the morning after a tryst. In fact, he rarely stayed the night here, preferring to return home rather than share the intimacy of slumber.

Until Clara.

It had been an amazing pleasure to awaken at dawn with her warm body spooned into his. He had lain there for a long time, aroused but content to watch her sleep. Everything about Clara fascinated him, the curl of her dark lashes, the faint dusting of freckles on her arms, the slow rise and fall of her breasts. He had been tempted to kiss her awake, to join their bodies while she hovered in that dreamy state between sleep and awareness. With her sensual nature, she would have thoroughly enjoyed the experience.

But he had restrained himself. Clara was just as likely to leap out of bed and insist upon returning to Warrington House at once. She was a strong, independent woman, and stubbornly determined to labor for a pittance rather than accept the role of his mistress. Her scorn for his wealth and title intrigued him. And made him all the more determined to lift her out of a life of drudgery.

So he had left her asleep. The hour had already been too late for her to leave, he'd reasoned. Clara would simply have to accept her new life with him.

So why the devil did he feel a twinge of guilt?

"Your newspaper, m'lord."

Simon glanced up to see the gangly form of his manservant. Hiram Bagley was as wiry as his wife was stout. He had curly salt-and-pepper hair, a beak nose, and a strong sense of loyalty and discretion.

Setting down his fork, Simon took the newspaper and gave a nod of thanks. "It looks to be a fine morning. Why don't you and Mrs. Bagley take the day off? Go to the shops or to the park."

Then Simon and Clara would have the house to themselves. Undoubtedly, they would quarrel when she awakened to discover the lateness of the hour. It would take a considerable effort to smooth her ruffled feathers. But he would enjoy the aftermath. They could make love anywhere they fancied, on the hearth rug in the drawing room or in the upstairs passageway or—*yes*—on the desk in his study.

"Thank ye, m'lord. I'll go and tell the missus at once." Bagley's manner was respectful. But as he walked away, his blue eyes twinkled with understanding.

Simon found himself grinning like a fool. A fool in love. *Was* he in love?

He was seriously in *lust,* that much was certain. Maybe because Clara had been a virgin, he felt intensely protective of her. Yet those powerful feelings had ruled him even before he'd seen the proof on the sheets. Her lie had been a punch in the gut. He had been wild with the fear that she had played him for a fool. Not his Clara. She was principled, considerate, and delightfully impudent.

You may fall to your knees and beg, my lord, but I'll never be your wife.

Hell, why *not* marry her?

Like the warmth of her embrace, the notion wrapped around him. Clara deserved better than to be a kept woman. She had been less than forthcoming about her background, yet he felt certain she had been raised a lady.

His family already liked her. She would be a fine mother, too—and she might already be pregnant with his child. The thought deepened the tenderness inside him.

Clara would resist him, of course. She valued her autonomy. But he greatly looked forward to changing her mind.

Satisfied with his decision, Simon poured himself another cup of coffee and settled back to read the newspaper. One headline in particular caught his attention. It was a story on the robbery at Havenden House.

The reminder slapped him in the face. Bloody hell! He'd been so distracted that he'd forgotten all about the quotation. It put an irksome wrinkle in his plans for the day. Somehow, he had to find time to go to Bow Street Station and show that note to the magistrate. But not before Clara awakened. If he left now, she might be gone when he returned.

She *would* be gone. He knew her too well.

He scanned the article. The first paragraph accurately recounted the incident and described the missing necklace. The second one, however, slammed into him like a load of bricks.

> Does the Wraith have an accomplice? According to the magistrate at Bow Street Station, the only daughter of the infamous Gilbert Holly-brooke is being sought for questioning in the Havenden burglary. Over a fortnight ago, Miss Claire Hollybrooke abandoned her position as Instructress of Literature at the Canfield Academy in Lincolnshire. Her whereabouts are presently unknown. A reward of twenty pounds sterling is being offered for information leading to her apprehension. She is a tall female, five-

and-twenty years of age, with dark brown hair
and piercing blue eyes . . .

Claire scrambled out of the large four-poster bed. She
glanced at the clock on the marble mantelpiece and
moaned. Nearly eight.

Dear heavens, she would lose her position!

Throwing on her clothes, she tried not to panic. Rosabel always slept late, especially after a ball. And in the
message to Lady Hester yesterday evening, Claire had
claimed to be ill. It was possible—just possible—that no
one had noticed her absence today.

But Lord Warrington expected her in the library at
eight. What if he sent a footman to find her? She would
have to come up with a plausible excuse—perhaps that
she had been quietly sewing in Rosabel's dressing room.
Yes, that would do the trick.

Then another scenario made her giddy with fear. What
if she were caught sneaking in the back door in her wrinkled ballgown? What explanation could she give for *that*?

Her heart pounded, and Claire leaned against the bedpost while she took several deep gulps of air to calm herself. Breathe in, breathe out. It was something she made
her pupils do before they took exams.

The dizziness cleared from her head, unfortunately
making her aware of the tender ache between her legs. Instead of organizing her thoughts, she found herself flush
with the memory of her extraordinary night with Simon.

Oh, why hadn't he awakened her? And where was he
now? Had he gone out?

Had he destroyed that note?

A sense of purpose drove her. She had no time to fret
about her job. The first order of business was to check his
study and see if his coat was still there.

Claire made a desultory effort to smooth her gown, stepped into her slippers, and collected the scattered pins from the rug. On her way out of the bedchamber and down the corridor, she arranged her hair in a haphazard pile at the back of her head. Tiptoeing down the broad staircase, she felt a rise of hope at seeing the door to the study was still closed.

But maybe Simon was inside.

Instead of alarm, a shiver of anticipation rippled through her. Would he kiss her again, invite her back upstairs to make love?

She banished the errant longing. Her time with Simon was over—it had to be. If, by the grace of God, she managed to squeak out of her present dilemma, she must never take such a risk again.

As she stepped onto the marble floor of the foyer, the delicious smells of coffee and bacon drifted from down the corridor. Was he eating breakfast? If so, she might have a chance.

Her skin prickling with tension, Claire silently crossed the elegant hall with its tall white columns. Without knocking, she slipped into the study and closed the door behind her.

The room was vacant. Morning light streamed past the opened venetian blinds, illuminating the walls of books and the cozy green chairs. The scent of leather bindings perfumed the air.

She rushed to the desk. To her vast relief, the dark gray coat and cravat lay draped over the chair, exactly as he'd left them the previous night. But instead of looking for the note, Claire found herself burying her nose in the fine cloth, inhaling the spicy masculine aroma of Simon. A strange reluctance to find out the truth ached inside of her. She could leave right now, walk out the front door.

And then her father might be sentenced to death.

Resolutely, she opened the front of the coat. There were two pockets in the lining of smooth, dark blue silk. The first one was empty, but the other held something crinkly.

The note.

Other than that, the pocket was empty. She could have sworn Simon had picked up something else, too, a small object from beneath Lady Havenden's bed. But it was gone now, so Claire concentrated on the note.

Her heart thumped madly. With trembling fingers, she unfolded the paper. It held a message neatly penned in block letters.

Words without thoughts never to heaven go.

Her shaky knees gave way, and she collapsed into the chair. Her mind automatically supplied the source of the quotation. *Hamlet*, Act III, Scene Three. She had her class study that play every year. Her father had devoted a chapter of his book to Hamlet as a hero.

So the Wraith really *had* struck again. Her mind whirled with unanswered questions. Why topple the elaborate scheme to put the blame on Papa? Why would Lord Warrington orchestrate another robbery if it would exonerate her father?

Words without thoughts never to heaven go.

What did the Wraith mean by it? And why had Simon kept the note? Why had he not turned it over to the Bow Street Runner?

Her stomach rolled with queasiness. Simon had to be protecting the true identity of the Wraith.

Then another thought arrowed straight into her breast. Maybe *Simon* was the Wraith. Maybe he'd left the note, then changed his mind.

Preposterous. Her heart summarily rejected the wild speculations of her mind. Desperation must be playing games with her imagination.

And yet . . .

There was something secretive about Simon. He had a way of creeping up on her without making a sound. He had gone to Newgate Prison yesterday—to visit Papa. Had he been intending to gloat at his success? Then last evening, he had appeared upstairs at Havenden House, claiming to be looking for Claire. Had he stolen the emeralds and secreted them somewhere, intending to collect them later?

Madness. The theory was sheer, utter lunacy. She couldn't believe it of the man who had been her perfect lover.

Yet for Papa's sake, she could leave no stone unturned. Subduing her qualms about invading Simon's privacy, she opened the top drawer of his desk and searched through a miscellany of pens and inkpots. He didn't have a cache of stolen jewels, thank heavens. Nor did his blank stationery match the paper used by the Wraith. Two more drawers yielded nothing out of the ordinary.

But the bottom drawer was locked.

Claire tried to think where he would keep the key. Nearby, where it would be handy. She checked the other drawers again, reaching all the way into the farthest corners. No luck.

She peeked beneath the blotter. Empty.

Looking around, she spied a carved wooden box sitting within arm's reach on a bookshelf. She opened it—and there lay a small, shiny key.

Quickly, she inserted it in the lock and opened the drawer. But there were only orderly packets of paper with writing on them, each neatly bound with string.

Picking up the topmost pile, Claire untied it and looked through the papers. They appeared to be notes of some sort, pages and pages of detailed writings in Simon's hand. A weight lifted from her as she realized that his penmanship was firmer and more precise than the author of that note.

Then her sense of relief vanished.

Leafing through the papers, she found herself gazing down at a list of Shakespearean quotations.

> "The game is up."
> —*Cymbeline*, III:iii

Chapter Twenty-two

Angry disbelief spurred Simon upstairs to the bedchamber. But the big four-poster was empty, the covers rumpled, the pillows in disarray. Only a single hairpin glinted on the rug as evidence that Clara had been here.

Claire, he grimly corrected himself. *Claire Hollybrooke.*

The pain of her lies clawed at his chest. How had she duped him—and everyone else? And why the devil had she taken a post in Warrington House? Did she intend to rob her own grandfather?

He choked on an extension of that thought. *She was Warrington's granddaughter.*

He surged out of the bedroom and back down the stairs. She couldn't have been gone for long. He would catch up to her before she reached Warrington House. He'd haul her straight back here—

His gaze flashed to the door of his study. The note. Had she seen him put it into his pocket yesterday evening?

On the drive here, she had been nervous, edgy. Later, she had been distressed when he'd shed his coat and left it on the chair.

She must have slept with him in order to steal that note. But *why*? What did it mean to her?

In a black rage, he made a sharp detour across the foyer. With instinctive caution, he quietly opened the door.

Clara—Claire—was sitting at his desk.

For an instant, his fury dropped away and he felt a dizzying clutch of emotion. She had the look of a woman who had been thoroughly loved. In the morning light, her skin had a radiant glow. Feathery tendrils escaped the slapdash arrangement of her dark hair. Her breasts were mounded above the low blue bodice.

And she was engrossed in rifling through his desk. His files were strewn over the mahogany surface. She must be intending to steal all the information he had collected on the Wraith.

Simon stood stunned. How the devil had she guessed about his secret work with Bow Street?

Any last hope that he was mistaken about her vanished in a wintry blast of disillusionment. By God, she was even more cunning and devious than her father.

"Miss Hollybrooke."

She started. Her head jerked up. Her lips were parted in surprise, and her gorgeous blue eyes made him feel as if he were drowning. Damn her for looking so beautiful!

Damn himself for wanting to make love to her again.

He stalked forward and flattened his palms on the desk. "Nothing to say, darling? You ought to have your denial ready since you're so adept at lying."

Her gaze wavered, but only for an instant. As prim as a princess, she sat up straight in the chair. *His* chair. "How did you find out?"

"This morning's newspaper carried a report about you. Miss Claire Hollybrooke has gone missing. She's being sought for her possible role in the Havenden burglary."

And Simon was going to strangle the magistrate for not informing him of that little tidbit.

Claire had gone pale. "*What?* Why would they think that I—"

"The apple doesn't fall far from the tree, Miss Hollybrooke."

Her lips compressed into a thin line. "Oh? Well, it was *you* who took the Shakespearean quote that was left beneath Lady Havenden's jewel box. How do you explain the fact that the Wraith has struck again?"

Simon had a theory in mind, all right. A diabolically clever one. It made him so restless that he prowled the length of the study before returning to voice it. "You stole Lady Havenden's necklace. And you left the quotation. You wanted to spring your father from prison by making everyone believe that the wrong man had been captured."

"That's ridiculous!"

Ignoring her, he continued. "You saw me take the note, and you were angry that I'd foiled your plan. So you agreed to sleep with me. Because you guessed that I'm—" *With the Bow Street Runners. And I'm gathering a case against your father.*

Simon clamped his mouth shut. He couldn't explain it, but something felt out of kilter. For one, Claire looked appalled, as if he'd sprouted horns and a forked tail. Certainly, she was a brilliant actress, but . . . what if she didn't know about his work? What other possible reason could she have for wanting that note back?

It couldn't be that she feared he'd pass it on to the authorities because that would only fit into her scheme.

"You're right, I did suspect the truth about you," she said heatedly. "At first, when I saw you pocket the note, I thought you were merely protecting the real Wraith. After all, you aristocrats stick together. Why would you care if an innocent man is put to death so long as you keep one of your own kind out of prison?"

Her lies made him livid. "At least now I can understand your resentment of the nobility. You learned it at your father's knee."

She sprang to her feet. Leaning across the desk, she jabbed her finger at Simon's face. "Don't you dare speak a single harsh word against my father! You of all men!"

No woman, not even his sisters, had ever provoked him to the verge of violence. He stared coldly until she withdrew her finger. "I believe you have the wrong villain in this story, Miss Hollybrooke."

"Rather, I've finally found the right one." With jerky movements, she gathered the papers into a pile. "It was blessed providence that I found these papers in your desk."

"I'd call it burglary."

"And I'd call it proof that my father isn't the Wraith. *You* are."

Incredulous, Simon thought at first he'd misheard her. Then he threw back his head and laughed. "I've heard some outrageous lies in my time, but that one is the work of a virtuoso."

Claire didn't look amused in the least. Picking up the papers, she tapped them on the desk to make the edges straight. "You may laugh all you like, my lord. But you have a list of the quotations in here. You have floorplans of the houses where the robberies took place. You have detailed descriptions of every piece that was stolen."

Watching her retie the string around the papers, he frowned. "What the devil do you think you're doing?"

"I'm taking the evidence to the magistrate at Bow Street. These papers will prove my father's innocence once and for all."

He chuckled again. She truly must not know he was a Runner—because Thomas Cramps would find her *evidence* highly amusing.

Holding the packet, she marched past him, and Simon seized her arm. "Don't you think you're carrying the charade a bit too far, Miss Hollybrooke?"

"Remove your hand. Or I'll scream bloody murder."

"Go ahead, but the Bagleys aren't here to rescue you. I've given them the day off." He doubted they'd left yet, but she didn't know that. Menace in his voice, he added, "And you aren't going anywhere with my file."

Claire clutched the papers in a white-knuckled grip. Unexpectedly, she flinched, her shoulders hunched and her eyes wide with fright. "Don't hurt me. Please don't."

Her cringing manner disconcerted him. The trembling of her body gave him a twist of self-disgust.

Did she really think he would strike a woman?

He loosened his fingers slightly. "I assure you, all I want is my—"

Pain exploded up his leg as she jammed her foot down hard on his instep. At the same instant, she wrenched herself free and made a dash for the door. He dove after her and brought her down in a flying leap, locking his arms around her body and cushioning her fall.

The impact jarred his teeth and hammered his shoulder. Ignoring the discomfort, he rolled quickly and caught Claire beneath him. She lay on her stomach, the papers beneath her. She twisted and squirmed, but between the weight of his body and tangle of her skirts, he had her trapped. Nevertheless, she thrashed futilely, panting with effort, stubborn to the core.

Simon was breathing hard, too. And it wasn't from exertion. Or fury—though he cursed himself for not anticipating her ploy.

It was her soft body that starved him of air. Despite her treachery, he still felt a powerful, mind-swaying lust. Her every movement caused a tantalizing friction against his groin. It made him remember the glory of being inside her.

He wanted her to remember, too.

Bending to her ear, he spoke softly, seductively. "Clara . . . darling . . . I wouldn't advise you to wriggle quite so much."

She went instantly still. Over her shoulder, she flashed him a bitter look of loathing. "Craven toad. If you try to force me, I'll bloody your face. I'll tear off your . . . your man parts."

Simon didn't know whether to chuckle or grimace. No doubt she'd follow through with her threat. Not that he would give her cause. What kind of man did she think he was? "If you promise to hand me those papers, I'll get off you."

She lay silent a moment, no doubt struggling with her pride. Then she ground out, "As you wish, my lord."

Simon didn't intend to grow gray hair waiting for a more docile response. He eased off her at once, but crouched on his haunches, ready to spring. Claire untwisted her skirts and sat up. Her hair had come undone on one side, a long, dark strand cascading down her shoulder and curling around her breast. He tried not to stare hungrily.

His notes on the Wraith lay on the carpet, amazingly still tied together in a bundle. He could have picked them up himself. But he extended his hand instead.

Claire glowered. Then she seized the packet and thrust it at him.

"You can take the evidence, but you can't stop me from going to Bow Street," she said fiercely. "I'll tell them everything, and they'll investigate you. Maybe you're rich and powerful, but you'll have made some mistake. They'll find it, and my father will go free."

Good God. Was she sticking to that overblown story? Did she still think she could play him for a fool?

"Walk into Bow Street Station, and you'll be the one arrested."

She blanched, though one eyebrow arched in disdain. "I'd sooner take my chances there than with *you*."

He didn't understand her persistence. She had to know the game was up. Just as *he* knew she must have committed the heist herself. It was the most logical solution to the mystery of the Wraith's reappearance. He ought to take her into custody and escort her to Bow Street for arraignment.

But the thought of Claire confined to a prison cell made his gut clench. He couldn't shake the uneasy instinct that he was missing a key piece to the puzzle.

If she didn't know he was a Runner, then why *had* she come after the note he'd found? Why not simply let him give it to the authorities? That would have suited her plan to free her father by proving the Wraith was still on the loose. And why had she searched his desk? If she'd been seeking valuables, what had induced her to read through his files?

A more painful dilemma badgered him. If Claire Hollybrooke was a deceitful schemer, why had she made love to him with such heartfelt tenderness? Why had she looked at him with stars in her eyes and given him the gift of her virginity?

The powerful ache to hold her close threatened to overwhelm him. Angry at his own softness, Simon jumped to his feet. He wanted to drive his fist through the wall. He offered a hand to her instead.

Naturally, she ignored him and rose on her own power. She gave him a final, challenging stare before turning her back and walking to the door. A webwork of wrinkles marred the dark blue ballgown. Despite her dishevelment, she moved with the innate grace of a lady.

How dared she pretend *he* was the one in the wrong?

Intensely frustrated, he called out, "There's only one problem with your scheme, Miss Hollybrooke. I'm a wealthy man. I've no gaming debts and no motivation to steal jewels."

Her fingers on the doorknob, she turned, her chin high. "Then perhaps you're helping someone else. I'll be at my father's trial next week. I'll tell the judge that you found the quotation in Lady Havenden's chamber. I'll make him summon you as a witness."

By God, he ought to call her bluff and let her do just that. But what if he was wrong about her? Claire would have the shock of her life when she walked into that courtroom.

Fool that he was, he couldn't be so cruel to her.

"I'll be there already," he said grimly.

"I beg your pardon?"

"I have this file for a legitimate purpose. I work under-cover for Bow Street. No one knows that—not even my family. Unfortunately, all that will change when I testify in court as a witness for the prosecution." Slapping the papers down onto the desk, he steeled himself for her re-action. If she didn't already loathe him enough, he'd give her cause for undying hatred. "You see, Miss Holly-brooke, I'm the man who arrested your father."

Claire returned to Warrington House through a side door that led past the butler's pantry. Hearing the clink of ac-tivity within, she hastened past, keeping her head down and casting a glance from the corner of her eye. The long, narrow room was a beehive of activity, with an army of footmen polishing a mountain of silver under the stern di-rection of the aging butler.

She had forgotten about the masquerade ball for Ros-abel's eighteenth birthday. It was only three days away. And maybe, with all the bustle of preparation, no hue and cry had been raised over Lady Rosabel's missing companion.

Claire slipped unnoticed into the servants' staircase.

She felt no sense of relief, only numbness. Her feet were leaden, every step an effort up an endless slope to her tiny bedchamber in the attic. She needed to change into something more appropriate for the day. Only then could she seek refuge in Rosabel's chamber. While her cousin slept, Claire could sit undisturbed in the darkness of the dressing room. But instead of mending ripped hems, she'd try to repair her shattered heart.

Simon had arrested Papa. Next week, he would give testimony under oath that would send her father to the gallows. The horror of his revelation resonated like the muffled clappers of a funeral bell.

Simon, a Bow Street Runner. It seemed impossible in light of his high rank—and yet it made terrible sense. She thought back to his habit of moving stealthily. His mysterious appearance at Newgate Prison. The way he had examined Lady Havenden's bedchamber with the efficiency of an expert. His furtive act of slipping the quotation into his pocket.

Claire shuddered. Of course he had laid claim to the evidence—he was the officer in charge of the case.

She could even hazard a guess as to why he practiced a profession that any other nobleman would have scorned. Lady Havenden had revealed that brigands had murdered his father and shot his mother. That act of violence must have driven Simon to devote his life to hunting criminals.

Under ordinary circumstances, Claire would have admired his dedication. Yet she could never forgive him for his bullheaded belief in her father's guilt.

She had attempted to argue Papa's case, but Simon had not a shred of sympathy for those who had broken the law. He had scoffed at her theory that Lord Warrington was the culprit. His mind was made up. He himself had gathered all the evidence, gone to her father's flat, and made the arrest.

Not even this most recent robbery had swayed him. Instead, he had blamed it on Claire. He had accused *her* of taking Lady Havenden's treasured emerald necklace. The icy condemnation in his eyes had frozen any last lingering warmth in her.

How she hated him!

How she ached for him, too.

Crippled by the pain of loss, Claire stopped at the top of the stairs to lean on the wooden railing. Memories inundated her. Last night, he had held her with such loving passion. He had kissed her and stroked her and taken her to heaven.

Now, on the basis of her real identity, he had tarred her as a villainess.

The only thing she couldn't fathom was why Simon hadn't taken her into custody, too. He had allowed her to leave on the warning that he would be watching her every move. Maybe he thought he could seduce her again.

He wouldn't succeed. Devil take him!

Fortified by righteous anger, Claire marched down the narrow corridor of the attic. The Wraith had to be someone in this house—most likely, her grandfather. If Simon was too mulish to help her, then she'd find the proof herself.

Another fear gripped her. What if her grandfather had read that article in the newspaper? What if he too made the connection and realized that Mrs. Clara Brownley was really his granddaughter?

Perhaps it would be prudent to stay out of his path for a day or two. There were other things to investigate, that safe in his bedchamber, for one. She must try to think of a way to sneak in there . . .

Opening the door to her tiny attic chamber, she strode inside. Only to see Rosabel curled up asleep in a pink dressing gown on the bed.

Claire froze. She mustn't be seen in this gown.

But it was too late.

Rosabel's drowsy blue eyes flew open. "Brownie, you're back!"

Springing up, she threw her arms around Claire, enveloping her in soft arms and a flowery scent. Their closeness caused an untimely heat against Claire's eyelids. More than anything, she longed to spill out her anguish and be comforted by a friend.

But she mustn't trust anyone in this house. Not even her cousin.

Forcing a wary smile to her lips, Claire stepped away. "What are you doing up here?"

"When I found out you'd fallen ill, I had to check on you as soon as we came home from the ball. But you weren't here—and I've been so very worried! Where have you been?"

Collecting her composure, Claire went to the tiny window and opened it, letting a brisk breeze into the airless room. She couldn't think of anything to do but turn the tables on Rosabel. "I was worried about *you* last evening," she said severely. "You were dancing with Mr. Newcombe, and then you disappeared. I looked all over Havenden House for you."

An appalling thought struck Claire. Had Rosabel been stealing the emerald necklace?

Her cousin had the secretive, satisfied look of a cat with cream on its whiskers. "I don't know why everyone goes on about Lewis," she said airily, plopping back down onto the narrow bed. "He's so much more fun than any of the other gentlemen."

"Lewis, is it? And exactly what sort of *fun* do you mean?"

The girl sat there, swinging her bare feet and eyeing Claire speculatively. "You're one to talk. You spent the night with Lord Rockford, didn't you?"

Alhough Claire fought against it, heat rose to her cheeks. "We were speaking of *you*."

"So you did stay with him. Was it lovely? Or is he a beastly dry stick of a lover?"

It was wonderful. The most marvelous experience of my life—until he found out the truth.

Claire resolutely focused her attention on her cousin. "That is no way for a young lady to talk."

"Oh, bother the rules. You must tell me everything. And I promise I won't let on to anyone about you and his lordship."

Claire prayed the girl would keep that vow. She sat down beside Rosabel, taking her hand and looking earnestly into her eyes. "Listen to me. Mr. Newcombe is a scoundrel and a gambler. If you continue to associate with him, I'm afraid you'll find yourself in serious trouble."

A woeful look came over Rosabel's doll-like features. "But *you're* the one who's in trouble, Brownie."

Claire's heart skipped a beat. "What do you mean?"

"That's what I came here to tell you. Mama suspects you went off with a man. I tried to plead your case, but she *knows*." Tears welled in Rosabel's china-blue eyes. "Oh, Brownie, I don't know how to say this but . . . you've been sacked."

"Now is the winter of our discontent."
—*King Richard III*, I:i

Chapter Twenty-three

Two days later, Claire was sitting at the desk in her father's tiny flat, studying the list of quotations for the umpteenth time, when an eerie tapping startled her.

She tensed, her pulse pounding. Looking up, she spied the source of the noise. Outside, the wind had loosened the rope that her next-door neighbor, Mrs. Underhill, used to hang her laundry. The rope slapped once more against the window near the bed; then another gust sent it whirling off into the rainy gray afternoon.

Blowing out a breath, Claire ordered herself to relax. She had to stop jumping at every sound. But she couldn't help feeling like a rabbit caught in a trap. Waiting for the hunter to appear.

The unfortunate state of her finances had prevented her from finding another place to live. And her father's flat was the most obvious place for the law—which meant Simon—to track her down. Ever since she'd found out about that description of her in the newspaper, she had been living in a state of suspense, terrified of being arrested for having committed the Havenden robbery.

She couldn't free Papa from inside a jail cell. And he had no knight in shining armor but her.

The only useful part about leaving Warrington House was that Claire had plenty of time on her hands. She had called on Mr. Mundy, but the naïve young barrister had found no new information to bolster the case. She had gone to visit her father twice, letting him believe that her grandfather had read that article and dismissed her.

And she had spent hours poring over the list of quotations.

Now, Claire propped her elbows on the desk and returned her attention to the paper in front of her. Each snippet was labeled with the name of a victim and the stolen jewelry associated with it. The list now included the passage that had been left beneath Lady Havenden's strongbox. Claire had studied each word in hopes of finding some hidden meaning. She had gone back to the plays where the quotes had originated and searched for clues in each scene. She had tried to find ways to interpret the quotes as coded messages sent by Lord Warrington to chastise her father.

Nothing had worked. The answer to the puzzle remained locked in the mind of the Wraith.

The days until her father's trial were vanishing like smoke. Less than a week remained, and Claire was no closer to unraveling the truth—in fact, matters had worsened. She was barred from her grandfather's house, forbidden access to the one place where she might have found the elusive proof.

Fighting despair, she went to make herself a cup of tea. It took a few minutes of patient work with the flint and tinder to light the spirit lamp. While the water heated, Claire gazed around the tiny flat and fiercely promised herself that Papa would be back. Soon he would be scribbling madly at his battered oak desk, stopping now and then to dip his pen in the inkpot. Or reading in his favorite brown chair by the hearth, the wire-rimmed spectacles perched on the tip of his nose.

Abruptly, her mind conjured up another picture: Simon, furious and formidable, dwarfing the place, intimidating her father. Simon would have been methodical in his search for the stolen jewels, peering under the narrow cot in the adjoining bedchamber where Claire now slept, moving the books on the shelves, lifting the lid of the chest where she kept a few spare articles of clothing for her visits here.

It enraged her to think of him handling her personal items, touching the pitcher and basin where Papa shaved each morning, bending down to look through the cabinet with its meager array of dishes. For all she knew, he had poked his finger in the sugar container or into the small wooden box that held Papa's tea.

Scowling, Claire scooped up a spoonful of leaves and sprinkled them into the brown crockery pot. Imagining Simon standing in this very spot unsettled her. He might have held this very spoon.

With the same fingers that had stroked her so tenderly.

In a rush, she was back in his bed, lying beneath him, their bodies joined and her heart filled with an amazing sense of oneness . . .

Her eyes swam with tears, but Claire savagely blinked them away. Better she should think about him invading the home of an innocent man. He was an arrogant aristocrat who would readily believe that Papa—kind, unassuming, good-natured Papa—would nurse a grudge against the nobility and steal their precious jewels. He had refused even to consider that Papa might have been the victim of an elaborate ruse.

She poured a cup of tea and marched back to the desk. In the bottom drawer, Simon had found his mother's diamond bracelet. Who had planted it there?

Had it been that odious valet, Oscar Eddison, here on orders from Lord Warrington? The notion made her fume.

When her mother was alive and writing to Lord Warrington every year, they had lived in a larger flat with two bedchambers in addition to a sitting room and study. After Mama's death, Claire and her father had found smaller quarters, and later, after Claire had taken the position at the Canfield Academy, he had moved to this little, two-room flat.

Had her grandfather kept track of Papa all these years? He must have.

Had he also kept track of Claire? She banished the pang in her throat. He was a mean, sour, despicable old man.

Rain tapped at the windows, a fitting backdrop for her dismal thoughts. The afternoon was growing dark, so she lit a tallow candle and set it on the desk. She wrapped her cold hands around the warmth of her cup, sipped the tea, and forced herself to think. Her father spent his days at the library, and no matter how she'd chided him about safety, he often forgot to lock the door. It would have been a simple matter for someone to watch him, to wait for the right moment to walk in here, take the grocery receipt, and leave the diamond bracelet.

On impulse, Claire put down her cup and slid open the bottom drawer. It squeaked a protest, but revealed its meager contents: a ream of plain paper, yellowed and discolored, the cheapest type offered by the stationer around the corner.

Transferring the paper to the top of the desk, she examined the empty drawer, reaching into the shadows at the back. To her amazement, she pulled out a small, folded note.

Her heart began to pound. Quickly, she opened the note. A single line made goose bumps prickle her skin.

Heaven hath a hand in these events.

Claire identified it at once. *Richard II,* Act V. And the penmanship belonged to the Wraith.

She didn't know whether to be joyful or to cry. Oh, why hadn't Simon found this message? It would have cast doubt on his case against her father! Now, if she told him, he would accuse *her* of planting it there.

He could rot on his sanctimonious pedestal for all she cared.

With a renewed sense of purpose, Claire added the passage to the others, inserting it above the one left at Havenden House. It was then, for some reason she couldn't explain, that a stunning observation caught her attention.

She quickly scanned the list. Her hands trembled with excitement. By the heavens, she was right. The first letter of each quotation matched the first letter of the next victim's last name.

It couldn't be a coincidence. Not eleven times.

Was it possible the quotes were anagrams? Had the Wraith hidden the name of his next target in each quotation he'd left?

Energized, she seized a piece of blank paper and set to work to test the theory. She had only begun on the first one when a knocking on the door penetrated her reverie.

The quill slipped from her nerveless fingers. In two days, she'd had no visitors. Not even Rosabel knew where she was staying.

Had Simon come to arrest her at last?

Claire swallowed hard. Her first impulse was to hide, but that would be an exercise in futility. Better she should hold her head high and get the ordeal over with and done.

Rising, she headed across the room to turn the key and open the door. Lifting her gaze to glare at Simon, she found herself staring at a tall black hat. She adjusted her eyes slightly downward to her visitor's pale blue eyes, thick sandy mustache, and receding jaw.

"Miss Hollybrooke," he said, removing his dripping hat.

"Mr. Grimes!" Claire hid a twinge of dismay. Though she itched to return to her task, it would be ungracious to leave her father's colleague standing on the stoop. "Do come in out of the rain."

Vincent Grimes stepped inside, bringing with him the smell of wet wool and expensive cologne. He hung his overcoat and hat on a hook by the door. He was dressed smartly in a dark green coat, an elaborate cravat, and tan pantaloons. "My dear, I'm relieved to see you're safe."

"I presume you read that article in the newspaper."

He took her hands in his. "Yes, and I was furious that those idiots at Bow Street would make such an accusation about *you*."

He really did appear angry. His lips were compressed and his eyes flashed in a way that made Claire realize he was an attractive man, rather like a drawing she had seen of the poet Lord Byron.

Although his concern touched her, she didn't care for his overly familiar manner. Especially since they were alone. Wresting her hands free, she said, "Thank you for believing in me." *At least someone did.*

"I'd have come sooner, but I thought you were staying with a friend. I saw the light of your candle as I was passing just now."

"Oh, I'm only here for a little while." To ward off the curiosity in his eyes, she quickly expanded on the fib. "I'm off shortly to return to my friend, but perhaps I could offer you a cup of tea."

He beamed a smile. "That would be most kind."

As Claire headed to the small table that held the teapot, a memory popped into her mind. Mr. Grimes had been at Havenden House. She had spied him leaving one of the bedchambers. In all the turmoil of her night with Simon, she had forgotten the incident.

Alarm made her fingers tighten around the brown mug. Was *Mr. Grimes* the Wraith? Did he carry some unknown grudge against Papa? Was the source of his newfound wealth not an inheritance, but thievery?

With effort, she kept her hand steady as she poured from the pot. No, Mr. Grimes had been leaving a room at the opposite end of the floor from Lady Havenden's. There had to be another explanation.

When she turned around, he was standing over the desk, looking at the list. "Oh, sorry," he said sheepishly, accepting the cup from her. "I hope you don't mind my prying, but are those the actual quotations left by the Wraith?"

"Yes. I was trying to make sense of them." Claire motioned him toward the unlit hearth. "Do sit down."

He waited respectfully for her to take one of the brown chairs before settling himself in the other. "Perhaps I could help you. My expertise is Elizabethan poetry, but I've read all of Shakespeare's plays."

Claire kept quiet about the anagrams. Her theory might be wrong, and she didn't want anyone looking over her shoulder.

Nor did she wish for Mr. Grimes to linger. "That's very generous of you. However, I'm in a bit of a rush, so perhaps another time."

"Oh, certainly." In a flustered manner, he took a quick gulp from his cup. "I only came to ask about your father. How is he bearing up?"

"As well as can be expected." Remembering Papa's thinness, she felt a lump choke her throat. "He's cheerful and keeps busy writing."

"Writing?" Mr. Grimes frowned. "Why, at a time like this, how can he manage to get his thoughts in order?"

"It's a way to keep his mind off his troubles." And Claire needed to distract herself, too, or she'd be bawling all over Mr. Grimes's dark green coat. "May I ask you a question?"

"Anything, my dear."

"I believe I may have seen you at a ball recently. It was at Havenden House."

His hand paused with the cup halfway to his lips. His eyebrows lifted in surprise. "Well, doesn't that beat all! Is your friend a member of society?"

"Yes. You *were* there, then."

He nodded rather self-consciously. "Remember my great-aunt, the one who left me the inheritance? I don't wish to be a braggart, but . . . she was a baroness and a dear friend of Lady Havenden's."

"Ah." So that explained it. In her anxiety, Claire was seeing ghosts and goblins in every shadow.

"Lady Havenden has been terribly distraught about her emerald necklace," he said, shaking his head. "But even worse, *you've* taken the blame. It can't be wise for you to be here. The Runners are sure to come looking for you."

"I won't be much longer, I hope."

Luckily, he took the hint and put down his cup. "Well, then, I shan't keep you." He donned his outerwear, then turned to look hopefully at her. "Might I offer you a ride to your friend's house?"

"Thank you, but someone is coming by very soon to fetch me." Heaven help her, she risked fire and brimstone for all the lying she'd done of late. "Good-bye, Mr. Grimes."

He went back out into the rain, and with a sigh of relief, Claire locked the door and returned to her father's desk. It had grown darker, and the candle created a little island of light over her papers.

She had scarcely picked up her pen and dipped it into the inkwell when a rapping on the door once again broke her concentration. Good grief. Mr. Grimes must have thought of another reason to disturb her peace. Arming herself with a well-bred smile, she opened the door.

Simon knew he had his work cut out for him when the corners of her mouth turned instantly downward. Despite the gathering dusk and her dowdy gray gown, there was no mistaking Claire for anything but a lady. She stood proudly, her chin lifted at a haughty tilt. She was the judgmental Mrs. Brownley again, and he hadn't realized just how starved he had been for the sight of her.

Or how intensely he still resented being duped by her.

"Have you come to arrest me, my lord?" she asked politely.

I'd like to give you a life sentence. "No. But I've some issues to discuss with you. May I come in?"

"As you wish." She stepped back, but her stiffly proper manner made it plain he wasn't welcome.

In the cramped confines of the flat, Simon shucked his greatcoat and dropped it on a chair, tossing his hat on top. He gritted his teeth to keep from lashing out like a jealous fool. That wasn't in his plan.

But having recognized the fancy black carriage parked out front, he'd been standing in the shadows of the neighboring building for the past fifteen minutes, rain dripping from the brim of his hat and trickling in icy rivulets down his coat.

"What's his name? The man who just left."

"Mr. Grimes? He's a friend of the family."

"You were with him once before." Simon remembered the day he'd happened upon them near Piccadilly Circus. It had been raining then, too, and Grimes had kissed her hand in a way that was anything but brotherly. She stood by the unlit hearth, and Simon advanced on her. "Is he your friend or your father's?"

She held her ground, one eyebrow arched in scorn. "Is

this an interrogation? Hadn't you best take me to Bow Street first?"

Frustrated, he ran his fingers through his wet hair. He had to get a hold on himself or he'd ruin his own scheme. "No. It's just that—dammit, I won't have any other man touching you."

At once, an aura of intimacy enclosed them. Maybe admitting the truth had been good, because Claire had that dreamy look in her eyes, a look that scorched his blood. It vanished in an instant, but he rejoiced to know he still had the power to invoke her desires.

He intended to use the knowledge to his own purpose.

She regarded him frigidly. "You would dare say that— after accusing me of stealing the Havenden emeralds?"

"That's why I came here—to apologize for leaping to the wrong conclusion the other day."

"Oh? What brought about this miraculous change?"

She folded her arms, her eyes narrowed with mistrust. But at least she was listening. "For one, you didn't know I was a Bow Street Runner. So naturally, when I took that note, you would think I was concealing evidence."

"Then who did steal the emeralds?"

A copycat. It had to be. "I don't know," he said honestly. "I've a team of men working on the problem at this very moment."

With a sniff, she walked to the window and back again. "Find the thief and you'll find the Wraith. And I would suggest you direct your search toward Warrington House."

Simon clenched his jaw. He was supposed to be placating her, but he couldn't ignore such a flagrant mistake. "I've known your grandfather for a long time, Claire. He's a strict, principled man. Even if he'd nursed a grudge all these years, he wouldn't have acted upon it."

"But my father would?" Abruptly, her mocking tone softened, and she took a step closer, her eyes large and intense. "Oh, Simon, you don't know Papa. He wouldn't steal a quill pen, let alone diamonds. Look at how he lives." She waved her arm around the tiny room. "If he'd truly taken all those jewels, then where is the money from selling them?"

"I've wondered that myself," Simon admitted. "I've questioned every pawnbroker and jeweler in the city to no avail. But the courts will place great heed on my mother's diamond bracelet being found here."

"By you." Claire eyed him speculatively. "And I'm beginning to wonder if you're the one with the vendetta."

"What do you mean?"

"Your father was killed by brigands and your mother seriously injured. Is that why you're so narrow-minded about criminals?"

His blood ran cold. Where had she heard about that? *How much did she know?* A wild fear gripped his chest in a vise. "That topic is forbidden. I won't discuss it with you."

Giving him a look of keen disappointment, Claire whirled away and stalked to the door. "I can see we're at an impasse, my lord. Unless you've something new to say . . ."

His heart thudded. Damn, he was ruining it, letting his temper get the best of him.

"Forgive me," he forced out. "I shouldn't have snapped at you. And there *is* something else. Something extremely important." Going to Claire, he took her resisting hands in his. And he voiced the words he couldn't imagine saying to any other woman. "Darling, will you do me the great honor of accepting my offer of marriage?"

Her lips parted in shock. Her skin turned pale. A lifetime passed before she said faintly, "Why? Why would you want to marry *me*?"

Because I need you. I love you. "Because you're Warrington's granddaughter, and I took your virginity."

Not the right words. What had happened to his finesse? His plan?

At once, Claire stepped away from him, walking to the center of the room to cross her arms and scowl. As if she regarded marriage to him as a fate worse than death. "My grandfather has never acknowledged me. And I gave myself freely. So you're released of any obligation."

Approaching her, Simon tried again. He placed his hands on her shoulders and lowered his voice to a husky murmur. "It's more than that, and you know it. I'm mad about you, Claire. You've fascinated me since the moment we met."

"You hardly know me."

"I know enough. We're well-matched, you and I. I can't imagine any other woman standing up to me the way you do."

"We'd quarrel."

"And have a glorious time making up in the bedchamber." He traced the outline of her lips, rejoicing when her eyes grew slumberous.

Thrusting his hand away, she stepped back, accusation on her face. "I can't live by your Countess Code. And I *won't* live with the man who has condemned my father to death."

Simon laid down his trump card. "If you marry me, Claire, I won't testify against him."

She stood very still, her enormous blue eyes fastened on his face. "You would vow that to me?"

"On my honor as a gentleman." Triumph leaped in Simon. He hadn't realized until that moment how afraid he had been of her refusal. Sliding his arm around her, he tenderly kissed her brow. "If that is a *yes,* then where is your coat? We must make haste."

"Haste?"

"I've procured a special license. We're getting married tonight."

She protested, but Simon was desperate to have her as his wife, now, before the trial turned her against him. He had no intention of giving her the chance to change her mind.

He also had no intention of telling her that his partner, Islington, had returned unexpectedly from the north of England. And that Islington would testify in Simon's place.

"My only love sprung from my only hate!
Too early seen unknown, and known too late!"
—*Romeo and Juliet*, I:v

Chapter Twenty-four

Feeling caught in a dream, Claire stood beside Simon in the drawing room of the house in Belgravia. In front of them, a balding minister intoned the wedding service from the Book of Common Prayer. A lavish array of candles flickered and glowed. Masses of wildflowers cast perfume into the air. The pattering of rain on the darkened windows made the scene cozy and romantic.

Mrs. Bagley and Sir Harry Masterson flanked them as witnesses. The stout housekeeper beamed with pleasure, occasionally using a corner of her apron to wipe away a happy tear. Standing beside Simon, Sir Harry looked positively gleeful.

Claire noticed them only peripherally. It was Simon who held her attention. Simon, whose arm felt strong and solid beneath her fingers. Simon, who had stunned her with his offer less than an hour ago—both of marriage and the boon to Papa's case.

Why had he done it? Did his feelings for her run so deep? *I'm mad about you, Claire. You've fascinated me since the moment we met.*

The memory thrilled her anew. Though he hadn't spoken precisely of love, her heart abounded with hope. She too had felt reluctant to give voice to all the soft, tender emotions hidden inside of her. The right moment would come, though. *Soon.*

They spoke their vows, his tone deep and sure. The minister pronounced them man and wife, and she bowed her head for the blessing. Then Simon was clasping her in his arms, his mouth claiming hers in a deep kiss that went on and on, until the minister cleared his throat and they sprang apart to smile dazedly at each other.

Mr. Bagley played a rusty tune on the pianoforte, while his wife hastened to fill the crystal cups from the punch bowl and serve a cake with a fancy white glaze to the newlyweds, Sir Harry, and the minister.

"You'll join us, won't you?" Claire asked the Bagleys, but they demurred and said it wouldn't be fitting.

"Nonsense," Simon drawled. "If Lady Rockford wishes your company, then you're obliged to obey her."

He smiled lazily at Claire, and it took a moment to realize he meant *her*. *She* was Lady Rockford now. Her legs shaky, she had to sit down on the chaise. The cake and punch lay untouched in her lap. Did she *want* to be a countess? Could she join the social whirl, arrange dinner parties, exchange gossip with all the other matrons?

She had no choice. It would be expected of her. Panic nibbled at the edge of her happiness, but resolutely, she pushed it away.

When the refreshments were finished, and the minister had taken his leave, she and Simon walked Sir Harry to the door. Sir Harry clapped Simon on the shoulder. "Well done, old fellow. You won the bet, after all. Who would have guessed that you'd run into Warrington's long-lost granddaughter in Stanfield's garden that night?"

"You're not to mention our marriage to anyone. I've promised Claire we'll keep quiet about it for now." Simon regarded her with warm exasperation. "For the time being, she's my Countess Confidential."

That had been Claire's one demand. She didn't want word of her identity getting back to her grandfather. Not until the Wraith was caught and her father was freed. She looked at Sir Harry. "We do appreciate your being here on such short notice."

"I wouldn't have missed it for the world," Sir Harry said with relish, giving her a peck on the cheek. "Adieu, Lady Rockford. Make sure your rascal of a husband behaves himself—or he'll answer to me!"

Harry vanished into the rainy night, and they were alone in the foyer. Simon stood gazing at her, and the darkness of his eyes made all of her misgivings melt away. The world lightened in a rush of hope and love, and nothing seemed impossible anymore.

"My lady," he said, his voice low and caressing.

He slipped his arm around her waist, and they headed toward the stairs. Leaning against him, Claire felt a thrilling heat at the prospect of the night to come—and all the nights ahead of them.

And with Simon on her side, surely soon Papa would be free.

It wasn't until the following morning, while Claire was lying abed, admiring the sight of Simon in his breeches, shaving at the washstand, that she remembered her theory about the Shakespearean quotations.

They had shared long hours of extraordinary pleasure, talking in between bouts of lovemaking. They'd traded names they would never inflict upon their children, having a contest to see who could come up with the most outrageous example. Then Claire had told anecdotes about the girls at her school, and Simon had related boyhood stories about Holyoke Park in Hampshire, the seat of the Earls of Rockford. By tacit agreement, they'd steered clear of all unpleasantries.

But now, they needed to talk about the Wraith. She threw on a white silk robe from the dressing room, and together they went down to Simon's study to examine his copy of the messages.

Seating himself in the chair behind the large mahogany desk, he drew her onto his lap, a position she would have appreciated more had she not been so intent on proving her hypothesis.

"Look," she said, "each quotation is an anagram of sorts. The first letter matches the first letter of the next victim's last name. The other letters of the name are scrambled within the phrase."

He frowned, scanning the list. "A coincidence."

"Not eleven times."

"Ten," he corrected, "and that's if we include the one left at Lady Havenden's."

"Eleven," she repeated. "Yesterday, I found one that you missed in my father's drawer. Hand me a quill from the drawer, please."

As she dipped the nib into the inkpot and made the addition to the list, he leaned forward to read over her shoulder. " 'Heaven hath a hand in these events.' Perhaps the Wraith was predicting our marriage."

Beneath the cascade of her hair, his fingertips made light circles over the back of her dressing gown, causing a frisson of pleasure over her skin. But he wasn't taking her seriously yet.

Quickly, she solved the puzzle, then triumphantly showed it to him. "There, you see? It *does* work. *H* is for Havenden, the next victim, and the rest of the letters are present in the quote."

"Let me see that." Simon took the paper, and gradually,

a stunned look came over his handsome face. "The other ones work, too. It's so simple. Why didn't I see it before?"

"Because it isn't obvious at first. It only becomes noticeable as the quotations accumulate."

"If this is right," he said, "then the quote from Lady Havenden's house should reveal the location of the next robbery." His gaze snapped back to the paper. " 'Words without thoughts never to heaven go.' "

They both stared down at it, but Simon was quicker. "Warrington."

Claire's heart pounded. "Rosabel's birthday ball is tonight."

"I'll have my men stake out the upstairs during the party. If there's any thievery going on, we'll stop it at once." Standing, Simon held her up by the waist and twirled her around. "Well done, my lady. I do think I'll keep you, after all."

A smile curved his mouth. At the admiration in his eyes, she felt a flush of happiness. "Then you really do believe my father is innocent?"

A cool mask descended over his features. He set her down and placed his hands on her shoulders. "It means that I'll do everything in my power to uncover the truth, Claire. I promise you that."

His answer disappointed her. But tonight . . . surely then he would realize that he'd imprisoned the wrong man.

He folded the list of quotations and put the paper in his coat pocket. "I must be off now to make all the arrangements."

An alarming thought occurred to her as she walked him to the door. "How will you manage to put your men on the scene? You aren't planning to alert Lord Warrington, are you?"

His quick frown told her he'd intended to do just that. "Darling, why would the Wraith rob his own house?"

"To put you off his scent, of course."

"If it pleases you, then, I'll figure something else out. Warrington wasn't happy, anyway, when I withdrew my suit of Lady Rosabel the other day." Simon gave her that lordly stare. "But he'll have to know sooner or later that I'm married to his other granddaughter."

She matched his stare. "Not yet."

The standoff lasted only a few seconds. Then he shook his head in exasperation and gripped her close. "I abhor this secretiveness, darling. I want to tell my mother and sisters our news. They'll be appalled to find out they missed our wedding—and eager to plan a huge reception."

Framing her face in his hands, he gave her a quick kiss. Then he was gone.

Claire leaned weakly against the doorjamb. A huge reception? It was a jarring reminder of her new status. This cozy house felt like an oasis from the world of society. Yet they couldn't stay here forever. She would be expected to move into Simon's huge town house, to direct a large staff of servants, to play hostess to countless guests.

What had she gotten herself into?

She took a slow, deep breath. There would be time aplenty to make those adjustments. For now, she must focus on Papa. She had no intention of leaving his fate in Simon's hands—especially if Simon was looking for a stranger.

The ball was a masquerade. By acquiring a costume, she could slip unnoticed into Warrington House and keep a watch on matters herself.

Simon stood in the gloom of the servants' staircase. With the door cracked slightly, he had an excellent view of the corridor and all approaches to both Lady Hester's bedchamber and Lady Rosabel's.

When he had returned to his house in Belgravia in late afternoon, Claire had drawn him a map of the upstairs at Warrington House. Then she had pleased him again in the bedchamber—and herself as well. He had lingered until the last possible moment before donning his monk's costume, leaving Claire in bed with an order to stay put until his return.

By the time the first guests had arrived, he had smuggled Islington through a side door, stationing him in a linen closet at the other end of the passageway. He had posted additional men outside at intervals to watch for anyone slinking through the shrubbery.

Now, by his pocketwatch, the hour neared midnight, and his every nerve felt strung taut. Usually, surveillance was a damned tedious business. It required staying alert and watchful for hours at a time.

It felt a thousand times worse tonight. Tonight, Simon had a personal stake in the outcome.

If the Wraith did indeed put in an appearance, then Simon could give Claire the gift she craved most. Her father's freedom.

If the Wraith failed to show, then Gilbert Hollybrooke's trial would proceed as planned in a few days. And Islington would give the testimony that would send Claire's father to the gallows.

Icy fear gripped his chest. He would lose Claire—she would hate him for the rest of her life. But worse than that, he would hate himself—for the possibility of being instrumental in condemning an innocent man.

Had Hollybrooke been set up? For a long time, Simon had ignored his gut instinct. But maybe Claire was right; maybe he had been too stubborn to see past the solid evidence. Had the murder of his father hardened him to the point of being inflexible?

Perhaps. Yet she didn't understand that his job allowed

him no room to take her word on faith. He had to rely upon cold, clear logic.

But he could at least consider her conviction that someone in this household was the culprit. And he'd place his bets on Lord Frederick—who had gaming debts up to his jug ears. For that reason, Simon had taken the precaution earlier of slipping into the bedchambers of both ladies and taking an accounting of their jewels. He would know if a piece had gone missing before or after the guests had arrived.

A nun in white robes glided into view. Simon went on the alert. Could the Wraith be a woman?

He peered closely through the opening in the door, but the winged wimple and a mask concealed her face. Damned costumes! He'd always disliked masquerade balls, but tonight, he especially loathed them. The disguises worn by the guests made it difficult for him to identify anyone.

The nun proceeded past the chambers of both ladies and turned the corner. He blew out a breath of frustration. And tried not to think about Claire home in bed, waiting for him.

As Claire rounded the corner, she kept a sharp watch for Simon. He had hidden himself well; she hadn't so much as glimpsed a tall monk in a brown, hooded cassock.

It was ironic that they'd chosen costumes so similar. She'd used a set of spare bedsheets to devise the enveloping robes of a nun. This afternoon, when he'd returned unexpectedly, he'd almost caught her finishing her sewing. She had stuffed it all in a chest, played the adoring wife, and tried not to feel guilty for deceiving him.

Reaching her destination, she glanced up and down the deserted corridor. Then she quietly let herself into her grandfather's rooms and shut the door.

A short while ago, she had been downstairs, keeping

an eye on Lord Frederick, who played cards in the drawing room, Lord Warrington, who discussed politics with a group of men in the library, and Rosabel, dressed as a princess and dancing every set, including two with a masked, fair-haired cavalier, undoubtedly Lewis Newcombe. Claire had decided it was the perfect opportunity to check out that safe. If she could find the other stolen jewels, maybe Simon would finally believe her.

She hurried through the small antechamber and into the bedchamber. The demi-mask over the upper half of her face restricted her vision, but the oil lamp on the bedside table showed the room was unoccupied. She would never have a better opportunity.

On the massive four-poster bed, the dragon-embroidered coverlet was drawn up to a row of pillows. Shadows cloaked the collection of exotic artifacts around the chamber. To her right, the dressing room was dark. To her left, a pair of glowing red eyes watched from the gloom.

She froze, her heart hammering, before recognition struck. It was her grandfather's table, the base formed by a brass tiger with ruby eyes.

Releasing a breath, Claire steadied her nerves. The absolute quiet sent prickles over her skin. But now was no time to turn coward.

She headed across the room to a brass shield on the wall. Lifting it from its hook, she propped it against a chair. The dark square of a safe showed against the paleness of the wallpaper. The handle didn't budge.

Where would her grandfather keep the key?

Opening the top drawer of the bedside table, she moved the lamp closer to shed light inside. Books, a handkerchief, a brown bottle of laudanum, exactly as the last time she'd searched here. No key.

Crouching down, she examined the bottom drawer,

again to no avail. As she prepared to rise, a male voice immobilized her.

"Looking for this?"

Gasping, she glanced over her shoulder. Behind her stood a short man holding up a ring of keys. Her grandfather's valet, Oscar Eddison.

A furtive movement at the far end of the corridor caught Simon's attention. Islington's burly form crept in the direction the nun had taken only a few minutes ago.

Simon checked the impulse to go after his partner. Something suspicious must have drawn Islington out of his hiding place. But he'd call out if he needed assistance.

Simon remained at his post. His legs were beginning to cramp from standing for hours. Shifting position, he settled his shoulder against the doorframe and continued to scan the empty passageway. Music drifted from the ballroom on the floor below. He could hear the distant hum of voices and laughter.

And he wondered what Islington had seen.

Trapped, Claire crouched by the opened drawer. The light from the lamp fell on her face, and she thanked heaven for her demi-mask.

The valet flicked a glance at the exposed safe. "Thieving wench! I heard you come in, so I hid in the dressing room. Take off that mask and show your face."

She shook her head without speaking. Eddison mustn't recognize her. *Dear God.* How could she escape him?

"Do as I say!" he thundered.

He stalked forward, gripping the iron keys like a weapon. Claire pretended to cower. When he was almost upon her, she lunged. With all her strength, she drove her shoulder into his abdomen.

Groaning, he crashed to the carpet. The keys flew out of his grasp and clinked somewhere in the shadows.

She kept right on going, hiking up the skirt of her costume and racing for the door. Her fingers groped for the handle, wrenched it open. And she collided with a burly man.

The impact made Claire see stars. In a twinkling, he had seized her, marching her back inside the bedchamber and over to the lamp. She wriggled and fought to no avail. His beefy hand formed a manacle around her upper arm.

"The name's Islington, miss. I'm an officer of the Crown."

With that, he reached up and tore off her mask. He had a squat nose, ruddy features, and spiky brown hair. He looked vaguely familiar.

Claire instantly went limp. Islington must be one of Simon's men! "Sir, you must fetch Lord R—"

"Mrs. Brownley?" Eddison had scrambled to his feet.

"Miss Hollybrooke?" Islington said at the same time.

Claire's throat went dry. *Oh, no*.

"Her name is Mrs. Brownley," the valet insisted. "She was a servant here until she was dismissed for licentious behavior."

"She's also Gilbert Hollybrooke's daughter," Islington stated grimly. "I saw her at the station a few weeks ago, arguing with the magistrate."

Eddison's weaselly face went chalk white. "I don't believe it . . ."

Islington ignored him. "We've been searching for you, miss. My superior's been keeping a watch on your father's rooms."

Simon. He must have been protecting her. Dear God, could he get her out of this fix? Or would he go back to believing she was a thief?

"I'll fetch Lord Warrington," Eddison said, marching to the door. "He'll want to know who was robbing him."

Claire panicked. She wasn't ready to face her grandfather, not without proof. "Take me to your superior at once," she commanded the Runner. "I won't speak to anyone else."

"You're in no position to give orders, miss." Gravely, Islington produced a length of cord from inside his coat. "You're under arrest."

Not fifteen minutes after he'd seen his partner creeping along the corridor, Simon spied Islington again, motioning urgently from the other end of the corridor.

Simon took off running, and they met halfway. "What's wrong?"

"This way, m'lord." Beaming, Islington led Simon around the corner. "I've caught the Wraith, I have. The phony one, at least. She was right in the midst of cracking open Lord Warrington's safe."

"She?"

"Aye, looking all pious and proper, dressed like a holy sister. And the best part is—well, I'll let you have a look at her yourself."

That nun. The one he had dismissed as insignificant. How wrong he had been to assume the thief would go after Lady Hester's jewels.

Who was she?

Simon was in no mood to play guessing games. But they were already at the doorway, so he let Islington enjoy his moment of success.

He himself felt a rush of elation. Finally, he had the proof to free Claire's father. How thrilled she would be! He'd have to eat crow, but then, he'd have a fine time making it up to her.

He entered the dimly lit bedroom, taking in the array

of exotic objects in a glance. His gaze fixed on the nun, sitting in a chair, her hands bound behind her.

A thunderbolt destroyed his euphoria. *Claire?*

She gave him an appealing look, but at least had the sense to remain silent. Fear and anger choked him. What was she doing here?

" 'Tis Miss Hollybrooke, m'lord. Assisting her father, no doubt."

"Go on outside, tell the other men. I'll see to this matter."

Islington nodded, then addressed Claire. "I'll see you in the docket with your sire, miss. Now I'll be testifying against the both of you."

As Islington stalked out of the chamber, Simon stood in the grips of absolute shock. *Islington had given it away.* And Claire's beautiful face showed the starkness of disbelief and pain.

"Is this true?" she whispered. "*He's* going to testify? Instead of *you*?"

Hell. Bloody, bloody hell. "Yes, but I'll explain everything later." Spurred by urgency, Simon crouched behind her to work at the knot securing her wrists. "Right now, you're in serious trouble. Why the devil did you come here, anyway?"

"I was looking for the stolen jewels in my grandfather's safe. But Simon . . . you tricked me."

"I had no choice. You wouldn't have married me otherwise." Doubts wormed into his mind. Was she telling the truth? Or had he been duped again? Had she been intending to steal from her own grandfather in order to spring Gilbert Hollybrooke from prison?

Simon could think only of protecting her. No matter what.

She yanked her hands free and rubbed her wrists. Then she tore off the wimple and threw it to the floor. A few dark tendrils flowed down over her nun's habit. Hurt in her voice, she repeated, *"You tricked me."*

"You need that wimple to disguise yourself. You have to go now—and quickly. I'll say you escaped me."

She made no move to replace her headgear. Her voice rose in anger. "You *lied* to me. You led me to believe you were on my father's side. How could you *do* that?"

Her every word hammered into him like nails. "You've lied to me, too, Claire. More than once."

"Every falsehood I've told has been to protect my father. But you aren't going to help him, are you? You never intended to."

"We'll speak of this later, dammit. There isn't time—

It was already too late.

Leaning on his cane, Warrington hobbled into the bedchamber, followed by his sour-faced valet. With the prerogative of old age, the marquess wore no costume, only a suit of dark gray with a white cravat. His piercing blue eyes skewered Claire. "It *is* you!"

Eddison pointed a bony finger at Claire. "She's an imposter and a thief! I knew there was something suspicious about the wench from the very moment—"

Craving an outlet for his pain, Simon caught the valet by the throat and slammed him against the bedpost. "Be careful how you refer to my wife."

Behind him, Claire gasped. He had revealed their marriage and earned more of her ire. But he'd break a thousand promises if it meant saving her from prison. "Apologize."

Eddison made choking noises. "Sorry—m'lord—"

"Not to me, you oaf, to *her*."

"Sorry—m'lady—I didn't know—"

Claire marched over and snapped, "Let him down, Simon. You're every bit as vile as he is."

Her scornful tone cut through the red mist of his rage.

Relaxing his fingers, he let the valet loose and swung to her. "Claire, darling, hear me out. I needed you to be my wife . . . I'm in love with you."

He reached out to touch her cheek, but she flinched from him, mistrust written in the accusation of her eyes. "Keep your distance, sir."

Warrington stood watching with one bushy gray brow elevated. He stared intensely at Claire, but spoke to Simon. "Is this true, Rockford? You've married her—my granddaughter?"

"Yesterday, by special license."

"I see." Warrington shifted his enigmatic gaze to Claire. "You and I must settle some matters. Shall he stay?"

She sent Simon a look of utter loathing. "No. And I want the marriage annulled. It was made under false pretenses. I don't ever wish to see him again."

"The private wound is deepest."
—*The Two Gentlemen of Verona*, V:iv

Chapter Twenty-five

Lord Warrington ordered everyone from the room. Claire was left alone with her grandfather—and he knew her true identity. But she could think only of the agony of Simon's betrayal.

Simon had lied to her. He had deceived her in the most despicable manner. He'd never had the slightest intention of freeing Papa. He had only married her for—

Claire, darling . . . I'm in love with you.

Heartache gave birth to anger. His cruel fraud invalidated his soft words. He had wed her out of a sense of obligation, that was all. Because she was Warrington's granddaughter. When he'd thought her a commoner, she had not been worthy of an honorable offer.

"Sit down," Lord Warrington growled. "You look about to swoon."

Dazed by the blow of Simon's treachery, Claire sank onto the chair opposite her grandfather. The lamp rested on the table between them. When had he moved it? In the throes of unreality, she focused on him. He stared back, his eyes sharp blue daggers in his weathered face.

"So you're Emmy's daughter," he said. "I was right to think there was something familiar about you."

Emmy. Had he always called Lady Emily by that pet name? It was too warm, too personal, and Claire rebelled at the suggestion that he had been anything but a cold, distant father. "You would have known me for certain had you seen fit to acknowledge my birth."

Something twisted in his face. Then he leaned forward, his gnarled hands wrapped around the knob of his cane. "The past is gone. We will speak only of the present. Why were you stealing from me?"

"I wasn't. I was looking for what *you* had stolen." In the wake of the shock delivered by Islington, Claire felt utterly fearless. Let this mean old codger try to silence her. Let him!

His shaggy gray eyebrows drew together in a frown. "Are you referring to Emmy's dowry? You're welcome to it—along with another for your own marriage to Rockford."

"You can't buy my silence," she said heatedly. "I don't want your money. I want you to clear my father of all the charges against him."

"You're making no sense, girl. I've no power to release him from prison. I'm sorry for your sake, but the fellow's a thief."

"No. He isn't the Wraith—*you* are." When the marquess stared uncomprehendingly, Claire clenched her fingers into fists in her lap. "You planned all those robberies in order to ruin him. You arranged for the evidence to be placed in his desk. Because you've resented him all these years for stealing your daughter."

The muted ticking of a clock marked the silence. She watched her grandfather fiercely, seeking even the smallest sign of guilt.

But he held his head cocked to the side in a pose of disbelief. Releasing a ragged sigh, he leaned tiredly back in his chair. "I don't know how you came by such a notion, but it isn't true. Rather, I've become an admirer of your father's writings. I've a copy of every treatise he's published over the years in addition to his book."

His blatant remark flabbergasted Claire. He had to be playing on her sympathies. "You've kept track of him, all right. We've moved several times, yet you knew how to find him."

"I've kept track of *you*, not him." He paused, then added slowly, "I would have liked it if you'd answered my letters."

"Blast your lies!" Her eyes burned with incipient tears, but Claire blinked them back. "I've never received so much as a line from you. Nor did my mother—no matter how many times she wrote."

Lord Warrington looked visibly shaken. His knuckles were white from gripping the cane. "Emmy wrote to me? When?"

"Every year, on the anniversary of her elopement. She would weep over those letters. Because she knew you wouldn't acknowledge her."

He stared at her another moment. In agitation, he attempted to rise, but sank back down and said hoarsely, "Pull the bell rope."

She might have refused, but his face looked gray, his eyes watery, his posture shrunken. A pang of guilt overrode her anger. Had she made him ill with her accusations?

The twisted cord dangled by the bedside. After giving it a yank, Claire poured a glass of water from the pitcher on the table. She handed it to her grandfather and helped him take a few sips.

"Eddison distributes the mail in this house," she said slowly. "Do you suppose he took all the letters?"

He grunted an assent. "Would to God I'd suspected it long ago."

• • •

In short order, Oscar Eddison stood before his master. Simon had come into the bedchamber, too, and from her chair, Claire had a clear view of him standing in the shadows. He had discarded the monk's habit, and in his shirt and breeches, he resembled a pirate. From his determined expression, she knew he wanted to talk to her. But her heart felt too fragile to endure the assault of his charm.

Warrington fixed Eddison with a fearsome glower. "My granddaughter has never received my letters. Nor have I received hers."

The valet's beady brown eyes darted to Claire, then back again. "M'lord, I—I always put your correspondence in the post. I cannot imagine what happened—mail does get lost from time to time—"

"Enough! If you don't confess, I shall give Rockford permission to choke the truth out of you."

Simon stepped forward, his face taut with menace.

Eddison blanched. He fell to one knee before Warrington. "Pray forgive me, m'lord. You were furious when Lady Emily left. You said she was dead to you! As well she should have been. She dishonored you!"

The marquess narrowed his eyes. "Craven bootlicker! Get on your feet. How dared you destroy my daughter's letters?"

Eddison sprang up, wringing his hands. "No! I—I have them. All of them! Unopened, in a box in my room. I'll—I'll fetch them at once."

As he darted toward the door, Simon seized him by the scruff of the neck. "You thought ill of Lady Emily, did you? I'm wondering if you're the one who wanted revenge on Hollybrooke for taking her from this house."

Eddison's mouth worked like a fish's. "R-revenge?"

"Yes. We'll go get those letters together. Then I'm

escorting you to Bow Street Station on suspicion of being
the Wraith."

Claire sat frozen, floored by the notion that Eddison
might have acted without her grandfather's knowledge.
Simon ignored the valet's stammering protests. He gazed
at her with an intensity of purpose that tugged at her wayward heart. Undoubtedly, part of his plan for the night involved getting her alone. The wretch!

Claire looked at her grandfather, who sat slumped in
his chair, lost in his own thoughts. "May I stay here for
the night?"

His eyes brightened, lighting his wrinkled features.
"My dear, you may stay for as long as you like."

The next morning, Claire arose late, feeling drugged by a
fitless sleep. She had only meant to occupy her old bed in
the attic, but Lord Warrington had insisted on giving her a
large chamber directly across from Rosabel's. With its
rose-hued draperies and dainty furnishings, it was a room
fit for a princess.

Or at least the granddaughter of a marquess.

Claire dressed slowly, donning the plain gray gown
that she had worn beneath her nun's habit. An emotional
whirlpool had sapped her of energy. Her grandfather had
wanted to be a part of her life all along.

And he was *not* the Wraith. He had *not* plotted to throw
Papa into prison. She had been so horribly mistaken.

It had been Oscar Eddison who had nursed the grudge.
Before leaving, Simon had explained that a signed confession from the valet would be needed to free her father.
With paperwork and permissions to obtain, the process
would likely take the better part of today.

In the meantime, she felt cast adrift in uncharted wa-
ters. The ache in her heart kept pulling her mind back to
Simon. Although she realized he was trying to make up

for his betrayal, the magnitude of it chilled her to the core. What if she hadn't talked to her grandfather? What if they hadn't discovered Eddison's complicity?

Papa would have been sentenced to death on Islington's testimony.

She could never forgive Simon for taking that risk. *Never.*

She couldn't live with a man who had deceived her so grievously. Yet the prospect of living without him left her desolate.

A knock sounded on the door. A footman delivered astonishing news. The dowager Lady Rockford waited in the blue drawing room.

Simon must have told his mother about the marriage.

Her hands shaking, Claire smoothed her hair. What if Simon's mother disapproved of the marriage? Claire hadn't spared a thought for the reaction of his family—or hers. As she hastened out of her chamber, she glanced at Rosabel's closed door. How surprised she'd be when she woke up to discover she'd acquired a cousin!

Downstairs, Claire took a deep breath and entered the huge drawing room to find her mother-in-law sitting on a chaise near the hearth. Her graying brown hair was done up in an elegant twist, and her fine gown of blue silk made Claire feel instantly dowdy.

She curtsied. "Lady Rockford, what a pleasure to see you again."

A warm smile lit her face. "My dear, *you* are Lady Rockford now, a fact which pleases me immensely. Will you sit beside me?"

Claire complied. To soothe her frayed nerves, she decided to be frank. "You're not unhappy that Simon didn't marry Lady Rosabel?"

"Rather, I'm delighted he's found the woman he loves."

Claire bitterly doubted the depth of his love. But she

could hardly say *that*. "You can't approve of me. My mother created a scandal when she ran off with her tutor. And now my father is an accused felon."

"Your mother was in love. And your father was unjustly accused and is soon to be released—the moment that odious valet confesses." The dowager pursed her lips. "To think he kept your mother's letters from Lord Warrington for all those years."

Dismayed, Claire focused on one bit of news. "So Eddison hasn't yet admitted he's the Wraith?"

"No, but Simon is certain he will." Her thin hand reached out to touch Claire's. "You mustn't worry, dear. Simon has gone to Bow Street himself to oversee the matter."

Her serene brown eyes showed no knowledge of his secret. *I work undercover for Bow Street. No one knows that—not even my family.*

Yet Simon had told Claire. Why had he disclosed that fact when he'd believed her to be a criminal? Merely because he'd known she'd find out at the trial?

"I hope you won't think me meddling," the dowager said, "but my son told me the two of you have quarreled, and that the blame is his. I won't ask for particulars, but I thought perhaps you should understand the reason why he can be so stubborn and harsh at times."

"Do you mean . . . what happened when he was fifteen?"

"He's told you, then?"

Claire shook her head. "I heard a snippet of gossip. When I asked Simon, he said the subject was closed."

"It's a very difficult memory for him." The dowager looked away a moment, her eyes sad, as if she were peering into the past. "It's not often that a boy witnesses the murder of his father."

Claire gasped. "Simon was *there*?"

"Yes. You see, he'd been expelled from school for

fighting. We didn't believe in entrusting such a matter to servants, so my husband and I went to fetch him ourselves. On the way home, while Simon and his father quarreled, our coachman stopped to assist a disabled carriage on the side of the road. My husband got out to aid the gentleman."

She paused, her hand to her throat. Horrified, Claire guessed, "But he wasn't a gentleman. He was a highwayman."

Lady Rockford gave a shaky nod. "It was a trick. He had a brace of pistols. He ordered us all out of the coach. When my husband tried to shield me, the brigand shot both of us. Simon and the coachman captured the thief. But it was too late to save my husband."

Claire's stomach twisted. "You were gravely injured, too."

"Yes, and I fear Simon has never forgiven himself."

"It wasn't his fault!"

"So I've told him. But he persists in blaming himself for being a wild youth. In his mind, had he not been expelled, we would not have been on that road. And from that day onward, his behavior has been exemplary—almost too exemplary. He's trusted no one outside his family." Her face softened with a smile. "Until *you*, my dear."

Claire couldn't allow herself to believe herself special to him. But she kept her qualms to herself while she and her mother-in-law chatted about other matters, mainly how impatient Simon's sisters were to welcome her into the family. After a time, the dowager grew visibly tired and took her leave. In a rush of tenderness, Claire embraced her at the door.

Yet her heart ached with painful regrets. How could she tell the dowager that the marriage was over before it had even begun?

She walked slowly back upstairs. No wonder Simon

was so dedicated to fighting criminals. And no wonder he didn't trust the fact that Papa was a harmless scholar. Simon had seen his parents gruesomely tricked while performing an act of charity.

But that didn't absolve him.

As Claire headed toward her room, Lady Hester ran out of Rosabel's chamber at an alarming pace. She was panting, her pudgy face pale, her hazel eyes wild. Spying Claire, she stopped dead in her tracks. "Mrs. Brownley! What are *you* doing here?"

Claire didn't waste time explaining her new status. "Is something amiss?"

Her aunt dabbed her brow with a handkerchief. " 'Tis Rosabel. Her bed's not been slept in. I fear she's run off. With that scoundrel, Lewis Newcombe!"

"For ever and a day."
—*As You Like It*, IV:i

Chapter Twenty-six

Within half an hour, Claire was heading north in the Warrington coach, on her way to Gretna Green.

Across from her, Frederick sat sulking beside Lord Warrington. Her cousin had been rousted out of bed after a late night. Consequently, his fair hair was mussed, his blue coat wrinkled, and his cravat askew. "She's likely in town somewhere," he complained. "Rosie wouldn't go all the way to Scotland with Lewis. This is a wild-goose chase."

"Claire found that anagram in your sister's chamber," the marquess said. "Not only did your friend run off with my granddaughter, but I'd venture to guess he's the Wraith."

Frederick gulped and fell silent.

Claire had been horrified to discover the message propped against Rosabel's pillow. *Good night, good night! parting is such sweet sorrow. That I shall say good night till it be morrow.*

It had taken her a few moments to realize the quotation from *Romeo and Juliet* didn't reveal the next victim. Rather, this anagram referred to Gretna Green, a village on the Scottish border where marriages were performed without the banns required by English law. She had written a quick note to Simon to apprise him of the situation.

No wonder Oscar Eddison hadn't confessed. He wasn't the Wraith, after all. When her grandfather had grimly presumed Newcombe to be the guilty party, Claire had kept her own dark thoughts to herself. What if Rosabel herself had committed those robberies? What if she had been helping Lewis Newcombe pay his gaming debts?

Lord Warrington glowered at his grandson. "'Tis your fault, you scalawag. Newcombe wasn't invited to the ball, so you must have let him in. Claire saw him there, dancing with your sister."

Frederick twiddled with his watch fob and nervously eyed Claire. He had been less than thrilled to discover they were cousins. "*I* didn't see him. Lewis had another engagement. And he isn't the Wraith, I'd swear he isn't."

Gripping his cane, Lord Warrington gave his grandson a strangely intent stare. "Then who is, eh? Is it you, boy? I know about those things that have gone missing."

Visibly shocked, Frederick stammered, "M-missing?"

Claire started in surprise. "What things?"

Lord Warrington turned his attention to her. "I've too many artifacts to display all at once, so I keep the rest in a locked storage room in the cellar. A few weeks ago, I noticed things were disappearing. A box inlaid with precious stones. A gold statue of a Hindu god. A collar encrusted with diamonds." His sharp blue gaze shifted to Frederick. "And don't deny your guilt. I've had you followed. You've been selling my treasures to pawnbrokers to finance your gambling."

Frederick glanced wildly around as if seeking escape from the plush confines of the coach. Then he flared, "It's *my* inheritance. If you weren't so blasted tight with your purse strings—"

"Silence!" His grandfather struck the tip of the cane on the floor of the coach. "You will tell me if you've stolen from others as the Wraith. You and that rascal Newcombe."

Frederick shrank against the seat. "M-me? No! I swear it!"

"That had best be the truth. As it is, you're joining the King's navy. A few hard years at sea will make a man out of you."

"No!"

"I've already purchased your commission. You're leaving next month. Now sit up. For once in your sorry life, show some pride!"

Frederick straightened as if a red-hot poker had been thrust into his spine. "F-forgive me, Admiral. I—I'll get your things back. I will!"

"Admiral," the marquess muttered. "My family is the only crew I could never manage."

He looked old and gray, drained by the angry exchange, and Claire felt a softening in her heart. Though her grandfather was a harsh man, he could suffer like any man. He reminded her of Simon, authoritative and brusque, yet with hidden tenderness lurking beneath the arrogant mask.

Simon. A vortex of pain pulled at her. But she refused to let it overwhelm her. Not now, not when she had to find Rosabel.

The journey stretched on interminably. Since the ball had ended near dawn, the couple had had perhaps a five-hour lead. Claire and her grandfather stopped at every inn along the road to make inquiries, thrice receiving the encouraging news that a man and a girl fitting Rosabel's description had tarried there for refreshment. At the third

place, Claire realized they were less than two hours behind the elopers.

The coach rocked and swayed, but she felt too anxious
to be lulled. As the afternoon wore into dusk, the tension
in her squeezed tighter. At Lord Warrington's order, the
coach pressed onward.

While Frederick dozed in the corner, her grandfather
told Claire about the letters. His voice halting at times, he
admitted to staying up half the night to read them. Lady
Emily had written many anecdotes about his granddaughter. And he had found the invitation Claire had written,
asking him to attend her tenth birthday party.

"I would've come, you know," he said, his weathered
face a pale shadow in the gathering gloom. "Blast my
pride! I should have called on you regardless of never
hearing from your mother."

"Perhaps Mama should have done the same," Claire
murmured, surprising herself with the realization. Was it
the same for her and Simon? Did blame belong on both
sides?

She had given Simon every reason to doubt her, yet he
had trusted her with the secret of his work. He had openly
declared his love for her in front of an audience. He'd had
the frantic look of a desperate man.

It was a balm to her heart to know that he loved her so
dearly. And yet she had never voiced her own deep feelings for him. Was she, perhaps, the one who did not trust?
Because she'd hated the nobility?

She would face all that later. Now, nothing mattered
but finding her cousin, capturing the Wraith, and freeing
her father.

The coach slowed, and Claire pressed her face to the
window glass, expecting to see another inn. It was near
dark and no lanterns shone through the gloom. But there
was something else . . .

She caught her breath. "It looks like . . . it *is* Rosabel. Something must have happened to their carriage."

"Praise God!" Lord Warrington poked Frederick awake. "Get up, you slugabed. You have to rescue your sister."

Frederick groaned, covering his head, but Claire didn't wait for him. She threw open the door and hurried straight to Rosabel, who sat dejectedly on a boulder beside the road.

"Brownie!" She launched herself at Claire, nearly bowling her over. "I was *wishing* you were here. Eloping sounded romantic when Aunt Emily did it. But it's cold and dark, and I just want to go home."

Stunned, Claire unpeeled her cousin's arms. A fancy black carriage loomed in the shadows a few feet away, tilted into a ditch. "Are you alone, then? Did Mr. Newcombe abandon you?"

"Lewis? Oh, but he's not—"

"Stop your jabbering." The dark figure of a man stepped out from behind the carriage. "Neither of you are going anywhere without me."

Claire stood petrified. It was Vincent Grimes.

And he was aiming a brace of pistols straight at them.

Simon rode hell-bent down the Great North Road. The darkness was thickening, and he needed to slow down or risk a tumble.

He took the risk, urging his mount onward, the gelding blessedly swift for a hack obtained at the last posting inn. His heart thrummed in rhythm with the pounding hooves. The cold evening wind nipped at his face. And his mind raced with the dread that he might be too late.

Although Claire was accompanied by Warrington and Frederick, Simon feared that an old codger and a shiftless pup were no match for a cunning criminal. And Lady

Rosabel might resist being rescued. All along, the little minx had been in love with that rascal Newcombe.

The Wraith.

Simon had spent the morning in a fruitless attempt to obtain Eddison's confession. In frustration, he'd gone to the Old Bailey to ask for a postponement of Hollybrooke's trial. But he'd had to cool his heels, waiting for an audience with the judge before arguing his case. By the time he'd returned to Bow Street, Claire's message had been hours old.

The few lines informing him of Rosabel's elopement with the Wraith had been terse, without a hint of warmth. Now, with every strike of the hooves, Simon felt the agony of her loss. With his own stupidity, he had betrayed Claire's trust. He wanted her safe in his arms again. He wanted to spend the rest of his life making up for his folly.

If she would allow him. *If*.

Far ahead in the gathering darkness loomed the black, boxy shape of a coach, stopped in the road.

Drawing on the reins, Simon slowed his mount. He squinted, seeing another carriage and the figures of several people. Ice pumped through his veins, making him sluggish with shock. It looked exactly like the scene when his father had been murdered.

And in an eerie echo of that night, a shot rang out.

Claire stood still, hardly daring to breathe, the cold circle of the pistol pressed to her cheek. Grimes held her like a shield in front of him. A short distance away, Frederick lay groaning on the ground.

He had made a valiant attempt to overpower the villain, only to be felled by a bullet from one of the two pistols. Rosabel hovered over him, whimpering and wringing her hands.

The stocky coachman knelt to examine Frederick's arm.

Balancing on his cane, Lord Warrington leaned creakily over his grandson. "Brace up, boy. It's only a flesh wound."

Frederick yipped in pain as the coachman staunched the bleeding.

Claire was conscious of Grimes's arm clamping her against him. The smell of his expensive cologne made her nauseous. "You had better let me go," she said, willing her voice not to waver. "You're in enough trouble already without having murder on your hands."

"I've no intention of murdering *you,* my dear. We'll take the coach north. I've had enough of that sniveling cousin of yours."

Take the coach? He was pushing her toward it, but Claire stalled for time. "How did you meet Rosabel? I thought she was in love with Lewis Newcombe."

"Lewis is my cousin, and a very obliging bloke in arranging our romance. Our mothers were sisters, you see, both stage actresses. Alas, mine didn't marry a viscount." His hot breath seared her ear. "But I'll make up for it. I'll marry a marquess's granddaughter."

"I'll see you in hell first." Lord Warrington stepped forward, his crippled leg slowing his progress.

His intent look warned Claire to say nothing of her marriage to Simon. Grimes might kill her in a rage.

"Stay back, old man. Lest I shoot her and seize your other granddaughter instead."

The marquess froze in place, glaring.

As he pushed her toward the Warrington coach, Claire tried not to panic. He couldn't tie her up, not with so many watchers ready to spring on him if he laid down the gun. She'd have to sit with him in the driver's seat. And he'd release her while she clambered up there . . .

"So you're the Wraith," she said. "How could you put the blame on my father? He was your friend!"

Grimes snorted. "Not since he published his book. I've tried for years to sell my manuscripts, but Gilbert succeeded on his first attempt."

Despite the danger, her voice vibrated with disgust. "Do you really think I'll marry the man who put him in prison?"

He caressed her cheek with the tip of the gun. "A pistol, my dear, can be very convincing. Now climb!"

They had reached the coach, and his arm fell away. Claire hitched up her skirts to give her legs more freedom. She started the ascent to the high seat, using the iron step as a boost. Halfway, she glanced down, saw him watching the others, and put all her strength into a quick, backward swing of her foot.

Her heel caught the pistol and it went skidding into the darkness. Grimes yelped in surprise. At the same instant, a black shape surged out of the night and tackled him.

Simon!

The two men grappled in the road, but Simon had the advantage of size. In a matter of moments, he had Grimes pinned to the ground, his face in the dirt. "Get me a length of rope," he said over his shoulder.

The coachman made haste to assist him.

Claire jumped down to look for the pistol. But Lord Warrington already had it trained on Grimes. "Truss him up tight," he ordered the coachman. "We're taking the scoundrel back to London. He'll sign his confession and Gilbert Hollybrooke will be released."

Her father was free! But in the midst of her relief, Claire felt the sharp pain of her separation from Simon. He rose to his feet while the coachman finished his task. His hair was mussed and his shirt filthy, but he had never looked more wonderful to her. *Her husband.*

His face solemn, he walked to her side. Quietly, he said, "You *did* marry the man who put your father in prison."

"You heard?"

"I was hiding in the shadows. Waiting for my chance. And dying inside at the thought of losing you."

To her amazement, he knelt in the dirt, lifting his head to gaze up at her. Behind her, she heard a gasp from Rosabel, but Claire was too enraptured to pay heed.

"You told me once that you wouldn't marry me if I went down on my knees and begged," he said. "But I'm begging, anyway. Take me back as your husband, Claire. I love you with all my heart. I'll devote the rest of my life to showing you how sorry I am for deceiving you."

Her heart melted and her eyes overflowed. Simon wasn't simply a nobleman. He was a *noble man*. How could she not have known that?

She knelt down with him. "I've told my share of lies, too. So I'll meet you halfway. I love you, Simon."

Afterward, she couldn't have said who initiated the kiss. All she knew was that his arms were around her, and their mouths were joined in a burst of emotion that lit her soul with a blaze of glory. Long moments later, he drew back, a devilish glint in his dark eyes. "We've an audience, darling."

Claire turned and blushed, for Rosabel clapped her hands. "Grandpapa says we're cousins! And you're married to the earl, exactly as I wanted. It's more romantic than an elopement!"

"Now, don't be getting any more foolish ideas," Lord Warrington chided her. Then he grinned at Claire. "I knew you weren't serious about that annulment business."

"Hush, Grandpapa," she said sternly. "You'll give away all my secrets."

His face softened. "One thing's for certain, Rockford. My granddaughter will keep you on the hop."

"She's already done so," Simon said with a mock grimace. "She's prickly, waspish—and utterly delightful."

" 'If I be waspish, best beware my sting,' " Claire said, quoting Kate in *The Taming of the Shrew*.

Simon gave her a brash grin. "I'll cite one from the Bard, too, darling. One that speaks of how long I intend to love you." He brushed a tender kiss over her lips. " 'Forever and a day.' "

Coming in June 2006...

New York Times bestselling author Barbara Dawson Smith

THE ROGUE REPORT

Dear Reader,

I have a secret. Several, in fact...

Most people know me only as the headmistress of a charity school. Having a son but no husband has made me a social outcast, which is no great inconvenience since I despise Society, especially those "gentlemen" who seduce naïve young women. My contempt for such knaves leads us to Secret the First: I am the anonymous author of The Rogue Report, *a newsletter that exposes these scoundrels and their exploits. My busy life leaves no time for romance, or so one might think.*

This brings us to Secret the Second: I have lately carried on a flirtation with the school's new mathematics professor. Mr. William Jackman is altogether too charming and mysterious for anyone's good, particularly mine. Though I'm tempted to indulge my desires, I cannot help but wonder if my darling "Jack" hides secrets, too.

You see, not everyone appreciates The Rogue Report, *and at least one of its subjects is out for revenge. Is Jack bent on protecting me, or is he really the villain who seeks my ruin? Is it possible that I've fallen in love with the most notorious rogue of them all?*

Lady Julia Corwyn

"A first-rate romance with characters who come alive and draw the reader into this seductive story."
—*The Oakland Press* on *The Duchess Diaries*

ISBN: 0-312-93240-5

Visit *www.barbaradawsonsmith.com*

FROM ST. MARTIN'S PAPERBACKS